BROKEN
FAITH

LOIS CLOAREC HART

DEDICATION

Day
We leapt in faith
We landed in love

ACKNOWLEDGEMENTS

Revising *Broken Faith* was a trip back in time. When I originally wrote the novel, Facebook didn't exist, smart phones were in the early stages of development, texts still referred to books, and only birds twittered. I chose to keep the technological anachronisms intact, so don't be shocked when a couple of characters don't even carry cell phones.

One thing that hasn't changed is how much my writing improves with the skilled input of my trusted long-time collaborators. *Broken Faith* was the first story that my wife, Day Petersen, worked on with me from concept to completion. Kathleen GramsGibbs, who has spent years editing my stories, was also involved in *Broken Faith's* revision process. They are a joy to work with, and I am deeply grateful to both.

This time around I also had the benefit of working with Ylva's Renaissance woman, writer-editor, Sandra Gerth. Sandra, you took on the task of breaking me of a lot of bad habits, and you did it with kindness, tact, and a great sense of humour. I don't know when I've enjoyed a challenge as much. Thank you for all you taught me and for making it fun and (relatively) painless. I look forward to our next collaboration, *The Rise of the Autonomous Body Parts.*

CHAPTER 1

MARIKA LEANED AGAINST HER APARTMENT door, her shoulders slumped as she listened to the muted rumble of the elevator down the hall. Long after the sound died, she pushed herself upright and returned to her living room. She stood silently until Spooky wound himself through her legs. With a faint smile, she stooped and picked up her feline companion.

She stroked his soft fur as she wandered to the sliding door that opened onto a small balcony. She pushed the door open and went outside. Usually, she found the breathtaking panorama of distant mountains and winding river soothing, but on this day, it did nothing to calm her heart or mind.

With a sigh she turned back into her apartment and raised the cat to eye level. "I sent your buddy away, Spooky."

The cat blinked.

"You know I had to, Mister." Marika cradled the cat against her shoulder and whispered into his fur, "It was the right thing to do. She doesn't love us, Spook. At least not that way."

When the feline began to squirm, Marika set him on the floor. They parted company: the cat headed for his favourite perch on the couch and Marika for her piano under the large bay window.

Marika trailed her index finger over the shining mahogany of the Baldwin baby grand, circled it, and pulled out the bench. Once seated, she contemplated the keys for a long moment, then began to play.

The melancholy sounds of Chopin's *Prelude in E Minor* filled the room. Suddenly, Marika slammed her hands down on the keys and startled her somnolent cat with the discordant cacophony.

"Well, Spooky, I told Terry I had a date tonight. I wouldn't want to be a liar, would I?" She strode to the phone and punched in a number. "Cass?"

Marika winced at the burst of triumphant laughter in her ear.

"The last time I saw you, you said you wouldn't be back," Cass said. "Changed your mind?"

Marika rubbed the fine furrow that had appeared in her forehead and pinched the bridge of her nose. "Yes. Look, are you up for some company tonight?"

"I trust you remember what to bring?"

"I do." Marika's voice was sombre.

"All right. Then I'll expect you within the hour. Don't make me wait."

"I won't. I'm leaving now."

A click sounded on the other end of the line.

Marika hung up the phone and glanced over at her cat. "Guess you'll have to look after yourself tonight, Spook." She grabbed her handbag and stopped to deposit an affectionate caress on her pet. "You be good, and I'll see you in the morning."

Spooky stretched and purred under Marika's hand.

She whispered, "I'm sorry," then turned and walked out.

The grocery bag held only essentials, but it felt heavier than usual to Rhiannon. Even the backpack slung over her opposite shoulder was unusually burdensome. She raised her downcast eyes and looked down the street for her bus. *I must've missed the 7:40. Figures. What else can happen to screw up this lousy day?*

Someone rushed around the corner of the plaza and slammed into Rhiannon.

The impact drove the breath from her lungs and the pavement from under her feet. She flew back and lost the contents of her bag all over the sidewalk.

Rhiannon raised herself on scraped elbows and stared at the oranges rolling across the sidewalk. *Shit. They weren't even on special.*

"Oh my God, I'm so very sorry," the person who had slammed into her said. "I wasn't looking where I was going."

Rhiannon accepted the proffered hand and stumbled to her feet. To her surprise, she knew her inadvertent mugger.

"Are you all right?"

"I'm fine, Ms. Havers. No harm done." Rhiannon knelt to gather her scattered groceries. *Except for my oranges.* She frowned at the sight of her now less than perfect produce.

Marika Havers helped with the recovery process. "Do I know you, Miss?"

"I work for Mr. Owen." Rhiannon stuffed her groceries into the rumpled brown bag.

"Oh, of course." Ms. Havers' voice was uncertain.

She has no idea who I am. Not that it matters. Rhiannon rose and balanced her bag.

Ms. Havers tucked the last couple of items into the top and picked up the backpack. She hung it over Rhiannon's shoulder and peered at her with concern. "Are you sure you're okay? May I offer you a ride somewhere?"

"No." Rhiannon realized her rejection sounded brusque, but she lacked the energy to allay her assailant's guilt. "Thanks anyway, but my bus just arrived." She hurried to catch her bus. When she was on-board, she looked back at the plaza in time to see Ms. Havers disappear into the liquor store.

Rhiannon settled back and decided that the collision had been an appropriate end to a very bad day. She leaned her head against the window. She felt as if she'd run a marathon, though she'd been at her desk the entire day.

Rhiannon flexed her back, but stopped when a musc' threatened to knot.

When the bus approached her stop, she picked v grocery bag and swayed toward the middle exit.

As she approached her house, Rhiannon glanced across the street. She wasn't aware she held her breath until she released it in a sigh of relief.

The King brothers and their cronies were mercifully absent. Winters were usually quiet on her street, but spring and summer drew the thuggish brothers out into their filthy, littered yard. They would lounge on their motorbikes and drink beer with their buddies to the raucous accompaniment of cranked up music.

Neighbours had long ago learned to stay out of the brothers' way. Mrs. Greeley had called in a noise complaint to the police three years ago, only to have most of her windows mysteriously broken, garbage strewn about her yard, and her Corgi hung from a mailbox two nights later.

When the police came to question the King brothers in the matter, their pals provided alibis. The neighbours, who had gathered when the police arrived, watched helplessly as the officers drove off while the brothers laughed and sneered. Mrs. Greeley moved away, and since then, everyone else played deaf, dumb, and blind while the brothers lorded it over their small, captive kingdom.

Rhiannon kept her head down, scurried to the gate leading into her yard, and nudged it open with an elbow. She stepped deftly around broken pavement, and went up the creaky wooden steps to the front door. She pushed her way in and winced at the sound of voices coming from what her aunt grandly called the parlour.

"Anne," her aunt called.

Rhiannon cursed inwardly, but responded to her aunt's summons.

Her aunt stood in the parlour doorway and clutched the arm of a tall, weedy man Rhiannon had never seen before.

For a long moment, Rhiannon eyed the stranger, struck by the sheer homeliness of the man. Well over six feet tall, and spare to the point of gauntness, he had thinning blond hair, deep-set pale green eyes, and a prominent Adam's apple. Wire rimmed glasses perched on a prominent beak, and he reminded her of a caricaturized Ichabod Crane.

She glanced past him and her aunt's bulk.

towel and bathing suit over the shower rod and then rinsed her dishes in the sink.

Rhiannon finished drying her dish and spoon and returned to her room. Voices droned downstairs, and, aware of her aunt's fondness for talking people's ears off, she smirked in sympathy for the captive priest.

Back in her room, she browsed the stack of library books on the table. She'd read most of them already, and neither of the two still unread caught her attention tonight. Instead, she opened the bottom drawer of the legless bureau to retrieve a bankbook.

Rhiannon snapped on the naked overhead bulb and lay down on her bed. She doubled the thin pillow behind her head and opened the well-thumbed book to the last page with notations on it.

She stared at the balance and did some calculations in her head. *Won't be too long now. Maybe six or seven more paydays and I'm at the magic five figures.* Rhiannon laughed softly. *I can just see the look on Hettie's face when I toss her the house keys. I won't even say goodbye. I'm sure as hell not going to tell her where I'm going.*

With every payday, Rhiannon's dream drew a little closer; and, safe within her locked room, she allowed herself the luxury of dreaming of the day she had been working toward for so long.

***

David awkwardly disengaged from the clutches of the nattering women and made his exit.

He breathed a sigh of relief as he shook off the stultifying after-effects of an hour in his congregants' company. As was his custom, he lost himself in contemplation while he walked to his church and the rectory, situated a few blocks away in the inner city.

What an odd duck Hettie Walker's niece is. Just this side of hostile, Rhiannon was an enigma. Her intelligent, penetrating eyes held a deep reticence, but David sensed that was their usual state and not directed specifically at him. He wondered what caused such wariness in one so young, and felt a budding compassion for her.

Miss Walker had deflected his initial attempt to inquire about her niece, which only made him more curious. David had allowed the subject to drop, but his inquisitive mind refused to let go of the memory of Rhiannon's suspicious eyes. If he were to believe Hettie and her friends, Miss Walker had heroically borne the burden of her ungrateful niece's care because it was her Christian duty. But David had honed his instincts through two decades of ministry and he knew he'd only heard one, very slanted side of the story.

Tupper. The thought made David smile. If anyone would know both sides of the story, it was the ancient, garrulous sexton who did everything around the church from sweeping floors to setting out hymnals.

Deep in his ruminations, David stepped off the curb without looking and barely avoided being hit by a car. The angry driver signaled his outrage in no uncertain terms. David waved sheepishly as he chastised himself for his lack of attention, well aware that he was prone to lose sight of the outer world while he wandered happily in his inner one. Determined to at least make it back to his rectory in one piece, David carefully checked the street before starting across it again.

Across town from her condo, Marika stopped before Cass' door and drew a deep breath. She didn't allow herself time to reconsider as she quickly knocked and waited.

The door swung open. Cass leaned against the frame and eyed Marika for long moments before she smirked and held out her hand.

"It's Walker Cardhu." Marika handed over the brown bag.

Cass checked the contents and grinned. "Aren't you such a good girl." She twisted the cap off the scotch.

Marika wondered again why she had come. Even so, she knew she wouldn't leave. She had tried to stay away. It certainly wasn't as if Cass put a gun to her head to force her return. Not that Cass ever showed surprise when Marika did reappear. Most of the time Cass wasn't even at home if Marika turned up unannounced, but when she was, Marika knew she'd be greeted with the same knowing smirk. .

Marika studied Cass as she drank from the bottle. *What is it about her? What pulls me back here?* Marika knew the answer to that, but shied away from admitting it, even to herself.

Cass replaced the bottle's cap and pinned Marika with her gaze.

Marika flinched. Cass would never stand out in a crowd. Her appearance was utterly mundane, but her eyes...her eyes were those of a predator; hungry, manic and focused intently on her.

Marika shivered, but was about to push past Cass when the sound of women's laughter coming from inside the apartment made her stop.

Cass regarded her with an insolent grin.

"You didn't tell me you had company."

Cass shrugged. "So?"

Marika retreated to the hall, and Cass made no move to stop her. They stared at each other until finally Cass called into the apartment, "You two get the hell out of here."

Loud complaints sounded until Cass turned and took a few steps inside. "Don't make me tell you twice."

Responding to Cass' snarled command, two women stumbled by Marika's averted eyes and down the hall. "She don't mean shit," one of them said to her friend. "We'll be back here before Monday."

Marika winced and quietly closed the door behind her.

CHAPTER 2

MARIKA CALLED UP ANOTHER FILE on her computer and shook her head. Her client had a weak case for being granted refugee status, and she was hard pressed to find adequate substantiation for his hearing in three weeks.

A knock sounded on her open door. Marika looked up.

Len Owen stood in the doorway, his usual easy-going grin absent.

"Hey, stranger. I haven't seen you for a while."

"Hi, Marika. Do you have a moment?"

"For you, anytime. Come on in. Have a seat. What brings you down from Corporate?"

"I don't know if you've heard, but I've taken a position in the Vancouver office, and I'll be leaving in a couple of weeks. I'm pretty much just wrapping things up right now."

"I had heard something about that. Congratulations. I'm sure you're going to enjoy living out on the coast."

"It'll be different, that's for sure," Len said. "I'm going to take quite a hit on housing costs out there, but I sure won't miss Calgary winters. Look, I'm hoping we might help each other out here. Human Resources said that your legal assistant is leaving soon on maternity leave, is that right?"

"Yes. Marion starts her leave in two weeks, though I'm not entirely sure she's going to last that long."

"She does look ready to pop any day now. I was wondering if you've found a replacement for her yet."

Marika shook her head. "I haven't really had time to look into it. I was going to call Human Resources and tell them to send me floaters for now. I might even go that route for the entire six months until Marion's back."

"I think I have a better idea. I have a top notch assistant, and I think you'd be very pleased with her work if you take her on. I'd really like to find her a position before I leave, and with you in the market for a replacement assistant, I thought this might work out perfectly."

"Since Marion plans to come back after her leave is up, I'm not looking for anyone permanent. Can't your assistant go into the floater pool?"

"Certainly that's what she'll do if you're not interested, but she's a good kid. I'd like to see her settled with someone who'll treat her right, even if it's only for a limited time."

Marika considered the case Len made for his assistant. She wasn't surprised that he was trying to do something nice for the woman. His reputation as an all-round nice guy was well established. But his voice held an unusual undertone of urgency that made her curious. "What is it you're not telling me?"

"I'm not trying to put one over on you. Rhiannon really is the best assistant I've ever had. She's got a first-rate mind, and she's probably the hardest worker in this building. She never balks at overtime, and countless nights I've left here when she's still hard at it."

"Maybe she can't get her work done within regular hours."

Len shook his head. "That's not it at all. Her output is phenomenal. I couldn't begin to tell you how many times her research has bailed me out. Sure, that's what she's paid for, but, damn, Marika, she really makes me look good in front of the clients. I'd take her with me to Vancouver if I could."

"So what's the drawback to this paragon of legal assistants?"

"Well, to be blunt, Rhiannon's people skills aren't the greatest." Len hastened to add, "Don't get me wrong, she's always perfectly polite and correct in her behaviour with me and toward the clients."

"But?"

"But she's the oddest duck I've ever run into."

"Odd how?"

Len stood and paced to the windows, which overlooked the heart of downtown Calgary from seven floors up. "Well, for instance, even after two years, I can't get her to call me anything but Mr. Owen. I've told her dozens of times to call me Len, but she always nods agreeably and treats me as formally as always."

"That doesn't sound all that bad. I know it's outdated, but office formality has its place. Maybe she's shy."

Len shook his head and turned to face Marika. "No, it's not shyness, exactly, though she is reserved. I'd almost say she doesn't like people, but once she comes to know you enough to let down the barriers a little, you can tell it's not that she's a misanthrope, she just doesn't trust people." Len resumed his seat. "Look, the thing is, if you're looking for someone warm and fuzzy to have cheerful morning chitchats with, Rhiannon isn't it. If you're looking for a dedicated, talented worker, she's your girl. I'd like to see her with you because you treat your people decently. I'm afraid that if she goes into the floater pool, she'll end up working for someone like Nolan."

Marika grimaced. She despised the way Troy Nolan treated his assistants. He was petty, disdainful, and spiteful to anyone unlucky enough to be assigned to his office, and as far as she was concerned, a disgrace to the entire firm. *Unfortunately the partners can't seem to see what's so clear to the rest of us.* "I suppose I could give her a chance. I'd need her to work with Marion for at least a week before Marion goes on maternity leave, so that she's up to date on our procedures here in Immigration."

Len beamed. "Excellent. I know you won't regret it. And there's no problem sparing her to start training right away. As I said, I'm in the process of wrapping things up right now, and I can always grab a floater if necessary." He stood and shook Marika's hand. "I'll send her down later this morning. She's running an errand for Henry right now. One of his witnesses showed up here rather than at the courthouse. His assistant had already gone over, so he borrowed Rhiannon to escort the lady there since he was still busy."

"He couldn't have just given her directions?"

"I don't think her grasp of English was very good. She was wearing one of those Middle Eastern robes, you know—where you only see her face?"

"You mean a chador?"

"Yeah, I guess that's what it's called. Anyway, when Rhiannon gets back, I'll have her come down and introduce herself, all right?"

"That's fine. I'll have Marion begin briefing her on our procedures." Marika escorted Len out.

He stopped at the door. "You won't regret it. Treat her fairly, and you'll never have a more dedicated employee."

After Len departed, Marika filled Marion in on her replacement.

A raised eyebrow greeted her announcement. "Rhiannon Davies? Are you sure about this, Marika?"

"Why? Len said she's a very hard worker."

"Well, yes, she is that, but she's about the most unsociable person I've ever met. I don't think I've ever heard her utter a single word that wasn't work-related, except maybe to ask if there's more coffee. Hell, she doesn't even come to our monthly luncheons. It's gotten so we don't bother asking her anymore."

"I know Len said she's not much of a people person, but as long as she's competent, I can put up with anything until you're back." Marika smiled at Marion. "Besides, no one could really replace you."

"You got that right. Okay, if you're willing to put up with Miss Ice, I'll train her up right."

"Miss Ice? No, forget it. I don't want to know." Marika returned to her office.

An hour later, Marion poked her head into the office. "Rhiannon is here. May I bring her in?"

Marika looked up from her computer and nodded. "Sure." She rose to greet her new assistant.

Marion walked in followed by a slight young woman. Short, brown hair with gold highlights framed her gamine face, and freckles splashed across an upturned nose. There was a stubborn tilt to her small, square chin, and her dark blue eyes had a look of perpetual wariness. Her clothes were business beige, perfectly suitable for the office, but drab and unflattering.

Marika's eyes widened. *I know her. Oh, my God. She's the woman I knocked over at the plaza.*

Rhiannon showed no signs of being nonplussed. Apparently, she had already made the connection between her assailant and her new boss.

Marika took a deep breath and extended her hand. "Rhiannon? Come in, and we'll talk about what your responsibilities will be."

Rhiannon stepped forward, gave Marika's hand a single, firm shake, and sat down.

Marion hovered, until Marika dismissed her with a nod.

Marika resumed her seat and regarded her new assistant. She didn't appreciate feeling off-balance, though she couldn't in fairness blame Rhiannon. *I was the one who knocked her ass over tea kettle. If anyone should hold a grudge, she should.* Marika took in the rigid, wary set of Rhiannon's shoulders and the clear, cool eyes that returned her gaze steadily.

They sat in silence for long moments. Rhiannon didn't squirm under her scrutiny.

Marika consciously projected her stern "I will tolerate no fools" look. She had used that expression to induce a cold sweat and trembling knees in grown men, but Rhiannon did not flinch. *She'd probably sit there like a stone until dismissed.* "You come well recommended. Len thinks highly of your work habits. I trust his opinion, and I'm sure you'll extend the same quality of performance to this office." Marika paused.

Rhiannon gave no indication of accepting the conversational opening, but the intensity in her eyes assured Marika that her new assistant was paying attention.

"Over the next couple of weeks, I want you to work with Marion and get up to speed on our procedures. I know that Immigration will be quite a change from Corporate, but I'm sure you'll handle the transition smoothly."

That at least got a nod.

Marika sighed softly. This was the point where she would normally engage in some polite conversation to elicit something of the new employee's personal history, but she doubted that any such attempt would be welcomed. *I wonder if Len knows anything of Rhiannon's background. I'll have to ask him.* "All right. You should join Marion and get started."

Rhiannon stood. "Thank you, Ms. Havers."

She withdrew abruptly and was almost out of the office when Marika said, "You can call me..." She trailed off weakly, "Marika."

Rhiannon stopped and looked at Marika over her shoulder. "Yes, ma'am." She closed the office door quietly behind her.

Marika stared out her office windows. Rhiannon had stopped to talk to Marion at her desk, and Marika studied her new assistant. *Did I just make a very big mistake? Damn it, Len. What have you gotten me into? This is going to be a long six months. I guess she and I won't be having any heart-to-hearts anytime soon.*

It was almost noon when a cheerful voice sounded at the office door. "Nose to the grindstone, eh? Good to see it."

Marika looked up with a smile.

Lee's tall, solidly muscled frame loomed in the doorway. A dark blue company blazer was tossed over one shoulder, and she sported a wide grin.

"Well, as I live and breathe, if it isn't the notorious Lee Glenn. I thought for sure they'd toss you in jail down there in Mexico, and I'd have to come bail your ass out."

A deep, contagious laugh erupted from Lee. She strolled over to perch on the edge of Marika's desk. "Nah, though I did have one run-in with an overly enthusiastic customs agent."

Marika stood and hugged Lee. "That's quite the tan you have. I thought you were going down there to work. Looks like you put in some time on the beach."

"Not you, too. Ever since I got back, I've been trying to convince Dana that I wasn't on holiday without her and Eli."

"Uh-huh, well, if I were that lady of yours, I'd put a long leash on you the next time you claim you're heading out of the country on 'business.'" Marika poked Lee's solid thigh. "So, did you bring me anything from your southern sojourn?"

Lee winked. "I brought back a bottle of tequila, so fresh from the factory that the worm is still doing cartwheels."

"That sounds interesting. Bring it over sometime this week, and we can catch up."

"Sure, but I was also thinking I might take my favourite lawyer out to lunch, if you're free, that is."

Marika glanced at the stubborn file she had poured over all morning and then back at her friend. She firmly closed the file. "I'm all yours." She chuckled at Lee's comical leer. "God, you're incorrigible. How does Dana put up with you?"

"Dunno. I ask myself that pretty much every day," Lee said as she trailed Marika out of the office.

Marion waddled back to her cubicle, followed by Rhiannon with an armful of binders.

Marika gestured at her assistants. "I'm just going to let them know that I'll be out for lunch." When Lee didn't answer, Marika glanced over her shoulder.

Lee stood staring at Rhiannon.

"Lee?"

"Huh? Oh, yeah, okay. Sorry, I didn't realize she was one of yours."

Marika raised an eyebrow at the cryptic remark, but didn't stop to ask for clarification. "Marion, I'll be out of the office for the next hour. May I bring you back anything?"

"No thanks, Marika. Have a good lunch."

Lee and Rhiannon exchanged grins.

"You two know each other?" Marika asked.

Lee shook her head. "Not well. Lady Mouse and I only met this morning. How are you doing, Miss Rhiannon?"

"Fine, thank you. And you, oh great saver of women in distress?"

Banter from Miss Ice? Oh, Lee is so going to tell me this story.

Lee bade Rhiannon goodbye and secured a shy smile and a nod of farewell in return.

Marika tried not to gape, but as they walked to the elevator, she laid a hand on Lee's forearm. "What was that all about?"

"I'll tell you the whole tale over lunch. Now c'mon, before all the tables are gone."

They left the office tower and walked two blocks over to the Tudor Rose, an English style pub that they both enjoyed. They were fortunate to get an empty booth in the popular lunch spot. Lee immediately ordered ale, but Marika opted for coffee.

Marika eyed her old friend affectionately. She couldn't suppress a snicker at how far away Lee had to hold the menu to read it. Lee stubbornly refused to admit that she needed reading glasses, which forever exasperated her long-suffering partner, Dana.

Marika found her friend's quirk endearing, and it really was Lee's only personal vanity. *But I don't have to live with her.* "So, why do I have the pleasure of your company today? I thought after your trip, you were going to take some time off."

"I was pretty tired, all right. Setting up a consulting company in Mexico is a whole new experience. We had to twist ourselves into some pretty strange knots to get the contracts signed. I was relieved to finally wrap it up and drop it in Juan's capable hands." Lee shot Marika a grin. "But you know how indispensable I am. We're considering bidding on the security contract for your building when it's up for renewal next month, so Willem dispatched me to look things over. I'll be hanging around and poking into corners for the next week."

"That's wonderful. It'll be a treat seeing you around the office. Maybe we can get together for coffee breaks."

"Or go out for lunch again," Lee said. "It's on you next time."

"Not the next couple of days, though. I have hearings scheduled, and they're pretty unpredictable in length, so it's hard to make plans. How about we look at Friday?"

"Great." Lee's eyes brightened as the waiter placed her meal on the table. She finished long before Marika and eyed the tempting dessert menu at the end of the table.

Marika smiled to herself. She loved that Lee had a huge appetite for life and all its pleasures.

"The mud pie looks pretty good, doesn't it?"

"It's meant to," Marika said dryly. "They're trying to entice you."

"And doing a damned fine job of it, too. I'd certainly hate for someone to have done all that work for nothing." Lee signaled the waiter and ordered dessert and another ale.

Marika pushed her plate aside and reached for her coffee. "So, you were going to tell me the story of how you know my new assistant."

"Right. I was. Well, it all started this morning when I was on my way to your building. I was a few blocks away when I noticed two women turn down an alley. The only reason I paid any attention is that one of them was wearing a chador, and you don't see that in Calgary every day, but I didn't think too much of it until I saw a couple of punks follow them in. It was Pike and Eddie King."

"The guys you had a run-in with when you were a military policewoman?"

Lee nodded. "Yeah. They know better than to cross me, but this morning they thought they'd come across a couple of likely victims. By the time I reached them, Pike and Eddie had them trapped between the wall and a dumpster."

"Oh, no. What happened?"

"Pike taunted and threatened them, but I gotta say, Rhiannon didn't give an inch. She wasn't going to let the two lowlifes get at Mrs. Khalil either. She was between the King brothers and the lady, and she ordered them in no uncertain terms to back off." Admiration shone in Lee's eyes. "So I came up from behind and scared the bejesus out of them. Not to mention that I irritated the hell out of Pike.

He hates his real name, so of course I called him Francis right off the bat."

"Do you think it was wise to antagonize him, Lee?"

"Might not have been wise, but it sure was fun." Lee laughed. "Besides, they're just your basic, garden variety bullies. I threatened to call their PO and let him know what they were up to. That pretty much took the wind out of their sails. Like all bullies, Pike has a healthy sense of self-preservation when the odds aren't heavily in his favour. He's meaner than a hungry rat, and while Eddie's got the brawn, he doesn't have two spare brain cells to rub together. He does whatever his brother tells him."

"Still, I wish you wouldn't take chances."

"I wasn't taking a chance. Your new assistant was. If I hadn't come along, I'm not sure what would've happened, though I wager she'd have given as good as she got if it had gotten physical."

"Oh, I don't know, Lee. She's awfully small. I doubt she'd have stood a chance."

"If there's anything I've learned in my business, it's that size isn't everything. Pike called her a mouse, but she's one mouse with a lion heart. I'm telling you, there's more to that woman than meets the eye."

Marika sipped her coffee as she pondered Lee's assessment. "I don't know if she told Len about the incident, but she certainly never said a word about it when I interviewed her."

"Does that surprise you?"

"No. She strikes me as somewhat reticent." *To put it mildly. She never even mentioned that I ran over her like a bulldozer.*

Lee chuckled. "She strikes me like a sphinx."

"But not with you." Marika smiled. Lee had a gift for connecting with people from all walks of life.

"True. Anyway, that's how Rhiannon and I met. I had no idea she worked for your firm until I saw her in your office."

"She only started this morning. But on a completely different topic, I've come up with the perfect gift for you to give Dana this weekend."

Lee looked up with a guilty expression "Um, I sorta already took care of that."

"Oh, no. Lee, you swore after the last disaster that you'd never buy Dana another birthday, anniversary, or Christmas gift without consulting me first. Have I ever steered you wrong?"

"No, no, you haven't," Lee said. "But I came up with the perfect idea, and I know she's gonna love it."

"Okay, let's hear it. What did you get for the love of your life this time?"

"I got her a new motorcycle helmet."

"You got her what?"

"I had it custom painted in the Sukuzi's colours. You should see it; it's gorgeous—all black and purple, with her name on it."

"I'm sure the helmet is lovely, but this is your anniversary. Perhaps a more...romantic gift is in order."

Lee frowned as she poked at the remnants of chocolate on her plate. "It's romantic," she said, though with a noticeable lack of conviction. "After all, it says I'm thinking about her safety when she's riding with me, and that I want her alive and kicking for a long, long time."

"If that's really what you wanted to say, you'd get rid of that damned bike. Now that would be a great gift."

Lee stared at Marika as if she'd just proposed that Lee offer her first born in sacrifice. She loved her Suzuki 1100 touring bike almost as much as she loved Dana and Eli.

Marika started to laugh as a pout emerged on Lee's face. It looked so out of place.

"Okay, so maybe the helmet wasn't the best idea," Lee said. "Aw shit, I don't know what to get her."

"That's what you have me for. Lee, have you thought that maybe it's time to consider a ring for Dana?"

"A ring?"

"Yes, a ring. After all, how long have you two been together now?"

Lee frowned at the ceiling. "Well, how long ago did you and I break up?"

"About five and a half years ago."

"Okay, so this is our fifth anniversary."

"Then don't you think she might be expecting some sign of commitment from you?"

"We bought a house together. We're raising her son together. If that isn't commitment, what is?"

Marika patted Lee's hand. "I know, and I agree. But I really think Dana might like a ring and a ceremony to formalize your union in front of all your friends and family. I think she would like to know that you're fully committed to her and Eli."

"You think so?"

"I do."

"I'll think about it." With a grin Lee added, "But I'm still giving her the helmet."

Marika rolled her eyes. *Sorry, Dana. I tried, but a helmet it is. Maybe next year.*

"So, what'd you do with yourself this weekend?" Lee asked.

Marika flinched. "Oh, not much. Pretty much stayed in most of the weekend. Me and Spooky kept each other company."

Lee studied her.

Marika quickly sought to change the subject. "The party is still on for Saturday, right? I told Dana I'd be there early to help set up."

"Uh-huh." Lee regarded her intently. "What's going on, Marika?"

"Nothing's going on." Marika refused to meet Lee's eyes. "Why do you ask?"

"Goddamnit. You went to Cass, didn't you?"

Marika sat perfectly still and stared at the table.

"Sonuvabitch. You promised you'd stay away from her."

Marika shrank into her seat and crossed her arms over her chest. "I am an adult, in case you hadn't noticed. I have a right to see whoever I choose."

Lee reached out, took Marika's hands, and gripped them tightly. "She's bad for you. Please, please, stay away from her. Jesus, you're so much better than that."

Marika looked away. "Am I?"

Lee sighed and gentled the grip on her hands. "Yes, you are. She uses you, my friend. It's not healthy."

"Maybe I use her, too."

"I suppose in a way you do, but you don't hurt her the way she hurts you. Frankly, I don't even think she has a heart to hurt. But you do. Of all people, I know you do. Oh, Marika, why?"

"There's no expectations, no confusion. We both know what we're getting out of it."

"You have so much more to give than that. Why do you settle for someone like Cass when you could have someone like Dana?"

"Could I?"

Lee frowned. "Of course you could. Why would you question that?"

"Why? Look at my track record."

"I admit that you haven't had much luck, but that doesn't mean you should stop trying."

"It's not a matter of luck. Every time I meet someone I might be interested in, I either end up bored and can't wait to get rid of them, or I go the opposite way and smother the life out of the relationship."

"So you're just going to give up and go to Cass when you need to get your jollies, is that it?"

The barb hit home, and Marika fought back tears.

"Aw shit, I'm sorry. Sometimes my big mouth gets away from me." Lee released Marika's hands. "Look, I just think you deserve a lot better than Cass. I know you've had romantic issues, but you know what? You're great at friendship. Maybe that's the problem. You need to concentrate on being friends with a woman first and see if anything else develops, rather than trying to get all hot and heavy the moment you meet someone."

"When did you become Dear Abby?"

"I know you'll do what you want, but I don't have to like it. I hate watching you treat yourself like this, or even worse, allow her to treat you like that. She's bad news. Nothing good can come of seeing her."

"I have to get back to work." Marika motioned for the check, which the waiter swiftly brought.

Lee took the check and laid down some cash. She regarded Marika somberly but said nothing. Silently, they rose and made their way out of the pub.

CHAPTER 3

DAVID'S FOOTSTEPS RESONATED IN THE vaulted nave as he and Tupper shuffled along each pew, straightened hymnals and the occasional Book of Common Prayer, and raised padded prayer kneelers back into their stored position.

They reached the last pew at the same time.

"Tupper, do you have a minute?"

"Yup. Som'pin on your mind?"

"I've been meaning to ask you about Miss Walker's niece."

"Little Anne? Where'd ya meet her? I haven't seen her in church for a couple of years now."

David gestured to a pew. "Sit for a moment?"

"Sure." Tupper slid onto the hard wooden bench.

David took a seat beside him. "I met her at her aunt's house when I was doing visitations last week. She seemed..." David hesitated, unsure how to express his unease. "Unhappy." It wasn't entirely accurate, but it was the best he could come up with.

"Well, would ya be happy if ya'd spent twelve years livin' with Hettie Walker?"

I'd be unhappy if I'd spent ten minutes living with Hettie Walker. David ducked his head. *Sorry 'bout that, God. I know better. She's one of your children, too.*

"Ya know, I was here when that little girl come ta live with her auntie. I don't know that I've ever seen her with a real, face-splittin' grin. Never met such a quiet kid. I'd try talkin' ta her after services, but her aunt would always come and pull her away. Don't think she thought I was a proper influence or sum'pin.'"

"Do you know why she stays with her aunt? Hettie said her niece was twenty-three now, so she could certainly move out if she wished." David's curiosity had been stoked by Hettie's complaint about the miniscule rent Rhiannon paid despite her good job.

Tupper rubbed his grizzled cheek. "Seems like ta me that the girl's parents died, so the authorities asked Hettie to take her. Not real sure 'bout all the details, but I 'member Hettie makin' a big deal out of what a sacrifice it was, takin' the child in and all."

David considered that a moment and then recalled another oddity. "You and her aunt both call her Anne, but she insisted her name was Rhiannon. Is one short for the other?"

"Dunno. I just went by what Hettie called her. Kid never said nothin' different ta me." Tupper frowned. "Ya know, far as I could see, that kid never gave Hettie a lick of trouble, but ta listen t'her and her crew, you'da thought Hettie Walker was a pure saint for takin' the child inta her home. I know it ain't Christian, Reverend, but I got no time for folks making themselves out to be martyrs. She usta haul the little girl ta all her church lady meetin's, and the kid would just sit in the corner drawing away 'til Hettie was done. Kid was the durndest thing for drawin'. I usta save the old leaflets and give 'em to her for scrap paper." His face darkened. "Saw Hettie whaling on the child for drawin' during a service one time. Hell, I don' blame the kid. We had Reverend Alwyard then, and his sermons could put the saints ta sleep."

David was disturbed by the picture Tupper painted. "Why do you think she stays with her aunt now that she's grown? You'd think she would've left as soon as she could."

"Well, could be home is home, even when home stinks, ya know?"

"Perhaps," David murmured, unconvinced. His mind began to wander as he pondered ways to reach out to someone who obviously had no interest in being reached.

"Speak of the devil."Tupper pointed out the side window to the street beyond. Hettie and two of her cronies walked down the street. "Goin' ta their regular Saturday afternoon meetin'. They all go over ta Miz Carter's house right as rain for a prayer meetin'. I'm thinking there's more gossip than prayer, but they love ta tell folks how they're prayin' for the lost sheep of the world. Hell, if I wuz a lost sheep, I'd rather wait on Jesus' comin' than have them lookin' fer me."

David grinned, and an idea surfaced. "So how long do these meetings normally last?"

"Dunno 'zactly. I think they usually have dinner together. That's how they get away with callin' it fellowship. Gotta have food."Tupper looked at him quizzically. "Why?"

"No particular reason, but, Tupp, I do believe I'm going to find a little fellowship myself."

***

David walked down Rhiannon's street and was delighted to spy her sitting on the front stoop of Hettie Walker's house. He'd suspected that the combination of the brilliant spring day and her aunt's absence might draw Rhiannon out of her lair.

He pushed open the gate, strolled up the pathway, and ignored the forbidding frown on Rhiannon's face. With her slight frame and gamine features, she reminded him of a short, truculent Audrey Hepburn. He knew he would never get an invitation to sit, so he chose to plop down without permission.

Rhiannon promptly drew away. "My aunt's not here."

David nodded. "I know." *Let's see what wins out—her hostility or curiosity. I think I'll wager on the latter.* He tilted his face back to absorb the welcome warmth of the sun. *Reminds me of the time me and Jimmy waited out that badger one warm July night. Took almost three hours before it came out of its tunnel. I sure hope she's not going to be as stubborn.*

Finally, Rhiannon broke the stillness. "So what do you want, Ichabod? Out recruiting?"

Eh, I've heard worse insults. At least she acknowledged my existence. "Not at all. I was out for a walk, enjoying a lovely day."

"You want something. Everyone does."

"Nope, not me. Just looking for a place to rest my weary feet." David waggled the extraordinarily long feet he had crossed in front of him.

Rhiannon snorted, but she didn't retreat into the house or throw him out of the yard.

David waited.

"I'm not going to church, you know? There's nothing you say can change my mind on that."

"Wasn't trying to." David voice remained placid.

"If you've got anything else in mind, you can forget that, too."

David threw his head back and laughed until his eyes welled over. Then he noticed that Rhiannon had edged as far away from him as she could. *Uh oh. C'mon, Davie. You don't want to scare the kid.* Slowly, David sat forward and folded himself into a smaller space, careful not to make any sudden move in her direction. "Rhiannon, I have a daughter not all that much younger than you. I assure you, I have no ulterior motive. I simply felt like sitting in the sunshine and chatting with a friend."

"I'm not your friend." Despite Rhiannon's caustic words, she no longer looked poised to flee.

"No, but you could be."

"I don't need any friends."

"You mean you don't need any 'more' friends."

Rhiannon refused to look at him. "Meant what I said."

"That's an unusual attitude." David was careful to keep his tone neutral.

Rhiannon shrugged but said nothing.

"What about your old school friends? Don't you see them anymore?"

"Good joke, Ichabod."

Unmistakable bitterness under laid the words, but David had long ago learned the value of patient silence. He waited to see whether she would add anything to her cryptic comment.

"I was one of the school freaks. There weren't many kids who'd even talk to me, unless they wanted me to draw something for them. Then they'd be nice, but only until I delivered. Took me a while to understand my role. At first I thought when I drew something for them, they'd be my friends afterwards. I learned different."

"Surely there must have been someone who didn't go along with the crowd?"

Rhiannon shot David a quick glance, then looked away again. "There was one—Patsy. They made her a pariah, too, because she was a native kid. We used to hang out some."

"Do you ever see her now?"

"She dropped out of school in tenth grade. I think it just got to be too much for her. We were only school friends, so I never saw her outside. I always wondered what happened to her. The day she left, she gave me a dream catcher she made. I wish I'd known she wasn't coming back, so I could've drawn something special for her."

David allowed himself time to let the lump in his throat diminish. He knew any sympathy he offered would be rejected and could undermine what small gains he had made. Instead, he turned the conversation on a safer tack. "So, you just sitting out here working on your tan?"

Rhiannon shrugged and looked out across the street. "I was thinking about my new job."

David allowed a note of cautious interest into his voice. "What do you do?"

"I'm a legal assistant. I'm still with the same firm, but I transferred from corporate to an immigration lawyer this week."

David tucked one long leg under the other and studied Rhiannon. *Something's bugging her, but this time I don't think it's me.* "That's quite a switch. How's the new boss?"

"Okay." Rhiannon shrugged. "She's decent, at least so far. She pretty much tells me what she needs and leaves me alone to do it."

Somehow I get the feeling being left alone is exactly what she wants...at home and work. "So what don't you like about the job?"

"Who said I don't like it?"

David raised an eyebrow.

"Okay, so the work itself is fascinating, a lot more so than the corporate work I was doing." Her voice trailed off, and she stared into the distance.

"But?" David prompted.

Rhiannon pulled herself back from wherever her thoughts had taken her. "My job is to dig up research and help my boss substantiate cases for immigrants requesting refugee status. A couple of days ago, the woman I'm replacing gave me a case to work on, and I haven't been able to get it out of my head."

Rhiannon fidgeted, and David waited. *I wonder if she's ever confided in anyone.*

"It was the case of a Romany man, you know, a Gypsy?"

David nodded. He remembered a Romany family from his posting in Fort St. John.

"His name is Marius, and he's in his mid-thirties. He had a pretty rough time growing up as a Gypsy in Romania. His father was a political prisoner for a few years, and his uncle was executed. Even after his dad came home, he had to report in every month to the Romanian secret service. Anyway, this guy grows up, gets married, and even has a couple of kids. After the revolution in '89, he thought things were going to get better, but they didn't. He lost his job because he's Rom, and because of his family's dissident history."

Rhiannon slipped into her narrative so completely that she unconsciously rested one hand against David's knee for a moment. "Finally, Marius had enough. He joined the Roma Party with his brother, and they were assigned to go around to the Gypsy communities telling them of their rights and teaching them how to vote. Immediately, the authorities started harassing the brothers. They're stopped, beaten, arbitrarily arrested, but still they keep up their political work."

"Sounds like he and his brother were very committed to their cause."

Rhiannon instantly stiffened and drew back. "You're not getting the whole picture. Marius wasn't the only one to suffer. The police went to his parents' house to look for him. When his mother tried to stop them from ransacking the place, they beat her, too. At the hospital, the doctor told Marius' father that it wouldn't be any loss if a Gypsy woman died. By four in the morning, she was having trouble breathing, but the nurse wouldn't do anything without a doctor's authorization. She died an hour later."

"That's terrible. No wonder he emigrated."

"Hell, that's not the worst of it. After the autopsy showed his mother died of a clot on the brain, her husband was sent to prison for beating his wife to death. Sometime after that, Marius and his family were walking home from a Roma Party meeting when four men came up and forced them into a car. They were taken to a fenced-in yard, where they beat him and raped his wife in front of their children, while they cried and begged for mercy. When they were thrown back out on the street, they realized they'd been in the backyard of a secret service building."

Rhiannon's story chilled David. *God, what can I say? No wonder it haunts her. It would haunt me too. It has haunted me, too.* "What happened then?"

"I guess it was the last straw. Marius bought a fake Hungarian passport on the black market, and a contact smuggled him out across the Hungarian border. Everyone figured that with him out of the country, his family would be safe, but the police came looking for him, and when they didn't find him, they beat his wife up and raped her again. She hid out all summer until her family could save enough money to get her and the children out of the country."

"So now they're together...here?"

"Yeah. But don't you see? He failed them. If it was just him, on his own, giving everything for his political beliefs, then I could understand. But what he did hurt his family. His mother died, his father was put in prison, his wife was raped and his kids terrorized, but he didn't stop. All he cared about was his little crusade. What kind of man puts that ahead of his family?"

And so we arrive at the crux. Tread carefully, Davie, m'lad. "Maybe he felt he was doing what was best for them in the long run. You know, working for a better future where things like that wouldn't happen. Maybe he felt the price was worth it."

Abruptly Rhiannon stood and paced in front of the small stoop. "Did he ever ask them if they were willing to pay the price? Or did he just make that decision for them?"

"I don't think we can second guess what happened, not knowing him or the circumstances, but I'd assume that at least he and his wife talked it over and decided supporting the cause was worth the risk." When Rhiannon turned on him, David was struck by the anger in her eyes.

"And what about the little kids? Who was looking out for them? They were the parents. They're supposed to be doing what's best for their children!" She sank down next to David and rested her head in her hands. "It never does any good anyway. One man can't stand against the tyrants."

"I don't believe that. One man can stop a line of tanks."

"Only if the tanks choose to stop for him, Ichabod. Otherwise, they keep on rolling and squish him into a puddle of nothing. Then what good is his noble gesture?"

"It matters, Rhiannon, it matters." David shook his head. Her disillusionment sat painfully at odds with her youthful passion. "It matters because one man stood up, and if he can, then more will stand after him, until so many stand up that the tanks can't possibly run over them all."

A tiny, unwilling smile flirted with Rhiannon's lips. "You're okay. You're wrong, but you're okay."

Startled, David smiled back. "Aw, you're not so bad yourself, for a baby cynic."

"Who're you calling a baby?" Rhiannon growled, but there was no heat behind her words.

David was about to tease her in return when Rhiannon's shoulders stiffened and she turned her head to stare down the street. David followed her gaze. A motorcycle came toward them. Rhiannon watched it intently and relaxed only as it continued past them and up the street.

"Problem?"

Rhiannon shook her head. "No. I just thought it might be my neighbours coming back early. They're usually gone all day on Saturdays."

"Not your favourite people, I take it."

"Not anyone's favourite people around here. I had a bit of a run-in with them earlier this week, and I've been trying to avoid them ever since. I changed my route coming home, and so far they haven't seen me."

David straightened. "If you're really afraid of them, then maybe we should call the police."

"We? You really are new around here. Trust me, there's nothing the police can do. Pike and Eddie are very good at covering their tracks, and they always have alibis."

"Well, we can't sit still and allow this to go on. Maybe I should call a neighbourhood meeting to deal with the issue."

"God, you're such an innocent. Believe me, the people around here are too cowed to stand up to the King brothers. You call a meeting, and no one will come. You go to the police, and maybe they'll run a patrol car through here once a night, but they can't do anything until a crime is committed. We don't fork over a lot of taxes around this area, so it's not like they're going to pay a whole lot of attention to a couple of neighbourhood bullyboys. You just don't get how it works down here."

"This isn't the first inner city parish I've been assigned to. Nothing worth having ever came easily, but that's what it's going to take. Do you really want to live like this for the rest of your life, scared of every street sound?"

Rhiannon looked at him with a glint of defiance in her eyes. "I'm not going to be living like this the rest of my life. A year from now, I'm going to be a million miles away from the King brothers."

"And your family?"

"Especially my family." She practically spat the words.

She does not like her aunt. While David understood the sentiment, it also saddened him. *She seems so alone.*

"What about your family? You said you had a daughter."

David was caught off guard by the change of topic. "Liz, yes, and a son, Dylan. They're back east in Nova Scotia."

"Why aren't they with you?"

Fair's fair, I guess. "Because my wife took my son and daughter with her when she left me ten years ago to move back to her home in Halifax."

"Huh. So why did she leave?"

"She didn't like the assignments I was given. She was tired of raising our children in rundown neighbourhoods and decided to take them home to her folks."

"Couldn't you have asked for parishes in better locations?" Her eyes were alight with interest.

"Yes, I suppose I could've asked, but no one else was willing to take those postings. I felt the work I was doing was worth a few broken windows and stripped down cars."

"Worth more than your family?"

I've asked myself that a thousand times since Hannah left. I still don't have an answer. Don't know that I ever will.

When he didn't speak, Rhiannon snorted. "You're no better than Marius." She shook her head and stood up in a single, sharp motion. "I've got work to do." Rhiannon went into the house and closed the door behind her.

David stared at the door. Finally, he stood and walked back down the path to the sidewalk. He pulled the gate closed behind him and started down the sidewalk. "Well, that went brilliantly, didn't it?"

CHAPTER 4

LEE'S LAUGHTER DRIFTED THROUGH MARIKA'S open office door. She looked up.

In the outer office, her friend was deeply in conversation with Rhiannon, who had a smile on her face.

Damn it. I hope she doesn't bring up Cass again. Two days had passed since lunch together at the Tudor Rose had ended on a strained note. Marika had ducked several of Lee's calls in the interval. *What now?*

Lee winked at Rhiannon and walked to Marika's door.

"Good morning, Lee. I didn't expect to see you today."

"And good morning to you." Lee took an envelope from her pocket. "I won't keep you long, but Dana asked me to drop this off."

Marika took the envelope and opened it. A list and a handful of twenties fell out. She looked up at Lee with a raised eyebrow.

"Hah, you should see the list she gave me. You got off lucky." Lee took her customary perch on the corner of the desk. "She said to ask you if you could be over at our place by one thirty or two on Saturday afternoon. She plans to put you to work."

Marika looked over the list and drew a deep breath. "I'd be happy to pick everything up, but I don't know if I'm going to stay—"

"Stop it." Lee's voice was serious. "I hate that you still see her, but I love you, and I'm not mad at you. Just don't hide from us, okay?"

Marika shook her head. Frustration at being stymied warred with affection for the friend who knew her so well. Affection won out. "All right. Tell Dana I'll be her kitchen maid for the day."

"Good. And look, I might as well tell you this now. Dana's invited her whole team to the party."

Marika's hands trembled, and she could feel Lee watching her. "The whole team?"

"Yes, and everyone's accepted."

"Everyone?"

"Yes. Terry and Jan are going to be there."

Marika shot Lee a pleading look. "Maybe I can just help Dana out, then leave before everyone arrives."

Lee sighed. "You're going to have to see them together sometime, and it might as well be when there are tons of people around and you're with friends."

"It's stupid, isn't it? I mean we only went out for a month last year. It's not like we had this huge committed relationship."

Lee came around the desk, knelt in front of Marika, and took her hands. "It's not stupid. I know how you felt about her. I know you had high hopes for that relationship."

Marika looked at Lee with tear-filled eyes. "It was crazy. I did everything wrong. I even made Terry so angry that she went psycho on me at Oly's. Why do I do that, Lee? How do I screw up so terribly?"

Lee's grip on Marika's hands tightened. "Whatever you did and whatever Terry thought, she had no right to humiliate you in front of everyone. If I'd been there that night, I'd have...well, I don't know what exactly I'd have done, but she'd have apologized, I can tell you that. I like Terry, but that was just damned mean."

"My protector." Marika squeezed Lee's hands. "And please don't blame Terry. She was going through so much herself. I didn't really understand until months later."

"She's lucky that you forgave and befriended her. I'm not sure she'd have gotten through all that shit without you."

"I'm sure she would've. Terry's family's really close, and she has a lot of friends. She didn't need me."

"Yeah, she did. Terry told me so when I ran into her at Oly's one night a few months ago and we got to talking. She said you should've been a counsellor, and she didn't mean the legal kind."

"Well, I'm glad I could be there for her, then. I tried to do my best. I never tried to steer her wrong or damage what was happening between her and Jan. I swear I didn't."

"I know that. That's not who you are." Lee stood and stretched her back. "So you'll come to the party, then?"

Marika tried to smile, but the sympathy in Lee's eyes was almost her undoing. "I will."

"Good. Now give me a hug. I've got to get back to work."

Marika stood and accepted Lee's embrace. Despite the familiar comfort of Lee's arms, her emotions churned. *Please, don't let me make a fool of myself. So Terry is in love, and it's not with me. What's new? I can handle this.*

When Marika pulled up in front Lee and Dana's house, she noted with relief that she was the first guest to arrive. Dana's fourteen-year-old son was shooting baskets in the driveway when she exited the car. "Hey, Eli, would you mind giving me a hand here?"

The boy turned with a half-glare, but Marika knew it was more an adolescent reflex than directed specifically at her. She and Eli got along well, even if children in general baffled her.

Eli set the ball down and trotted over to grab some bags.

"Thanks. I appreciate it. Your mom must be expecting quite a crowd today. I think I bought out half the town."

"No kidding," Eli said sullenly. He pushed his glasses up his nose and juggled the bags. "There's so much junk piled in the kitchen, I can't even get to the fridge."

Marika eyed her unhappy helper as they carried the bags toward the house. "So, what's got your tail in a knot?"

Eli kicked at a pebble. "Aw, she won't let me go over to Tony's house for a sleepover. I don't want to be around a bunch of women all night. I'd rather hang out with the guys."

"Any particular reason your mom wants you here?"

Eli mumbled something under his breath, and Marika couldn't stop a smile. She had known the boy since he was eight and knew when he was hiding something. She waited him out.

He stopped and scowled. "I'm kinda grounded this weekend."

"I see. Want to tell me why?"

Eli scuffed at the walkway. A hank of sweaty hair fell over his forehead. "She caught me smoking with Tony." Finally meeting Marika's eyes, he burst out, "It's so unfair! They weren't even my cigarettes, they were Tony's."

"But you were smoking too?"

"Yeah, but just to try one. I don't know why Mom's gone ballistic. Lee used to smoke."

"Uh-huh, and Lee had the good sense to stop, didn't she? I doubt very much that your mother wants you to go through what Lee did when she finally quit. Do you remember what a bear she was?"

Marika and Eli shared a grin as they recalled how it had taken Dana banishing Lee to the basement guest room before her partner stopped taking out her withdrawal pains on her family.

"I suppose," Eli said. "Still, if she doesn't lighten up, I think I'm gonna have to hire you to fight for my freedom."

"Not sure you could afford my fees, squirt. Tell you what, if you're still grounded by the time school ends, I'll consider taking you on, pro bono, okay?"

"If I'm still grounded by then, I'm hitting the highway."

"If you hit the highway, I'm turning you into road kill, son of mine," Dana said from the front door.

Marika chuckled. She was struck anew by how much mother and son resembled each other.

They had the same stocky build, chestnut hair, and dark brown eyes behind thick glasses. Usually, they had the same cheerful expression, but as soon as Eli saw his mother, his smile faded, replaced by a scowl.

Dana ignored her son's sulkiness. "Take the bags to the kitchen, then Lee could use some help in the backyard."

Eli stalked by, deliberately keeping his distance.

Dana shook her head as he disappeared down the hall. "Adolescents. I don't suppose I could interest you in fostering him for the next four years, could I?"

Marika accepted the hug Dana offered. "No thanks. Besides, if he's going to hire me to take you to court, it would be a conflict of interest."

They chuckled and went to the kitchen. Marika set her bags on a crowded counter and looked out the sliding glass doors that led out onto the deck. Lee was wrestling with a patio umbrella that stubbornly refused to unfurl. Eli watched her, his hands jammed in his jeans pockets.

"Why do I have a hunch he's not going to be much help?" Marika surveyed the kitchen and Dana's efforts to clear a workspace on the island. Weaving her way through bags scattered all over the floor, she joined Dana.

"I know. It's getting so even Lee is exasperated with him half the time, and you know he's always had her wrapped around his little finger." Dana drew a knife out of the drawer and pushed a cutting board over to Marika.

"Oh, don't worry about it," Marika said. "He'll be human again...someday. You only have to get through the next few years with your sanity intact, and he'll probably turn into a delightful adult."

Dana rummaged through bags until she came up with a few blocks of cheese. "It's the 'getting through with my sanity intact' that I question." She handed the cheese to Marika. "Here, start slicing these and then start on the pickles and the meat. There are about six different kinds of crackers in one of these bags, and I want to have those trays done first so they're ready when people start arriving."

They worked together to arrange trays.

"Did Lee give you your anniversary gift yet?" Marika looked up to see Dana roll her eyes. "I'm going to take that as a yes. I'll have you know I had nothing to do with it this year."

"I knew that without asking. I can't say much, though, since I got her a new leather riding jacket."

Marika laughed. "Actually, that's right up her alley. Good choice. So, Lee was saying your whole softball team will be here tonight."

"Uh-huh. Are you going to be all right with that?"

Marika shrugged. "Why shouldn't I be?"

Dana went to the fridge. "Gee, maybe because Terry will be here with Jan? Not to mention that you also have a history with a few others on the team." She returned to the island with several meat rolls for slicing.

"It's a small community. If I tried to avoid everyone I had a history with, I might as well just stay in my condo all day."

"You've got a point. But you and I both know that Terry was special to you, and it's not going to be easy."

"She was, and she still is, but only as a friend. I got over her a long time ago. Really." Marika hoped her words sounded more convincing than they felt. She busied herself with a new tray and was grateful when Dana allowed the subject to drop.

They worked steadily for the next couple of hours. After Lee wrestled the patio furniture into submission, she dropped in long enough to kiss Dana, hug Marika, and announce she and Eli were going to go pick up the keg. They'd just returned and were setting up the keg on the deck when the doorbell sounded.

Dana looked up. Her hands were deep in a huge bowl of raw hamburger meat and spices.

Marika took the bowl from her. "Go. I'll finish this up and make the patties while you see to your guests."

Dana smiled gratefully and washed her hands before she went to the front door.

Guests began arriving steadily. Most found their own way to the backyard. Marika chatted with those who dropped in to the kitchen but didn't venture out to the yard, where the party was now in full swing.

She was preparing the large coffee maker when Terry and Jan entered the yard from the alley. One look told her that Terry had, indeed, followed her directive to resolve matters with Jan.

Terry had an arm wrapped tightly around Jan, whose arm encircled Terry's waist. Jan laughed at something her lover said and reached up to affectionately brush back Terry's hair. Marika's chest tightened as Terry bent to kiss Jan before the couple joined their friends.

Marika turned away and busied herself at the counter farthest from the doors.

Dana came back into the kitchen. "C'mon, Marika. Leave everything and come on out. You're missing the party."

"I'll be out in a few minutes. I just want to finish a couple of things."

"Okay, but you know we really didn't ask you here so you could be our maid." Dana went back outside.

Marika closed her eyes. *How long before I can make a graceful exit?*

The kitchen door slid open again. "I'm coming, Dana. Just give me a few more minutes."

"Hey, Marika, you're missing all the fun."

Marika stiffened and turned. "Hi, Ter, how's it going?"

Terry crossed the space between them and wrapped Marika in a hug.

Marika returned the hug, then quickly stepped back out of the embrace.

"It couldn't be better," Terry said. "You were so right to throw me out. It was just the push I needed."

"I take it that you've resolved any lingering doubts." Marika was impressed with how calmly she managed to speak.

Terry leaned back against the counter and grinned. "And how. God, I was such an idiot. Jan's incredible. I've been floating on cloud nine for the last week."

"I can see that." Terry had such a look of joy in her eyes that Marika couldn't begrudge her friend's happiness. "I'm so glad for you. She's a very lucky lady."

Terry shook her head. "Believe me, I'm the lucky one. I've never, ever felt like this before. She's it. She's the one I'm going to spend the rest of my life with." She popped a piece of cheese into her mouth. "I guess that means I can drop by your place again sometime, eh?"

"You're always welcome, you know that. Spooky sends his best, by the way." Marika was profoundly grateful that her years of legal training had her on automatic pilot as she chatted casually. "Hey, you'd better get back to your lady. You don't want some of those vultures getting a fix on her now, do you?"

"Wouldn't do 'em any good. So, are you coming out? I'd really like you to meet Jan."

"I'll be out in a moment. I've still got a few things to do. Besides, we have met before, you know?"

"Nah, not really. Besides, I want you two to get to know each other and be friends. You're both so special to me."

Her words stung, but Marika simply gave Terry an affectionate nudge toward the doors. "Go. I'll be out shortly, and I'd enjoy a chance to talk to your partner."

"My partner. Yeah, I like the sounds of that. Okay, don't be too long, or I'll have to come in and get you." She left and made a beeline for Jan, who was talking to Dana. Terry came up behind Jan, wrapped her arms around her, and pulled her back against her body. Jan rested her hands on Terry's arms and leaned her head back against her lover's shoulder.

Marika's gaze lingered for a long moment before she turned away. A short while later, she ran out of things to do. She snagged a beer from the fridge and sat down at the breakfast nook. She sipped the brew as she watched the crowd of people in the backyard.

Eli entered the kitchen, digging into a huge bag of chips. Marika hid a grin.

"Lee says you're to bring out the hamburgers so she can start them," Eli said around a mouthful of chips.

"All right." Marika went to the fridge to retrieve them. "Why don't I give them to you to take out?"

Eli backed away from the tray she offered. "Nuh-uh. Lee said *you're* supposed to bring them out, and she meant it."

Looks like Lee's patience has officially expired. Damn.

Eli opened the door for Marika, and she took the hamburgers to where Lee tended the grill.

Lee glanced at her. "'Bout time."

"Sorry. I didn't know you were ready for the burgers." Marika ignored Lee's sarcastic grunt. "Oh, there's Tory. I haven't seen her in ages. Excuse me, will you?" Without giving Lee a chance to reply, Marika hastened away. She sidled up to a clutch of women she knew and joined their conversation while she kept an eye on the whereabouts of Terry and Jan.

As soon as possible, Marika eased away from the group and threaded her way back to the house, smiling and greeting people as she went.

A quick check confirmed that Lee was busy at the grill, and she made her escape. Dana and two others were in the kitchen, so Marika turned left into a small washroom. She closed the door and leaned against it. *This is so damned hard. I should've made an excuse...any excuse.* She shook her head. *Not that Lee would've bought anything I came up with.*

The buzz of the crowd and bursts of laughter floated in through the high, open window.

Marika sat down on the closed commode lid and rested her head in her hands. After several minutes, she reluctantly decided she couldn't stay in there much longer.

Then voices filtered through the window and caught her attention. "So, who was the fox?"

"What fox?"

Marika recognized the second voice as Val Menninger, a woman she'd briefly dated on the rebound from Terry the previous year.

"You couldn't have missed her. She was just out here. Hair so blonde it's almost white, legs so long they go on forever, and the most gorgeous ass I've ever seen in jeans. I didn't notice her before, but she was over talking to that bunch by the punch."

"Aw, shit. You don't mean Marika Havers, do you?"

Marika sat upright.

"I dunno. Like I said, I've never seen her before. I know she's not on the team, that's for sure. God, she was gorgeous, though. I wonder if she's single."

"You do not want to go there."

Marika cringed at the anger in Val's voice. *She's never forgiven me. I don't think she ever will. Guess I can't really blame her.*

"Why not? What's wrong with her?"

"Oh, nothing, if you don't mind being used and discarded like an old tissue when she's tired of you. Believe me, she's as cold as they come."

Marika shuddered at the venom in her ex-lover's voice.

"Damn, that's a shame. Still, it might be kinda fun while it lasted, as long as you knew what you were in for. Was she always cold?"

The insinuation was clear, and Marika stood to make her exit, sure she didn't want to hear anything else.

"No, I guess not," Val said grudgingly. "She knows her way between the sheets, but trust me, the bitch ain't worth it."

The rest of Val's assessment was lost to Marika as she hurried from the washroom.

Dana glanced up when Marika entered the kitchen, then did a double take. "Hey, are you all right?"

"Um...sure. Why do you ask?"

"Because you're so pale. Why don't you sit down here and keep me company for a few minutes?" Dana pushed a stool toward her, and Marika sank down on it. "Wanna talk about it?"

"There's nothing to talk about. I think it was the beer on an empty stomach. I don't feel all that well."

Dana laid a practiced hand on Marika's forehead. "Why don't you go lie down in the guest room for a bit, and I'll call you when it's time to eat."

About to decline, Marika realized it was a perfect out, for a while, at least. She walked down to the basement, where it was pleasantly cool and quiet. She stretched out on the bed in the guest room, and her mind drifted to the conversation she's overheard..

I'm so tired of all this. I never start out to hurt anyone, but just once I'd like a good relationship that lasts longer than a month. Marika wiped her eyes. *I have to find someone who will look at me the way Terry looks at Jan. No, not just that. I have to find someone who I'll look at the way Jan looks at Terry.*

Marika gathered the pillow under her head and stared at the ceiling. *There's always Cass. We've lasted longer than anyone since Rosalie. It's what...nine or ten months now?* She snorted. "Not that it's much of a relationship, and it sure as hell isn't love."

Marika rolled over, buried her head in her arms, and, emotionally exhausted, fell asleep.

She had no idea how much time had passed when someone shook her shoulder. She turned on her side and blinked up at Lee.

"Hey, are you all right? Dana said you were ill."

Marika yawned and swung her legs over the edge of the bed. "Yes, I'm fine now. Sorry about bailing. I didn't mean to fall asleep. What time is it?"

"Going on nine. I've been so busy, I didn't even notice you weren't around until Terry asked me if I'd seen you. I thought you were in the kitchen, but she said you weren't there."

"Probably just a little bug. I think I'll bow out, if you don't mind. Give me a good night's sleep, and I should be fine in the morning."

"Okay. Do you want me to drive you home?"

"No, you have guests to attend to. I'm fine, just very tired." Marika followed Lee upstairs, where the party was still going strong. "Would you mind saying goodnight to Dana for me?"

"Are you sure you don't want to tell her yourself? She'll be disappointed she missed you, not to mention that Terry is probably still looking for you."

"Tell Dana I'll call her in the morning, and tell Terry... well, just say I wasn't up to the party, okay?"

Lee nodded.

Marika hugged Lee. "Thanks for everything. I'll see you later." She made a rapid exit and exhaled when she reached the sanctuary of her car.

Many hours later, when the last of their guests had departed, Dana surveyed the clutter in their backyard. She shook her head at the mess and looked up at Lee. "Tomorrow?"

"Tomorrow." With a grin, Lee spun Dana into her arms. "Besides, I've got better things to do with my best girl than pick up garbage."

Dana melted into Lee's embrace. Her partner smelled of grill smoke, beer, and an indefinable 'Lee scent' that she could've picked out blind-folded in a crowd of thousands. "You know, after all these years, you still make me weak in the knees."

"Does that mean you'll be extra easy to tumble into bed, love of my life?"

Dana laughed as Lee took her hand and urged her toward the house. They had barely gotten inside the doors when her eager partner began to unbutton her blouse. Both of them jumped when an awkward cough sounded from behind them.

Dana dropped her head onto Lee's chest.

Lee cleared her throat. "Eli...what are you doing up at this hour?"

"My stomach's bothering me, and I couldn't find anything for it in the bathroom."

Dana discreetly rebuttoned her blouse and stepped around Lee. "I've got more. Considering all the junk you ate tonight, I'm not the least bit surprised you have a bellyache."

When Dana finally got Eli settled and returned to the master bedroom, Lee was already in bed. Dana washed up quickly, shed her clothes, and slid in beside her silent partner.

When Lee didn't move, Dana poked her shoulder. "Hey, is everything okay? Eli didn't mean to interrupt, you know? I'm sure he was more embarrassed than we were."

"Yeah, I know. Wasn't the first time, won't be the last. It's no big deal."

Dana snuggled close and laid her head on Lee's shoulder. "Then what's wrong, my love?"

Lee had a distracted look on her face. "I figured since I had a few minutes, I'd give Marika a call, just to make sure she got home all right."

"It's awfully late," Dana said. "We could've called in the morning."

"I know. I didn't think of the time. I was just..."

"Worried. You're a good friend. So, how was she?"

"She didn't answer. She's not there."

Dana rubbed Lee's belly. "She's probably just asleep and turned off the phone so she wouldn't be bothered."

Lee stilled Dana's hand and shook her head. "I don't think so, hon. I think she went to that bitch again."

"Who? Cass? But she hasn't seen her since that time, has she? Surely..."

"I didn't think so either." Lee gathered Dana into her arms. "I didn't tell you, but Marika confessed she was with her last weekend."

"Oh God, no. Why would she do that? Jesus, when I think of how we found her..." Dana blinked back tears.

"Yeah, I didn't think she'd ever go back after that, either, but she has, and nothing I say seems to reach her."

They lay in silence, and Dana drew comfort from Lee's embrace. "What can we do, love? I'm afraid for her."

"So am I. And I don't know if there is anything we can do."

CHAPTER 5

L EE TURNED HER MOTORCYCLE INTO the driveway of
Marika's condo tower and pulled into visitor parking
beside a battered silver Toyota.

Terry sat on the brick edge of the raised flower gardens
that bracketed the covered entranceway.

Lee took off her helmet, locked it to the bike, and
dismounted.

There was a despondent look on Terry's normally
cheerful face. Lee suspected that she was there for much the
same reason as Lee.

"Hey, Terry, how's it going?"

"Not bad. Are you here to see Marika, too?"

"Uh-huh. I take it she's not answering her intercom?"

"No, she's not. She didn't answer her cell this morning
when I called, either. Because of the stupid security, I can't
get into the garage to see if her car's there. I tried to ring
through to the superintendent, but no one answered." Terry
frowned at Lee. "What if she's seriously sick and can't get to
her phone or something?"

"I've got keys. Let's go check." Lee unlocked the door
and held it for Terry to precede her inside. They crossed
the lobby to the dual elevators and pressed the button. "So,
where's Jan this morning?"

"She and my mom are brainstorming over coffee and
doughnuts. They're both on the organizing committee
for the summer food bank drive, and they have some big
meeting tomorrow night that they're getting ready for."

The elevator arrived, and they entered. Terry pressed the button for the fifteenth floor. "Where's Dana this morning?"

"She's monitoring Eli's grounding. She's got him picking up garbage and stuff in the backyard."

"It was a terrific party. Jan and I had a great time."

"Glad you did. I wouldn't want to do it every week, but we had fun putting it on. The turnout was pretty impressive."

"I'll say. I ran into people there I haven't seen in ages. I don't know how you fit them all in your yard. I hope your neighbours weren't too bothered by the noise."

"No. We solved that problem by inviting them to join us. Did you see the man wearing the wild red Hawaiian shirt?"

"You mean the guy that just about knocked Robyn's cake off the table when he tried to limbo?"

"Yeah, well, that's the dentist who lives next door to us, and somehow I don't think he was in any shape to complain about anything."

They chuckled as they stepped out of the elevator on the fifteenth floor and walked down the hall to Marika's door at the far end of the corridor.

Terry tapped on the door. She cocked her head and listened for any sounds from within.

When several repetitions failed to elicit a response, Lee used her key to open the door.

"Marika?" Terry called softly. She did a quick check of the living room and kitchen before she walked down the hall.

Sure that their friend wasn't at home, Lee didn't bother to follow her. Instead, she bent to stroke Spooky, who had come to greet them. "Hey, Spook. Did your momma leave you alone? Bet you're hungry, aren't you?"

Spooky padded to the kitchen and looked at Lee expectantly.

Lee fed Spooky, and by the time she'd finished, Terry had returned.

"She's not here," Terry said. "Do you think she's all right? I mean, if she wasn't feeling well last night..."

Lee ran a hand through her hair and sighed. "Let's sit down."

Terry trailed after Lee and took a seat on the couch.

On the other end of the couch, Lee studied her hands as she tried to decide how much to divulge.

"What's going on? Do you know where Marika is? Is she okay?" Terry's words held an angry edge.

Lee leaned back and faced Terry. "I think I probably know where Marika is, and no, she's not okay." At the instant look of alarm on Terry's face, Lee held up a hand. "I don't mean that she's in any immediate danger." She hesitated for several moments. "I probably shouldn't say anything. I doubt very much that Marika would want you to know, but God knows I haven't been able to reach her, and maybe you can."

"What are you talking about? If Marika's in trouble, we have to help her."

Lee smiled sadly. "She doesn't want any help, and frankly, other than hogtying her, I'm not sure what we can do."

"Damn it, Lee, stop being deliberately obtuse and tell me what the hell is going on."

Lee regarded the agitated woman. "You do care about her, don't you?"

Terry glared at Lee. "Of course I do. I may not have known her as long as you, but she's my friend, too."

"Relax. I'll tell you what I know." Lee rubbed her temple to ward off an incipient headache and tried to decide where to start and how much to reveal. "Marika's gotten herself into a bad relationship and either doesn't want to or can't break free." She grimaced at the startled look on Terry's face. "Let me start from the beginning. About two months ago we dropped by on a Sunday morning. We'd decided on the spur of the moment to go out to brunch so we thought we'd see if Marika wanted to come."

Terry nodded but remained silent.

"I always just use my keys to let myself in, so we went upstairs. We saw a woman leave Marika's apartment. No big deal, right? I mean Marika's an adult, and if she's had overnight company, it's none of our business."

"Did you recognize the woman?"

"No, I didn't. She really wasn't anything out of the ordinary—brown hair, brown eyes, average height and build. But there was something about her." Lee scowled.

"What? What was there about her?"

Lee shook her head. "I'm not sure if I can describe it, but it was her eyes. They were dead cold, kinda like that picture of Karla Homolka. You know the one I mean?"

"You mean that picture when she was going into court, and her eyes were so flat, you wondered if she even had a soul?"

"That's exactly it, but it was also the way she sauntered down the hall—as if she owned the world and it existed only to serve her. Not to mention the smirk on her face when she saw us. She wasn't the least bit fazed. She walked right past us like we were nothing. Not even a nod of acknowledgement."

Terry had edged closer during the narrative. "Did you go in?"

"We did. We found Marika huddled in a corner of her bedroom, naked. She was just staring into space. I'd never seen her like that before. She was totally unresponsive. Didn't even blink when I waved my hand in front of her face." Lee's throat closed as she remembered the lost, desolate look in her friend's eyes.

"Do you think she was...?"

Lee knew Terry couldn't say the word. "I don't know. She had some bruises, both old and new, on her body."

"So you think she was abused?" Terry sounded as if she'd be ill.

Lee sympathized. She'd had nightmares long after. "She was definitely abused, but I think most of the damage that bitch did was internal."

"Not...?"

"I can't say for sure. She wouldn't tell us what happened or let us take her to the hospital, so I don't know. No, what I mean is, the damage that bitch has done to her heart and spirit."

"Jesus." Terry was pale. "I had no idea this was going on. *Is* it still going on?"

Lee nodded sadly. "Yes. At least I know that she was with her last weekend. Her name is Cass, by the way, but that's all I know about the woman. Marika won't say how they met or how long ago they got together or where that she-devil lives. After that morning, Marika promised she wouldn't have anything more to do with her. I think she tried to stay away, but Cass has some weird hold over her."

"But why? Why would she go with someone like that? She's got so much to offer someone, and she sure as hell deserves a lot better than that."

"Exactly what I keep telling her. But she won't listen to me. Hell, she won't even allow Dana or me to mention that day, except to say that she appreciated our concern, but she was fine."

"Doesn't sound like she was fine to me."

"No, she wasn't, but she's too damned proud to admit she needs help."

They were silent for a long time, lost in contemplation. Finally, Terry shook her head. "I still don't get it. I mean, she's beautiful. She could have anyone she wants."

"Not anyone." Lee grimaced at her unguarded words. "I mean, yeah, but she's never had much luck with relationships, in case you haven't noticed."

Terry glanced up sharply.

Lee shifted uneasily and hoped that Terry wouldn't pick up on unvoiced truths. "You know, I think the answer to why she has gone to Cass might be in her past."

"Her past? What do you mean?"

"Has she told you much about her family, about her youth?"

"Not really. She's never been one for reminiscing, that's for sure. I know that her parents split up because her mother was an alcoholic. I know her father is a prominent, wealthy lawyer in Toronto, and that he's remarried. And I know that she's estranged from her family because of some scandal when she was a teenager, and she hasn't seen them in years. Why? What do you know?"

"Pretty much the whole story, I think, but we'd been friends for about four years before Marika opened up about her past." Lee paused and regarded Terry solemnly. "Marika's a very private woman, and I'm only telling you because I know you care about her, and, frankly, I'm bloody well at my wits' end."

"I would never hurt her. And anything you say, I'll keep in strict confidence. She was there for me through some hard times. I want to be there for her, too, if I can."

"I know you'll talk to Jan, and that's okay. There's nothing I keep from Dana either, but keep it between you two, okay?" When Terry assented, Lee launched into her story. "You were right about her folks splitting up, and, because her mother was an alcoholic who could barely look after herself, Marika's father took custody. I got the impression the relationship between them was okay until her dad remarried, and then he got wrapped up in his new family. I guess there were a couple new babies in quick succession, and Marika got shuffled off to the side. Her father is this legal big shot, and they lived pretty high on the hog. I mean they had a cook, a driver, a nanny, and a part-time maid. What the hell was her name?" Lee racked her memory. "Rosanna...Rosalie... Rosalind... I dunno, I can't remember exactly, but the maid was really nice to Marika. She talked to her, encouraged the kid, told her how wonderful her piano playing was, but most of all, she listened to Marika."

"Bet she didn't get much of that."

"No, I don't think so. Inevitably, Marika started regarding this woman, who's probably twice her age, as a friend."

"Oh shit. I know where this is going."

"Yeah, you got it. Our sixteen-year-old girl falls head over heels in love for the first time in her life, and when Rosie seduces her, she's all too willing. Hell, she handed over her innocent heart and body, lock, stock, and barrel."

"Please tell me that bitch got what was coming to her."

"I wish I could. Unfortunately, this isn't a fairy tale, and the wicked witch doesn't eat the poisoned apple. Marika started meeting Rosie outside of the house. She even cut classes to go to the woman's apartment."

"Wait a minute. I think I do remember Marika saying something about this. She got caught in bed with her, didn't she?"

"Uh-huh. It was a weekend, and Marika was just waking up when Rosie came into her room. She told Marika that her family had gone out and promptly stripped down and crawled into the kid's bed for a little early-morning lovin'. Except that her parents hadn't gone out, which Rosie damned well knew. They were just getting into it when Marika's father came in to wake his daughter. It was a pretty ugly scene, from what I understand, and he ordered both of them to get dressed and meet him in his den. Marika was terrified, but Rosie kept telling her everything was going to be fine and to trust her."

"Why do I get the feeling it'd be safer to trust a snake?"

"You'd be right. They got down to the den, and the old man read them the riot act. He threatened to send Rosie back to wherever she came from, and Marika started screaming at him that she'd go with her. I guess Rosie just stood back while they yelled at each other, but finally she hauled a big envelope out of her purse and threw it on the desk. The pictures that spilled out were all of Marika and Rosie in bed at the bitch's apartment. Turns out she had her boyfriend taking photos every time they met."

"God. That must have devastated Marika."

"She told me she couldn't believe it. She was so shattered that she never said a word while her father brusquely paid the woman off, threatened her if copies ever turned up, and banished her. Dear old dad then proceeded to inform Marika that she was a fool and that he couldn't allow her indiscretions to taint his name or influence her little brother and sister. He told her that arrangements would be made for her to go to a boarding school overseas, and in the meantime, she was to remain in the house."

Tears welled up in Terry's eyes.

"Oh, it gets better. Marika's stepmom found her cuddling her baby sister not long before she flew out and threw a fit. Bloody woman probably thought Marika was going to pass 'lesbian cooties' to the kid. Anyway, it was all sort of a blur until she was on a plane for Geneva. They wouldn't even let her call her mother to say goodbye. Marika never knew if her mother even realized that she had gone."

Terry was quiet for long moments. "It was a terrible thing to happen, but how do you figure it relates to Cass?"

"Think about it. The first time Marika fell in love, her whole world collapsed around her. The object of her affection broke faith with her in the worst manner possible, so what lesson does she take from that?"

"Love sucks?"

"Not exactly. I think she longs for love as much as any of us, maybe more, but I don't think she trusts love. At some level, she's convinced she's going to be betrayed again, just like the first time. God knows she has yet to have a single long-term, successful romance. I think that, unconsciously, she needs to stop the pain before it begins, so she always does something to sabotage the relationship before it gets too serious. Hell, you and I can attest to that."

Terry nodded. "We can. So you think she goes to Cass because she doesn't trust anyone enough to have a normal relationship?"

"No, not really. I think, in some convoluted sense, she believes someone like Cass is all she's worthy of."

"But that's just dumb."

"I agree," Lee said. "You and I can see that, but I haven't had any success trying to get Marika to realize it."

Marika tugged on her jeans and took her shirt off the hanger. She found her purse next to a large suitcase near the bedroom door. She picked up her purse and looked back at the bed.

Cass's cold, half-lidded eyes watched her. Without a word, Cass rolled over.

Marika stared at her back, then left the bedroom and pulled the door closed behind her. She went to the kitchen and opened a cupboard to look for a clean glass. The shelves were almost bare, but she found a mug.

As she ran some water, she contemplated the empty state of the entire apartment. It hardly seemed as if anyone lived there. There were no dishes, few towels or amenities, and only bare-bones furniture, except in the bedroom. When she'd once worked up the nerve to question Cass on her minimalist decorating, Cass sneered and said she had no intention of wasting money on a trick pad.

Marika quickly rinsed and dried the mug and returned it to the cupboard. She had learned early that Cass wouldn't tolerate slovenly habits. She made her way to the front door to retrieve her jacket and shoes. Cass' coat was the only other garment hanging in the closet. Eager to leave, Marika exited the apartment.

On the ride home, Marika resolutely kept her mind off the activities of the previous night. She focused instead on the long, hot bath she planned to take as soon as she got back to her condo.

Once her car was parked in the underground garage, she jogged to the elevators and sighed with relief when one of the doors opened promptly for her. Grateful that the lift was empty, she leaned against a wall and closed her eyes.

When she got out of the elevator, Marika hurried to her door. She fumbled with her keys, and only when the door closed behind her did she relax. She tossed her jacket and purse on the hallway chair and walked down the short corridor to the living room.

At the sight of Lee and Terry staring at her, she came to an abrupt halt. Marika groaned inwardly. "What are you two doing here?" Her voice came out more harshly than she intended.

Lee spoke first. "We were concerned when you didn't answer your phone and thought we would check to make sure you're all right."

"I'm fine. Thank you for your concern. Now if you don't mind, I'd like to get cleaned up."

Terry stood and walked toward her, holding out a conciliatory hand. "Lee told me what's going on, and we want to help."

Marika whirled to glare at Lee. "Goddamnit! Just couldn't keep your mouth shut, could you? Who asked you to stick your nose in, anyway? Last time I checked, I was well over the age of consent and didn't need to check with Mommy whenever I want to go out."

Terry froze.

Lee jumped to her feet. "Jesus, you know we're just worried about you."

"Well, don't bother. I'm perfectly capable of looking after myself." Exhaustion washed over Marika. *Just go. Leave me alone. I can't deal with you right now.*

"Yeah, you're doing a helluva fine job looking after yourself," Lee said. "You look like something Spooky dragged in."

"I'm tired. I just need some sleep, and I'll be fine."

"What you need," Lee said sharply, "is to stay a million miles away from that parasite. She's eating you alive, and you don't even see it."

"What I need," Marika said, her anger escalating, "is for you to stop lecturing me."

When both Lee and Terry both began to speak at once, Marika's temper boiled over. "Stop it!" she yelled, distantly aware of the shock on their faces as she backed away and wrapped her arms around herself. She stopped when she hit the wall. "I don't need your approval. You're both so bloody smug because you've found 'true love.' Well, guess what, ladies. Some of us never do and never will, but we would get along just fine if you'd stop gloating and crowing."

When Terry tried to speak, Marika shook her head. "Just leave. Please, just leave." Marika turned, strode down the hall to her bedroom, and closed the door.

Lee locked Marika's front door behind them, and they walked silently to the elevators.

"Well, that went well, didn't it?" Lee said.

"Do you think it was all right to leave her alone?"

"I don't think that was up to us," Lee said. "She made it crystal clear that she didn't want us there."

"So, what do we do now?"

"I don't know. Marika will withdraw for a while now, and I think it might be best to let her. Give her some time to cool down. It won't take her long to realize that whatever we did, we did because we love her. Then it'll just be a matter of breaking through her damned pride to get things back to normal, because she'll isolate herself for the next ten years before she'll admit that she needs us."

CHAPTER 6

WHEN LEE SLAMMED THE PHONE into its cradle, Dana jumped. She raised a sympathetic eyebrow. "Still not answering?"

"No, damn it. How many times have I called her since last weekend's fiasco?"

"I haven't kept count, love, but it has to be a dozen or so. I think you're going to have to go see her in person."

Lee scowled. "Why does it always have to be me who makes the first move? Why can't, just once, Marika pick up the phone and call me after we've had a fight?"

"You know why." Dana knelt in front of Lee's chair and took her hands. "She's terrified of what would happen if you rejected her if she were to make the first move."

"She should know better than that. When have I ever blown her off?"

"Never. But she needs to be certain of your forgiveness before you can resume your friendship."

"It's stupid. All I want to do is apologize. I'm not going to say one damned word about Cass."

"I know that, Lee, but she doesn't. She wants your approval, and she knows she's not going to get it where Cass is concerned. But you've also seen what happens when you get stubborn and try to wait her out. You two didn't speak for almost two months three years ago, and you were miserable the whole time. So was she."

Lee sighed. "Sometimes I feel like we're in kindergarten again. It's a good thing we don't argue often."

Dana rose to her feet and ran a hand through Lee's hair.

Lee promptly pulled her down onto her lap.

Dana laughed and wrapped her arms around Lee's neck. She let herself get lost for long moments in the softness of Lee's lips. Then she laid her head on Lee's shoulder. "Marika knows how lucky she is to have your friendship. The thought of losing you terrifies her. Toss that fear and her guilt over Cass together, and it's a pretty toxic brew. She's not up to making herself vulnerable right now, and she's not going to get beyond it without your help."

"I know." Lee squeezed Dana gently. "Remind me again why I put up with her?"

Dana deposited a kiss on Lee's neck. "Because you love her, and so do I. And because we both know how wounded she is. She needs us. Mostly, she needs you, so are you going to go see her?"

"I guess. I'll drop by her office tomorrow after work."

"You could go over to her condo tonight."

"Mmm-hmm. I could." Lee slid her hands under Dana's T-shirt. "But Eli's at his dad's tonight."

Dana smiled. "He is, isn't he? You know, I think you're right. Tomorrow will be soon enough." She slid off Lee's lap, stood up, and offered her hand. "Care to join me?"

Lee grinned and jumped to her feet.

Dana was relieved to see the distress on her partner's face vanish as she led Lee to their bedroom. *Mission accomplished.*

As Lee walked down the hall toward Marika's office, she rehearsed what she should say. She tried to decide whether to apologize or act as if the previous weekend had never happened. *Six of one, half a dozen of the other. Dana's right, though. It is up to me to take the first step.*

She turned into the large open area which held a bank of lawyers' offices along the windows and multiple cubicles for their assistants and clerical staff.

Rhiannon was at her desk in front of Marika's empty office. She frowned at her computer screen and scrawled some notes on a yellow legal pad.

Lee drew even with Rhiannon's open-sided cubicle. "Good afternoon, Lady Mouse."

Rhiannon leaned back in her chair and smiled. "Hello, Ms. Glenn. I haven't seen you around in a while."

Lee perched on one corner of the desk and idly noted the complete lack of personal items in the small enclosure. "No, I had to do the paperwork on our bid this week, so I haven't had time to drop in. If all goes well, though, you may see me around more often."

"I'm sure Ms. Havers will be pleased to know that."

"I hope so. Is your boss still around anywhere?"

Rhiannon shook her head. "I'm sorry, she left early today."

"She did? That's not like her, even on a Friday."

"Extenuating circumstances. Marion had her baby last night, and Ms. Havers was going to visit her at the hospital."

"Last night? That was early, wasn't it?"

"I'm not exactly sure, but I know that today was supposed to be Marion's last day. They'd planned a going-away luncheon in the conference room."

"Sounds like the baby jumped the gun a little. So you're in the hot seat now, are you?"

"I guess so," Rhiannon said. "But it was only a day earlier than I would've taken over anyway."

"Think you'll like working here?"

"Yes, I think so. The work is very interesting."

"And...?"

"And?" Amusement sparkled in Rhiannon's eyes.

"And how is the formidable Ms. Havers to work for? Does she crack the whip, or is she really a pussycat in disguise?"

"I'm sure you'd know more about that than I would, Ms. Glenn."

Lee burst into laughter. "Check and mate."

Rhiannon's smile eased her habitually serious expression.

"Okay, so you're not going to spill the beans. Can you at least tell me if you expect her back later?"

"I don't think so. Ms. Havers took a bunch of files that she wanted for the weekend, so I assume she was going directly home from the hospital."

Lee shot a glance at her watch. "You're probably right. Day's almost over, anyway. Okay, no problem, I'll catch her at home." She rose and stretched. "You gonna wrap it up soon and head off for a hot Friday night on the town?"

Rhiannon dropped her gaze and gave a quick shake of her head.

Lee tapped a finger on the desk and waited until Rhiannon looked up at her. "Hey, none of my business, right? I just hope you're not letting your new boss work you too hard. You have to have some time for yourself, too."

"I don't mind overtime, but actually, I'm about done for the day." Rhiannon nudged a backpack from under the desk. "I was just going to go over to the Y for a swim after work."

"You like swimming?"

"Uh-huh. I usually go every day, though sometimes I run along the river paths instead of swimming."

"Well, they're both great exercise. I have a small gym set up in our basement at home, but I'd like to have a backyard pool, too. Somehow I don't think my partner would be too thrilled with the idea, but her son would probably love it." Lee waited to see if Rhiannon picked up on the significant pronoun.

"How old is her son?" Rhiannon's calm expression didn't change.

Lee relaxed. "He's fourteen. His name is Eli, and hers is Dana."

Rhiannon smiled. "A teenager, then."

With a small groan, Lee nodded. "Oh, yeah, and I'm not sure I'm going to survive his teen years in one piece. He has this uncanny ability to push every button I have. Dana's so good with him. She hardly ever loses it, but I swear that boy's responsible for most of my grey hairs." She riffled the abundant silver that streaked her dark locks. "He really is a great kid, though, and I keep reminding myself that this too shall pass."

Rhiannon nodded, but Lee saw a brief flash of sadness in her eyes. On impulse, she asked, "Would you like to come over for dinner this weekend? I'd love for you to meet Dana and Eli, and, believe me, Dana is a great cook." Lee patted her solid middle.

"Um, me? You want me to come to dinner?"

"Absolutely." *Why do I think you don't get many invitations?*

"I…um… Don't you want to check with Dana first?" A myriad of emotions played across Rhiannon's face.

"Dana never minds when I bring friends home for dinner."

The uncertainty in Rhiannon's eyes faded, and she smiled. "Thank you. I would like that."

"Excellent. Let's see. Tomorrow's out, because Eli's baseball team is playing, so how about Sunday, around five? Here, let me give you the address."

Rhiannon slid a piece of paper and a pen across the desk, and Lee scribbled down her address and phone number. Then she tore the paper in half and extended the pen. "Why don't you give me your phone number, too, just in case something comes up?"

Rhiannon frowned as she jotted down a number and held it out.

Lee took the piece of paper and tucked it in her wallet.

"That's my aunt's number, but you can leave a message for me if you like."

"You don't have a phone?"

"I, uh, never needed one of my own, but my aunt lives in the same house." Rhiannon fiddled with the pen without meeting Lee's gaze.

"Okay. I look forward to seeing you on Sunday."

Lee marched down the hallway, determined not to let Marika evade her this time. *No way in hell is a lowlife like Cass going to ruin our friendship.* She knocked on Marika's door and almost lost her balance when it opened immediately.

Marika stood there, hands thrust in her pockets, not meeting Lee's gaze.

"Hi," Lee said.

"Hi."

Lee waited an endless moment. "May I come in?"

Marika stepped aside and allowed her to enter.

Lee brushed by, shrugged out of her jacket, and tossed it on the hall chair. Despite the long-suffering sigh behind her, she continued into the living room.

She greeted Spooky, who padded up to sniff at her. The cat evidently determined the brown bag Lee carried did not contain anything of interest and wandered off.

Lee turned to meet Marika's bleak gaze. They regarded each other until Lee broke the impasse. "I've missed you." Lee was gratified to see warming in those sombre eyes.

"Me too, you." Marika nodded at the brown bag. "Something interesting in there?"

Lee drew out a very large bottle of tequila. "Right from Mexico. You did ask me to bring it over." When Marika chuckled, Lee dug farther and pulled out a bag of limes. She handed that over and extracted the last of her treasures. When she flourished a large saltshaker, Lee was rewarded with a genuine laugh.

"I do have salt here, you know?"

"Yup, I know that, but I figured that if you threw me out, I'd need all the ingredients with me to go drown my sorrows."

Marika's head dropped, and for an instant Lee regretted her off-handed quip. *No, we need to face the elephant in the room.*

Lee set the bottle and saltshaker on the coffee table and stepped forward. She cupped Marika's face in her hands. "I'm sorry. I was out of line. And my only excuse is that I care very much about what goes on with you. Forgive me?"

The limes dropped to the floor, and Marika leaned into Lee's welcoming arms. They held each other silently.

"Why do you put up with me?" Marika's words were muffled.

"Oh, I dunno. Could be because I like a challenge." There was a burst of laughter against Lee's shoulder. She tightened her embrace. "Or maybe I just think you're worth it."

Marika stilled, then released her breath in a barely audible sigh. She pulled back and stared at Lee. Disbelief and hope warred in her expression.

Lee held Marika's gaze steadily until she won a tiny smile.

Marika stepped back and wiped her cheeks with the back of her hand. "I'll slice up the limes. You know where the glasses are." She retrieved the limes and went to the kitchen.

It's a start. Lee pulled two small glasses out of the china hutch and carried them back to the coffee table. She twisted the cap off the bottle and filled both shot glasses.

Marika returned with a tray of sliced limes, set them on the coffee table, and sat down next to Lee.

Lee handed Marika a glass and nudged the shaker across the coffee table.

Marika sprinkled salt in the webbing of her hand, licked it off, downed the shot, and sucked on a lime wedge. Her eyes widened, and she stifled a cough. "Your turn."

Lee quickly followed suit. They downed two more shots in rapid succession before they leaned back and grinned at each other.

"Pretty potent stuff there." Marika fanned herself with one hand.

"Yup. I went right to the factory for that one. Told you the worm was still doing cartwheels."

Marika scrunched up her nose.

"You don't believe me?" Lee grabbed the bottle and swirled the contents until the translucent coil in the bottom of the tequila appeared to dance.

"Ugh. Why did I let you talk me into drinking this stuff? And why on earth do they put that thing in there, anyway?"

Lee stopped playing with the tequila and poured two more shots. "Dunno. I never thought about it before. Maybe to test its potency?"

"So if the worm lives, it's too weak?"

"Sounds like as good a theory as any," Lee said. "Bottoms up."

They finished the round, and Marika laughed. "You keep pouring like that, and you will have me bottoms up."

Lee did her best Groucho Marx impression. "Ah, but what a lovely bottom it is, my dear."

Marika snorted and threw a pillow.

Lee casually batted it aside as she set up another round. "Slow down a bit. I'd like to at least last until sundown." Despite her admonishment, Marika picked up the saltshaker in preparation for the next round.

"Why? Do you turn into a vampire then?" Lee asked.

Marika swallowed her drink, sucked on the lime, and bared her teeth. "You'll have to wait and see. I've been known to bite."

Lee followed suit and downed her shot. "Tell me about it. Do you remember the first time we had tequila shooters together? I think we'd only been together for a few weeks at the time."

"I remember. You were showing me how to make your own special style of shooters."

"And how did you repay me for that privilege? You bit me!" Lee pulled up her rugby shirt and peered at her belly. "I think I still have the scar to prove it."

"Aw, poor baby." Marika patted Lee's solid belly. "I apologize for missing the lime."

Intent on her search for the scar, Lee jumped when Marika laid a kiss on her exposed abdomen, then blew a loud raspberry.

Lee pushed a laughing Marika away and wiped her stomach. "Evil wench. How am I going to explain hickeys on my belly to Dana?"

Marika grabbed the tequila and wavered as she aimed at their glasses.

Lee took the bottle from her. She filled the glasses with a marginally steadier hand. "Featherweight." She was delighted to see the relaxed look on Marika's face. *We are so going to pay for this in the morning.* "Feel like ordering a pizza?"

"Vegetarian?"

"What's the point of having pizza if all you're going to put on it is vegetables?"

Marika shot Lee a cockeyed grin.

"Oh, all right. Vegetarian on your half only, though."

Lee called in their order as Marika stood, swayed, and walked down the hallway. With the order placed, Lee hung up and hit the speed dial for her home. Eli picked up. "Hey, buddy, can I talk to your mom?"

There was a brief pause, then Dana came on the line.

"Hi, hon. Just checking in to see how things are going."

"Things are going fine here, love. I take it they're going fine there, too." Amusement was clear in Dana's voice.

"Oh, yeah. We've been talking, and everything's cool again."

"Uh-huh. Talking, eh?"

"Well, we shared a couple of drinks, too, and we've ordered pizza."

"Lee, darling, I want you to go put your keys in the freezer right now and promise me you won't drive tonight."

Lee frowned. "But how will I get home?"

"I'm not sure I'm going to want you home tonight. Maybe you should spend the night at Marika's."

Lee blinked several times. Her vision was slightly out of focus. "You want me to stay with another woman?" She glanced up as Marika returned to the room. "Dana doesn't want me to come home tonight." She hit the button to put it on speaker.

Marika flopped down beside Lee. "Hi, Dana."

"Hi, sweetie. Don't you let that big goof drive, all right? If you're going to get her drunk, you have to keep her."

"Okay. But I can't keep her, because she belongs to you."

"Yes, she does. But I have a very strong suspicion that you two are going to deserve each other tonight."

Marika looked at Lee. "I think she thinks we're inebbb... innneeeb...drunk."

"Aw, honey, we've only had a few."

"Sure you have. Look, my love, I have to go. I promised Eli I'd take him and Tony to McDonald's and then the movies, and he's waving my car keys at me. Promise me you'll either stay with Marika or call me to come and get you."

"I will," Lee said. "Love you."

"Love you too, you big goof. See you later."

Lee hung up.

Marika grinned. "You really should marry Dana. She's one in a million."

Lee picked up the now half-empty bottle and poured two more shots. "I love her, ya know." She pushed one glass toward Marika.

"I know, and she loves you, too. I think it works best that way, don't you?"

Lee rolled the glass between her palms. "Doesn't always work, though, does it? It didn't work for us."

Marika regarded Lee for a long moment, then downed the shot without the salt and lime. She leaned forward and laid an unsteady hand on Lee's thigh. "No, it didn't. But that was my fault. You're the best, Lee, and you deserve the best. You should marry Dana. She makes you happy, and I need you to be happy."

"Why?"

Marika blinked.

"Why do you need me to be happy?" Lee clarified.

"Cuz you're my best friend, you idiot." Marika's lopsided, but affectionate grin took any sting out of the insult.

"But if you want me to be happy, why can't you understand that I want you to be happy, too?" Lee spoke slowly and strove for an elusive coherence.

Marika's brow wrinkled.

The phone rang from the lobby. Pizza had arrived.

Dana was about to ring the buzzer for Marika's apartment when an elderly gentleman stepped up behind her, unlocked the door, and held it for her. Dana exchanged smiles with him and crossed the lobby to the elevator.

After dropping the boys at the movie, she had decided to check up on Lee and Marika. She planned to either bring Lee home or take her keys and return the next morning.

Dana arrived at Marika's door and tapped lightly. When no one answered, she tried the doorknob. To her surprise, the door opened. *That's weird. It's not like her to leave it unlocked.* When Dana entered, laughter came from the living room. She rounded the corner and grinned at the sight.

Lee was sprawled at one end of the couch. On the other end, Marika tilted an almost empty bottle to her lips. Spooky nosed about a solitary piece of pizza that lay abandoned in a box. Chewed lime wedges littered the floor, and an overturned saltshaker had spilled crystals over the coffee table.

Still unseen, Dana leaned against the wall and watched.

Marika wiped her mouth and handed Lee the bottle. "Your turn. Worm's still there."

Lee held the bottle over her head and peered at it closely. Then she looked up, and her face split in a wide grin. "Dana!" Lee stumbled to her feet and lurched over to envelop Dana in a hug. She tried to whirl her around but only succeeded in almost falling down.

Dana steadied her with an arm wrapped around Lee's waist.

"Did ya mish me?" Lee nuzzled Dana's hair.

"Oh, absolutely."

Lee gave her a doe-eyed look. "I love you sooooo much."

"Love you, too, sweetie. Now, why don't we sit down before you fall down?" Dana steered Lee back to the couch.

Marika held the bottle out to Dana. "We're playin' tequila roulette. You hafta take a swallow, and whoever eats the worm loses."

"Eww, no thanks." Dana pushed the bottle away. "I'll leave it for you two." She knelt in front of Lee and patted her knee. "Where are your keys, love? I'll take them with me and come back tomorrow morning to pick you up, okay?"

Lee stared at the ceiling with a look of intense concentration. "Keys, keys... Where'd I put 'em?"

Dana shook her head and looked around. She spotted Lee's jacket on the floor, her wallet half out of the pocket. A search of the garment turned up the keys, and Dana stuffed them in her pocket. She returned to Lee and Marika and regarded them with mock pity. "Oh, you two are so going to pay for this in the morning."

Lee and Marika blinked at each other and started to laugh.

Dana rolled her eyes, dropped a kiss on Lee's forehead, and dodged flailing hands when Lee made a grab for her. With a chuckle, she shook at finger at Lee. "Oh no, you don't. You're sleeping here tonight."

"But I only have one bed." Marika's protest was slurred.

"You have the daybed in the den. For that matter, it's fine if Lee sleeps in your bed. All she's going to do is keep company with the white porcelain goddess tonight, anyway."

Lee tugged on her hand and drew Dana's attention to her stomach as she pulled up her shirt. "Marika blew bubbles on my belly."

Dana pulled the shirt down and patted Lee's stomach. "I'm sure she's very sorry and will never do that again. Right, Marika?"

"Never, ever again. I promise." Marika crossed her heart, then collapsed in helpless laughter.

"You definitely deserve each other." Dana was about to leave when Lee waved wildly at her. "Yes, love?"

"I forgot to tell you. Lady Mouse is coming to dinner on Sunday, and so is Marika." Lee turned to Marika, who nodded in agreement.

"A mouse is coming to dinner?" Dana cocked her head.

"Not *a* mouse...Lady Mouse."

Dana rolled her eyes, waved goodbye, and left the apartment. *Note to self—ask Lee tomorrow why a rodent is invited to Sunday dinner.*

CHAPTER 7

GAO QUI-JIAN LOOKED UP FREQUENTLY from his corner position to survey the smoky bar. None of the bar's shabby patrons appeared to pay any attention to his table. Dim lighting and loud jukebox music further obscured Gao's activities.

He had barely touched the beer in front of him while Pike and Eddie were on their third of the last half hour. He studied his tablemates. *Barbarians. Unkempt, uncivilized, uneducated. The day I can wash my hands of you two can't come too soon.*

"So, when's the next shipment coming in?" Pike asked.

"It will arrive Wednesday night, and you're to transport it Thursday morning on your regular run to Montana. However, your contact will meet you in Missoula rather than Kalispell this time." Gao issued his orders in precise, lightly accented tones.

"Shit," Eddie said. "Why the hell do we have to take 'em that far instead of dumping 'em in Kalispell like we always do?"

"Because you fools created such a debacle last time. You may consider yourself lucky that you're even allowed to take another shipment. How many times have I warned you not to tamper with the cargo, to simply deliver it to your contact and continue on with your business?"

Pike refused to meet Gao's gaze. "Hell, we were only having a little fun. Wasn't no harm done. We let her go when we was finished. Besides, no way an illegal's gonna run to the cops."

"No, she didn't run to the police, but she did run. She was so traumatized by your little bout of entertainment that she bolted into the woods. The contact had to leave her there and take the rest of the cargo. She wandered into Kalispell a few days later and is now in INS custody. Fortunately, my sources tell me that she didn't know enough about her transport arrangements to damage us."

"So no harm done, right?" Pike said.

"That is hardly the point. Had your inability to control your baser urges jeopardized our business, I assure you that my associates would have been greatly displeased. If you wish to keep your heads on your shoulders, I strongly suggest you attend strictly to your instructions from now on."

Eddie swallowed audibly.

Pike paled and held up his hands. "Yeah, man, no problem. We'll just pick 'em up and drop 'em off. You can count on us."

Gao dropped a piece of paper on the table. "Here are the contact instructions for Missoula." He stood and plucked his jacket from the back of his chair. "And, gentlemen, if I hear of any further transgressions, I will not run interference on your behalf again. I will go directly to the Chameleon with a full report on your activities." *The idiots need not know that meetings with the Chameleon are detrimental to one's health... and life span.*

"What's she gonna care if we pick up a little action?" Pike's bluster did not camouflage his nervous eye tick or the way his fingers beat a ceaseless rhythm on the table top.

Sweat dotted Eddie's upper lip, and he kept his gaze fixed on his older brother.

They may dismiss me; they won't dare dismiss her. "I do think she would take exception to you two endangering her profits, don't you, gentlemen? And she really isn't very nice when that happens...or have you forgotten the fate of the fools who held your jobs previously?"

Terror flashed over their faces. Gao knew they remembered the flayed and vivisected corpses of their predecessors, which had been dumped in a wheat field not far off the snakehead route they now ran.

Gao smiled coldly at their reaction, left the table, and exited the bar. He automatically glanced about as he made his way down the street. *Idiots. If they last another year in her service, I'll be amazed.* He stopped and waited for the crossing light to turn green. *If they fail again, I will eliminate them. Foot soldiers are easily replaced.*

∼⌒⌒∽⌒∼

Gao received a summons to Vancouver late Friday night. He was ordered to meet the Chameleon at a specified address Saturday afternoon.

His first thought was of the most recent shipment to Missoula, but the transport had gone smoothly and the cargo was in transit to New York. Pike and Eddie had followed their orders to the letter, so Gao was sure he wasn't being called on the carpet because of his feckless subordinates.

After a sleepless night in which he endlessly reviewed his performance and any potential trouble points, Gao caught the first available flight from Calgary. When his plane landed, he immediately rented a car.

Forty minutes later Gao entered a primarily industrial area. He rechecked the instructions he had scrawled on a scrap of paper and pulled into a nondescript strip mall. His destination was a shabby coffee shop tucked discreetly between a florist and a pharmacy.

Gao parked and entered the coffee shop. He was pinned by a deceptively casual glance from the counterman, who gave a nod and returned to his newspaper. Gao ignored the two customers and made his way down a short hall to the door labeled "employees only."

He passed through into a small antechamber piled with cardboard stock boxes. On the opposite wall, a man Gao recognized as one of the Chameleon's inner circle sat next to another door and watched him. Gao had met the man several times when instructions had been conveyed to him, but he had never been told his name and knew not to ask.

The Chameleon's man stood and advanced. Gao remained impassive as he was subjected to a quick but thorough frisking.

The guard gestured to the door beside his chair. "Go in. Keep your eyes front and focused on the lamp."

Gao nodded and surreptitiously dried his palms on his trousers. He opened the door and entered a darkened room. The only illumination was tiny slivers of sunlight that edged blackout shades and a dim lamp on a metal desk directly in front of him. He kept his eyes fixed on that lamp and stood silently.

"Gao Qui-jian." The voice sounded from a corner behind him. The tone was neutral, but Gao barely restrained a flinch.

"Yes, madam." Gao tried to breathe normally. *I haven't done anything wrong. She cannot fault me.*

"Did you have a good flight?"

"Yes, madam."

"Good. You were very prompt."

There was a hint of approval in the voice. For an instant, Gao relaxed, then he stiffened again. *Fool. Remember where you are.* "Yes, madam."

A light chuckle sent chills down his spine, and Gao consciously locked his knees.

"You've done well by us." The voice became coolly businesslike. "I'm pleased with your performance in keeping the Calgary end of our transactions running smoothly. However, I have a couple of local problems that require your personal touch."

Gao allowed himself a modicum of relief as it became apparent he wasn't here to be disciplined. "I'm at your disposal, madam."

"Yes, you are."

Gao was wrenched out of any complacency by the amused malevolence in the Chameleon's tone.

The voice sharpened. "Your cousin Rhongji has become something of a liability. You brought him on board, and he is your responsibility."

Gao blinked as images of his amiable, fun-loving younger cousin flooded his mind. "May I ask what he's done, madam?"

"He has taken to an...ostentatious lifestyle, which has brought him to the attention of the wrong people. You will either bring him to heel and remind him that our people maintain a low profile, or you will eliminate the problem."

The icy tone left no room for misunderstanding, and Gao nodded. He cleared his throat and fought for an impassive tone. "You referred to a couple of problems?"

"One of our customs agents has lately displayed a rather disturbing degree of avarice and needs to be reminded for whom he works. His health and happiness continue at our pleasure. You are to remind him of that fact. Liang will provide you with the details. Once these matters are taken care of, you are to leave the city immediately."

Gao was sure he had given no visible reaction to the orders, but the Chameleon chuckled. "Do you have a problem with that?"

"No, madam. Of course not."

"It's a shame to miss the opportunity to see your eldest brother's new son." The voice was deceptively mild.

It is. The child carries our line forward, but what would one such as you care about family? Gao was not surprised that the Chameleon knew his family details. "It's not important, madam."

"You would like to return to Vancouver someday."

It wasn't a question, but Gao nodded again.

"That's a future possibility, but for now, I require your talents in Calgary. You have been a very competent lieutenant, and I value that in an employee. Besides, Calgary isn't so bad, is it?"

"It's not Vancouver, madam."

"No, but it has its...attractions. See Liang on your way out. Send your report through the usual channels. I'll expect to hear from you within twenty-four hours."

Gao nodded and turned away from the voice.

"What happened in Kalispell must never happen again. Is that clear, Gao?"

Gao froze.

"My lieutenants are responsible for the conduct of their subordinates...and Gao...I do not give second chances."

"Yes, madam." Gao returned to the antechamber. He ran his sleeve over his face and addressed the guard. "You have some information for me?"

Liang removed a large envelope from his inner pocket and extended it.

Gao opened the envelope and glanced at the two typed sheets of paper and the single photograph within. "Can you tell me what exactly my cousin has done?"

Liang's gaze was as cold as the Chameleon's voice. "Rhongji is a player in high stakes gambling circles. He fucked up big time this week, and I had to pull his ass out of the fire. Everything you need to know is in there. Basically your cousin is fast becoming a loose end."

Gao nodded, tucked the envelope into his pocket, and made his exit. *Why summon me here? I am pleased Rhongji lives, but why is that so? Why did they not simply eliminate him? It's unlike the Chameleon to tolerate such stupidity.* Gao started the car, then stilled. *I'm being tested. First Pike and Eddie, now Rhongji. She holds me responsible for their transgressions. I either fix the problems or...*

Gao's mind refused to fill in the blank. His hand trembled as he shifted his car out of park and pulled out of the lot. *I cannot allow Rhongji's excesses to jeopardize my future...or his. There is no alternative. He must be made to understand the razor we balance on, no matter what it takes.* Ruthlessly, he excised memories of the chubby little boy who had hung on his every word and drove to Rhongji's apartment.

When Gao rang his cousin's apartment for entry to the building, Rhongji buzzed him in without questioning his identity. Gao shook his head at his cousin's foolish complacency.

At the nineteenth-floor apartment, an emaciated, slip-clad woman with unfocused sloe-eyes opened the door in response to his knock.

Gao brushed by her. Rhongji was sprawled on a couch, clothed only in scarlet boxer shorts, his eyes closed as he drew deeply on a pipe.

"Hey, you're not Billy. You can't come in here." The woman laid a hand on Gao's arm.

He shook her off.

She turned to the supine man. "Ronnie—"

Gao snapped, "Get out."

Rhongji's eyes flew open, and a smile lit his face. "Quijian! Shit, man, I didn't know you were coming to the coast. Why didn't you call me?"

Gao fixed an icy gaze on his cousin. "Get rid of her."

Rhongji sat bolt upright. "Uh, sure. Look, honey, why don't you take a hike, and I'll give you a call later."

"But, Ronnie, we were supposed to—"

Gao wordlessly backhanded the woman's face.

Rhongji stared at him as Gao's victim whimpered.

Gao never took his gaze from his cousin.

Rhongji grabbed his companion's clothing, purse, and shoes and thrust them into her arms. She struggled into her dress at the door and had barely fastened it before Rhongji pushed her out into the hall.

Turning back to Gao, Rhongji held out a hand in supplication. "Hey, you didn't have to do that. She didn't mean no harm."

"Shut up."

Rhongji shifted from foot to foot.

"Sit." Gao pointed at the abandoned couch, and Rhongji hastened to do as he was bid. "You are a fool."

Rhongji glanced up at him quickly, then averted his gaze without a word. For a fleeting moment, his hangdog expression reminded Gao of the boy he had grown up with. *No sympathy. If I can't get through to him, neither of us stand a chance.* "Do you have any idea the danger you've put both of us in?"

Rhongji looked up with alarm.

Gao shook his head. "You don't have a clue, do you? The Chameleon summoned me here to clean up your mess. We get one chance, and you are not going to fuck this up."

Rhongji cringed. "I didn't think—"

Gao took two steps and cuffed Rhongji.

"Ow! Fuck, man…"

Gao ignored his protest. "That's right, you didn't think. You've never thought in your life, and you're not going to try now. When I took the assignment in Calgary, what did I tell you?"

Rhongji rubbed his ear. "You told me to keep my nose clean and to tend strictly to business."

"Exactly, and what have you done?"

"I do tend to business. We haven't had one break in distribution since I took over."

"Which is probably the only reason you are still alive." *Other than to serve as a test of my loyalty.* There was growing panic in Rhongji's eyes. "You do not cross these people. You know the Chameleon insists on discretion. She permits you to go elsewhere to gamble and whore around, but she will not allow you to draw attention in her backyard. Do you understand?"

Rhongji hung his head.

"Get your clothes. You're coming with me."

Rhongji's eyes widened. "Don't do this, man. We're cousins; we're blood. I always done what you told me, even when we were kids. I can make this right, I swear. Gimme another chance. You know I'd follow you into hell, man. Fuck, I wouldn't even be in this life if not for you. Please don't..."

"Stop babbling. If I intended to kill you, I'd hardly have left a witness alive."

Rhongji stood and stumbled to the bedroom.

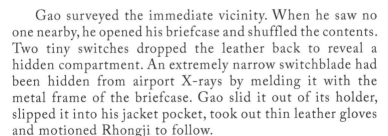

Gao surveyed the immediate vicinity. When he saw no one nearby, he opened his briefcase and shuffled the contents. Two tiny switches dropped the leather back to reveal a hidden compartment. An extremely narrow switchblade had been hidden from airport X-rays by melding it with the metal frame of the briefcase. Gao slid it out of its holder, slipped it into his jacket pocket, took out thin leather gloves and motioned Rhongji to follow.

He left the car unlocked in an alley behind a bar and led Rhongji in a circuitous route around the parking lot. They slipped between the rows of cars and approached a Grand

Prix. Gao punctured all four tires with his blade, then they retreated one row over and waited.

It was no more than five minutes later when the customs agent entered the lot. Weaving a little, he made his way to the Grand Prix. He started to open his door, then paused and looked at his front tire. The agent swore and kicked at it. He cursed as he walked around the car, his tirade getting louder with each flat tire he discovered.

Gao and Rhongji approached him. "Is everything all right?" Gao asked.

Kneeling beside his front tire, the man didn't look up. "Some asshole slashed my tires!"

Gao was on him instantly. He held his blade to the man's throat and leaned over him as the customs agent froze.

Rhongji hung back, his gaze darting around.

"I have a message from the Chameleon," Gao whispered into the man's ear. The terrified man squeaked but didn't move. "Your demands are unacceptable, and the Chameleon wishes to remind you who it is you work for."

With his blade still pressed to the man's throat, Gao stepped on the man's hand. "You and your family exist at the Chameleon's pleasure, and if you need help remembering that fact—" He slashed downward with his blade, severing two of the agent's fingers. Before his victim could scream, Gao slammed the agent's head against the side of the car and dropped him into a gathering pool of his own blood. He kicked the sundered digits under the car and strode away, followed by his stunned partner in crime.

CHAPTER 8

R HIANNON STUDIED HER BUS SCHEDULE and picked up the well-worn city map that lay beside her on the stoop. She worked out how to get to Lee's place on public transit, then tossed the map aside and stretched, twisting her head from side to side.

Reverend Ross walked down the street toward her house.

An involuntary smile crossed Rhiannon's face, but she quashed it before he entered the yard, bag in hand.

He sauntered up to the stoop and flopped down beside her without saying a word.

Rhiannon eyed him with a half-amused, half-irritated grin. "You never know when to give up, do you, Ichabod?"

"Nope." David took a can of Coke out of the bag and passed it to her before taking a second one for himself. He popped the tab, tilted his head back, and took a long drink. His prominent Adam's apple bobbed with each swallow. He lowered the can and pressed it to his face. "Hot one out today." He gestured at the unopened can in Rhiannon's hand. "It's cold. I just picked them up at the 7-11."

Rhiannon pulled back the tab and took a small sip. "'s good." They sat in amiable silence and drank their Cokes.

David pointed at the bus schedule. "Going somewhere?"

"I was invited to dinner tomorrow, and I was just figuring out how to get there."

"You haven't been to your friend's house before?"

"Friend? I barely know these people. Heck, I've only met Lee a few times, and I've never met her family." Rhiannon shook her head. "I still don't know why she asked me."

"It's entirely possible that she simply likes you and would like to get to know you better." Amusement danced around David's mouth. "Did you meet her at work?"

"Sort of." Rhiannon related the story of her initial encounter with Lee and how she had intervened against the King brothers. "So then, when she's there to see my boss on Friday, right out of the blue she asked me to come to dinner. I thought maybe I heard wrong, but she really meant it."

"She sounds like a good person. You'll probably enjoy the chance to get to know her and her family."

Rhiannon pinned David with a defiant stare. "She's gay. She lives with her partner and her partner's son."

David nodded and took another sip of his Coke.

"Isn't this where you're supposed to warn me off?" Rhiannon wasn't sure why she pressed the issue.

"Warn you off what? Having dinner with a very nice woman who saved you from a couple of thugs? I suppose I could caution you to check the potato salad twice. You never know with that stuff. Won't touch it myself. I've heard a lot of horror stories about potato salad and ptomaine poisoning. I remember going to a church picnic one time in Fort St. John, and Old Aggie had brought her world-famous potato salad. Well, it got left out in the sun too long, and darned if it didn't end up sending a dozen people to hospital." David's tone was tranquil and his body language relaxed.

Rhiannon stared at him. He never reacted as she expected. *How do you fight with someone who won't fight back?* "Why are you talking about stupid salad? Shouldn't you be launching into a sermon about the evils of homosexuality? God knows I've heard Hettie raving that 'sodomites will never enter the kingdom of heaven' often enough."

"I suspect your aunt and I may not agree on a lot of things. She strikes me as woman who adheres more to the letter of the law than the spirit." David pulled himself upright. "Let me tell you a story. Many years ago, before you were even born, I arrived at the seminary as a green and gangling prairie kid, wet behind the ears, with bits of hay still sticking out of my hair."

Rhiannon grinned.

David smiled back. "Yup, I know it's hard to believe I wasn't always the suave and sophisticated man of the world you see before you."

A giggle slipped out before Rhiannon could stop it.

"I was scared to death. I knew I wanted to be a priest—had known that for as long as I could remember—but I wasn't sure I had what it took. God must have been smiling on me that day, because I was assigned quarters with another new seminarian. His name was Conor, and if ever a man was born to be a priest, he was."

David fell silent, a faraway look in his eyes. After a moment, he shook himself. "Conor was beautiful, inside and out. It was like his soul was so brilliant it shone right through his skin. Even the strictest of our instructors weren't immune to his charisma. He was a few years older, and he took me under his wing. Everything came easily to Conor, but he never used that as an excuse to slack off, and he was always ready to help those of us less gifted. That definitely included me." David drained his Coke and pulled two more out of the bag. "Want another?"

"Thanks, but I'm not finished with this one."

David put one Coke back. "Anyway, I've never been sure if I'd have gotten through seminary without Conor's help. As it turned out, when we graduated, we were assigned to the same large inner city parish. We spent the next couple of years working closely together." He regarded Rhiannon earnestly. "He could've been, or done, anything, you know? If he'd wanted, he would be a bishop today, heck, maybe even an archbishop, but that wasn't Conor's path. He genuinely felt his calling was working with people in need. He once told me that he had been torn between a career in medicine or in the church." David looked down. "He should've chosen medicine."

"Why? What did he do?"

"You read the last page of a book first, don't you?"

"I do not. Well, not all the time. So what happened next?"

"I was posted to a northern parish after a couple of years, but we stayed close friends. Conor was my best man when I got married, godfather to my kids, and he helped pick up the pieces when Hannah left me and took my children back to Halifax." David stood and paced back and forth in front of the stoop. There was anguish in his eyes. "About four years ago, a brother priest told me that Conor left the priesthood and that he had AIDS. I couldn't believe it. I took a leave of absence and flew out to the coast. I found Conor on Salt Springs Island, living with a man he'd never mentioned to me. I was so angry. I yelled at him, said terrible things I never meant to say, even threw a punch, and he bore it all quietly."

"Why were you angry? Because he was gay?"

"In part, maybe. He was my hero and everything I wanted to be—as a priest and a man. More than that, though, I was furious that he hadn't told me, when we were as close as brothers."

"You were scared."

David stared at Rhiannon for a long moment, then collapsed on the stoop beside her. "Yes. Conor was the one thing in my world I depended on. He was my rock. And now this horrible disease was going to take him from a world that needed him…and from me." His voice was so quiet that Rhiannon had to strain to hear him.

She reached for his hand. They sat in silence for a time until Rhiannon asked gently, "Did he die?"

"No, he's still alive, but he's so thin now that a good wind would blow him over. His partner died two years ago."

"Did you ever make your peace with him?"

"Eventually, but it took me a year. Conor put up with my nonsense until finally he came up to see me and made me sit down and talk everything out. He humbled me with his grace, and he taught me, just as he had been doing for over twenty years. Since then, I get out to see him every chance I can, and we talk on the phone all the time. He showed me how to live, and now he's showing me how to die. He's not bitter, and he's determined to make his life count right up to his last breath."

Rhiannon released David's hand. "So how do you square Conor with what your church teaches? Do you think he's going to hell?"

"If ever a human being was heaven-bound, Conor is. And it's not like he's the only one. At least three hundred priests, mostly Catholic, have died of AIDS-related causes in the US alone, and that's only the ones they know about. I doubt our numbers are that much different in Canada."

"I'm sorry, David. That's an awful lot of people. So Conor made you rethink your attitudes about gays?"

"Not just that. He really inspired me to figure out why I got into the ministry, and what I hoped to offer. Ultimately, I decided that church dictates didn't necessarily correspond to the spirit I want to emulate and illustrate to others."

"Geez, who knew you were such a rebel." Rhiannon furrowed her brow. "I'm the farthest thing from an expert, but couldn't trash-talking the Bible lead to you getting the boot?"

David chuckled. "Give me some credit for subtlety. I uphold the eternal truths of love, compassion, and faithfulness." His expression grew serious. "But in all honesty, there may come a day when the church and I part ways. If Conor taught me anything, it was to honour my conscience."

"Huh. So bottom line is that you're telling me you don't have a problem with Lee—or Conor—being gay?"

"Does Lee love her partner? Is she devoted to the woman and the woman's child? Are they a solid, faithful union?" A hint of a smile played on David's face.

"How should I know? I've never even met them. But I get your point. Besides, from what little I know, I'll bet Lee is great with her family."

"You really like her, don't you?"

"Yes, I do. I bet you would too. She's got this warmth about her that you just can't help liking. When you talk, she listens like she's really interested in what you have to say." Rhiannon glanced at David sharply, ready to forestall any hint of pity. There was none.

"I'm sure you'll have a terrific time tomorrow."

Rhiannon squeezed the empty Coke can into an hourglass shape. "I don't know if I should go."

"Surely it doesn't bother you that Lee is gay?"

Rhiannon glared at him. "Of course not, Ichabod."

"Then what's the problem?"

"I won't know what to say. I'm terrible at small talk. I'll probably make a total ass of myself. I don't even know what to bring." She picked up a pebble and threw it at the gate. "Am I supposed to bring something? Don't people bring things when they're invited to dinner?"

David blinked at the flood of words. "Whoa, slow down. Yes, it's often customary to bring a small gift for your hosts."

"Like what?"

A grin lifted the corner of his lips, but he raised a calming hand. "A bottle of wine is nice or some flowers."

"Wine?" Rhiannon gulped nervously. "I don't know anything about wine. I'd probably get something they hated, and then they'd think I'm an idiot, but they'd drink it just to be polite, and I'd see them forcing themselves to swallow. And if I bring them flowers, they'll probably be allergic to them—"

David stared at her, and she stopped. "It's an invitation to dinner, Rhi, not an audience with the Queen."

Rhiannon fell into a sulky silence.

David sighed. "Why don't you just forget about bringing anything this time? Next time you'll have a better idea about what they're like and what they enjoy."

"You're assuming there'll be a next time."

David laughed.

Rhiannon joined him. "Okay, okay, I'll chill."

Out of the blue, David asked, "Why does your aunt call you Anne?"

Rhiannon raised her eyebrows at the non sequitur. "When I came to live here, Hettie decided my name was too fancy and would just give me airs about being better than everyone else, so she enrolled me in school as Anne and insisted that everyone call me that. I tried to tell people my name was Rhiannon, but no one would listen to me. Eventually, I gave up. Even my bloody high school diploma has Anne on it, but as soon as I left school and registered in career college, I used my given name."

David shook his head. "Now why would she do that? Taking away a child's identity is hardly going to help them make such a big adjustment."

"I think she hated my dad and felt my mom married way beneath her. He was a Welsh immigrant without a penny to his name. He named me after his mother, and probably Hettie didn't want any reminders of his heritage in her house. I guess plain old Anne sounded more proper to her."

David grunted his disapproval, and Rhiannon was warmed by the support. Her earliest battles, the beginning of half a lifetime of conflict with her aunt, had been over her insistence on keeping her name. She had lost, mostly because every time she refused to answer to "Anne," she was harshly punished. *If he'd been the priest then, I'd have had an ally. Sure could've used one.*

"I have a proposition for you."

They looked at each other with identical grins.

"The answer's still no, Ichabod." Rhiannon smirked as David rolled his eyes.

"Story of my life." They chuckled together. "No, I was wondering if you would be interested in earning a little extra money by helping Tupper and me with a church improvement project."

"What kind of project?"

"Well, let me tell you a little story," David said.

Rhiannon didn't try to hide her smile. *He'll be telling stories on his deathbed.*

"Do you know Mrs. Kristen?"

"She and her husband are the English couple, right? He always looks like a bird is nesting in his hair, and she always bosses him around."

David nodded. "That's them. Well, last Sunday they were in the congregation when I preached on the good Samaritan." He grinned. "You can never lose with the classics. Anyway, I'm giving it my all, trying to show them how the old story relates to our lives today. I'm hammering on the theme that we must be Samaritans to the unclean and outcast of our society and that we have a responsibility to care for them, too, not just those sitting beside us in the pews. I'd just gotten to the part where I'm talking about how dealing with people you don't normally like makes us deal with ourselves and our own prejudices when all of a sudden I hear a shriek that darn near broke the stained glass windows." David paused.

"What? What was it?"

"The very thing I asked myself," David said soberly. "I looked out over the congregation, and Mrs. Kristen was jumping up and down in a rear pew, batting at her husband, who appeared to be pawing her rear end."

Rhiannon chuckled. "What did you do?"

"For a moment, I thought I should ignore it and go on, but honestly, having a lady jumping around in the middle of your sermon tends to distract your audience, so I was about to ask what was wrong when Mr. Kristen pipes up, ''Ere, not to worry, Rev'ren'. The old girl just 'ad a splinter in her arse.' She turns and hits him over the head with her purse. He starts cussing her out in very descriptive Cockney, and by that time, I've completely lost control of the situation. He's ducking and trying to get away, and finally she chases him right out of the church."

Convulsed with laughter, Rhiannon wiped at her eyes. David's mimicry of the old Englishman's accent was dead-on. "I'm surprised she even felt it."

David tried to look reproving, but there was a twinkle in his eyes. "She is a lady of substance, to be sure. I still don't know how I made it through the rest of the sermon, but after the service, when the church had cleared, Tupper and I went back to check on the pew she was in. It looked like someone had relieved their boredom one day by carving into the wood. I guess Mrs. Kristen didn't notice when she sat down, and she must have moved at just the wrong angle and been impaled."

"So, how does this relate to me earning some money?"

"Well, Tupper spent this week sanding and smoothing that pew and a few others that needed it. They just need to be stained now, but the problem is that Tupper can't do it because his asthma acts up when he's exposed to the smell of paints and lacquers. I don't want to leave it, and I won't have time this week to get it done myself, so I wondered if you'd be interested."

"I've never painted or stained anything before."

"How hard can it be? Besides, Tupper will show you. He just can't stay in an enclosed space once you start."

"What's the pay?"

David chuckled. "I had a feeling that would be one of your first questions. I'm afraid that all my budget allows for is minimum wage, but I'll throw in a meal allowance too."

"When would you want me to start?"

"Monday after you've finished work, if that's good for you. They'll take a couple of coats, but you should be done in a few days."

"Let me think about it, and I'll let you know tomorrow."

David nodded and pulled a card out of his shirt pocket. He handed it to her, then stood and brushed off his trousers. "I'd better be going. Give me a call when you make up your mind."

Rhiannon waved as David strolled down the path and out to the sidewalk. She turned the business card over. He had scrawled "David" and another number on the back. She compared it to the official church number on the front. He had given her his private number.

Rhiannon stared at the card for long moments. *Why do I feel like my life is being turned upside down?* She tucked the card into her wallet and picked up the bus schedule.

Dana arrived at Marika's door and knocked loudly. She grinned as the door opened and Marika stood there, scowling. "Good afternoon."

Marika winced. "Yeah, yeah. Here to pick up that bad influence you call a partner?"

Dana trailed after Marika into the living room, where Lee was sprawled on the couch, a forearm over her eyes despite the shades-darkened room.

"I'm a bad influence? Who invented tequila roulette?" Lee asked.

Dana stifled a smile. Lee's hair was damp, though she was still in yesterday's clothes, and the room had been tidied since her last visit. A couple of empty coffee mugs sat on the table. Dana pushed Lee's feet off the couch and took a seat beside her. "Well, you look like you survived."

Lee grunted. "Barely." She uncovered her eyes and peered at Dana. "I'm not going to get any sympathy today, am I?"

"Not in the least. Self-inflicted injuries, my love. You know the policy on that." Dana laughed at Lee's woebegone countenance. "Don't worry. I'm sure by this time tomorrow, you'll feel almost human again."

With a tiny shake of her head, Lee slid her arm back over her eyes.

Marika spoke up quietly, "About tomorrow—"

Before she could finish the sentence, Lee dropped her arm and pinned her with a fierce scowl. "Don't even say it. You're coming, and that's that."

Dana looked between the two.

Marika dropped her gaze and nodded.

Lee swung herself upright and stood. "Let's get going." She stopped beside Marika's chair and rested a hand on her shoulder. "See you tomorrow, right?"

Marika gave a half-hearted smile. "Okay. I still think it's a bad idea, but I'll be there."

Dana followed Lee out of the condo. As soon as they were in the hall, she asked, "What was that all about?"

"She thinks it's a bad idea to fraternize with Lady Mouse outside of the office. Frankly, I think the kid scares her."

"Lady Mouse? You mentioned that name last night. What or who is Lady Mouse?"

"Oh, yeah, I forgot to tell you. I invited Marika and her assistant, Rhiannon, to dinner on Sunday. I didn't think you'd mind."

"Of course not. You know you can invite anyone to our home anytime. But why is Marika upset about it?"

Lee slung an arm around Dana and hugged her as they waited for the elevator. "You really are the best, you know? Rhiannon is the one I told you about who faced down those thugs in the alley. She also happens to be Marika's temporary assistant. She's not the most sociable person in the world, but I'd like us to give her a chance."

"Okay. Is Marika upset because you're fixing her up?"

Lee started to laugh and then flinched. "Ouch. No, that's not it at all. Hell, I don't even know if Rhiannon is family. I just think that it'd be good for both of them to get to know each other outside of the office. We're about the only people who can make that happen. God knows Marika will never take the initiative on her own, and neither would Rhiannon." Lee shot Dana a serious look. "They're both good people, love, and I just have this gut feeling that they'd be friends, given half a chance. I'd like to see them get that chance."

The elevator arrived, and they entered. After Dana punched the button for the lobby, she leaned against the back wall and gazed at Lee. "You really are a big marshmallow."

"Marshmallow? I'm no marshmallow."

"Yup, you are." Dana poked Lee's stomach. "A big, lovable, soft-in-the-centre marshmallow."

"Cut that out, woman."

Lee wrapped her arms around Dana and dropped a kiss on her head. Dana returned the embrace, and they rode the rest of the way in peaceful silence.

CHAPTER 9

C LUSTERS OF SOAP BUBBLES DRIFTED and collapsed around Marika's body while the soft sounds of Enya filled the air. It had taken over twenty-four hours, but the effects of her hangover had receded.

Marika smiled. *I wonder if Lee has recovered yet.*

Spooky jumped up on the counter and began to groom himself.

"Hey, mister, you leave hair all over my towel, and I'm turning you into a throw rug."

Yellow eyes flicked to Marika, but he ignored her threat.

"Why do I bother? I might as well talk to myself." Marika settled deeper into the bathtub, and hot water rose around her neck. She snapped her fingers on the surface of her bath and sent a small geyser of water toward her cat.

Spooky hissed, then stalked over her towel before he leaped to the floor and left the room.

She laughed, stretched, and settled back into the bubbles as her mind drifted lazily over her plans for the day. *I'd better get some work done since I did nothing but couch-surf yesterday. And I'm supposed to be at Lee and Dana's by five.*

Marika frowned. *Why did Lee have to invite Rhiannon? Don't I see enough of her during work hours?* She ducked under the water, then surfaced and wiped the water out of her face. *At least Lee and Dana will be there, and for some reason, the formidable Ms. Davies actually seems to like Lee. Who doesn't, of course, but Lee likes her back. I suppose that's not all that surprising either. Ugh. Why couldn't they have left me out of it and just had her over for dinner? Oh well, she'll probably leave before dessert, anyway. She's not exactly the sort to hang around until nightcaps are served.* "All right, Plan A. Let Lee and Dana try and carry on the conversation tonight. If the past two weeks are any evidence, even Lee's skills will be tested to the limit."

Marika lounged in the tub until the water cooled. She got out, dried off, and observed her naked form critically in the mirror. *At least all the hours at my desk haven't hurt me yet, but I really should take up golf again.*

Sadness threatened to overwhelm her as she remembered her father teaching her the game when she was little. *That was a lifetime ago.*

Marika pushed the memory away and dried herself off. She donned shorts and a faded T-shirt, then went to the kitchen to make a fresh pot of coffee. When she turned on the coffeemaker, Spooky wound himself around her legs and purred.

"Oh sure, now you're going to suck up. I don't suppose it would have anything to do with food, would it?"

Spooky padded over to the pantry and sat in front of the door.

"Aw, my poor starving boy," Marika said. "You're just wasting away to nothing, aren't you?" She nudged him aside, opened the door, and was about to grab a tin of cat food off the shelf when the buzzer sounded from the lobby. She ignored Spooky's protests and left the kitchen to answer her intercom. "Hello?"

"Hi, Marika. It's Terry." There was an atypical note of hesitancy in her voice. "Can I come in?"

"Of course. Come on up." Marika entered the code to open the entrance. She unlocked her door, then returned to the kitchen. She finished filling Spooky's dish just as a knock sounded. "It's open."

Terry entered and came to the kitchen.

Marika straightened and smiled at her visitor.

Terry thrust a brown paper bag at her. "I brought bagels."

"Thank you." Marika opened the bag and inhaled the aroma. "Mmm, they smell wonderful. I just made a fresh pot of coffee. Would you like some?"

Terry sniffed appreciatively. "Hazelnut?"

"It is. Why don't you get the mugs down while I set the bagels out?"

They took their coffee, bagels, and cream cheese to the kitchen table. Marika set out the plates and knives and smiled as she realized how naturally they slipped into their old habits. "Oh, these are great. You must have gone down to Castle's." Marika bit into a cinnamon raisin bagel so fresh that it still held a hint of warmth.

Terry mumbled confirmation around a mouthful and then washed it down with coffee. "It's not a bad drive on a Sunday morning. The traffic was pretty light."

"It's at least an hour return trip, even in Sunday traffic." Marika laid a hand on Terry's arm. "Thank you for going to all that trouble."

Terry covered Marika's hand with hers. "Are we okay?"

"We're absolutely okay."

Terry's shoulders relaxed, and she smiled. "Good. I'm really sorry I butted in. What you do is your business. We were just worried..."

"I know, but everything's all right—really."

Doubt was clear in Terry's eyes, but Marika ignored it. She held up another bagel. "I think I like your idea of an olive branch better than Lee's. It's much easier on the constitution."

Terry laughed. "I heard about that. I was talking to Dana last night, and she said Lee was suffering severely, although she didn't sound too sympathetic about it. I take it you two over-served each other on Friday?"

"You'd think by now I'd know better than to get into a game of tequila shooters with that woman. I swear she could drink a whole regiment of soldiers under the table."

"I think she has."

The last of the residual tension slipped away, and soon they bantered as if the past couple of weeks had never occurred. When Spooky jumped on Terry's lap to take his accustomed position, they both chuckled at the sheer familiarity of it.

"Another cup?" Marika rose to refill her coffee.

Terry held out her mug.

"So, what's Jan up to this morning?"

There was no answer.

Marika tilted her head. "Ter? Is something wrong?"

Terry sighed and shook her head. "Not really. She is a little miffed at me, though."

"Do you want to talk about it?" Marika resumed her seat and studied Terry.

"It's stupid, really."

"If it's bothering you or Jan, then it's not stupid." Marika basked again in her role as Terry's sage. *Oh, my God. This is what I feared losing. It was never about our abortive affair.* Startled, Marika had to wrench her concentration back on Terry's words.

"Jan can't understand why I won't sleep at her house, why we always have to stay at my place. I mean, she's fond of Michael and Claire, but she would like to make love where we don't have roommates one floor down."

"Why don't you want to stay at her place?"

Terry fidgeted and caused Spooky to jump off her lap. "Because it's his house."

Marika wasn't surprised. She took a long sip of coffee and considered her answer. "Rob's gone, Ter. It's Jan's house now. You've spent a lot of time over there, both before and after he died. What exactly makes you so uncomfortable?"

Terry grimaced. "I can't make love to his wife in his bed. It's...it's...icky."

"That would be the proper psychological term, would it?" Marika ignored Terry's half-hearted glower. "Have you talked this out with Jan?"

When Terry didn't respond, Marika raised one eyebrow. "Terry? You have told Jan this, haven't you?"

"No."

"How do you expect Jan to understand if you don't explain your feelings to her?"

"She'll think I'm an idiot."

Marika regarded Terry affectionately. "That woman is so much in love with you that she thinks you walk on water.

And before you end up disillusioning her, maybe you should think of compromising."

"Compromise? How?"

"I assume there's more than one bedroom in the house." Terry nodded.

"Why don't you try spending the night in one of the other bedrooms? Make one of the other rooms yours and hers. It doesn't matter if it's smaller, just that you can be comfortable there and keep your mind on Jan and your future, rather than the past. I'm sure if you explained this all to her, she would be more than willing to adapt."

Relief and excitement blazed across Terry's face. "That could work." She jumped up and hugged Marika, who squawked as her coffee spilled. "Oops, sorry 'bout that." Terry grabbed a dishtowel and dabbed at the spreading stain on Marika's T-shirt.

"Go on, go home and talk to Jan." Marika took the cloth from Terry's hand and finished mopping up.

"I don't know how to thank you."

"Consider it a fair trade for the bagels. Now get going, I've got work to do today."

Terry planted a quick kiss on Marika's forehead.

Marika walked her to the door. When Terry left, she turned and leaned against the door as she considered her minor epiphany. "All this time. How could I be so blind? It was never the sex. It was the friendship."

Spooky ambled up to her, and she scooped him up with a laugh. "We're going to be okay, mister. We don't love Terry after all. Well, we do, but not like that. Who knew?" She held Spooky up to eye level. "Did you know? Were you just not telling me so I could figure it out for myself?" She snuggled him into her chest and kissed his head. "Wise cat."

With a laugh Marika set Spooky down and peeled off her wet shirt. Suddenly even the prospect of dinner with her taciturn assistant didn't seem daunting.

Rhiannon keyed her bedroom padlock and picked up her battered backpack. As she walked down the stairs, she wrestled with a strap that she had repaired countless times, but which had broken again.

The front door opened as she neared the base of the stairs. Hettie and her friends entered.

Damn it. I thought I'd get out here before she came back.

"Hello, Anne," Hettie said. "Are you on your way out?"

"Yes. I'm going to a friend's place for dinner." Rhiannon tied the strap ends together as a temporary fix.

"Dinner? You're going out to dinner? With who?"

Rhiannon grimaced. "You wouldn't know them." She tried to edge by the women crowding the door.

"Well, you be cautious now, dear. Young girls can't be too careful out there. There are far too many deviants in the world, and you know how I worry about you. You really shouldn't go anywhere without letting me know the address and the phone number, just in case."

Rhiannon had no illusions about her aunt's solicitude. Hettie burned with curiosity about her unprecedented dinner invitation. *That'll be the day I tell you anything.* She pushed past them.

Hettie raised her voice. "Girls, I think we should offer a prayer to keep our little Annie safe."

Rhiannon gritted her teeth and kept walking. Her nostrils flared as she recalled years of incessant prayers for her ungrateful soul. *Wonder what exactly they wanted me to be grateful for: the theft of my name, all the nights I cried myself to sleep, or all the times I had to wear long sleeves and pants so no one saw the bruises. Yeah, I'm grateful all right—grateful I'll be out of this hellhole before another year is gone.*

On her way to the bus stop, Rhiannon amused herself by imagining their faces if they knew. *You wanted to know where I'm going, Hettie? Well, I'm off to have dinner with a wonderful couple and their son. And, oh, did I mention that it's a couple of women? Yup, I'm off to have Sunday dinner with a lesbian family. I'll be sure to tell them you said hello.*

Rhiannon laughed out loud. *Wouldn't that just give them all heart palpitations.* She was still smiling as she boarded the bus.

Marika downshifted as she neared a small park a few blocks from Lee and Dana's home. She drove slowly, watching for small children who often frequented the playground, then she did a double take.

Rhiannon sat on a bench under a tree, reading a book.

Should I stop? Marika was past the park before she could make up her mind. *I'm not her keeper. She'll find her way there.*

When Marika arrived, there was a note on the front door that read, *We're out back.* She walked around the side of the house to the backyard.

Dana was at the grill. Lee and Eli were tossing a football. Eli saw her first and whooped a greeting.

Marika waved, then chuckled as he missed Lee's next toss.

Lee walked over to greet her. "Glad to see you're still in the land of the living."

Marika returned Lee's hug. "No thanks to you, you old reprobate. The next time you go out of the country, try bringing back something a little less lethal."

Dana joined them. "Oh, don't worry. She paid for your little soiree, too. You should've seen her yesterday. She—"

Lee's hand cut off the rest of her words. "No telling tales out of school."

Dana's eyes twinkled. She squirmed out of Lee's grasp, gave Marika a quick hug, and linked arms with her as they strolled over to the deck. "Can I get you something? A beer?"

Lee and Marika groaned, and Dana laughed. "Okay, how about a Coke or some lemonade?"

"Do you have something like ginger ale?" Marika's stomach was still sensitive.

"I'll get it," Eli said.

Dana called after him, "Bring two."

"Oh, I almost forgot," Marika said. "Your other guest is sitting down in the park."

"Rhiannon?" Lee asked. "What's she doing there?"

"I have no idea. I just noticed her when I drove past."

Lee frowned. "Why didn't you stop and offer her a ride?"

Marika fidgeted, then looked up at Eli's return. "Thanks." She opened the can he offered. Lee's and Dana's gazes were still on her. "I don't know. I mean, I didn't know why she was there instead of here, and I didn't know what to do."

Lee stood. "C'mon, Eli. You and I are going for a walk." They left out the back gate.

Marika glanced sideways. "I'm sorry."

Dana met her gaze. "What gives with you and your assistant?"

"Nothing 'gives.' I don't even know her that well."

"Well, that's the whole idea of tonight—for you two to get to know each other better." Dana forestalled Marika's protest with a raised hand. "I know you're not thrilled with the idea, but I want you to consider something. Lee thinks there's something very worthwhile about Rhiannon, and if I've learned anything in our years together, it's to trust Lee's people instincts. I've never seen her be wrong about anyone. Have you?"

Marika shook her head. "No. You're right. It's probably why Lee gave me a second chance at being friends after I screwed up so badly."

"Do you want to talk about it?"

"It?"

"Why you have a problem with Rhiannon. Is she bad at her job?"

Marika sighed. "No. No, she's very good at it. She's been like a sponge the last couple of weeks. I can't believe I'm saying this, but she might even be better than Marion."

"Really? That's very high praise."

"I know, and I certainly can't fault her on her work ethic, but—well, for instance, we had a case last week, a Jordanian woman. She fled an arranged marriage with a man she despised to stay with an aunt here in Calgary. She's seeking refugee status based on a fear of familial persecution should she be sent back. I've filed her paperwork, but her case won't be adjudicated for months yet."

Dana nodded as she watched Marika.

"On Wednesday, she rushed into the office in tears. I was on a call, but I could see she was terrified about something. I got off the phone as quickly as possible. By the time I went out to see what was going on and bring her into my office, Rhiannon had the situation well in hand."

"What was the woman so scared about?"

"Her aunt received word from family that her brother has flown to Canada, intent on either bringing Ms. al-Rashid back to get married or avenging the family honour."

"God! No wonder she was terrified."

"Exactly. But I'd barely gotten the story out of her before Rhiannon came into my office. She'd already made arrangements with the Immigrant Women's Shelter. She told the client not to worry and volunteered to take her over. The situation was resolved before I could even get involved."

"That's good, isn't it? She sounds like an exemplary assistant."

"She is." Marika frowned.

"But?"

"But...well, when she got back, I tried to compliment her on how well she handled the situation."

Dana smiled. "I take it that didn't go well?"

"She was absolutely polite as she brushed me off and returned to work." Marika shook her head. "She's so prickly, so...stand-offish. I miss Marion."

"Tell me, do you treat her the way you treated Marion at the office?"

"I'm perfectly civil to her."

Dana snorted. "Uh-huh. And when was the last time you left a treat on her desk?"

Marika stared at the oak-stained planks beneath her feet. It was a longtime habit of hers to leave a latte or a muffin or a flower on Marion's desk now and then.

"You've always gone the extra mile to let Marion know how much you appreciate her."

"But that's different."

"How? Aren't they both very competent assistants?"

"Yes, but...I like Marion. She's my friend as well as my assistant."

"You know," Dana said, "it can't be easy for Rhiannon, either. If she has an ounce of sensitivity, she has to be aware that you're comparing her unfavourably to Marion. She was probably sitting in the park, trying to work up her nerve to join a bunch of near strangers for dinner."

The thought was troubling. Marika shot Dana an apologetic glance.

"All I'm saying is to give her a chance. She may surprise you."

Marika nodded. *I'm going to do better—I'm really going to try.*

Lee's laugh boomed from the alley. Lee, Eli, and Rhiannon entered the yard.

Rhiannon's eyes widened when she saw Marika.

I bet she wouldn't have accepted Lee's invitation if she'd known I was going to be here. "Hello, Rhiannon. I'm glad you could make it."

"Hi, Ms. Havers." Rhiannon shot Lee an anxious glance.

Lee grinned at her. "Oh no, Lady Mouse. No formality at our house. Here, she's Marika. Now let me introduce you to my partner. Dana, this is Rhiannon Davies, a.k.a. Lady Mouse. Rhiannon, this is Dana Cochrane, Eli's mom."

Dana extended her hand, which Rhiannon shook. "Hi, Rhiannon. Lee speaks so highly of you that I've been looking forward to meeting you."

Rhiannon blushed and jammed her hands into her pockets.

Marika smiled. *She looks a lot less formidable out of the office. Eli's almost as tall as she is. Next to Lee she looks downright elfin.*

"Come have a seat. May I get you something to drink?" Dana led Rhiannon to a chair.

Rhiannon glanced at their pop cans. "Ginger ale is fine, thank you."

Lee dropped into the seat next to her. "You don't have to have it if you don't like it. We got a little bit of everything. What's your favourite drink?"

"Coke, thank you."

"Then Coke it is." Dana nodded at Eli, and he went into the kitchen. He was back in a moment with an armful of Cokes and ginger ales. He popped open a Coke and handed it to Rhiannon.

"Thank you." She gave him a shy smile.

"Did you have any trouble finding our place?" Lee took a Coke from Eli.

"Not really. I've got a pretty good city map."

Marika took a seat across from Rhiannon.

Dana and Lee kept up a string of small talk, striving to make their new guest comfortable. Rhiannon grew more animated as time passed. She even initiated a topic or two.

When Dana announced that dinner was ready, Rhiannon jumped up to help her set the table. They disappeared into the house.

Lee shot Marika a smug grin.

Marika smiled. "Yes, yes, I know. You were right."

"I do so like to hear you say that." Lee ducked the peanut Marika threw at her. "Tut tut, what kind of example are you setting for the child?"

"Hey, who're you calling a child?" Eli said.

Lee wrapped an arm around him and knuckled his head affectionately.

Rhiannon returned with an armload of dishes, cups, and cutlery.

Marika rose and held the door open for her. "May I help you?" She extended a hand to take some of her load.

A dazzling smile lit Rhiannon's face and illuminated her eyes as she handed over the plates.

My God, she's got gorgeous blue eyes. Marika stumbled back a step when Rhiannon stepped around her. Flustered, she deposited the plates on the table, where Eli helped Rhiannon set them around.

They all took their seats and serving dishes began to make the rounds. Marika was quiet and concentrated on her food.

It was only when Eli returned to his ongoing campaign to get a dog that she began to relax. For a year, he had been agitating for a dog. His parents were amenable to getting a small dog, but he had his heart set on a big dog and wasn't about to settle for less.

Marika stifled a smile as Eli launched into his arguments. She knew them by heart. He had confided to her that he was pretty sure he was wearing them down, but she had her doubts.

"C'mon, Mom. C'mon, Lee. Just think how great it would be to have a guard dog—like a wolfhound or an Alsatian. No one would dare mess with our home cuz he'd chew their legs off."

Lee laughed. "You do know we have the most up-to-date security system my company can provide, right?"

"I know, but what if the electricity goes out and the bad guys were just waiting for a chance to pounce? A dog won't lose power."

"Battery back-ups, son. Our security system won't lose power, either."

Eli heaved a big sigh and turned to Rhiannon. "Did your parents let you have a dog?"

Marika sat up and listened intently.

"Not a dog, no. I did have a white mouse named Elrod, though."

"Ewww, Elrod?" Eli's nose wrinkled.

The others laughed.

Rhiannon smiled. "My dad named him. He had a thing for funny names. I'm amazed I didn't end up as a Hermione or Hildegard."

"Or Phyllis." Dana chuckled.

Lee gave her an indignant stare. "Like Timothea is all that great."

Rhiannon cocked her head and glanced at Marika.

Marika said sotto voce, "Their middle names."

"Oh." Rhiannon's expression cleared. Then much to Marika's surprise, she asked shyly, "What's yours, Ms.—um, I mean, Marika?"

Marika was pleased that Rhiannon had finally used her first name. "Kathryn. Marika Kathryn. What's yours?"

"Ardith. It was my mother's name." Rhiannon lowered her gaze.

Lee and Dana exchanged glances.

Dana rose to her feet. "Well, who's for dessert? I've got ice cream and fresh strawberries."

Lee and Eli began to clear dishes.

When Marika started to stand and help, Dana shook her head and glanced significantly at Rhiannon, who still stared at the table.

Marika nodded her understanding and sank back in her seat. "So was it a good weekend?"

Rhiannon looked up and nodded. "It's certainly ending well. Actually, I picked up some extra work, so it was a good weekend."

Marika raised one eyebrow at her definition of a good weekend. "What, I don't keep you busy enough?"

"No, that's not it. It's not really a big deal. I'm helping a…friend…at the neighbourhood church. I'm going to be refinishing some pews. It's only a few days' work, but he's going to pay me for it."

"Have you ever done that kind of work before?"

"No, but David—Reverend Ross—assures me it's not hard and that he and Tupper will show me what to do."

"I wouldn't worry too much. I don't think there's anything you couldn't do once you set your mind to it."

Rhiannon flashed her a smile.

God, she's cute when she does that. She should smile more often. Marika blinked. *Okay, where did that come from?*

Rhiannon scrambled to open the door for Dana, who carried a tray of ice cream, strawberries, and small dishes. Lee trailed after with a pot of coffee, and Eli followed with cups, sugar, and cream.

"Dig in, there's lots." Dana heaped a pile of berries on ice cream and passed the bowl to Rhiannon. "Don't be afraid to ask for seconds."

Rhiannon did ask for seconds.

Lee smirked at Marika, who stuck out her tongue. Lee just laughed and winked.

The rest of the evening passed in pleasant chat until Rhiannon checked her watch. "It's been wonderful, but I'm going to have to go to catch my bus."

Marika stood. "I'm about to head off myself. Why don't I give you a lift home?"

A look of near-panic crossed Rhiannon's face. "Oh no, that's all right. I mean, thank you, but I don't want to take you out of your way. It's no problem to take the bus."

"Don't be stubborn, Rhi. Let Marika give you a ride home." Lee's grin erased any hint of criticism.

Rhiannon obviously didn't want Marika to take her home, but she also clearly didn't want to offend Lee.

Marika laid a hand lightly on Rhiannon's arm. "Come. It's silly for you to have to take a long bus ride when I've got my car here. Let's go."

For an instant, Marika thought her offer would be rejected, but Rhiannon picked up her backpack and joined the others as they walked around the house and out to Marika's car.

Marika hugged Lee and Dana. "Thank you for another wonderful evening. I'll call you later this week, okay?" While she unlocked the car, she kept an eye on Rhiannon.

Rhiannon offered her hand to Dana. "I really had a good time. Thank you very much for inviting me."

Dana ignored the hand and pulled Rhiannon into a warm hug. Marika almost laughed aloud at the look of surprise on her assistant's face, but she noticed with approval that Rhiannon returned the embrace and even produced another of those smiles that Marika found so charming.

Lee beamed and swept Rhiannon into a bear hug, lifting her off the ground. "So, will you honour us with your presence again?"

Rhiannon grinned. "If you ask, I will come."

Lee and Dana laughed. Lee slid an arm around Dana, and they waved as Marika and Rhiannon climbed into the car and pulled away.

"Which way should I go?" Marika asked.

"Just head downtown." A smile lingered on Rhiannon's face.

"They're wonderful people, aren't they?"

Rhiannon nodded. "Yes, they sure are. Have you known them long?"

"Quite a while." Marika pulled up to a four-way stop and checked in all directions. "Lee and I dated several years ago, and we've been friends ever since." Marika's eyes widened as she realized what she'd done. She had been so relaxed by the end of the evening that she forgot that Rhiannon might not be aware she was gay. She wasn't necessarily closeted at work, but neither did she advertise her orientation. She generally kept her personal and professional lives well separated. The senior partners knew, as did Marion, but she doubted any of them had been indiscreet. When it was necessary to attend social functions concerning the firm, she went alone.

Marika cleared her throat nervously.

"I'll bet she was a lot of fun to go out with."

"Yes, she was." Marika shot a glance at Rhiannon.

Rhiannon smiled and stroked the leather seat beneath her. "This sure is a nice car."

Grateful for the change of topic, Marika nodded. "I like it. It handles beautifully, inside and out of the city. Do you have a car?"

"No. Actually, I don't drive."

"Not at all?" *Who doesn't drive in today's world?*

"I never had a car to practice on, so I never bothered to get my licence. I get around well with public transit, so I don't miss having a licence, though I imagine I'll want to get one someday."

Marika was approaching the centre of the city. "Where do I go from here?"

"You can drop me anywhere downtown."

Marika shook her head. "Oh no, I'm not about to explain to Lee how I dumped you out in the middle of nowhere. Where do you live?" For a moment Marika didn't think Rhiannon would answer.

"Victoria Park."

Marika raised an eyebrow, but said nothing as she took the next right. Victoria Park was one of the poorest sections of town and usually made the news only when the police tried to move the hookers off their stroll in the district.

Marika followed Rhiannon's mumbled instructions and drove through the impoverished neighbourhood, keenly aware that the closer they got to their destination, the more Rhiannon slumped down in her seat.

Finally, halfway down one shabby street, Rhiannon jerked her thumb at a tall, narrow house. "That's it, but if you don't mind, could you drop me at the alley?"

Marika eyed the seedy house as they drove past. She turned the corner and was about to pull into the alley when a hand on her arm stopped her.

"I'll get out here," Rhiannon said.

Marika could tell that this time she wasn't going to be swayed. She pulled the car to the curb and stopped. "I'm really glad you joined us tonight. I enjoyed the chance to get to know you outside the office."

She found herself pinned by intense, searching eyes, and she held still. She was rewarded by Rhiannon's slow smile and warm gaze.

"I had a good time too. See you tomorrow."

"Tomorrow," Marika said.

Rhiannon opened the door and stepped out.

Marika waited until she was well down the alley before pulling away. On her way back to the condo, she mulled over the mystery of Rhiannon's home and the woman's obvious reluctance to have her boss see it. *I know she makes enough to afford better accommodations. I wonder why she stays there. She's quite the puzzle, isn't she?*

Marika shook her head. "I may not know much about her, but I do know Rhiannon would resent having her life under a microscope." She sighed. *And her opinion now matters to me. Darn that Lee.*

CHAPTER 10

DAVID PEERED AT THE CHICKEN, which was browned to perfection. He poked it with a fork several times. Pleased, he closed the oven door and surveyed the rest of his preparations. He left the rectory and walked next door to the church. When he saw legs jutting out from underneath a pew, he grinned. "Hey, Rhiannon?"

"Yes?"

"Are you hungry yet?"

"I could eat."

"Good, because I've made enough dinner for two, and I would be honoured if you'd share it with me."

Rhiannon wriggled out from under the pew, brush in hand and a painter's mask over her face. She tugged the mask down and studied him. "You didn't have to do that. I could've grabbed something when I got home."

David shrugged. "I have to eat, you have to eat. It seemed to make sense to eat together, particularly since you're working so hard on my behalf."

"You're paying me, but okay, thanks." Rhiannon set her brush on the tin beside her. She stood and dusted herself off. "I'd better clean up first."

"Sure. Come on over to the rectory when you're done. Dinner's almost ready." David returned to his kitchen, set the table, and began to whip the potatoes. He had just finished carving the chicken when he heard a knock on the door. "It's open. Come in."

Rhiannon stepped inside and inhaled appreciatively. "Smells good in here."

"Take a seat. Everything's ready." David grabbed the butter from the refrigerator and returned to the table to set everything in place. He took a chair opposite Rhiannon and bowed his head. "Dear Lord, we thank You for this day and for the food that You've provided. We ask that You use it to strengthen our bodies for Your work. Thank You for my friend and for her help today, and please help keep me from scaring her off before she finishes all the pews. In Your Son's name, Amen." David ignored the look of amused scepticism on Rhiannon's face as he passed the chicken. "Help yourself."

She filled her plate and dug in eagerly.

David matched her bite for bite.

"This is good." There was a note of surprise in Rhiannon's voice.

David pushed the corn her way. "Thanks. When Conor came to see me after Hannah left, he was appalled at the way I was eating. He told me that man could not live on pizza alone, and before he went home, he made sure I knew how to make chicken, spaghetti, shepherd's pie, and omelets. It's simple stuff, but over the years I've learned a few more dishes and managed not to starve to death."

"I like to do stir-fry now and then. Usually, I make one, and it lasts me for at least three or four days."

"Stir-fry is good. I must admit I love homemade hamburgers, too. I make 'em about an inch thick and then grill them to perfection, just between medium rare and done. Piled with tomatoes, onions, and pickles, and you have heaven on a bun." David slapped his forehead. "Oh, I almost forgot." He retrieved a pitcher from the fridge. "Do you like lemonade?"

"Yes, please." Rhiannon held out her glass.

He filled it and then his own before taking his seat again. "So, did you have a good time at your friend's place yesterday?"

"I had a great time. Lee's family is wonderful. They really made me feel welcome." Rhiannon paused in mid-bite. "They even said they're going to have me back again sometime."

"That's wonderful, Rhi. They must have enjoyed your company too, then."

She cocked her head, then shrugged. "Maybe, or maybe they were just being polite." She stabbed another piece of chicken. "My boss was there too."

One of David's eyebrows rose. "Really? So she's a friend of Lee's?"

"Uh-huh. Actually, she and Lee used to date years ago, before Lee and Dana got together. They all seem to be very good friends." Rhiannon chuckled. "I think Eli—he's Dana's son—has a crush on Marika."

"How old is he?"

"I think Lee said he was fourteen now."

"Oh yes, I remember being that age." David rolled his eyes. "I think I fell in love with any female who'd give me a second glance. When I was in seventh grade, I was crazy about my English teacher. I used to go to school early just to leave a flower on her desk."

"Aw, that's so cute," Rhiannon said. "Did you ever confess your undying love to her in person?"

"Good heavens, no. I was so shy that I couldn't even put my hand up in class for fear she'd call on me. No, I'm afraid I was doomed to unrequited love for that whole year."

"Poor Ichabod. So what ever happened to the love of your life?"

"At the end of the term, she got engaged to the vice principal, an ox of a man with dandruff and terminally bad breath. I decided if her taste was that bad, she wasn't the woman for me."

Rhiannon broke out laughing, and David delighted at the sound. "Glad to see that my romantic trauma is so entertaining." When her giggles subsided, he asked, "So, any childhood crushes for you?"

Rhiannon shook her head. "None that I can remember." She traced her fork through the remaining kernels of corn, then looked at him seriously. "I don't think I have it in me to fall in love."

David stared at her. "Why do you say that? You're still very young. You have lots of time to find that one special someone."

"I don't think there's going to be 'that one special someone' for me. I've never had so much as a crush. I mean, it wasn't like I had a circle of friends to gossip with or anything, but I used to hear the other girls talking. They were always going on about who the cute guys were and who was going out with whom. I'd look at the boys they obsessed over, and I could never see it." She added wryly, "Not that I ever had to worry about any of them asking me out."

David studied his plate, his brow furrowed. "I think we all have the capacity to love. It's part of being human. Has there never been anyone in your life whom you loved?"

"My parents."

David looked up. Rhiannon's unblinking stare challenged him. He selected his words with care. "And I'm sure they loved you and each other."

Rhiannon snorted. "Oh, yeah. Mom loved me so much, she died for me, and Dad loved Mom so much, he wouldn't live for me."

David blinked, but Rhiannon held up her hand. "I don't want to talk about it anymore."

He honoured her reticence but burned with curiosity. They finished their meal in silence, and Rhiannon helped him clear the plates. He brought two small bowls of fresh peach slices from the refrigerator and set one in front of her.

"Thanks."

"You're welcome."

After several spoonfuls of the fruit, David said, "You mentioned earlier that Lee and your boss used to date. Are you all right with your boss being gay?"

"Sure, why not?" Rhiannon shrugged. "She's actually pretty decent, and she's fair to work for, so that's all I care about. Besides, Lee and Dana obviously like her."

"And their opinion means a lot?"

Rhiannon didn't hesitate. "Yes, it does. I think they're really good people, you know? Lee had no reason to ask me over for dinner except that she was being kind. I figure they wanted me to meet my boss on neutral ground, so I could get to know their friend sorta like they do. They went out of their way to include me and make me feel comfortable. I won't forget that."

No, you won't, will you? David suspected that, though hard won, once given, Rhiannon's loyalty would be unshakable.

"She left a muffin on my desk today."

He blinked at the non sequitur. "Excuse me?"

"Ms. Havers—Marika, she left a great big blueberry muffin on my desk this morning. I found it when I got in."

David registered the undertone of bewilderment. "That was nice of her."

"It was, wasn't it? Huh." Rhiannon shook her head and finished off her dessert. "Well, I'd better get back to work. I don't want anyone to think I'm not earning my pay." She stood and started to clear her things away.

"That's okay, leave it. I'll take care of them." David took the fruit bowl and cutlery from her hand.

"Okay. Thanks for dinner." Rhiannon left the kitchen.

"You're welcome," David called after her. "Any time." He laughed softly. *I got her to stay for a whole meal. Way to go, Dave.*

Rhiannon watched Marika escort the thin young Chechen and his interpreter out to the hall. She returned, dropped into the seat beside Rhiannon's desk, and heaved a dramatic sigh. Rhiannon eyed her boss curiously.

"Make a note to book a different interpreter for his next session. I'm afraid Mr. Ulyanov left something to be desired, not to mention that at one point I thought the two of them were going to come to blows."

"Any idea what it was all about?" Rhiannon asked.

"Not the least. But I was about two seconds away from calling security to break them up. Please tell me my day is going to get better from here on."

Rhiannon glanced at the appointment book. "Well, you have a Mr. Njenga last thing before lunch and then the Abu Masri deposition at two-thirty this afternoon."

Marika beamed. "Kefa's scheduled? Oh, that does make my day."

Rhiannon shot her a questioning look.

"That's right, you weren't here. Kefa Njenga is an Oxford-educated Nigerian civil engineer. He's from the Ogoni tribe in southern Nigeria. About ten years ago, he got involved in the tribe's struggle against the military dictatorship and Shell Oil. He was actually a youth liaison worker with Ken Saro-Wiwa's movement until he was nabbed by the military." Marika shook her head. "How he survived what they put him through amazes me, but somehow he did, and in the aftermath of the Saro-Wiwa and Ogoni Nine executions in '95, he managed to escape. He had to hide for two years before he could make arrangements to smuggle his family out of the country. Eventually, with the help of sympathizers, they made their way here."

"I take it he's one of your favourites?"

"Oh yes. You'll understand when you meet him, believe me. He and his wife are a remarkable couple. I don't think I've ever met more determined, hard-working people in my life." Marika smiled. "The first time I met Kefa, he was this tall, skinny beanpole. I think he's put on about a hundred pounds since then." She stood and regarded Rhiannon seriously. "Just so you're forewarned, the military messed his face up badly."

Rhiannon nodded. She would not shame her boss by anything less than a professional demeanor when the client arrived.

Marika stretched and glanced at her watch. "I'm going to run downstairs for a decent cup of coffee. May I get you one?"

Rhiannon rapidly calculated whether her budget would allow this small indulgence.

"My treat." Marika sounded amused.

"Uh, okay. Thanks." Rhiannon busied herself at her keyboard.

Marika returned to her office, reappeared with her purse, and left the office.

Rhiannon stared after Marika. *What's going on? First the muffin, now a coffee. This is so not like her. I wonder if Lee and Dana said something.*

She shook her head. The about-face in Marika's attitude was unsettling, but not unpleasant. It was an agreeable change from the previous two weeks. Marika had been terse and businesslike in all their communications, in clear contrast to her affectionate exchanges with Marion. Rhiannon had focused on proving her competence and projecting a professional bearing. She didn't do personal relationships.

Until now. First, I can't shake David, then Lee invites me to dinner, and now Marika's being nice. I don't get it. Did I miss the 'be kind to Rhiannon' memo this month? Rhiannon shook her head but put it all out of her mind as she pulled up the Njenga file.

Not long after Marika deposited a tall coffee on Rhiannon's desk and returned to her office, a very large man walked up to Rhiannon. He was well over six feet and, she guessed, closing in on three hundred pounds. Thick ridges of scar tissue stretched from his disfigured eye socket, across his jaw, and down over his throat, marring his round, friendly face.

Despite her best intentions, Rhiannon stared. "Mr. Njenga?"

"Yes, Miss, I am Kefa Njenga, and I have an appointment with Ms. Havers."

Rhiannon could hear the clear British influence in his deep, rich voice.

"Kefa! It's so good to see you again." Marika advanced toward him with her hand outstretched.

"Ah, Marika, you grow more beautiful every time I see you." They shook hands enthusiastically.

"And you're just as honey-tongued as ever. Does Mrs. Njenga know how you flatter all the ladies?"

Kefa regarded her with feigned apprehension. "You won't be telling on me, will you?"

They laughed together, and just before the office door closed, he added, "Besides, how do you think we ended up with eight children?"

Rhiannon smiled. It was easy to see why Marika favoured this client. She returned her attention to the file she was researching on a Kashmiri client. She scrolled rapidly through US State Department human rights reports before she switched to the Amnesty International website for additional information.

Rhiannon was deeply absorbed in her research and almost didn't notice the man who crossed to her desk just before noon. When she looked up, she was startled to find baleful eyes glaring at her.

"I am Salam al-Rashid. You have hidden my sister Tahia. Where is she?" The voice was imperious, demanding. The man's thick Middle-Eastern accent obscured his words.

Uh-oh. Rhiannon stood slowly and gestured to the chairs which lined the wall. "Won't you take a seat, Mr. al-Rashid? My boss is with a client at the moment, but—"

"I require nothing from you but the location of my sister!" The man's voice rose.

Rhiannon's mind raced as she took a deep breath.

"Is there a problem here?"

Rhiannon turned to see Marika at her office door. "Ms. Havers, this is Mr. al-Rashid. He is looking for his sister, Tahia." She stared into Marika's stern eyes and was relieved to see instant comprehension.

The man glowered at Marika. A vein throbbed in his forehead.

"My sister—where is she? Our aunt told me that she came to you, and you would know where she is. Tell me this instant."

Marika flicked her gaze to Rhiannon's phone before she stepped to one side and drew the angry man's focus with her.

Rhiannon discreetly punched in the code for security.

The man advanced toward Marika. He waved his hands in angry punctuation of his demands. The volume of his voice escalated, and he was clearly becoming more agitated by the moment.

Rhiannon kept her gaze fixed on Marika and the livid al-Rashid. *C'mon, c'mon, c'mon. Security, where the hell are you?*

The man plunged his hands into his jacket pockets.

Rhiannon glimpsed a flash of metal and instinctively threw herself across the short space between them. She tackled al-Rashid and bore him to the floor by sheer force of momentum and surprise.

A blaze of pain slashed across Rhiannon's back. She gasped and rolled away. A shadow burst past her. Through tearing eyes, she saw Kefa pin the screaming, writhing man to the floor, wrench the knife from the attacker, and toss it away.

In the bedlam of noise and movement, Rhiannon was conscious of fire lancing across the back of her right shoulder. Then arms cradled her.

"Call 911! Where the hell is security? Get me some towels!" Marika's voice sounded faraway, and her worried face swam in Rhiannon's vision.

Over the outcry of panicked, confused people, the agonized ululating of her attacker echoed through the office.

I wonder why he's screaming.

"God, Rhiannon, why'd you do that?" Marika murmured as she brushed Rhiannon's face with a gentle hand. "He could've killed you."

"Could've killed you, too." Rhiannon couldn't summon the energy to keep her eyes open.

"Damn it, where are those towels?"

She sounds so scared. Rhiannon couldn't stop shaking. The arms around her tightened. Something pressed firmly against the back of her shoulder, and Rhiannon cried out.

"I'm sorry, I'm so sorry. I've got to get this bleeding slowed down. Hang on, Rhi, hang on."

Rhiannon allowed the grey fog to take her under.

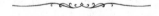

Lee whistled off-key as she entered the office tower. Despite the cool, drizzly weather, it had been a good morning, and she hoped to steal Marika and Rhiannon away for lunch. She was curious to see whether the Sunday gathering had made any change in the dynamic between them.

"Hey, Fred," she called cheerfully to the security guard as he waved her by with a grin. Lee approached the bank of elevators.

Fred's radio went off in a frantic burst of sound. "Code Red, seventh floor, 712!"

Lee's head snapped up, and she pushed through the crowd waiting for the elevator. Fred was right behind her, and another guard ran to join them.

Lee punched the button for the seventh floor and cursed at the slowness of their ascent. When they finally reached the floor, she burst out of the doors and ran down the hall, the guards hard on her heels.

Lee heard the clamour of excited voices long before they reached Marika's office, and her mind flashed through every instance her friend had shared with her about angry clients and confrontations in the office. After rounding the corner at a dead run, she slammed to a halt at the scene in front of her. *Oh God!*

A large black man stood with his foot on the chest of a man who was screaming and writhing on the floor.

A few feet away, Marika cradled Rhiannon. Blood soaked both of them and the carpet. For one awful instant, Lee was sure that Rhiannon was dead, then she saw the shallow rise and fall of her chest.

The two security guards ran to the downed man and tried to pin his flailing arms.

Marika looked up as Lee knelt at her side. Her eyes were filled with tears. "Thank God you're here. She's hurt."

Lee laid a hand on each of them. "I know, sweetie. The EMTs will be on their way. She's going to be okay." *Please, God, let that be the truth.*

"She did it for me, Lee. He had a knife, and she took him down. This should've been me."

"Jesus Christ!"

Fred's shocked voice grabbed Lee's attention. She looked over to where the two security guards had managed to get plastic cuffs on the assailant.

Lee felt her gorge rise as she saw the reason. When they'd rolled the man on his side, they'd exposed the scorched edges of clothing surrounding a circle of seared and bubbled flesh. Bits of broken glass lay on the blackened carpet.

"He was carrying acid." Kefa raised his head and regarded Marika sombrely. "You were very lucky, my friend. That little one saved you from a terrible fate."

Marika swayed as she stared at the mutilated flesh.

The writhing man gasped agonized screams.

Lee wrapped an arm around Marika's shoulders. "It didn't happen. Don't let your mind go there. Stay here. Rhiannon needs you now."

Marika renewed her hold on Rhiannon and pressed the soaked towel firmly against her.

There was tumult in the hall, and the crowd parted for two paramedics pushing a gurney into the office. One EMT went to al-Rashid, who had subsided to deep moans; the other dropped to her knees beside Lee, Marika, and Rhiannon.

"Any of that yours?" the paramedic asked, nodding at the blood on Marika's clothes. When Marika shook her head, the EMT eased Rhiannon out of Marika's arms and worked swiftly to assess the severity of the wound.

"Lee," Marika whispered.

"Hmm?"

"Can you get them out of here?" Marika indicated the crowd. "She wouldn't want them to see her this way."

Lee nodded and strode over to the onlookers, who now included one of the senior partners. "All right, everyone needs to leave now and give the emergency workers room to work. Go back to your offices and clear the halls."

The crowd dispersed, though there was a buzz of excited chatter as they moved away.

Two city police officers got off the elevator, and Lee motioned them her way. She knew the senior man and quickly briefed him on the situation. They made their way back into the office as the paramedics prepared to load al-Rashid onto the gurney.

Marika glared at the EMTs. "You should take her first. She's the victim here."

"That's not how it works, ma'am. He's more seriously injured, so he goes first. She's stabilized, and the second unit is on its way. It'll be here within minutes."

Marika scowled but stroked Rhiannon's hair.

"Sweetie, we need to contact her next of kin."

Marika nodded. "Call human resources. Dial 2100. See who's listed, and get their number."

The first gurney was wheeled out, and the second gurney arrived. While Lee waited for human resources to find the information, she scrutinized Marika. "Yes? What do you mean, there's nobody listed? There has to be." Lee listened a few more moments, then hung up.

Marika kept a hand on Rhiannon's arm as she was loaded on the gurney.

"There's no listing on her NOK," Lee said.

"How can that be? She lives with a relative or something, doesn't she?"

"I think so, but I got the impression they weren't close."

"Well, we have to inform someone." Marika turned to the paramedics who were buckling the straps around the unconscious Rhiannon. "Where are you taking her?"

"Foothills, ma'am. Do you have her health card?"

"No, I don't." Marika glanced at Rhiannon's desk.

Lee leaned over and tugged a backpack out from underneath. "Sorry, kid. No choice." She rummaged through the contents and came up with an old wallet, which held a bus pass, library card, social insurance card, birth certificate, and the required health card. She took it out and handed it to the paramedic, who hurried after her partner.

"Any sign of something resembling next of kin in there?"

Lee thumbed through the rest of the contents and found only five dollars and a business card. She took a closer look at the business card.

"Hmm, Reverend David Ross. He's a priest at St. Barnabas Anglican." Lee looked at Marika. "Her priest, do you think?"

"She did say something about working at a church," Marika said. "Come on, we should get going."

"Um, Marika?" Lee looked at her friend's bloody clothes as she began to punch in the number on the card. "You got anything you can change into?"

Marika glanced down and shook her head. "No. I've got wet wipes in my purse. I'll clean off what I can on the way over. C'mon, Lee, hurry!"

Lee made an exasperated face and focused on her call.

A woman answered, "St. Barnabas."

"May I speak to David Ross, please."

After a few moments, a warm masculine voice came on the line. "Reverend Ross."

"Hi, my name is Lee Glenn. Do you by any chance know a Rhiannon Davies?"

"Yes, why? Is something wrong? Is she all right?"

Lee hated being the bearer of bad news. "No, sir, not really. She was attacked in her office. I found your number in her things."

"Good Lord! Is she—?"

"No!" Lee hastened to assure the priest. "No, I think she's going to be all right, but she's been taken to Foothills with a knife wound. Her boss and I don't know who to notify as next of kin. There's no listing on her human resources files."

There was a noticeable hesitation. "She has an aunt, but I don't think... Look, I'm going to the hospital now, and I'll take responsibility for notifying her... family, if it's warranted."

"All right. We're on our way there, too. See you in the ER." Lee hung up the phone.

Marika had grabbed her coat, wrapped it around herself, and was hovering anxiously.

Lee picked up Rhiannon's backpack, stuffed the wallet back inside, and zipped it. "Let's go."

The words were barely out of Lee's mouth before Marika hustled her out of the office.

CHAPTER 11

L EE STOLE A SIDEWAYS GLANCE at Marika as they walked from the parking lot to the emergency room. Marika had been silent on the drive to the hospital, and Lee, wrapped up in her own thoughts, hadn't pressed her. *Probably not a great idea to let her brood, though. She's pretty shaken up.*

Lee couldn't get the image of the assailant's acid-seared flesh out of her mind. *Jesus, that's going to haunt Marika for a long time. That was way too close for comfort.*

Marika glanced at her hands, and anguish twisted her expression. Despite her efforts in the car, minute traces of blood lingered.

Lee put her arm around Marika's shoulders and led her through the automatic door and into the ER waiting room. There were few people at this time of day. Even had it been crowded, it would have been no problem to pick out Reverend Ross.

A tall, thin man in dark clerical garb sat on the far side of the room, his head down and shoulders hunched. Lee wondered if he was deep in thought or prayer. He absently pushed his glasses up his nose and ran a hand over thinning blonde hair. She noticed that his white cleric's collar was askew and found it disarming.

"C'mon. I think I see Rhiannon's church buddy." Lee steered Marika across the room. When they came within a few metres of the priest, he glanced up. Lee was struck by his compassionate, intelligent eyes as he stood and waited for them.

"Are you Reverend Ross?" Lee asked, extending a hand.

He took her hand. "David, please. And you're Ms. Glenn?"

"Lee. And this is Marika Havers, Rhiannon's boss." They, too, shook hands, and the three of them sat down.

"Have you heard anything yet?" Lee asked.

"I asked at the triage desk, and they're working on her right now. I left word that we were here and to notify us when we could see her." David's voice was calm. "Would you please tell me what happened?"

Lee quickly filled David in on the morning's events.

"The man who attacked her—he was brought here too?" David asked.

"I think so." Lee didn't care one way or the other.

"Oh, my God!" Marika's exclamation caught Lee by surprise. She and David stared at her. "The aunt! If al-Rashid got the information about his sister from their aunt, he probably forced it from her. She may be lying injured at her home right now. I have to talk to the police." Marika patted her pockets but failed to find her cell, so she hurried to the courtesy phone on the far side of the lobby.

Lee watched her for a moment before she returned her attention to David. They regarded each other with discreet curiosity.

Finally, Lee broke the silence. "So you're Rhiannon's priest, eh?"

"No, I wouldn't say that. She did attend St. Barnabas several years ago, but it was long before I arrived."

"Huh. So you're her…what? Employer, family counsellor, consigliere?"

David smiled. "I hope that I'm her friend. I'm working on it."

"Yeah, I know what you mean. Our young friend can be prickly at times."

David nodded. "It's rather like taking tea with a porcupine. You're never quite sure if you're going to have a perfectly lovely encounter or end up with a hand full of quills because you reached for the scones at the wrong time."

"She's worth the effort, though." Lee was even more convinced of that after the day's events.

"That she is," David said.

Marika returned, and Lee raised an eyebrow.

"I contacted the police and gave them the information. The office will give them the aunt's address. They're going to send someone over immediately to check things out."

"Good." Lee patted the chair beside her, and Marika sat. "How are you doing? You okay?"

"Just worried." Marika bit her lip. "Do you think she'll be all right?"

"I think so. Just before they took the other guy out, the paramedic said Rhiannon was stabilized. She's going to be out of action for a while, though, I suspect."

David sighed. "She's not going to like that. Somehow I can't see her turning to her aunt for help. Stubborn woman will try to take care of herself as she recovers."

Lee and Marika looked at him curiously.

"She lives with her aunt, who was her legal guardian while she was growing up, but Rhiannon despises the woman. I doubt that she'll even tell her, let alone allow Hettie to care for her. Frankly, I'm not sure her aunt would be inclined to help. They're not exactly on good terms, to say the least."

"There's no way she'll be able to manage alone, at least not for the first few days." Lee pondered the problem. "I know. I can take her home and put her in the guest room until she's better."

"Are you sure she'll agree?" David asked. "She's very independent, and that's putting it mildly."

Lee sat up, enthused. "It's perfect. We have lots of room, and my partner is a nurse. She works days at a clinic, but she could monitor Rhiannon at night. If necessary, I can take a few days off work while she gets settled in."

David nodded. "It could work, if we present it the right way."

"No." Marika's voice was quiet, but adamant.

Lee gaped at Marika. "Whaddaya mean 'no'? It's perfect. She can stay with us until she's ready to go home again. Dana won't mind."

"I mean that she'll come home with me."

Lee stared at Marika. "You? You're going to look after her?"

Marika nodded but said nothing more.

"That doesn't make any sense. We've got the room, and Dana can keep an eye on her wound. You've only got one bedroom, for crying out loud."

Lee's objections ceased when David laid a hand on her arm. He shook his head slightly and gestured at Marika.

Marika stared at the floor, her hands locked together so tightly that the knuckles were white. When she raised her head, her expression was determined. "She can have my bedroom. I'll take the daybed in the den. As far as appointments go, I can rearrange my schedule and work from home for a few days."

Lee was astonished that Marika would even offer, but in the face of such resolve, she capitulated. "Okay. I'll see if Dana will stop by in the evenings."

A doctor approached and drew their attention. David stood, and the doctor smiled at him. "We just can't keep you away from our fair facility, can we?"

"Not when you have one of my flock in here, Gilles. How is she doing?"

The doctor motioned David to sit and took the seat next to him.

David turned to the women. "Lee, Marika, this is Dr. Gilles Mathieu. Gilles, these are Rhiannon's friends, Lee and Marika."

They exchanged nods.

"Your friend actually got lucky," Dr. Mathieu said. "The blade that her attacker used appears to have been as sharp as a scalpel, so rather than ripping through flesh and muscle, it sliced cleanly. I put in fifty stitches, subcutaneous and surface. She's young and healthy, and I expect her to heal well. She'll have an impressive scar, of course, but she could check with plastic surgeons later if she wants some work done. Some physiotherapy might be needed, depending on her range of motion once the wound is healed."

"So she's going to be okay?" Lee asked.

Dr. Mathieu nodded. "She should be fine. It'll hurt like hell for a while, but I've written her a scrip for painkillers. She was in shock and had suffered some blood loss when she arrived, but we're treating her for that. We will keep her here overnight."

"When she comes home," Marika asked, "how should her wound be treated?"

"Well, it has to be kept clean, of course, and an antibiotic ointment should be applied twice a day for the first week. I've written a prescription for that, as well. Keep a close eye on it to make sure there's no sign of infection. I used dissolving stitches, so while she should see her family doctor for follow-up, she won't need to have the stitches removed." He looked questioningly at the three. When they all nodded their understanding, he stood. "You can see her anytime now, though she might be groggy. David, a pleasure, as always. Drop by sometime when you're not on duty, and we'll grab a coffee." The two men shook hands, and the doctor strode off.

Lee heaved a sigh. "Well, that sounded a lot better than I'd feared." She could see the relief on her companions' faces. "So...let's go see how our Lady Mouse is doing."

Rhiannon tried hard to concentrate. The pain medication had cut the fire in her shoulder to a dull throb but made it difficult to focus on making plans.

She rested on her left side, and a pillow supported her back. She tried an experimental wiggle of her right shoulder, only to gasp when pain shot through her. *Okay, bad idea.* She breathed shallowly and waited for the agony to subside.

She didn't mind that she was to stay overnight. It would delay her return to the house in Victoria Park and her aunt's scrutiny. Her gaze rested on the pile of bloody clothes the ER had cut off. *Wonder if they'll loan me some scrubs to leave.* Rhiannon tried to think of an alternative. *I guess I could wear this hospital gown home on the bus.* She couldn't suppress a chuckle.

"Hey, what's all the jocularity in here?" Lee's head poked through the curtains surrounding her cubicle, and Rhiannon smiled wanly. "Don't you know there's no laughing allowed when you've been sliced and diced like a piece of sushi?" Lee looked over her shoulder. "She's decent." She entered the cubicle, followed by David and Marika.

Rhiannon blinked at the trio.

Lee sat beside the bed and patted Rhiannon's hand. "Lady Mouse, what am I going to do with you? I thought I was the one who's supposed to slay the dragons."

"You were late. I had to throw myself into the breach, but believe me, next time the dragons are all yours."

Lee chuckled, and Rhiannon raised her eyes to David. "Hey, Ichabod. What are you doing here?"

"Lee called me, and I came to see what kind of trouble you'd gotten yourself into this time."

"Aw, when do I ever get in trouble?"

Lee snorted. "The very first time I met you, you were facing down a pair of thugs. I think your middle name is Trouble."

Rhiannon giggled. "Well, that's better than Phyllis."

Marika, who was standing silently behind Lee and David, laughed.

Rhiannon's gaze drifted to her. "Are you okay, Ms. Havers?"

Marika nodded. "Thanks to you, I am."

"I'm glad I was there at the right time."

David patted Rhiannon's ankle. "They told us they're going to keep you here overnight."

"Yes, I know. Look, could you do me a favour?"

"Of course. What do you need?"

"Some clothes. I don't think I'll ever wear those again." Rhiannon grimaced at the pile of bloody clothing. "The keys to my place are in my backpack, back at the office."

"I brought your stuff with me," Lee said. "I left it out in the car, but I can get it."

Rhiannon brightened. "Then you won't need to go to the house. I'll just wear my sweats tomorrow. Thanks, Lee. I appreciate you bringing it."

Her visitors exchanged glances.

"What?" Rhiannon asked.

David drew a deep breath. "We think it would be best if you didn't go home for a few days."

"They said they're going to release me in the morning, so I have to."

"No, you don't," Lee said. "Marika volunteered to have you stay with her until you're healed a little."

"Whoa. I can't impose like that," Rhiannon said. "I'll just go home."

"It's not an imposition. I really would like you to stay with me." Marika's voice was quiet but insistent.

"No, I can't. I can look after myself. Seriously, I'm perfectly capable." Rhiannon strove for an assured tone.

David shook his head. "You won't even be able to dress yourself for a few days. You either let Marika help you, or I'm going to have to tell your aunt and have her assist you."

Rhiannon stared at him. There was sadness in his eyes, but also intransigence. "Promise me. Promise me, David. Swear you won't tell her about this."

"I'll make that promise, but only if you agree to let us help you."

"Damn it, that's blackmail."

Lee squeezed her hand. "I know you hate this, but you're going to need assistance for a little while. Just accept that and allow us to help."

Rhiannon closed her eyes. When she opened them, she found her visitors watching her closely. "All right, but only until I can do things for myself." *Which won't take long!* "What time is it?"

Lee checked her watch. "Almost two."

"Good. That means Hettie has gone to bingo. Can you go over and grab me enough clothes for a few days? You can use the backpack to carry them."

David nodded. "I can do that, but won't your aunt report you missing if you don't leave some kind of word?"

Rhiannon groaned. "Please find me something to write on. You can pin my note on the corkboard by the kitchen phone. She'll see it there."

David went off to scrounge paper and pen.

Rhiannon looked up at Marika. "Are you certain you can tolerate a houseguest for a couple of days?"

Marika smiled. "I'm sure we can manage, as long as you don't have anything against cats. My cat has a bit of an attitude."

"That's an understatement," Lee said. "Spooky thinks he owns the place, and she's allowed to stay there at his pleasure."

"It's true. I live to serve that furry tyrant."

"Well, I'll try to be much less demanding." Rhiannon fought back the weariness that threatened to overwhelm her.

David returned with pen and paper.

Rhiannon wrote awkwardly as she tried to minimize the movement in her shoulder. *Staying with friends. Back in a few days. R.* She let the pen drop.

David slid the pad out from under her hand. "I'll be back as quickly as possible."

"I'll come with you," Lee said. "I've got her backpack in the car, anyway."

When Lee and David left, Marika slid into the vacated chair.

There was an awkward silence, until Rhiannon said, "I'm surprised."

"About?"

"I guess...well, if anyone volunteered to take me in..." Rhiannon's voice trailed off. *I just didn't expect this...from you.*

Marika nodded. "Lee wanted to take you home with her." She lowered her head. "I know you'd probably have preferred that. I'm sorry."

"Why?"

"Why am I sorry?"

"No. Why would you take me in? You really don't owe me, you know?"

"I disagree. I think I owe you a great deal, and for more than just today. I'd like the chance to make it up to you, but if you'd really rather, I know Lee will take you in a heartbeat."

Rhiannon was losing the battle with fatigue and the pain medication. "No, that's okay." Her eyes drifted shut. "Sorry. Can't keep my eyes open."

"That's okay. Must be good drugs, eh?"

"Good..." Rhiannon lost the battle, and as she fell asleep, she felt a light touch smooth the hair away from her face.

"She lives here?" Lee eyed the dilapidated two-story house. Broken pickets fenced thin grass that fought a losing battle against weeds and bare earth. A dirty plastic flowerpot without blossoms leaned crookedly beside the front door.

David put the old Volvo in park and turned the engine off. "Yes. Rhiannon's lived here with her aunt for over a decade."

They left the car, and Lee trailed up the walk behind the priest. "What a dump." David shook his head, and Lee decided to keep further observations to herself.

They climbed the front stairs, and David held his hand out for the keys.

Lee rummaged in the backpack and came up with them.

The interior of the narrow house was as unprepossessing as the exterior. The odour of fried foods hung in the warm, thick air. An ambience of decay permeated the hallway. Lee noted the peeling wallpaper, threadbare carpet, and naked light bulb, which dangled from the high ceiling.

David had walked down the hall to the kitchen, so Lee hastened after him. He pinned Rhiannon's note to the corkboard beside the phone, next to dozens of other notes.

Lee took in the slovenly tabletop, trails of crumbs on the cracked linoleum floor, and dirty dishes piled in the sink. *Rhiannon lives here?* She shook her head. *How can someone like her come from a place like this?*

"C'mon. Rhiannon's room is upstairs."

Lee followed David back down the hall and up the narrow staircase. He paused at the top and looked both ways down the hall. With a little shrug, he turned right and began to open doors.

"Bathroom. Closet. Her aunt's bedroom. Must be the one at the back of the house." David turned back the other way and came to a door with a sturdy padlock on it. "I think we found it," he said, lifting the lock.

Lee chuckled. "Now why doesn't that surprise me?"

David fumbled with the keys, then fit one to the lock and turned it easily. He pushed the door open, and they entered.

The afternoon sunlight illuminated Rhiannon's room. Lee gave a small whistle as she took in the set-up. "She's got a whole apartment in one room—kitchen, bedroom, and sitting room."

Two narrow windows with yellowed blinds pulled halfway down opened up on a view of the back alley. An ancient fridge and a squat, legless bureau sat against one wall. A frayed blue bedspread was neatly drawn over the single bed on the opposite wall. Under the windows, an old wooden kitchen table held a secondhand microwave, a battered electric wok, two cardboard boxes, and a stack of library books.

Lee's eyebrows shot up as she realized that every spare bit of space on the walls was covered by drawings. "Wow, these are really good. Look at the detail. You can almost feel that panther coiled to spring off the wall."

"Look." David gestured to several different pictures. "These two...they're in a lot of the pictures."

Lee peered closer. "Who do you suppose they are?"

"At a guess, I'd say her parents, but I don't know for sure."

"The woman in the picture does look a lot like Rhiannon. Our little friend is very talented."

"Yes, she is. Look, I don't want to be here when Hettie gets home. We should probably get Rhiannon's things and go."

Lee headed for the battered dresser. "Is her aunt really such a terror? The way Rhiannon reacted when you put the terms of the agreement to her, it was as if her aunt was the devil incarnate."

"No, I wouldn't say that Hettie's evil. She simply grates on people, especially Rhiannon."

Lee selected some casual clothes and pajamas and folded them carefully into the bag. "That include you, David? Does she grate on you, too?"

A heavy sigh sounded from behind her. Lee glanced over her shoulder.

David shuffled through a stack of books on the table. "Looks like these are due back at the library this weekend. I'll take them in for her."

"It appears to me you're ducking the question, Padre."

"I suppose. I've yet to be assigned to a church where there aren't any Hetties. I try to live up to my faith and accept them as God's children too, but they do try me at times."

"What exactly is a Hettie?"

"Outwardly devout. Inwardly, not so much. Usually much more interested in the social versus the spiritual."

"Hmm." Lee added a few more lines to the emerging portrait of Rhiannon. She opened the second drawer and reached for a stack of underwear. Her hand brushed against something unexpected, and she pulled it out. It was a bank book, its corners frayed and curled. Lee looked over at the priest, who was ostensibly absorbed in a library book. She couldn't resist a swift peek at the last page. *Jesus! She's got almost ten thousand dollars in there. What the hell is she doing living here?* Ashamed at her invasion of privacy, Lee tucked the book back into the drawer. *None of my business.*

"Got everything she needs?" David crossed the room with the books tucked under his arm.

Lee zipped the backpack closed. "I think I have enough. I don't know where her toothbrush and toiletries are, but I'll have Marika pick up some things." She grinned at David. "C'mon, Padre, let's get you out of the dragon's lair."

They left the room. David locked the padlock, and they started down the stairs.

"So, how come Rhi calls you Ichabod?"

"You can't see the resemblance?"

Lee stared at him and started to laugh. She was still chuckling when they exited the house and locked the front door behind them. She tossed the stuffed backpack into the back and slid into the passenger seat.

David started the car. As they pulled away, David said, "I'm glad you were along. I don't think I'd have felt very comfortable going through Rhiannon's things."

For a split second, Lee wondered if he had seen her look at the bank book, but then she realized what he'd meant. "Not into ladies lingerie?"

"They just don't make them in my size."

His deadpan tone set Lee off. Gales of laughter washed away the fear and anxiety of the day. She finally wiped the tears from her eyes and regarded him curiously. "I have to ask. Why did you veto my suggestion in the hospital? Doesn't it make more sense to you to have Rhiannon stay with Dana and me?"

"It was more instinct than anything else. I think...I feel that those two need each other right now. They went through the same trauma, and I believe they can each help the other heal." He shrugged and gave Lee an apologetic smile. "I didn't mean to interfere. I know Rhiannon thinks the world of you and your partner. I just...sometimes I get an overwhelming feeling about things, and I've learned to go with it."

Lee wasn't as convinced. "I know Marika will be kind to Rhiannon, but honestly, much as I love her, it's hard picturing her in a caregiver role."

"People often don't know what they're capable of until they're challenged."

"Maybe. She sure was determined to take Rhiannon home with her."

"What surprised me was that it wasn't nearly the battle I'd anticipated with Rhiannon. I thought we'd have to fight tooth and nail to make her accept help."

Lee smiled. "I think your threat to inform her aunt tipped the scales. Looked to me like she'd agree to just about anything to prevent that."

David nodded. "I was pretty sure that would be my ace."

"Well, Dana and I will make a point to drop over on a regular basis. I don't expect to be much help, but Dana is a terrific nurse, and I speak from personal experience."

"Don't underestimate your presence, Lee. Sometimes simple friendship is as much of a balm as the most skilled professional hands."

"That's the beauty of my partner—she brings both to the table."

"Then I expect Rhiannon will be up and about by this time next week." David signaled his turn into the hospital parking lot.

"From your mouth to God's ear, Padre."

CHAPTER 12

THE NEXT MORNING, MARIKA WENT to her office. She juggled appointments and picked up what she needed to work from home. She also instructed maintenance to replace all the carpet in her waiting room. The head of maintenance insisted they could excise the acid-damaged patch and steam-clean the bloodstains, but Marika rejected the suggestion. When Rhiannon returned to work, Marika did not want any reminders of the previous day's events in their office, not even a vaguely discoloured spot on the floor or an imperfectly matched piece of carpet.

When Marika arrived at Foothills Hospital, Rhiannon was dressed. She sat on the edge of the bed, with her bag and discharge papers beside her. She'd been staring out the window but stood as Marika entered.

"Hi, Rhiannon. Are you ready to leave this place?"

"I am, but Ms. Havers—"

"Marika, please. After all, you're going to be a guest in my home, so I think we should be on a first-name basis."

"Okay...Marika. About that, you really don't have to do this, you know? I'll be perfectly fine if you just drop me off at home. I really can take care of myself, and I'm sure with a day or two of rest, I can be back in the office. And it won't take me long to catch up. You'll barely know I was gone."

She's talking about going back to work? Marika decided to play her ace immediately. "I'm sorry. You know what David said. If you don't allow me to help you, he will go to your aunt. I don't know him well, but I get the strong impression that when he says something, he means it."

Rhiannon's expression fell.

Is a stay at my home so repugnant to her? Did I make a mistake? Should I have stayed out of it and let her go home with Lee?

Before Marika could offer the option of going elsewhere, Rhiannon nodded. "Okay. I guess we can go."

That's it? Just okay? Huh, that's a pretty powerful ace. Marika hid her amusement. "I brought a wheelchair up from the lobby in case you didn't feel up to walking to the car."

In a second surprise, Rhiannon sat down in the wheelchair without protest.

Marika picked up the backpack, placed the discharge papers on Rhiannon's lap, and pushed her out of the room.

At the condo, Rhiannon eased out of the car, wavered, and leaned against the door.

Marika took her backpack and considered offering an arm. *Don't push your luck. That might be the proverbial straw for Miss Independence.* She stayed close to Rhiannon as they walked to the elevators.

On the elevator, Marika glanced at Rhiannon, taking in her pale face and the way she held her right arm against her body. *I hope she won't resist having a nap. I know she won't be comfortable right away, but she'll feel a lot better if she doesn't fight me on this.*

When they entered her apartment, Spooky strolled over and sniffed Rhiannon.

"Behave yourself, mister. Try to keep the attitude to a minimum." Marika tossed her keys on the side table. She was pleased when Rhiannon knelt and held out her left hand to the cat.

Spooky ducked his head and ran his body under her outstretched hand with an audible purr. Rhiannon stroked his fur several times before she stood and swayed.

Marika slid a hand under Rhiannon's left arm. "Why don't I show you where your room is? If you want, you can lie down for a nap. I'm just going to catch up on a few things in the den, and I'll wake you later for lunch."

Rhiannon leaned on Marika. "Thank you. I guess I'm more worn out than I thought."

Marika helped Rhiannon down the hall. "Kitchen, living room, and dining room are that way. The den is next to the master bedroom, and the bathroom and utility/laundry room are across the hall. When you need towels, you'll find the linen closet next to the bathroom." She opened her bedroom door and steered Rhiannon inside. "This is your room. There's an ensuite with a shower, but you'll probably want to use the bathtub in the main bathroom to keep the stitches as dry as possible. Dana will be over tonight to take a look at them and show me how to care for your wound until...well, while you're here."

Rhiannon surveyed the room, then turned to her with a frown.

Did I forget something? "Is everything okay?"

"This is your bedroom."

"Well...yes, but it's yours while you're here, and I'll take the daybed in the den."

Rhiannon shook her head. "I can't kick you out of your own room. I'll take the den."

Marika sighed. *I knew this was going too smoothly.* "It will be easier on your shoulder if you take the bed. The better care you take now, the sooner you'll be out of here and independent again, right?"

Rhiannon reluctantly nodded.

Score another one for me. Marika stifled a smile. *Good to know she'll respond to logic. It might just make this a lot easier than I thought.* Marika set Rhiannon's bag on the boudoir chair. "I cleared some space for you." She opened the top drawer. "Lee didn't know where your toiletries were, so I bought some basics and left them in the ensuite for you. Why don't you get yourself settled, take a nap, and I'll wake you in a little while?"

Rhiannon still stood in the centre of the room, but she gave a curt nod.

Marika closed the bedroom door and went to the den. *I don't know. Maybe I am certifiable. What the hell do I know about looking after someone? Especially someone who resents being looked after.* She sat at her desk and swiveled her chair from side to side. *Good thing Lee didn't ask me why I'm doing this. I couldn't have given her a good answer. I still don't have an answer—good or bad. I just...I don't know. I just had to.* With a shake of her head, Marika booted her computer and logged into her files.

Rhiannon put the last of her attire in the drawer and slid it shut. She turned and leaned back against the dresser as she surveyed the room. *You could almost put Hettie's whole house in here.* The queen-size bed was made up with rose-coloured sheets, a pale pink quilt, and an assortment of pillows. *Geez, how does she sleep with twenty pillows stacked halfway to the ceiling? Don't her fingers get caught in all that lace when she rolls over?*

An unexpected yawn persuaded Rhiannon to lie down for a few moments. She sank onto the soft bed. *Sure beats the hell out of my lumpy old mattress.* She grimaced and shifted to take the pressure off her shoulder. *I suppose it wouldn't hurt to rest for a bit.* She closed her eyes and was asleep in moments.

When Rhiannon woke, it was with an overwhelming sensation that she wasn't alone. Her eyes flew open.

Marika leaned against the open door with her arms crossed.

Rhiannon studied her watcher. *I wonder what she's thinking? Maybe she's changed her mind. Should I offer to go home again?*

Then Marika smiled. "Feel like some lunch?" Her voice was casual, but warm.

Rhiannon nodded and rocked slightly to get up before a wave of pain stopped her.

An involuntary moan instantly brought Marika to her side. With careful hands, Marika steadied her and assisted her to sit up.

Rhiannon blushed. "Sorry 'bout that."

"There's nothing to be sorry about. You're not going to be 100% for a while yet, that's why you're here. Please let me help where I can."

Rhiannon allowed Marika to assist her to her feet. Marika immediately stepped back; though as they left the room, she was never more than an arm's length away.

Lunch turned out to be a pleasant surprise. Marika filled Rhiannon's plate with chicken salad and pushed the tray of steaming, thickly sliced French bread toward her. When Rhiannon found it difficult to butter the bread with only one hand, Marika quietly took over.

"This is really good, Ms...I mean Marika." *Sure beats the hell out of my bologna sandwich and Cup-a-Soup.*

"Thank you. I'm glad you're enjoying it. Would you care for some iced tea?"

Rhiannon swallowed before answering. "I don't know. I don't think I've ever had any."

Marika raised an eyebrow. "Well, try it, and if you don't enjoy it, I'll find something else."

Rhiannon found she did like iced tea, as well as the fresh blueberries served over yogurt for dessert. There was little conversation during lunch, but Rhiannon didn't sense that silence made her hostess uncomfortable.

When they were finished, Rhiannon rose to clear the table.

Marika shook her head and took the plate out of Rhiannon's hand. "No, that's okay. I've got it. Once you've got two working arms, you can help out."

"Once I've got two working arms, I'll be out of your hair."

"You're not in my hair."

Rhiannon stared at Marika as she gathered up dishes. *She really doesn't seem to mind me being here. Huh. It must be true—what a difference a week makes.*

Marika closed the dishwasher, faced Rhiannon, and thrust her hands into her pockets. "I should get some more work done this afternoon." She shook her head. "And no, you're not allowed to help. You're supposed to be resting."

Rhiannon frowned. *I have to get back to work—the sooner the better.*

"You do know you're on full pay and benefits while you recover, don't you?"

"I am?"

"Considering that you could sue the firm for inadequate security on the job, I'd say it's the least they could do."

"I wouldn't sue!"

Marika smiled. "I know that, but they don't. Besides, you were injured on the job. You're entitled to be paid until you're able to work again."

Rhiannon fidgeted. She was no longer tired after her nap and wanted something to occupy herself.

"I have a small collection of DVDs and a better collection of CDs. You're welcome to use them, or you could watch TV or read."

"Read?" Rhiannon brightened. "Do you have books I could borrow?"

"You could say that. Come with me."

Rhiannon followed Marika to the den. As they entered the room, Rhiannon stopped short and stared. It was smaller than the master bedroom, but still twice the size of Rhiannon's own bedroom. One wall was lined with built-in floor-to-ceiling bookcases, and a mahogany, double-pedestal desk with a padded leather chair sat at the far end of the room. A daybed and side table were on the opposite wall, with a black leather recliner and reading lamp by the window. The condo's predominant colour scheme of grey and white with rose accents was carried over to this room. *I'll bet she spends a lot of hours in here. I sure would.*

"Help yourself to any of the books. I'm just going to get some work done." Marika turned on some music and took a seat at her desk.

Rhiannon listened to the mellow instrumental music for a moment, then began her inspection of the library. She moved swiftly past the legal and reference books to find shelves of fiction, non-fiction, classics and contemporary works. She gleefully opened one book after another before she settled on an old favourite she hadn't read in years. With the book in hand, she glanced at the recliner and bit her lip.

"You're welcome to read in here. You won't be a bother, and I can tell you from experience, that's the most comfortable seat in the house."

Rhiannon sat in the chair. The handle to recline the chair was on the right. Before she could ask, Marika knelt at her side and pulled the lever for her. Rhiannon grinned and wriggled into the plush depths. Marika snapped on the overhead lamp, and she nodded her thanks.

They spent the afternoon quietly, each intent on her own pursuits.

"Are you hungry at all? May I fix you a snack?" Marika finally asked.

Recalled from the streets of Victorian London, Rhiannon glanced at the wall clock and was surprised to realize that more than three hours had flown by. She shifted and winced as her shoulder throbbed. "I'm not hungry, but I think it might be time for another pill."

Marika pushed the lever back and offered a hand out of the chair.

Rhiannon accepted. No longer engrossed with Holmes and Watson, she felt the full effects of her surgery again. "If you don't mind, I think I'll go lie down for a while."

"Not at all. You do whatever you want to, Rhiannon. Rest when you need to. That's the whole point of you being here. Do you need any help?"

"No, thanks, I'm just going to take a couple of pills and nap for a while." Rhiannon stopped at the door to look back at Marika. "I don't think I've said it, but I really do appreciate all you're doing for me."

Marika's eyes widened.

Rhiannon smiled and left the den. She fell asleep almost immediately and was awakened by a gentle squeeze of her uninjured shoulder when Marika summoned her for dinner. Groggy, she allowed Marika to assist her out of bed again. "I'll meet you in the kitchen." Rhiannon yawned. "I just want to freshen up a bit."

Marika left as Rhiannon made her way to the ensuite. After she'd washed up, she dried her face and looked over the selection of toiletries that had been left for her on the counter. *Well, her definition of 'basics' isn't exactly mine, but I do appreciate the thought.*

Rhiannon's first impulse was to find out what she owed Marika and pay her back. But an unaccustomed inner voice—one that sounded remarkably like Lee—prevailed.

Marika was setting dishes on the table when Rhiannon entered the kitchen. "Thank you very much for everything you left in the bathroom for me. It really was generous of you."

"You're welcome. It was just a few things that Lee and I thought you could use."

Rhiannon grinned. "It sort of looks like Shoppers Drugstore erupted in there, but it was very kind."

Marika chuckled and pulled out a chair for Rhiannon.

She sat down. "Thanks." *Maybe we can get through this without driving each other crazy. The first day went okay. It's not like we're best buddies or anything, but we're getting along all right.*

Dana arrived after dinner and accepted a coffee as she joined them in the living room. "So, how is our hero feeling today?"

Rhiannon squirmed. "Okay, I guess."

"She was in quite a bit of pain earlier this afternoon," Marika said.

Dana nodded. "To be expected for a while, I'm afraid. Lee called Reverend Ross, who put me in touch with Dr. Mathieu. I told him I'd be monitoring Rhiannon's recovery, and he filled in the gaps for me. In some ways, you got off lucky, Rhi, but at its deepest point, you're looking at a twelve-millimetre incision. It's not going to heal overnight."

Rhiannon flinched.

Dana patted her hand. "Don't worry. We're going to make sure you're well looked after." She turned and gave Marika instructions.

Their voices faded as Rhiannon pondered the turn her life had taken. She could remember with vivid clarity the very last day she had felt genuinely cared for by another human being. It had been over a dozen years ago. *Now, virtual strangers are offering affection and concern. Why? When did I lose control? And shouldn't it bother me more?* Lost in her thoughts, Rhiannon didn't hear her name called until a hand touched her arm.

"Rhiannon?"

Rhiannon blinked at Marika.

"Dana was suggesting you might want to take a bath now, and then she'll show me how to clean and dress your wound."

"Okay." Rhiannon stood.

"Don't get your shoulder wet," Dana said. "Just wash what you can reach comfortably, and I'll take care of the rest."

Marika said, "Don't forget, the towels are in the linen closet, and if you want to use any of the bath oils—"

"Better to keep it plain soap and water for a few days, Rhi."

"No problem." Rhiannon didn't know if she'd ever used bath oils, certainly not since she'd joined her aunt's household. She left the living room and grabbed a towel from the linen closet. She bent to run the taps and grinned at Spooky, who was curled up on the thick, soft bath mat. Rhiannon stroked the somnolent feline. "Is this your favourite place in the house? You might want to move, Mister Cat. It could get pretty wet in here."

Spooky stretched and strolled out of the bathroom.

With the tub filling, Rhiannon began to undress. She was immediately glad that the nurse who helped her dress that morning had decreed no bra so as not to aggravate the stitches. Her left hand was clumsy, and it took her twice as long as usual to get her buttons undone. She knew she would've had to ask for help with a bra, and it galled her not to be able to handle such a basic task.

Rhiannon turned the taps off, lowered herself into the bathtub, and sighed. She longed to lay back and let the last two days soak away, but she stayed upright and used her good side to wash. Eyeing the extension hose, she was trying to work out how to shampoo her hair without getting her back wet when a light tap sounded on the door frame.

Dana poked her head in. "Okay to come in?"

"Sure." Rhiannon drew her knees up and leaned forward with her left arm wrapped around them.

Dana knelt at the side of the tub.

Marika followed but stayed back out of the way.

"Okay, sweetie, I'm going to peel the dressing off and then clean this up a bit. I'll go slowly, but you let me know if I'm hurting you."

Rhiannon hunched her shoulders.

Dana rubbed her back lightly, well away from the bandaged area. "Try not to tighten up. It'll just make it harder."

Rhiannon nodded but couldn't help stiffening when the tape was peeled away and she felt the first pressure of the washcloth. Dana's deft touch proved gentle, and the tension in her body eased.

"You're doing great there, Rhi. Your doctor did an excellent job with the stitches, nice and small and tight. Your scar should hardly be noticeable by the time it all heals."

Rhiannon listened to Dana's soothing tones as the nurse carefully washed away the dried blood. Absently, she realized that Dana's left hand kept stroking her back even as the right hand did the delicate work around her wound. *I wonder if this is what Spooky feels like when I pet him.*

"Marika, see what I'm doing here? Once I've gotten the worst of this cleared away, you won't have as much to do next time. Just be very careful not to snag any of the stitches, and keep the pressure light."

Rhiannon rested her head on her knees and found she actually enjoyed the procedure. She was disappointed when, all too soon, Dana pronounced her done.

"Would you like some help washing your hair?" Dana asked.

Rhiannon nodded. "That'd be great. I was just trying to figure out how to do that without soaking my back."

"Can you grab a small towel, Marika? We'll put that over the surgical area and have you lean forward, Rhi. I'll use a light spray and get you cleaned up, no problem." Dana unhooked the hose and adjusted the head for the mildest flow while Marika went to get another towel.

Rhiannon braced herself on her left hand, and Dana held the towel on her back with one hand and directed the hose on her head with the other as Marika washed her hair.

Eyes closed, Rhiannon enjoyed the gentle massage and lathering. *I could get to like this.* Part of her mind nagged her about the impropriety, but long-buried hedonistic responses reveled in the simple sensual pleasure. When she was clean, Dana helped her from the bathtub and wrapped her in a bath sheet almost as big as she was. She brushed back Rhiannon's hair and planted a kiss on her wet forehead.

Rhiannon smiled shyly.

Dana returned her smile. "Let's get you settled in bed, and then Marika will do the actual dressing so she knows how to change it tomorrow."

Marika lingered by the door while Dana helped Rhiannon into her pajama bottoms and guided her between the sheets to lay on her stomach with her right arm carefully positioned by her side.

"Okay, Marika, grab my bag and bring it here. I'm going to walk you through doing this. I brought some antibiotic ointment, Q-tips, a small roll of dressing pads, and a big roll of surgical tape. The clinic will never miss it, and I figured it was for a good cause."

Rhiannon closed her eyes. *I'm really glad Dana's my friend. Friend. I have friends. How cool is that?*

The mattress shifted beneath her as Marika sat.

"All right," Dana said. "Very gently use the Q-tip to spread a thin coating of ointment right over the stitches."

Rhiannon didn't flinch at the featherlight touch when Marika did as instructed. It took about five minutes, with Dana murmuring encouragement, but eventually the nurse was satisfied.

"Well done. We'll make an RN out of you yet. Now, cut off enough of the padding to cover the length of the wound. Uh-huh. Good girl. Now lay it over carefully and then tape it on."

Tape ripped, and Marika pressed the edges of the dressing down.

"Excellent. Johns Hopkins, here you come." Dana chuckled. "Okay, ladies, one more thing. Rhi, I'll bet you've been minimizing the use of your arm and shoulder, right?"

"Uh-huh. It hurts when I move it much."

"And that's good. Pain is your body's early warning signal, and it shouldn't be ignored. But, there's also a danger that if you shy away from using it for long periods, the muscles will stiffen. When the wound heals, you'll have to work twice as hard to get back full use of them."

Rhiannon frowned.

Dana shook her head. "Don't worry. It just means we have some adapting to do. What I want you to work on is small, passive movements—bring your right arm forward, back, and out from your body, about six inches to start with. Increase the movements a little each day, as much as you can comfortably tolerate. And, Marika, if you wouldn't mind, gently massage the muscles of her back twice a day. Don't touch the surgical area, but work around the perimeter."

"I can handle that," Marika answered without hesitation. "We can do it first thing in the morning and last thing at night."

"Great. Why don't you start now, and I'll see myself out. You both did really well tonight. You're a good team, and I don't foresee any difficulties."

"Thanks, Dana." Rhiannon shivered as Marika's warm fingers began a gentle stroking and probing of her shoulder and back and then down her right arm.

"You're very welcome. I'd say 'any time,' but I'd prefer to see you on a social rather than professional basis. You two have a good night, and if you have any problems or questions, call me at home or work right away."

"Thanks, Dana. You're an angel," Marika said.

"Ah well, wait 'til I send you the bill."

The room was much quieter after Dana left. Rhiannon drifted on the edge of sleep. *My boss is giving me a massage. How weird is that? Shouldn't it bother me? It should, right?*

Marika worked a knot out of Rhiannon's back, and she sighed.

"Are you okay?" Marika asked. "Did I hurt you?"

"No, not at all." *No, definitely not bothered.* Rhiannon's eyes closed. *I'll think about it later.*

Marika finished and stood.

"Thank you. That felt really good."

"Would you like some help getting your top on, or would you rather do without while you sleep?"

"I'm almost too comfortable to move, but I suppose I should put it on for a little added protection." Rhiannon rolled into a sitting position with Marika's help. It was only when Marika turned to get her top from the drawer that Rhiannon remembered she was half-naked. *Oh well. She saw all of me getting out of the tub. I don't think this will freak her out.*

Marika slid one sleeve over Rhiannon's right arm, pulled the top over her back, and let her work her left arm into the other sleeve. Then she knelt and began to fasten the buttons. Marika's forehead furrowed, and her fingers trembled.

Well, I'll be damned. She's nervous. My cool, calm, confident boss is nervous. Huh. As the last button was closed, Rhiannon laid her hand over Marika's. "Thank you."

Marika raised her eyes and took a deep breath. "You're welcome. How about another couple of pain pills and then lights out? I know it's early, but I suspect a good night's sleep would be just what Dana would order."

"You're right. I don't think she'd be impressed if we stayed up watching midnight movies."

Marika smiled, then stood and fetched a glass of water. She passed it to Rhiannon, shook two pain tablets into her palm, and held out her hand.

Rhiannon hesitated and looked up.

Marika waited.

Rhiannon shrugged, then nipped the pills off Marika's palm. She took a deep swallow of water and handed the glass back. She sank back onto the bed with a smile, then her smile faded. *Don't be stupid. Remember, this is just temporary. Don't get used to it.*

"Goodnight, Rhi. Call me if you need anything."

"I will. Thanks again, for everything."

"You're most welcome." Marika drew the covers up, tucked them around Rhiannon, and turned off the bedside lamp.

Dana sat in bed and watched as Lee tossed her clothes haphazardly toward the laundry basket.

"Honest to God," Lee said, "if Willem even thinks about countermanding Taylor's firing, I'm going to hit him over the head. Can you believe that idiot was drunk on the job? He's a bloody lost cause, and I'm not going to have him ruin our company's reputation one minute longer."

Dana couldn't remember the last time she'd seen Lee so upset. "Come to bed, sweetheart. You can go in tomorrow and fight with Willem. Right now, you've got to calm down before you blow a gasket."

Lee glanced at Dana. "Guess I have been going on, huh?"

"You have. And I certainly understand why, but I don't intend to sacrifice a good night's sleep because of your lame-brained employee."

"Ex-employee." Lee finished stripping off her clothes and slid under the covers. She opened her arms, and Dana snuggled into her.

They embraced quietly until Lee asked, "How'd it go tonight? Everything all right?"

"Uh-huh. I showed Marika how to clean and dress Rhiannon's wound and suggested a routine of slow, passive movement to keep her arm flexible. I also told her that it might be a good idea if she massages Rhiannon's shoulder and back twice a day."

"Is massage supposed to help rehabilitate the injured area?"

Dana chuckled. "It might not do much for healing the shoulder, but I suspect it'll do wonders for their relationship."

Lee rolled Dana onto her back. "Sweetheart, are you matchmaking?"

Dana turned serious. "No, I'm really not. What I'm doing is allowing two lonely people to connect and giving them an excuse to touch each other. If nothing more comes from it than the beginning of a friendship, I'll consider my work well done. Reverend Ross was right. Marika needs to take care of Rhiannon. She needs to be responsible for something more than a darned cat."

"And Rhiannon?" Lee stroked the side of Dana's face.

"And Rhiannon is even more isolated than Marika. Marika at least has Terry and us. I don't think Rhiannon has a single soul who cares about her except that priest, and from what you told me, he only came into her life recently. Lee, do you know what happens to babies denied human contact?"

Lee shook her head.

"The technical term is 'failure to thrive,' but what it means is they simply don't have much reason to live. Humans need to be touched, my love. That's the most basic expression of our humanity. I doubt that girl has been touched with affection in more years than she can remember. And Marika, hell, she's been touched all right. By the likes of Cass and others that don't give a rat's ass about her beyond her looks and her performance in bed."

"They need each other," Lee said.

"They do need each other."

"You are very sneaky, hon."

Dana grinned. "Maybe, but then I have to be with you and Eli around."

"Oh, is that right?" Lee tickled Dana's belly until she laughed. "So, about this touching theory, can the touches be anywhere?"

Dana waggled an eyebrow and cupped Lee's breast, circling her nipple. "Well, some touches are more effective than others."

Lee swallowed hard. "I think I'd like to explore your theories a little more thoroughly."

Dana wrapped her arms around Lee and pulled her down. "Excellent idea. Let's start by examining the many ways naked bodies can touch each other."

Then Lee started to apply her own theories of touch.

"Oh, my love. That's exactly what I had in mind..."

CHAPTER 13

"THAT SHOULD WORK, DAVID. I really appreciate this. What time do you think you'll be over? ... All right, we'll see you then. Goodbye."

Marika leaned back and swiveled in her chair. *Will this work? Rhi's not nearly as prickly as I thought she'd be. She doesn't even fuss when I have to help her. Mind you, she still prefers Lee's company to mine, but that's no surprise. I think Rhi has a big case of hero worship going on there.* She smiled. *Still, baby steps, right? I'm going to go with my gut on this one. After all, it's been very pleasant with her here.*

They had fallen into a comfortable daily routine. Quiet conversations, long peaceful hours in the den, walks along the river paths, and the evening news after dinner were staples of their days. *I'm actually going to be sorry to see her go home.* Marika shook her head. *Who'd have guessed? And the way she works at the exercises Dana gave her, it won't be long now.*

Marika left the den, and stopped short at the unfamiliar sound of Rhiannon chortling. She hastened to see what was going on.

Rhiannon sat cross-legged on the couch and laughed at Spooky, who was hopping around the carpet. She looked up at Marika and pointed. "Your silly cat is chasing invisible mice. All of a sudden, he started pouncing and jumping around, but there's nothing there."

Marika chuckled and took a seat beside Rhiannon. "I know. He does that occasionally. I think he sees his own shadow or something."

"Maybe he's chasing dust bunnies," Rhiannon said.

Marika gave her a look of mock horror. "In my home? Perish the thought."

Rhiannon burst out laughing as Spooky took off at a dead run toward the kitchen, where the click of his claws could be heard on the tiles when he skidded to a stop.

"You should see the Spookmeister when I give him catnip."

"I'll bet." Rhiannon craned her neck to see what the cat was doing. "How long have you had him?"

Marika cocked her head. "I guess it's been about four years now. I'd just gotten off work one night and was going to my car, when I saw a couple of kids tormenting twin kittens in the parking garage. I chased them off and found a tiny bundle of grey and white fur standing over his even smaller brother. He tried to bite me when I went to pick him up, but I wrapped my scarf around him and his sibling. I took them to a vet, but the smaller one didn't make it."

"So you took Spooky home?"

"I wasn't going to. I had no intention of adopting a cat, but, I...I just couldn't leave him there, you know?"

Rhiannon smiled. "Uh-huh. Got a thing for strays, eh?"

Marika blushed. "Anyway, the rest is history. He's now king of the castle, and allows me to feed and care for him at his pleasure."

Rhiannon laughed. "Sounds familiar. How'd he get his name? Did you find him on Halloween?"

"No, it came from *The X-Files*."

Rhiannon raised an eyebrow.

"You know, Mulder's nickname? Spooky?"

Rhiannon shrugged. "I've heard of the show, but I've never seen it."

"It wasn't to everyone's taste, but I liked it. What sort of programs do you watch?"

Rhiannon scowled.

Uh-oh. What did I say wrong this time? Damn, sometimes it's like walking in a mine field.

"I don't really watch TV. The only one in the house is in my aunt's parlour," Rhiannon said.

"And you don't like to watch what she does?" The anger on Rhiannon's face wasn't directed at her, so Marika didn't retreat.

"I..." Rhiannon drew in a deep breath and she trembled. "I prefer not to be in my aunt's presence for any reason at all."

"Yet you live with her." Marika was prepared to back off at the first signs that Rhiannon couldn't handle this line of conversation.

After long moments, Rhiannon answered. "It's a convenient arrangement for the time being. The rent's very cheap, and for the most part I don't have to see her, except sometimes going in and out of the house."

"Is she really that bad?" Marika was shocked at the bleak gaze that met hers.

"Yes."

Far enough. Leave it alone. "Hey, I came to tell you that we're going to have company this afternoon."

Rhiannon's body lost some of its tension. "Who? Or are you talking about Lee and Dana?"

"No. Lee and Dana will be over for dinner tonight, but David called. He wanted to drop by and see you, so I told him to come over whenever he wants." Marika was relieved to see a grin erase the grimness.

"Good. He's a nice guy."

David arrived an hour later. When Marika greeted him at the door, he passed her a small booklet that she tucked under her purse on the hall table. Then she led him into the living room.

Rhiannon beamed. "Hey, Ichabod. How's it going?"

"Pretty good. How are you feeling?"

"Much better actually. My boss has been taking good care of me." Rhiannon winked. "I think she just wants to make sure I'm back to work soon."

Marika raised an eyebrow and Rhiannon grinned at her. Marika shook her head and smiled. "So could I interest either of you in a cup of coffee?" When both accepted her offer, Marika went to the kitchen, eavesdropping as she filled the coffee carafe.

"I'm really sorry that I didn't get the pews finished. I hope it didn't cause any problems," Rhiannon said.

"Good heavens, it's not like you slacked off. Unfortunately, I couldn't leave it until you were well enough, so I finished them myself. But you'll get the full amount we agreed on, because it certainly wasn't your fault that you couldn't complete the job."

Marika stifled a laugh.

"No way. You only pay me for what I did. I'm not taking money for work I didn't do."

David heaved a sigh.

Don't even bother. You'd have more luck moving a mountain. Marika grinned and gathered coffee and cups on a tray.

When Marika returned to the living room David was counting bills and coins into Rhiannon's hand. Rhiannon frowned and handed two coins back. Marika smothered her amusement, set the tray on the coffee table, and began to fill cups. She handed one to David, then Rhiannon.

David sipped his coffee. "Did you ever find out what happened with the aunt of the assailant, the one that you called the police about?"

Marika nodded. "They responded right away, but they were almost too late. They found her badly beaten in her home. The last I heard, she was still in critical condition, but they think she'll survive."

David shook his head. "I'd like to visit her if I could get her name and location from you."

"I'm pretty sure they took her to Rockyview, but I'll have to check. Can I call you on Monday?" Marika kept half an eye on Rhiannon as they talked. *What's she thinking? She hasn't said a word about the attack or the attacker. I wish she'd talk to me. And I wish I knew more about PTSD. I don't know if she's handling it well, or just bottling it up. God knows I haven't had much luck repressing and I wasn't the one he hurt.*

Sleep had been elusive for Marika the first couple of nights. Every time she closed her eyes, she relived the feel of Rhiannon's bleeding, unconscious body in her arms and the sight of the raw, bubbled flesh on the assailant's body. Several times, she'd gone to the doorway of her bedroom and sought reassurance from the sight and sound of the peaceful sleeper in her bed.

"I was going to Rockyview for a visitation this afternoon, anyway, so I'll see what I can find out." David turned to Rhiannon. "I ran into your aunt yesterday. She asked if I knew where you were."

Rhiannon froze. "You didn't tell her, did you?"

"No," David assured her. "All I said was that you'd mentioned staying with a friend for a while."

Rhiannon's laugh was bitter. "And did that satisfy the old busybody?"

"Not exactly. Your aunt would've made an excellent interrogator."

"I think she was one in her last life, jackboots and all."

Marika and David exchanged glances. He made a subtle gesture toward the hallway, and she nodded. While David distracted Rhiannon with Tupper's observations about his latest Sunday sermon, Marika went to the hall for the booklet he'd brought with him. She stared at it and crossed her fingers.

When Marika returned to the living room, the booklet was behind her back. "We had an idea, and we wanted to talk it over with you."

"You did? What is it?" Rhiannon asked.

Marika held out the pamphlet.

Rhiannon took it. "Operator's Licence Information?"

"Yes, we thought... I know you mentioned that you'd like to get your licence, sometime...so David and I were talking..." Marika couldn't read the expression on Rhiannon's face.

David took over. "If you want to study for your learner's exam, once your shoulder is up to it, Marika and I will teach you how to drive. I'll take you out with my old Volvo, which is an automatic transmission, and she'll teach you how to drive a standard."

Rhiannon blinked and stared at the manual.

Well, at least she's not saying no. I hope she doesn't let pride stand in her way. When Rhiannon began to flip through the pages, pausing occasionally at brightly coloured illustrations, Marika's heart leapt.

Rhiannon looked from David to Marika. "Why are you... Are you sure you want to do this?"

Okay, that's not exactly a yes, but it's also not a no. "We are."

David nodded. "Marika and I talked it over, and even if you don't have a car now, you may want one in the future. You'll need a licence, so you might as well get it while you have two willing instructors. You can use the Volvo to take the test in."

"Because they're indestructible?"

David laughed. "No. Because it's an automatic, and it's easier not to have to worry about changing gears when you're trying to remember everything else."

Marika tried not to sound over-eager. "So? Will you let us teach you?"

Rhiannon stared at the driver's manual. "If you two are sure you know what you're getting into, then, yes." She looked up and smiled. "Thank you. I didn't expect this at all, but I really appreciate what you're doing."

David and Marika exchanged triumphant glances.

"Good." David checked his watch. "Oh, look at the time. I'm going to have to get going." Rhiannon began to stand and he shook his head. "No, don't get up. You've got some studying to do, and I can see myself out."

Marika walked David to the door where they exchanged a quiet high five.

"Call me once she's passed the learner's test, and we can coordinate what we're teaching her."

Marika nodded. "Sounds good. I'll talk to you then." She returned to the living room and found Rhiannon reading the booklet, a small furrow creasing her forehead. Marika left Rhiannon to study in peace while she went back to work in the den.

Marika grinned as Lee cut another slice of pie and went back for the apple slices left behind. Across the table Dana sighed.

"So Marika's really going to teach you how to drive?" Lee licked her fork.

"And David, too." Rhiannon shook her head when Lee slid the pie plate across to her. "No, thank you. One's enough."

"For some people," Dana said, but her gaze was affectionate.

"Growin' girl," Lee mumbled around the pie.

Marika laughed at Dana's snort and got up to get more coffee. She was delighted to see how enthusiastically Rhiannon had told Lee and Dana about learning to drive. *Guess we called that one right.*

Lee downed the remainder of her coffee and held out her mug for a refill. "Hey, if Marika and David are going to teach you how to drive a car, maybe I could show you how to handle a bike."

"No!" Marika and Dana said at the same time

Lee frowned. "Aw, c'mon, you two. I'm a good driver, and I'd teach her the proper way to ride."

Marika shuddered at the thought of Rhiannon trying to balance Lee's huge motorcycle. "It's up to Rhi, of course, but don't you think your bike might be a bit...oversized for her?"

Lee scratched her neck thoughtfully. "You might have a point. The Suke's pretty big. I've been thinking of getting Eli a dirt bike, so he and I could go riding on the weekends when he's not with his dad. Rhi could learn on that, and decide if she wants a street bike."

From the startled look on Dana's face it was the first time Lee had mentioned dirt bikes and Eli in the same breath.

"I really appreciate that, Lee," Rhiannon said. "But I think I should concentrate on one thing at a time and get my vehicle licence first."

"Okay, but let me know if you ever want to learn to ride, and I'll be glad to teach you."

Oh, Lee, I think you're going to get an earful when Dana gets you home tonight. Marika was grateful that Dana held back. The evening had been so pleasant that she didn't want to see it ruined. She steered the conversation to a safer topic. "So, is Eli coming with us to the Stampede this year, or is he too mature now to hang out with a bunch of old ladies?"

Dana shook her head. "I was informed in no uncertain terms that he was going with Tony and the boys this year, and I'm not allowed to acknowledge him in public if I see him there."

Marika and Rhiannon laughed, and Lee rolled her eyes.

"Naturally he didn't tell me this until after I'd gotten our tickets to the rodeo, chuck wagon races, and Grandstand show." Dana turned to Rhiannon. "If you don't have any plans, why don't you join us?"

"Me?"

"Sure, why not?" Lee said. "We always have a great time, and the tickets are already paid for, so someone might as well get some use out of them."

Marika was amused at how easy it was to read Rhiannon this time. *She wants to come, no doubt about it. It's that damned old pride thing.* "We really would enjoy having you join us."

Rhiannon regarded Marika intently. After a long moment, she nodded. "I'd like that, but I insist on paying for my tickets."

Lee straightened and leveled her most intimidating glare at Rhiannon. "Are you trying to insult us? We invited you as our guest, and you think that means you have to pay? I can't believe you said that. I'm outraged."

Marika stifled a smile. She laid a hand on Rhiannon's arm. "Let her do this or we'll have to put up with hearing about it the whole time we're there."

Rhiannon's face scrunched up. "Okay, but I'll make it up to you."

Lee grinned. "Sure, you can buy me a bag of those mini-doughnuts. I love those things."

"No kidding. You ate half a dozen bags last year, and then couldn't figure out why you felt like hell the next morning," Dana said.

Lee shook her head. "I think that had more to do with the beer tent than the doughnuts. Or it might've been a bad corndog or deep-fried pickle."

Rhiannon whispered to Marika. "She goes to the Stampede for the food, doesn't she?"

"I heard that," Lee said with a chuckle. "You don't get the whole Stampede experience unless you've tried all the rides, sampled all the food, watched the chucks and the bull-riding, and two-stepped your way through Nashville North."

Marika recalled Lee's enthusiastic "Stampeding" of previous years. *I wonder if Rhi's presence will tame Lee...no, never going to happen. Lee is Lee, and thank God for that.* She turned to Rhiannon. "Do you enjoy going to the Stampede?"

"Well, I sometimes go look around the grounds on preview night, and I like to watch the parade and the fireworks. I usually go to a couple of the pancake breakfasts, too."

Marika nodded. *All the free events—no surprise there. I wonder if I can wangle our corporate ride pass for her. I'll have to see.*

Dana looked up at the kitchen clock. "If we're going to make Eli's game, we're going to have to leave soon. I'm sorry to cut it so short, Marika. His dad will get him there on time, but I promised that we would show up to watch."

"Of course," Marika said. "I'm glad you were able to make it over for dinner."

"I want to take a quick look at Rhiannon's back before we leave. Would you excuse us for a moment?" Dana stood and motioned for Rhiannon to accompany her.

When they disappeared down the hall, Lee leaned forward and lowered her voice. "Do you know what July 5th is?"

Marika nodded. "Of course. It's Dana's birthday. Are we throwing her a surprise party or something this year?"

"Nope. This year I've reserved a cabin out at Emerald Lake. Eli's going to be with his father, and we're taking a couple days off work, so it's just her and me for four long, lovely days."

"That sounds wonderful."

"There's more." Lee's eyes shone. "It's not just her birthday."

Marika cocked her head. "It's not?"

"Nuh-uh. It's also the day I'm going to propose."

Marika gave a little shriek and launched herself at Lee, hugging her fiercely. "That's wonderful. I'm so happy for you both."

Lee embraced her back, then laid one finger across Marika's lips. "It's a secret, so you can't say anything."

"Not a word," Marika said as she slid back into her chair.

"I need your help, though."

"Of course, anything you need, you know that. What can I do?"

"Help me pick out the perfect ring."

Marika smiled. "You name the date, place, and time, and I'll be there."

"And also, I know Dana will agree that we would like you and Eli to stand with us the day of the ceremony."

A lump in her throat, Marika could only nod, eyes glistening. She struggled to bring her emotions under control as Dana and Rhiannon returned.

"So you should see this new centre fielder on Dana and Terry's team," Lee said, with a surreptitious wink at Marika. "That woman has a cannon for an arm."

"You talking about Darcy?" Dana asked, resting her hands on Lee's shoulders.

"Yup. I was just telling Marika that with her on your team, you might even win the championship this year."

"She's a helluva player, all right. Hey, why don't you and Rhiannon come to our game this week? Afterwards, we can all go out to Oly's."

Marika hesitated as she remembered Val's caustic words the night of the anniversary party. She wasn't keen to encounter her ex again, but a quick glance at Rhiannon's hopeful expression was enough to overcome her reservations. "Okay. If Rhi feels up to it and wants to go, then we'll be there."

Rhiannon beamed.

Marika smiled. *Somehow I think she's going to feel up to it.*

"So, have you memorized the study manual yet?" Marika matched her pace to Rhiannon's shorter stride as they strolled the walking path that followed alongside the Bow River.

"Not quite, but I'm working on it. Things like traffic signs are pretty basic, but I'm having a hard time with stopping distances, and the description of how to drive a car with a standard transmission is pretty confusing, too."

"Don't worry. Once you've got your permit and you start driving with David and me, it'll all make sense."

They moved aside to make way for a roller-blader as he whizzed by them, then walked on.

Rhiannon drew a deep breath. "I have to go home tomorrow."

Marika had been expecting it, but was saddened nonetheless. *Don't be ridiculous. You'll see her in the office every day.* "Are you sure?"

"Yes. I've imposed on you long enough."

"It was no imposition." Marika longed to tell Rhiannon how much she'd enjoyed her company, but the words stuck in her throat. "You know, even if you are ready to go home, you don't have to come back into the office until you feel up to it."

"Trying to replace me at work?" Rhiannon's voice held an undertone of uncertainty.

Marika stopped and turned to face Rhiannon. "No. Absolutely not. I'd miss you until you were ready to come back, but I don't want you to rush if you need more time to heal."

A smile lit up Rhiannon's face. "Dana said the healing has progressed really well, and that you've done an excellent job. I can move my arm without pain…"

Marika frowned at the blatant fib.

"Okay, almost without pain. But the point is, I can do my job, and believe me, I'd far rather be in the office than trying to avoid questions at my aunt's house."

Marika nodded. *It always comes back to that, doesn't it? I think you'd do just about anything to avoid Hettie the horrible.* "All right. But if you start getting tired, or your arm or shoulder hurt, or you simply need to lie down for a while—"

"I'll tell you."

"Deal." They resumed their walk. "It might be for the best anyway," Marika said. "That way, I can still change your dressing and keep an eye on how you're healing."

Rhiannon laughed. "That should go over well at the office."

"Well, I didn't mean I'd do it out in the waiting area. We can close my office door and draw the curtains or use the ladies' room."

"Probably the best idea."

The comfortable silence fell between them again as they began the circuit back to Marika's condo. When they passed the small ice cream shop that was still busy with Calgarians enjoying the summer evening, Rhiannon laid a hand on Marika's arm. "May I buy you an ice cream cone?"

Marika's initial instinct was to counteroffer that she would buy. *No, this is important to you, isn't it?* "Thank you. Pralines and Cream, please."

Rhiannon joined the line-up at the take-out window.

Marika leaned back against a tree and watched her. Rhiannon still favoured her right arm, but not noticeably so to the casual observer. *She probably is ready to resume work. And I do want her back at the office.* Marika sighed. *We have to return to normal sometime, even if this week has redefined 'normal.' I'm sure going to miss her, though.*

Rhiannon returned with a big grin and two double scoop sugar cones.

Marika smiled and shook her head, but accepted the proffered cone. They dawdled their way back to the condo as they enjoyed the ice cream. *I don't think she wants our last walk to end anymore than I do.* Marika's cone lasted until they reached the apartment door, while Rhiannon's had long since vanished. They entered and went directly to the kitchen to wash up.

With the water running over their hands, Rhiannon asked, "So, how come you never play that piano out there?"

"Actually, I do play it quite often."

"You haven't played since I've been here."

"I didn't want to disturb your rest, and I didn't know if you'd like my kind of music."

"What kind of music do you play?"

Marika handed Rhiannon one end of the towel and took the other for herself. "Classical, jazz, some modern stuff. Pretty much whatever I'm in the mood for when I sit down."

"Play something for me?"

Marika nodded. "All right. But just one piece and then maybe you should have your bath, okay?"

"Okay."

Marika led the way to the living room. Rhiannon sat on the couch and Spooky promptly crawled into her lap. Marika smiled. Her cat frequently curled up next to Rhiannon. *I'm glad they get along so well.*

When she began to play, Marika closed her eyes. A soft, mellow air filled the apartment and, as always, the music carried her away. She was startled to hear the sound of applause when she finished, but she opened her eyes and smiled at Rhiannon.

"That was wonderful. You're really very good."

"Thank you. I took piano lessons through most of my childhood and teens. I completed the Royal Conservatory exams, but I just play for myself now."

"What was that piece?"

"*Gymnopedie No.1* by Erik Satie. He's one of my favourites. Satie was a French composer at the turn of the last century, who had a rather odd fascination with gymnasts' feet. He would write his music to match the rhythms of their routines. He once wrote a very short composition with instructions that it be repeated 840 times in a row. Quite an oddball, actually, but then, aren't we all, in one way or another?"

Rhiannon raised an eyebrow, and Marika closed the lid over the keys. "All right, young lady," she said with mock severity. "Bath time."

"Yes, Mother." Rhiannon grinned. "Are you going to read me a story after that?"

"Only after you're all clean and tucked in." Marika's affectionate gaze followed Rhiannon out of the room.

An hour later, Marika worked the muscles of Rhiannon's back and shoulder. *I really am going to miss this...miss her. God, I hate the thought of her going back to a place she so obviously loathes.* She took extra care and extra time with the massage. Rhiannon's eyes closed and her breathing deepened into sleep. Still Marika continued, until at last she admitted she was prolonging the contact more for herself than for the sleeping woman.

Reluctantly she drew back and pulled the covers up to Rhiannon's shoulders. Marika laid a tentative hand on her hair and caressed the damp curls until she couldn't justify her presence any longer.

Marika turned off the lamp and walked to the door just as Spooky strolled into the room. She scooped up her pet and took him back to the bed, depositing him beside Rhiannon. Spooky immediately curled up and she nodded. "You keep her company, mister." *Wish I could.* Marika's eyes widened. *Where did that come from?* She studied Rhiannon for several long moments, then left the room.

CHAPTER 14

RHIANNON'S HEART SANK THE CLOSER they came to her home. "Could you let me off in the back alley?"

"Sure." Marika turned into the alley and stopped short of Hettie's backyard. She put the car in neutral and turned to Rhiannon. She lifted a hand, then dropped it. "You're sure about this?"

Rhiannon unlocked her seatbelt and tried to smile. "You know you've asked me that about twenty times today, right?"

Marika's gaze dropped. "I'm sorry."

"No, don't be." Rhiannon touched Marika's arm. "I can't begin to tell you how much I appreciate all you've done for me. But as great as you've been, I can't stay any longer. You've slept on that daybed long enough."

"It's pretty comfortable."

Impulsively, Rhiannon leaned over and hugged Marika. "I have to go. See you in the office tomorrow." She hopped out of the car and walked to the gate where she stopped and looked back.

The car hadn't moved.

Rhiannon squared her shoulders and entered the yard. *God, I hope Hettie's gone to bed already.*

When she opened the back door, Hettie loomed in front of her. "Well, look what the cat drug in."

Rhiannon froze at the familiar whiny sound, then closed the door.

Hettie's eyes glittered. "So where've you been?"

Rhiannon made no answer as she crossed the kitchen.

Hettie raised her voice. "I won't have a fornicator living under my roof, hear? If you're going to whore around, you can find yourself a new place to live!"

Rhiannon spun and glared at Hettie. "Not that it's any of your damned business, but I was staying with a friend. A female friend."

Hettie smirked. "Don't you be using that kind of language." She followed Rhiannon down the hall. "This is a God-fearing house, and I won't have you talkin' like that!"

The last thing Rhiannon heard as she mounted the stairs to the sanctuary of her room was the ancient litany of her failings, her questionable parentage, and the imminence of God's wrath descending upon her if she didn't repent and seek forgiveness—all delivered in her aunt's shrillest tones.

Less than an hour later Hettie's cohort gathered in the parlour. Hettie led them in prayers that outlined Rhiannon's latest transgressions for God's enlightenment. Then, guided by their leader, they launched into supplications for Rhiannon's redemption from temptation and lasciviousness.

Rhiannon curled her pillow up around her ears in a futile effort to block the noise. "Jesus, people on the other side of the city must hear them." She contrasted her homecoming to the peace and contentment of her time with Marika. *I miss that—I miss her.* "For crying out loud, you've been away from her for all of an hour. Grow the hell up. You knew it wasn't going to last."

She rolled on her side and thumped the mattress. Then she thumped it again, and again, until her shoulder was in agony. The pounding of blood in her ears obscured the relentless drone from below as she fought to control her breathing. *Okay, that might've been a mistake.*

Rhiannon staggered to her feet and found the pain pills in her bag. She threw two down in quick succession, and drank from an outdated milk bottle in her fridge. She grimaced. *Ugh. Even Spooky wouldn't drink that.*

She returned to bed and waited for the pain to subside. *Is this all a mistake? I'm so close to being out of here. They won't even be my friends for long. Maybe it's not worth it.* She tried to picture returning to life as it was before David and Lee and Dana...and Marika. But that pain was worse than her shoulder.

"She was so good to me. And she actually seemed to like spending time with me. I liked spending time with her, too." *I liked the backrubs most of all.* "Stop being a hedonistic little piggy. She only did it because she had to." Rhiannon shook her head. The acute memory of Marika's touch belied her words. Her gaze drifted across the drawings closest to her bed. She reached to touch one and an idea began to grow. "I think I know how to say thank you."

Rhiannon rolled the other way and reached for a tissue. She tore it in half and stuffed her ears. It cut the noise to tolerable so she switched off her lamp and pulled up the covers. She wriggled, trying to find a more comfortable part of the mattress. There wasn't one.

With a sigh, Rhiannon focused on the previous night's massage. *It was the best one of all. Kind of like a book where you don't want to turn the last page because it's too good to end.*

Rhiannon smiled in the dark and felt again Marika's hand caress her hair.

Rhiannon tried not to look obvious as she kept a surreptitious watch on her boss. Marika was working her way through a stack of mail that she'd just placed on her desk. There was a large manila envelope on the bottom of the pile that was responsible for the butterflies doing cartwheels in Rhiannon's stomach.

When she saw Marika pick up that envelope, Rhiannon dropped her eyes to her computer and tried to concentrate on the letter she was drafting. She deliberately kept her eyes on the screen, even when she sensed Marika walking toward her.

"Rhi, this is absolutely amazing. You did this?" Marika held a sheet of fine vellum as carefully as she'd have cradled a Faberge egg. When Rhiannon nodded, Marika gave a low whistle. "You are an incredibly talented artist."

Rhiannon had done a charcoal drawing of Marika petting Spooky curled up in her lap. It was deceptively simple, and portrayed her in a natural, relaxed pose, with a fond smile lighting her face. Signed and dated in the bottom right corner, it read simply: "Thank you, Rhiannon."

"When?"

"The last few nights." Rhiannon had gone to an art supply store on her Monday lunch hour and picked out the finest sheet of paper she could find, along with tissue paper to preserve the charcoal. She had an eidetic memory for images and it was easy for her to draw a realistic depiction of Marika and Spooky. "I just wanted to express my appreciation for all your kindness last week."

"It really was my pleasure, but this is incredible. I love it. I'm going to take it in for framing on my lunch hour."

Rhiannon flushed and stared at her hands. "I'm glad you like it."

"I much more than like it." Marika touched Rhiannon's shoulder. "So, do you think you're ready for the test today?"

Rhiannon looked up and nodded. "Uh-huh. I think I've memorized that book from cover to cover." She grinned. "What is the minimum stopping distance at a hundred kilometres per hour under normal driving conditions?"

Marika rolled her eyes. "Trust me, the vast majority of experienced drivers wouldn't stand a hope in hell of passing a learner's test."

"One hundred and eight metres. How many demerit points do you get for exceeding the speed limit by more than thirty kilometres per hour but less than fifty kilometres per hour?"

"I'm sure Lee could tell you that one." Marika laughed and returned to her office.

The rest of the morning was taken up with appointments that had been postponed from the previous week, and it was past one before they could leave for lunch. Rhiannon was elated when Marika carried the manila envelope out with her. *Maybe she'll hang it in the bedroom. It would be cool if it was the first thing she saw every morning.* "Okay, stop mooning, Davies. One more time through the study manual and it's time to go."

By the time Rhiannon returned to the office, Marika was already at her desk. She hurried out. "Well?"

Rhiannon grinned. "94%. You're looking at a legally licenced learner."

"Well done! So, would you like to go driving this weekend?"

"If you have the time."

"I think I can make time." Marika's eyes twinkled. "Listen, since we're going to the game tonight anyway, why don't you let me take you to dinner first? We'll celebrate."

Rhiannon glanced at her backpack. "I only brought casual clothes with me for after work."

"So we'll do casual. We can't let such an auspicious occasion go by unmarked. Why don't we go to the Pied Piper downstairs, and then head over to the ball field? Oh, and I want to change your dressing before we go, too."

"Okay."

Rhiannon slid behind her desk and tried to get her mind back on her job. It was difficult. Between her delight at passing her test, the pleasure of having her gift so well received, and the anticipation of the evening, her mind stubbornly refused to focus on immigration regulations.

She closed her eyes and let the day's exhilaration wash away the nastiness of the three days since she'd returned to her aunt's house.

Rhiannon opened her eyes. *All right, time to focus. You've got to finish the Leung deposition.* But even the sternest admonitions couldn't dent her smile.

Rhiannon examined the scene before her as Marika wheeled the Lexus into a parking spot. The dusty lot edged a large community recreational complex—with tennis courts, a soccer pitch, and the softball diamond that was their destination. The two teams clustered around their respective dugouts, and Rhiannon picked out Dana without difficulty.

As Rhiannon climbed out of the car, she asked, "What position does Dana play?"

Marika walked around to join her. "She's their utility player. She fills in wherever she's needed. Right now, I think she's playing shortstop because their regular player is pregnant."

Rhiannon glanced up as they headed toward the diamond. "Did you ever play?"

Marika laughed. "I'm afraid you could measure my athletic ability in sub-atomic particles. No, I just like to watch."

"What about Lee? Does she play, too?"

"She used to, but she blew her knee out in a bike accident a few years ago, so she had to join me in the rooting section. What about you? Did you ever play?"

"Just in school. I wasn't very good."

Marika gave her a little nudge. "Well, what's a game without a cheering section, right? They need us."

"Very good point."

"Why don't we wish Dana good luck, and then find some seats?"

They came to an abrupt halt when a woman stepped into their path. She wore the same uniform as Dana's—blue and white, with bright red lettering that read *Oly's*.

The woman glared at Marika. "What are you doing here?"

Marika sighed. "Val, I'm not looking for trouble. We just came to watch the game."

Val fixed her hostile gaze on Rhiannon. "Do you have any idea what you're getting yourself into, kid? If I were you, I'd run from this fucking bitch as fast and far as I could."

Before Rhiannon could utter any of the indignant words that surged to mind, a hand rested on her lower back and an arm settled over Marika's shoulders. "Are you having some sort of problem with my friends, Val?"

Relieved, Rhiannon looked up into Lee's stern features as she eyed their interrogator. Val tried to hold the cool gaze that pinned her, but failed and stalked away.

"Thanks, Lee. I was afraid that would happen." Marika looked at Rhiannon. "I'm sorry."

"Not your fault," Rhiannon said as Lee steered them toward the stands.

"Actually, it is, but I thought she would be over it by now."

Lee shook her head. "Val's not one to let bygone be bygones."

Rhiannon glanced between them.

Marika grimaced. "Ex-girlfriend."

They took their seats and Rhiannon studied Val as she leaned against the backstop, still glowering at Marika. *I wonder what Marika saw in her.*

"Rhi," Lee whispered. "You're staring."

Rhiannon flushed. "So is she."

"But we have better manners than she does, don't we?" Lee gave Rhiannon's knee a quick pat, then greeted a woman edging down the aisle toward them. "Hi, Jan. Want to join us?"

"Yes, please do," Marika said.

Rhiannon studied the newcomer. She was somewhat taller than Rhiannon, with auburn hair, dark green eyes, and freckles. A warm, friendly smile lit her face, and Rhiannon found herself instinctively liking the stranger.

Lee leaned back and gestured between them. "Jan Spencer, this is Rhiannon Davies."

Jan reached across Lee and offered her hand, which Rhiannon shook, still cautious of her shoulder.

"Hi, Rhiannon. Very nice to meet you."

"You, too."

Marika rested her arms on her legs and looked past Rhiannon and Lee. "I thought you were the equipment manager, Jan."

Lee snorted, and Jan laughed. "I was, until Eli discovered that Judy and Patrick's daughter, Tammy, was my helper."

"The boy's in love." Lee shook her head. "All we hear at home is Tammy this and Tammy that." She glanced at Marika with mock sympathy. "Sorry, my friend, you've been displaced. Prince Hormone is now looking elsewhere."

"Oh woe is me, I am forsaken again. Tis the lot of the older woman." Marika winked at Rhiannon, who laughed.

"And who am I to stand in the path of young love?" Jan nodded to where the two teenagers were in the end of the home team's dugout. They held opposite sides of the bat bag, their eyes only for each other.

"Uh-huh. Didn't have anything to do with Eli's promise to cut your lawn for a month, did it?" Lee asked with a grin.

Jan winked. "What can I say? I can be bribed."

As Dana's team took the field and the game began, Marika gave Rhiannon a quick overview of the players. "Jan's partner, Terry, is playing third. Dana's got shortstop tonight. Natalie's on second, and Robyn is catching. Her partner, Lisa, their regular shortstop, is the pregnant lady keeping score in the dugout. And, of course, you've already met Val on first."

Rhiannon grimaced.

"Gale's in right field, and Judy's in left. Her husband, Patrick, is their manager." Marika shook her head. "I don't know the pitcher or centre fielder. Lee?"

"They're new this year. Laurie Attfield is pitching, and the centre fielder is AJ Darcy. She's the one I said had an arm like a cannon."

"She can really belt them into the ozone, too." Jan's gaze rarely strayed from the woman at third.

"She's a great addition to the team," Lee said. "I think she's a firefighter or something."

"She is," Jan confirmed. "She can't always make it because of her shift, but we haven't lost a game yet when she's playing."

Marika studied the centre fielder.

Rhiannon followed the direction of Marika's gaze and examined the firefighter's athletic form. The woman was as tall as Lee, and while not as broad, except across the shoulders, had a look of strength and speed about her. Rhiannon couldn't see her features under the shade of the ball cap snugged down over her forehead, but she had to admit that the woman probably rated a second glance. *Just not Marika's second glance.* Rhiannon blinked. *It's none of your business if she wants to ogle some overgrown, muscle-bound, fatheaded firefighter.*

For a moment, the lustre of an unprecedented evening out with friends dimmed. But then Marika looked away from the firefighter and began to fill Rhiannon in on the team's performance the previous year when they finished third in the league's play-off tournament.

When the top of the inning ended without any score and the home team trotted in for their at-bats, Dana detoured to the fence and called up to Lee, "Hey, love, Patrick wants to know if you'll coach third."

With a big grin, Lee bounded down the stairs and out onto the field to take up her position.

"I think she misses playing." Jan slid over into Lee's vacated seat.

"She certainly does," Marika agreed. "But with everything that happened last year, it was probably better that she couldn't."

Jan nodded, but Rhiannon cocked her head.

"Dana had...a serious health scare. It was the first year neither of them could play, but things worked out all right."

Rhiannon caught her breath and studied Marika.

"Really, she's fine now," Marika said. "I'll tell you about it some other time, okay? Right now, we've got some cheering to do."

Terry, the lead-off batter, stepped up to the plate. She took a ball inside that made Jan glare at the pitcher, then rapped a clean single to left field. Jan was instantly on her feet, cheering loudly. When Terry held up at first, Jan sat down again and flashed Marika and Rhiannon an abashed glance.

Marika chuckled. "That's okay. We all know who Terry's biggest fan is."

Rhiannon laughed as Jan blushed but didn't deny it. She returned her attention to the field as Val stepped up to the plate. Much to Rhiannon's private delight, Val went down swinging on a full count, but Terry managed to steal second. Natalie stepped up next and flied out to centre on the first pitch. That brought the tall firefighter to the plate, batting cleanup.

Rhiannon stole a look from the corner of her eye, and scowled to see Marika's attention fixed on the batter, who had paused to take a couple more warm-up swings.

The firefighter coolly waited out the first two pitches, and then, with a smooth, powerful swing, gave the third offering a ride right out of the park. Her teammates whooped with delight as she jogged deliberately around the bases. Terry waited for her at home, her hand raised in salute as the centre fielder crossed the plate. Palms met, and Terry draped an arm over Darcy's shoulders as they headed for the dugout.

Jan and Marika clapped loudly. Rhiannon's applause was perfunctory.

Gale grounded out to short, and the home team returned to the field. The game proceeded quickly, with the score remaining two to nothing in favour of Oly's. The firefighter prevented a sure two runs for the opposition with a breathtaking diving catch in the top of the fifth, and then stole home while Dana was up in the seventh for an insurance run. The game ended in a three to nothing victory.

Rhiannon followed Jan and Marika down the steps, but hung back as they approached the victors, who were making plans to congregate at Oly's pub.

Jan rushed up to Terry, who pulled her into a tight hug. "Wonderful game, love." Jan brushed sweaty curls off Terry's forehead.

"Thanks, sweetheart. Good thing we had Darcy, though, or we might have blown it in the fifth." Terry smiled at Marika. "Hey, good to see you. Are you coming to Oly's with us?"

Marika nodded and drew Rhiannon forward. "Terry, I don't think you've met my friend, Rhiannon Davies. Rhi, this is Terry Sanderson."

Terry raised an eyebrow, then let go of Jan long enough to extend her hand. "Good to meet you, Rhiannon."

Rhiannon shook her hand. Lee and Dana joined them, and arranged to meet at the pub. She noticed Darcy leave with a group of women. *Maybe she has to go to work and can't go to Oly's.*

Rhiannon's hopeful thoughts were interrupted as Dana said, "Right, then, we have to tear Eli away from Tammy and drop him home first, so save us a couple of chairs."

They dispersed, and Rhiannon walked with Marika back to the car. She rolled her right shoulder several times.

"Is it bothering you?" Marika asked.

"Itchy. It's driving me nuts not being able to scratch it." Rhiannon knew that it was a sign of healing, but was still aggravated.

They reached the Lexus, and the automatic unlocking system clicked. But before Rhiannon could get in, Marika laid one hand on her left shoulder and began gently rubbing around the healing injury, using the dressing for soft friction without directly touching the stitches.

Rhiannon groaned and let her head drop. "God, that feels good."

Marika kept up the indirect scratching for another few moments, then released Rhiannon and stepped back. "Better?"

"And how," Rhiannon turned to face Marika. "Thank you."

Marika rounded the car to her side. Rhiannon was about to slide into her seat when she noticed an old silver Toyota pull out of a space one row over. Terry grinned at her from behind the steering wheel and Jan smiled from the passenger's seat. Rhiannon blinked and, with a shrug, got into the Lexus.

"Have you ever been to Oly's?" Marika asked, as she navigated out of the parking lot.

"I've never been to any bar."

Marika gave a short whistle. "Okay. Are you sure you want to go, because we don't have to."

"No, I don't mind. Besides, Lee and Dana are counting on us to save them chairs."

"You're right, they are, and it wouldn't do to let them down."

They found a spot two streets over from Oly's and parked the Lexus. Rhiannon shook her head in utter amazement as they approached the pub. She was going to a bar with friends. A month ago, the very concept would have been as foreign to her as boarding a space shuttle.

Rhiannon followed Marika through Oly's heavy front door and looked around curiously. She wasn't sure what she had expected, but the pub was clean and cool, albeit with a smoky haze in the air. Most of the noise in the bar was coming from a back corner of the common room, where the team had pulled several tables together and was making heavy inroads on four pitchers of draft.

Terry beckoned them over and pointed at two chairs across from her and Jan. "Hey, we saved you a place."

Rhiannon was glad that Val was at the far end of the table, huddled with the pitcher, Laurie. She glanced around, but didn't see the firefighter. She took the chair beside Marika and across from Jan. "What about Lee and Dana? Shouldn't we save them chairs?"

"Not a problem," Terry said as she bounced to her feet. "We'll just add another table for them." She went to drag another table over, and Rhiannon jumped up to help. They slid it into place, and Terry grinned at Rhi before she resumed her seat and put an arm around Jan.

A waiter set a clean, damp glass in front of Marika. He turned to Rhiannon. "Sorry, miss, I'll have to see some ID."

Rhiannon flushed, but pulled her birth certificate out of her wallet.

He looked at it. "Got anything with a picture on it? A driver's licence?"

Marika caught his attention. "She works for me, Solly. I can vouch for her being over the age of majority."

"Sorry, Marika, but you know Megan's rules."

Rhiannon offered her bus pass, and it was deemed acceptable. A glass was placed before her, too, and Jan reached across the table to fill both.

"You work for Marika?" Terry asked.

"She's Marion's replacement, and a darned fine one, too."

Rhiannon lowered her gaze as warmth surged through her. She took a cautious sip of the beer. She grimaced at the taste, and looked quickly to see if anyone noticed.

Jan regarded her with an amused smile.

Rhi gave Jan a sheepish grin in return and was relieved when Terry claimed her partner's attention.

Lee and Dana arrived to a chorus of greetings from the exuberant crowd. Lee made her rounds to joke with and tease her former teammates, while Dana took the chair beside Rhiannon.

"How's the shoulder doing?" Dana asked, after she accepted a mug from an attentive Solly.

"Healing well, according to my personal nurse, but driving me crazy with the itching."

"Well, don't scratch too hard." Dana took a drink and murmured appreciatively. "You don't want to ruin Dr. Mathieu's great handiwork. Besides, the stitches should be mostly dissolved soon, and you'll feel much better."

Rhiannon watched Dana's obvious pleasure in the beer and opted to try her drink again. *Yuck. Doesn't get any better on the second try. It must be an acquired taste.* She kept her hand wrapped around the glass while she listened to the din of conversations flowing around her.

Lee eventually made her way all around the table and dropped into the seat beside Dana. She snagged her partner's beer and drained it.

"Hey, you big goof, that was mine. Get your own." Dana slapped Lee's shoulder.

"And here I thought you loved me," Lee said. "Would you deny a woman dying of thirst?"

"Have some water if you're dying of thirst, but leave my beer alone." Dana refilled her beer and rested a protective hand over it.

"Water? Blechh." Lee beckoned Solly over and threw some bills on his tray as she ordered two more pitchers of beer.

Rhiannon leaned over to Marika and whispered, "How do we pay? Do I give my money to the waiter?"

"Already taken care of. I chipped in for both of us." Marika gestured at the pile of bills, one table down.

Rhiannon frowned and Marika shook her head. "Don't worry about it. I'll let you get the ice cream after driving lessons this weekend, all right?"

Rhiannon countered, "Ice cream and lunch." Marika had paid for dinner after work, asserting that it was her congratulatory treat. And while Rhiannon didn't have any illusions that she could match Marika dollar for dollar, she was determined to carry her own weight.

"Okay, ice cream and lunch, but I get to choose where we eat."

Rhiannon looked at Marika suspiciously, but nodded.

Marika nodded at Rhiannon's beer. "Would you prefer a pop?"

"That's okay. This is fine."

Marika smiled. "Then why do you look like you bit into a lemon?" Rhiannon had no ready comeback and Marika looked around for Solly. He was occupied with a table of newcomers, so she stood up. "I'll be back in a moment."

Rhiannon watched Marika walk to the long, room-length oaken bar before Lee asked her, "So, are you ready to hit the Stampede with us in a couple of weeks?"

"I think so," Rhi said with a straight face. "I've laid in a good supply of antacids, just in case."

Lee guffawed, and the others around the table joined in.

Rhiannon joined in the laughter until her gaze drifted to Marika, and the laughter caught in her throat. Marika leaned against the bar, deep in conversation with the firefighter, who was tracing one finger down Marika's arm.

Darcy had obviously taken time to clean up before coming to Oly's. She was no longer in the team uniform. Dressed in khaki shorts and a black tank top, she was an impressive sight. Lean muscles were clearly evident on long arms and legs; her short black hair was slicked back; and her gaze regarded Marika with obvious intent.

Stunned, Rhiannon watched as Marika laughed at something Darcy said. She was flooded with a desire to march over there and push the firefighter out of Marika's personal space. She had to fight to keep herself in her chair as she wrestled with the rage that threatened to overwhelm her.

Someone squatted beside her, and Jan asked quietly, "Want to take a walk? Get some fresh air?"

Rhiannon nodded. She followed Jan out of the bar without looking back at Marika. When Rhiannon reached the sidewalk, she sucked in a lungful of air and tried to tame the emotional onslaught.

Jan started down the street, and Rhiannon fell into step. She was grateful for the other woman's silence as she grappled with her confusion.

They had gone two blocks when Jan indicated a low, stone wall enclosing an old house that was now a realtor's office. "Feel like stopping for a minute?"

Rhiannon didn't say anything, but sat beside Jan, who looked up at the night sky.

"It's too bad the city lights wash the stars out so much, isn't it?"

Rhiannon grunted.

"If you never ventured out of the city, you wouldn't know their brilliance, yet they're there all the time. We just can't see them clearly."

Rhiannon turned and stared at Jan. *What's she talking about?*

Jan met her gaze. "May I tell you a little story?"

Rhiannon shrugged.

Jan smiled. "I'll take that as a yes. Last Christmas, I said some things to Terry that I regret to this day. I handled a difficult situation very badly, and sometimes it still amazes me that we got past it."

Rhiannon's eyebrows shot up. "But you seem so right together."

"Now, yes. But it wasn't a smooth ride getting to where we are." Jan sighed and leaned forward to rest her hands on the wall. "When I fell in love with Terry, I was still married to a man whom I also loved very much. I thought she was dating another woman, and even though I knew I had no right to feel the way I did, I couldn't help being overwhelmed with anger, hurt, and confusion. I lashed out. I can still see the pain in her eyes. To this day, I hate that I put that there."

"Why are you telling me this?"

"Because you were itching to tear Darcy's arm off, and I'm not sure what you'd have said to Marika right then." Jan laughed softly. "I know you don't know me, but I saw myself again so clearly that I had to get you out of there for a few moments." She gave a self-deprecating shrug. "Maybe I can save you some heartache, of learning the hard way, like I did. And…and sometimes it's just easier to talk to strangers."

"I don't…I mean, it's not like…" Rhiannon scowled and kicked her heels against the stone wall.

"I know. I've been there." Jan looked up at the sky. "Still, sometimes it's easier to think when you're out under the stars."

They sat there in silence, and Rhiannon's anger subsided.

Finally Jan said, "Maybe we should get back before they send out a search party, eh?"

On the walk back to the pub, Rhiannon still didn't understand what had happened, but she no longer felt homicidal. *Well, it's an improvement anyway.* She grinned. *Yeah, like I could've even put a dent in steroid-woman.*

They had almost reached Oly's when Rhiannon asked, "Who was the woman you thought Terry was dating?"

Jan smiled. "It doesn't matter. As it turned out, they were only friends." She held the door open for Rhiannon.

"Thanks, Jan. It probably was a good idea to get out for a bit."

Jan nodded. "Anytime."

When she glanced at their table, Rhiannon found a worried gaze focused on her. A quick scan found Darcy at the far end of the table, chatting with Laurie. Relieved, she and Jan parted company as she sat down beside Marika.

"Hey, where did you go? I was looking for you." Marika asked.

"Oh, Jan and I were just getting a breath of fresh air." Rhiannon grinned at Jan, who was snuggled under Terry's arm. Jan winked back.

Marika looked between them, but didn't question further. She pushed a Coke in front of Rhiannon. "Here. You'll probably enjoy that a lot more than the draft."

Rhiannon took an appreciative swallow. "That's good, thank you." She was startled by a chorus of boos that broke out at the far end of the table.

Gale and Natalie were weaving their way to the karaoke machine, arms slung over each other's shoulders.

Dana groaned.

Rhiannon eyed her curiously.

"You haven't lived until you've heard these two do karaoke," Dana said.

When Gale and Natalie broke into an exuberant, but wildly off-key rendition of *Bad Moon Rising*, Rhiannon understood. She winced, but laughed as she saw Marika and the catcher, Robyn, with their ears plugged until the end of the song.

Catcalls and flying peanuts rewarded the duo, who gave back as good as they got. They threatened to launch into another song if their teammates didn't show a little appreciation for their talent.

Rhiannon's jaw dropped when Natalie spun around and mooned the table. Whoops and cheers greeted the display. Lee chortled. "Now that's what I call a 'good moon rising'!" Dana cuffed her partner, but she was laughing just as hard as Lee.

Marika leaned closer to Rhiannon. "They're about to get rowdy. Do you feel like cutting out now? We have to work in the morning."

"About to get rowdy? They aren't there, yet?"

"Oh, not even close," Marika went around to hug Lee and Dana. "See you guys later."

They made their farewells, and Rhiannon locked eyes with Jan just before they left. She mouthed 'thank you' and got an understanding smile and a mouthed 'you're welcome' in return.

On the drive home, Marika asked, "Did you have a good time tonight?"

"Yes, I did. Thank you for taking me."

"You're welcome." Marika hesitated. "So...everything was all right?"

"Uh-huh." Rhiannon refused to look at Marika.

"Okay. I'm glad."

There was doubt in Marika's voice, but Rhiannon knew she wouldn't press it. When they reached her alley, she unlocked her seat belt. "It really was a good day. Thank you...for everything."

Marika's eyes softened. "You're very welcome. I enjoyed it too."

They were silent for a long moment as they regarded each other, then Rhiannon shook it off. "I'd better get going. See you tomorrow."

"See you tomorrow."

Rhiannon stopped at her backyard and looked back to where the Lexus idled. She raised a hand, then walked up the broken path to her aunt's house.

CHAPTER 15

"**W**AIT UNTIL YOU SEE THE picture, Spook. I had no idea that Rhiannon is this talented. Mind you, there's probably a lot more I don't know about her." Marika set the cat's bowl down. "One thing I do know is that she's a good person once you get past that prickly exterior."

Marika glanced at her watch. She had a little time before she was to pick up Rhiannon, so she went to the piano and began to play. The joyful sounds of Granados' *Spanish Dance* filled the room until the cacophony of the phone interrupted her music. Marika stopped playing to listen as the answering machine picked up.

"Hi, Marika. It's AJ Darcy. We met the other night at Oly's. I hope you don't mind, but I got your phone number from Natalie. I was wondering if you'd be interested in doing something together this evening. I'm working right now, but my shift is over at six. If you want to call me at the hall, it's 555-4782, or call me at home, 555-5214. We can maybe go for dinner or something. Hope to hear from you. Bye."

A beep signaled the end of the message. The voice had been sultry and self-assured, just like its owner. Darcy had made her interest clear at Oly's, but while Marika enjoyed the attention of the handsome woman, she politely rejected her advances and explained she was with friends. Darcy had accepted the rebuff, but there had been a determined glint in her eyes, and Marika half-expected the phone call.

Spooky strolled up to Marika and brushed against her leg. She petted him and stared at the phone. "I suppose I could go, eh? I haven't made any commitment for this evening once Rhi's driving lesson is finished." *Do I want to accept her invitation?* Marika closed the lid and rested her head on top of her crossed arms. *She certainly looks like she knows how to show a girl a good time. And she seems worlds apart from Cass. Darcy is sexy as hell and knows it. Cass is ... Cass.*

Marika hadn't seen Cass since the night of Lee and Dana's anniversary party. That wasn't unusual. She sometimes went many weeks without encountering her— *My...what? I never know what to call her. Lover? There's certainly no love between us.* Marika lifted the cat to her lap and stroked his fur. "Maybe I should call Darcy, Spooky. Lee and Dana would be thrilled, wouldn't they?"

She made no move to go to the phone. Her thoughts turned instead to Rhiannon, and she smiled as she remembered Rhiannon glaring at Val in her defence. *Don't think I'd want to cross Lady Mouse.* Marika set Spooky down and got to her feet. "See you later, mister. You behave yourself, okay?" She grabbed her purse and, ignoring the blinking red light on the answering machine, left the condo.

"When you ease up on the clutch, really focus on synchronizing with the gas pedal." Marika smiled at her pupil. "You did much better that time. Try it again."

Rhiannon's brow furrowed, and her hands clenched the wheel.

Marika tapped Rhiannon's fists. "Loosen up here. The car's not going to run away from you."

Rhiannon's frown eased. "It might. But at least it won't go very far."

They were in the parking lot of a large suburban church. The lot that would be filled the following morning held only two cars parked at the church's side entrance. Marika had chosen it as a safe spot to give Rhiannon her first instructions. Her student had mastered the basics and was now working on perfecting her starts.

Rhiannon revved the motor; the car lurched and stalled. "Sorry." She shot a sheepish look at Marika.

"That's all right. Try it again, and this time, go a bit slower when you ease off the clutch." *This is so much fun. She's listening to me like I'm Moses handing down the Commandments.*

When Rhiannon successfully drove around the perimeter and shifted from first to second and back down again, it was time to take a break.

"We've been going at this for an hour. Why don't you pull over under that tree where the picnic table is, and we'll take five," Marika said.

Rhiannon nodded, then brought the Lexus to a stop without stalling the engine.

"Well done. Now let's stretch our legs for a few minutes." They got out and leaned side-by-side against the table. "You're doing well, Rhi. I'm impressed. You're a very good student."

Rhiannon beamed. "Thank you. I have an excellent teacher."

They watched a pair of young skateboarders set up a homemade jump at the far end of the parking lot.

"This is a good place to practice," Rhiannon said. "How did you know it was here? Do you go to this church?"

"No. I haven't attended church since I left school in Switzerland. Attendance was compulsory there. Especially for me." Marika didn't like to think of the years spent exiled in a gilded cage. The headmistress had known exactly why the sullen sixteen-year-old was dumped on the exclusive boarding school mid-term. She had taken measures to ensure Marika's deviancy was held in check. Mandated church attendance and weekly therapy sessions were only two of the many regulations. "Actually, a couple of years ago I dated a woman who lived a block from here, and I passed it all the time. I knew it wasn't busy on Saturdays, so it seemed like a good place for a lesson."

"I take it the relationship didn't work out?"

Marika shrugged. "They never do."

"I…"

Marika looked at Rhiannon. "What?"

"Aw, it's none of my business."

"It's okay to ask. That's how new friends learn about each other, right?"

Rhiannon took a deep breath. "I wondered why you and Lee never made it. You seem like you really care about each other, and you're both such nice people."

"I think we both know at least one person who would violently disagree with that last statement, but thank you." Marika paused, unsure of how much she wanted to confess. "We are the best of friends…now, and maybe if we had started that way, things might have been different. I was fairly new to the city when Lee and I met, and we basically plunged into a relationship without taking time to get to know each other." Marika shook her head. "Story of my life. After about five months, she was ready to move in together, maybe make things permanent between us."

"So what happened?"

Marika sighed. "I blew it. I got scared. I had an affair and not very discreetly either. Lee later accused me of doing it deliberately to sabotage our relationship. She's probably right, but the upshot was that we broke up. Lee takes commitment very seriously, and it took me a long time to win back her trust. I'm profoundly grateful that she gave me the chance, because I don't know what I'd do without her in my life."

"I know what you mean. She's kind of a force of nature, isn't she?"

"That she is. Still, things worked out for the best, right? I mean, can you imagine Lee without Dana?" Marika straightened. "Which reminds me. Guess what Lee's doing this weekend."

"They went to Emerald Lake for Dana's birthday, didn't they?"

Marika smiled. "Uh-huh. And while they're there, Lee's going to propose."

"No way!" Rhiannon grinned. "That's wonderful."

"It is. I helped Lee choose the ring last week, and she picked it up from my place before they left."

"Do you think Dana suspects anything?"

"I doubt it. Lee can keep a secret with the best of them. She was determined to make this weekend one to remember for the rest of their lives."

"There's no question Dana will say yes, right?"

"None. She may occasionally act the long-suffering spouse, but she adores Lee, and so does Eli. I think Dana has wanted to formalize their relationship for a while now. She was just waiting for Lee to come around to the idea. And Lee asked me to be her 'best woman.'"

"Excellent choice."

"Would you be interested in coming to the ceremony with me? I know they'd love to have you, and you might be more comfortable going with someone you know."

Rhiannon stared at her feet. "Sorta like your date, you mean?"

Marika froze. "No. I mean, we could go as friends, right?" *Stupid, stupid, stupid. Now you've scared her.* "I'm sorry. I didn't really think that through—"

"I'd love to go with you."

"Oh...good. That's wonderful. I'm not sure when it will be, but I'll let you know." Marika's hands trembled, and she jammed them into her pockets. *Did I just screw things up royally? God, I hope not. Not again. Not with her.* "So, listen, I believe you owe me an ice cream. Feel like driving to a DQ? There's one at a plaza about five blocks from here."

"Sounds good." They started back to the car, and Rhiannon gave her a hip bump. "Besides, since you chose a hot dog stand for lunch, I think I owe you at least a Peanut Buster Parfait."

"Hey, those are the best hot dogs in town." Marika stifled a grin. *She is so not going to be good for my waistline.*

Lee stood on the balcony of their chalet and looked out over the brilliant green waters that had given Emerald Lake its name. Through the open door, she heard Dana puttering inside the cabin. They had just come back from dinner at the lodge, and Lee was at peace with her world.

The past few days had been wonderful. The lake was exquisite, its waters surrounded by verdant forest and soaring mountains. In the mid-1920's, the federal government forbade any additional development beyond the original hand-hewn log lodge and surrounding chalets. The result was a pristine wilderness setting and the most romantic backdrop Lee could think of for proposing to Dana. She hadn't done that yet, but it was their last night. She rested her hand over the small box deep in her pocket.

Glacier fed and crystal clear, Emerald Lake was too cold to swim, but they had canoed, fished, ridden horses, and hiked up to Takakkaw Falls. Evenings, they gathered with other guests around the fire pit, lounged in the fourteen-foot hot tub or returned to their chalet for more private pursuits.

Deep in reverie, Lee didn't notice Dana slip up behind her until warm arms encircled her waist and squeezed. "Hmphhp. Careful there, love—I'm still pretty full."

Dana chuckled and eased around in front of Lee. "I know what you mean. I never thought I'd turn down one of those desserts, but I didn't have an inch of available space left."

Lee wrapped her arms around Dana's neck. "Feel like walking off some of that meal? It's a beautiful night. Why don't we go for a stroll around the lake?"

Dana slid a hand up behind Lee's head and pulled her down for a kiss. When they finally drew apart, Lee grinned. "Or we could just stay here."

"Mmm, hold that thought for later. I think it's a good idea to go for a walk first. Just let me grab a sweater."

They set out down the path toward the bridge. From the bridge, it was an easy five kilometres to circle the lake. The night was warm, and the stars had started to emerge. Their brilliance and the full moon illuminated the well-trodden path. Hand in hand, Lee and Dana ambled along the lake's edge, pausing occasionally to admire the moonlight reflecting off the water.

Lee had seen just the spot for her proposal on an earlier walk, and as they drew closer to it, butterflies began to dance in her stomach. *God, I hope I don't fumble this.* She'd tried to come up with the perfect words but had given up and decided instead to simply speak from her heart.

They'd covered two thirds of the distance around the lake when Lee tugged Dana off the trail and down a small hill toward the water's edge. She guided Dana to sit on an ancient fallen tree, scoured alabaster by the wind and waves, and knelt in front of her, taking her hands. "Last year... when I thought..." Lee's throat closed, and her voice caught at the memory.

"Sweetheart, that's behind us now. I'm all right. You know I am."

"They said we have to get through five years to be sure." Lee's gaze drifted to Dana's left breast, where she had discovered a small, hard lump one terrible morning the previous spring.

Dana extricated one of her hands and cupped Lee's face. "I'm not going anywhere, my love. I won't leave you."

Lee drew in a deep breath. *This is supposed to be a proposal, you idiot.* "Promise?"

"Promise."

Lee recaptured the hand that caressed her face. "I love you. I love Eli, too, and I want us to always be a family. I need you to know how deeply I'm committed to you...to us...and to our family. Dana, will you marry me?"

The simple, heartfelt words generated a brilliant smile from Dana. She flung her arms around Lee and hugged her fiercely.

Lee held her as Dana's body shook. Finally, she murmured into her hair, "Do I take it that's a yes?"

Dana laughed and leaned back. "Yes, you big goof! Of course, yes!"

Lee threw back her head and whooped. "Yes! She said yes!" They embraced and tumbled to the sand, landing on the small stretch of beach between the log and the lake's edge. They gazed into each other's eyes and punctuated soft caresses with lingering kisses.

Suddenly, Lee bolted upright. "I almost forgot." She took the ring box out of her pocket and opened it.

Dana sat up and stared at the diamond solitaire. "Oh my God, Lee, that's beautiful."

Lee slipped it onto Dana's finger. "Hah, I told Marika I had the right size."

Dana chuckled as she inspected the band. "Marika?"

"She helped me pick it out," Lee said, "but I made the final selection."

"It's wonderful, love. You chose perfectly."

"I bought the wedding bands that match. Mine is being sized right now."

"You want to wear a ring? But you never wear rings."

"I never had a reason, but I want the world to know that I'm married to my best girl. This is a forever thing for me, Dana. I don't want anyone to doubt that."

"For me, too, love. For me, too." Dana leaned forward and took possession of Lee's lips. Her hands roamed over Lee's body.

When Dana began to unbutton Lee's shirt, Lee drew back. "I think we'd better take this back to the chalet."

Dana chuckled, but her hands didn't stop. "Lost your sense of adventure? We haven't made love outdoors in ages."

Lee's chest heaved under the unrelenting attention, and, torn between lust and concern, she glanced up at the trail. It was up the hill about ten metres, but even with the huge log for shelter, they wouldn't be well hidden from anyone hiking by.

Then warm lips closed over her hard nipple, and Lee forgot everything else. She tugged her laughing fiancée back down to the sand, and they raced to see who could remove impeding clothes the fastest.

Marika nudged her plate toward Rhiannon. "Be adventurous. Give it a try." *C'mon, you can do it.* "Look at it as one more new experience for today."

Rhiannon looked askance at the salmon mango roll on Marika's plate.

"Have I steered you wrong yet?"

"The day isn't finished yet." Rhiannon grinned and speared a bite. "Hmm. Not bad...for raw fish. What's that?" She pointed at a small dish that had come with their order.

"Wasabi. You may want to give that a pass."

"Why?"

"It's pretty powerful. If you're going to try it, just take a tiny bit."

Rhiannon dabbed some on the edge of her chicken and ate it. Her eyes widened; she fanned her tongue and grabbed for her water.

Marika chuckled. "I did warn you."

"Yeah, but you didn't tell me it would be like pouring dynamite through my nose."

"It is good for clearing congestion." Marika took another bite of her dinner. "So how are you feeling about your progress today?"

Rhiannon stopped a passing waiter and extended her water glass to be refilled, then drained the glass before answering. "I think it went pretty well, don't you?"

"I'd trust you to drive—at least if there weren't any dangerous dumpsters in the area."

"Hey!"

Marika grinned. *She's so easy to tease.* "No, seriously, I think you did really well for your first time out."

"Thanks. I was relieved when you took over to drive here, though. I don't think I'm up to downtown traffic."

"Maybe not yet, but it won't be long. So do you want to do anything after dinner?" *Say yes.* "I thought maybe we could go to a movie, if you felt like it."

"I'd like that. I haven't been to a theatre in quite a while."

"Wonderful. Do you prefer action, drama, comedy, science fiction?"

Rhiannon canted her head. "I just like a good story. The genre doesn't matter. Why don't you choose this time?"

And you can choose the next time. Marika smiled. "All right. Let's see what's on at Eau Claire, then."

The movie was lighthearted, and they exited the theatre laughing. Marika drove Rhiannon home, sorry to see the day end. *I wish it was last week.* Marika's desire to take Rhiannon home with her was all the more poignant for the pensive expression on Rhi's face as she gazed out the window.

Marika drove past hookers who lounged on street corners and stealthy men who congregated and dispersed with equal rapidity. Every dark alley seemed ominously alive with furtive movements.

"You turned the wrong way."

Marika realized she'd unconsciously turned in the direction of her condo. "Oh, sorry." She took the first left to get back on course. *You can't rescue her if she doesn't want rescuing.* She stole glances at Rhiannon as she tried to muster the nerve to offer the sanctuary of her home, even if only for tonight. *I hate that such a great day ends with her going back to that house.* They were nearly to Rhiannon's street. "Rhi, I was thinking—"

"Shit! Turn right! Turn right now!"

Heart pounding, Marika spun the wheel and screeched around the corner. She followed Rhiannon's instructions and drove away from the road that she had been about to enter.

"Pull over please," Rhiannon said.

Marika did and then turned. "What was that all about?"

Rhiannon just shook her head and unhooked her seat belt. She was about to climb out when Marika seized her arm. "Rhi? What the hell happened back there? What's going on?" For a long moment, Marika didn't think Rhiannon would answer.

Rhiannon's shoulders slumped, and she sat back in the seat. "It could've been dangerous for you to drive down my street right then."

"What? Why?" Marika's hand tightened on Rhiannon's arm.

Rhiannon stared out the front window and refused to meet Marika's eyes. "Some neighbours that normally aren't home on Saturday. Looks like they were having a party, and it's not safe to be around when they're partying."

Marika shook her head. "Neighbours? But I could have driven you around the back the way I normally do."

"You don't get it. Cars like this one don't come down here, at least not unless they're going to the 'stroll.' As soon as you drove past, they'd have seen you and been on you like flies on… Well, anyway, there's no way you could've stopped to let me out. This is better. I can approach the house from the rear, and they'll never see me." Rhiannon gently removed Marika's hand and reached for the door handle.

"Wait! You can't go out there if it's not safe. Just come home with me tonight, and I'll bring you back when it's daylight tomorrow, all right?"

Rhiannon shook her head. "No, but thank you." She pushed open the door and got out.

Marika leaned across the seat and held out a hand. "Please, Rhi. If it's not safe, I don't want you out there."

Rhiannon knelt by the side of the open door. "It's my world, Marika. I'll be fine. I'm used to it, remember? Look, I'll give the condo a call when I get in the house and leave a message so you know I'm safe, okay?"

Marika nodded miserably.

Rhiannon reached across the seat and patted her hand. "Go home. It was a wonderful day. Thank you again." She stood, closed the door, and started across the street. In moments, she had faded into the shadows left by broken streetlights.

Marika stared into the darkness. *I don't want this to be your world. I want so much better for you.* She shook her head, put the car in gear, and turned for home.

CHAPTER 16

MARIKA JOTTED DOWN NOTES AS she cradled the phone between her ear and shoulder. When Rhiannon poked her head in the office door, she motioned her in. "All right. We'll plan on being there Sunday, and we'll meet you in the offices on Monday. Good, see you then." Marika hung up and smiled at the excitement on Rhiannon's face. "Let me guess...parade time."

"Uh-huh." Rhiannon beamed. "Ready to go to the roof?"

"I need about five more minutes here. Why don't you save me a place?"

"Okay, look for me in the corner by the stairwell. That's the best spot." Rhiannon bounded out of the office. The vast majority of businesses adhered to the citywide edict to 'dress western' during Stampede week, and Rhiannon had complied by donning a denim skirt and embroidered denim vest over a plain white blouse.

She looks good in denim. Marika glanced down at her own caramel suede skirt and blouse with hammered silver buttons. She too enjoyed the western dress code and the excuse to get duded up. Marika quickly finished her notes, grabbed her cowboy hat, and hastened to the elevator. It was crowded with other employees heading for the roof of the building.

Marika exited onto the rooftop and surveyed the crowd. She spotted Rhiannon hanging over the edge of the parapet in the far corner, peering down at the street. Marika had been surprised at Rhiannon's enthusiasm, as she had assumed that Rhi would take the yearly excitement with her usual calm disinterest. Instead, Rhiannon had radiated eagerness ever since she'd arrived at the office that morning.

Marika edged through the crowd and came up behind Rhiannon, who turned to greet her with a grin. "Saved you a place." She indicated the open spot between her and the corner of the parapet.

Marika tugged her hat lower to protect her eyes from the bright sun and slid in next to Rhiannon. They leaned on the wall with their elbows touching as they surveyed the scene ten floors below. The streets were lined for blocks in each direction as far as Marika could see, often six and eight people deep. She glanced at adjoining rooftops and smiled. Every bit of usable space was filled with Calgarians eager to see the annual kick-off to the city's ten day party.

As they waited for the parade to wind its way past their location, Marika said, "The Tsang hearing has been moved up to a week from Monday in Vancouver."

"Tsang? Have I worked on that one?"

"No, that was Marion's baby, no pun intended. The hearing was originally scheduled for six months ago but was postponed. Now a spot has unexpectedly opened up, and the Tsangs have been slotted in. All the prep work is done, we just need to review it in the next week before we go to Vancouver."

Rhiannon's eyes widened. "We? Did you say before *we* go to Vancouver?"

"That's what I said. We. Marion was supposed to come with me, and since you're doing the same job, you're entitled to come in her place. The firm picks up all the costs: flights, hotels, and meals. It won't cost you a thing, unless you feel like playing tourist."

"Wow...Vancouver. I've never been to the coast. Heck, I've never been past Banff. We went there once on a school trip." Rhiannon beamed.

"We'll be working in conjunction with our Vancouver branch, so you'll get a chance to see your old boss, too."

"I'd like that. Mr. Owen was always very nice to me." Rhiannon looked down at the street. "But I like my new boss even better."

Marika caught her breath. "I'm glad."

Rhiannon leaned far forward and pointed. "Hey, I see the Grand Marshall. It's starting."

Alarmed, Marika grabbed the back of Rhiannon's vest. "Careful. I'd hate to have to explain to human resources how I let my assistant splatter on the pavement."

Rhiannon leaned forward at a less precarious angle. "I love parades."

"No, really?"

"When I was little, my dad used to take me to every parade there was in Toronto. I remember sitting on his shoulders so I could see over the crowd."

She's actually talking about her childhood. "Didn't your mother go with you and your dad?"

"Nah. Mom had to work days, and Dad worked nights, so they took turns taking care of me." Rhiannon smiled. "Sunday was our day to all be together. We would take the bus to the park or the zoo or down to the waterfront." Her voice trailed off.

Marika murmured encouragement, but it was apparent that Rhiannon had volunteered all the information she was going to.

The parade began to move past below them, and they compared notes on floats and bands. They admired the gaudily decorated horses, cheered the mini-chuckwagons, and laughed at the antics of the clowns running alongside and interacting with delighted viewers. But by the time the trailing street sweepers came by, cleaning up behind the horses, they were ready to leave the hot roof for the comfort of their air-conditioned office.

A couple of hours later, Marika was deep in a review of the Tsang file when Rhiannon came to the door of her office. Marika cocked her head.

Rhiannon glanced back over her shoulder. "There's someone here to see you. She doesn't have an appointment, but she said her name is Brooke Havers. She says she's your sister?"

Stunned, Marika looked past Rhiannon. A teenaged girl in a Highland band uniform fidgeted in the outer office.

The girl was tall and thin, with ash blond hair. It was like looking at a mirror image of herself, sixteen years in the past. This was the little sister she had last seen and held as a baby, a day before she had been sent in disgrace to Geneva. Marika tried to speak, but her throat closed up.

Rhiannon instantly crossed the office and knelt, resting one hand on Marika's knee. Her eyes shone with concern. "Hey, do you need me to send her away?"

Marika clutched at the hand on her knee. "No. No...I'll see her." She stood and made her way out of the office, Rhiannon close on her heels.

The girl turned as they reached the waiting area, and the sisters stared at each another.

"Brooke?" Marika's doubts vanished when she saw her father's big, grey eyes in the girl's nervous face. She held out her hand.

Brooke gave it a tentative shake. "I, uh...I'm in Calgary with my band, and I wanted to meet you."

"I'm glad you did," Marika said. "Why don't you come in, and we'll talk. Would you like something cold to drink?"

"Yes, please. It was a long, hot parade."

Marika looked at Rhiannon, who nodded and left. She gestured for Brooke to precede her into the office. Marika settled on her office couch, and Brooke sat at the far end. Her shock waned, and her manners kicked in. "Which band was yours?"

"Fifty-seventh Highland Cadet Band. We were right behind the float with the cartoon cowboy riding a bull. You know, the one with the steam puffing out of the bull's nostrils?" Brooke drummed her fingers on her legs and looked around the office.

"Oh, right. It was a good band. I've always enjoyed the pipes and drums."

"We took third in an Ontario band competition last year, and we're competing against the other Stampede bands this week. I think we might place even higher."

"What do you play?" Marika asked.

"A side drum, though by the time we finish marching, I always wish I'd chosen the fife. Still better than the bagpipes, though."

Marika smiled. "Drum, eh? So you're really popular when you practice at home?"

Brooke leaned back against the cushions and grinned. "Well, Bryce used to be a total jerk about it, and he kept threatening to punch a hole through my drum. But Dad built a soundproof practice room for me in the basement, so I don't get as many complaints anymore."

An old pain flooded Marika at the mention of their father, but she forced it back. "I take it Bryce isn't musical."

"Hah. If it's not on a computer screen, that weenie doesn't know it exists."

"I play piano myself, but I've never been in a band."

"Um, yeah, I knew that." Brooke looked at Marika with troubled eyes. "A few years ago, Bryce and I found some pictures of you in Dad's desk. There were some of you when you were little, playing the piano. We had no clue who you were, but there was a bunch of you with Dad and a woman I didn't know, so I kinda thought you were related. We look a lot alike."

"We do," Marika said. "May I ask how you found me?"

Brooke frowned. "Bryce and I asked Mom about the pictures. I don't think she knew Dad had them in his desk, because she got really mad. They had a big fight about it. Anyway, she told us that you were Dad's daughter from a previous marriage, but that you'd died in your teens."

To them I suppose I did. Marika had seen her father a few times since her banishment, but always well away from his wife and children. He paid her way through law school and gave her a generous allowance until she was on her feet but made it clear that was the extent of their relationship.

Brooke studied her face.

Marika tried to mask the hurt that she had never fully vanquished.

Rhiannon entered with two bottles of orange juice.

Marika accepted the drinks and passed one to her sister. Rhiannon held her gaze for a long moment, and Marika saw both sympathy and support there before Rhiannon left the office and closed the door.

"So, if you thought I was dead, how did you find me?" Marika sipped her juice.

Brooke drained half her bottle in one drink. "Sorry. I'm pretty thirsty."

"There's lots more if you want it."

"Nah, this should be good. Well, Bryce and I would talk now and then about the sister we had never known, and one day we even went back into Dad's study to see the pictures again, but they were gone. It wasn't until last year that I was looking for something in his cabinet, and I saw a file labeled Calgary. We'd just found out that our band was going to the Stampede, so I was curious to see what he had on the city. Was I ever surprised when I saw all the old pictures of you, plus some newer things—a newspaper article, a graduation program from Osgoode Hall with your name highlighted, things like that."

"That's how you knew I was in Calgary?"

"Since the file was labeled Calgary, that's where I started my search. It didn't take long to find out that you were an associate with McGregor, Cohen, and Kurst." Brooke grinned.

Marika smiled. "So, my little sister is a detective, is she?"

"The one thing I don't know is why my parents lied to us, and why you're not part of our family. What did you do that was so bad?"

Marika drew a deep breath. *Do I tell her the truth? What if she rejects me too?* She gave her head a tiny shake. *What do I have to lose? It's not like she was in my life before, so if she vanishes again, why should I care?* But Marika did care. "May I ask you something first?"

Brooke nodded.

"I know how you found me, but why did you look for me?"

Brooke canted her head. "I guess a lot of it was curiosity. I mean, you didn't seem like some big criminal or anything, and you obviously meant enough to Dad that he kept all his mementos even though Mom didn't want him to. It was the whole thing about having a sister I wasn't aware of. I wanted to know her…to know you, and fill in some of the blanks."

Marika's gaze drifted from Brooke to Rhiannon working at her desk. There was a small furrow in her brow that Rhiannon always got when she pondered something. The sight soothed Marika, and she turned back to Brooke. "Your parents didn't approve of who I am, and they didn't want me around for fear that I'd…influence you and Bryce."

"Who you are? Who are you really?" A hint of edginess crept back into Brooke's voice.

"I'm gay." Marika almost laughed at the way Brooke's eyebrows shot up. *It really is like looking in a mirror.*

"That's it? Just because you're gay? For crying out loud, this is the twenty-first century. I can't believe they'd banish you for that."

Marika warmed at the indignation in her sister's voice. "Well, it was only the twentieth century when it happened, and I was caught in a compromising position with an older woman in their house when I was sixteen." Marika shrugged. "They decided it was better for all concerned if I were educated outside of the country."

"That sucks!"

"They did what they felt they had to, to protect their children."

"Well, you were Dad's child, too, and he sure didn't do much to protect you."

Marika's eyes closed, and she fought back tears. The anguish of abandonment swept over her, and she was again the lonely, bewildered girl who had been deserted by her beloved father. She swallowed hard and was startled to feel a warm hand take hers. She opened her eyes.

Brooke gazed at her.

Neither said anything as Marika struggled for control. She finally took a deep breath and forced herself to relax. "Do you by any chance have any pictures of your family?"

"I thought you might want to see them, so I brought along a bunch of photos." Brooke took an envelope out of her purse. She pulled the first picture out and laid it on Marika's lap. "That's Bryce the weenie."

Marika studied the picture of her brother. He was cut from the same cloth as his sisters, tall and thin, with a shock of pale blond hair falling over a narrow face. He had been snapped sticking his tongue out at his sister, and Marika couldn't help laughing.

"This is Dad when we went to the cottage about a month ago." Brooke passed over another photo.

Marika studied her father. She hadn't seen him in years, but he hadn't changed much. Even squatting beside the sailboat moored at the landing, he clearly was still lean. A baseball cap covered his hair. *I wonder if he's bald or grey now.*

The next picture was of her father with Brooke's mother. Marika suppressed the vestiges of bitterness at the woman largely responsible for her estrangement and murmured noncommittally. They went through the rest of the photos, and when they were done, Marika looked at her sister. "Thank you. I really appreciate that." She held out the stack.

Brooke shook her head. "No, you keep them. I had them printed for you."

Marika's breath caught, and tears welled up in her eyes.

Brooke smiled, then glanced at her watch. "Darn! I have to go. I only got an hour's dispensation from Madame Gorgon, and then I have to meet everyone back at the school we're bunking in."

"Madame Gorgon?"

"Oh yeah. It's actually Mrs. Gordon, but that's what all the kids call her." Brooke rolled her eyes. "She's the wife of the band director, and she takes personal responsibility for keeping us all in line when we're on trips. Believe me, we don't get away with anything."

Marika stood up with her sister, amused at Brooke's aggrieved tone. *Why do I think Brooke and her bandmates make Mrs. Gordon's job as tough as they can?* "Are you here long? Do you think we could get together again?"

Brooke sighed. "I wish we could, but the next couple of days are booked solid with activities and competitions. This was pretty much the only time I could get free before we fly home again."

Marika tried to smile. *Stop hoping for more. Just be grateful she came by.*

Brooke regarded her. "Would you like my e-mail address? We could maybe write now and then, if you want."

"I'd like that. I'll give you mine, too. But won't your folks be upset if we correspond?"

Brooke stiffened. "I have no intention of telling them. Do you?"

Marika was uneasy at deceiving her father and Brooke's mother, though not for herself.

"What they did wasn't right," Brooke said. "I can't do anything about the past, but I can reclaim my sister...if she'll let me back in her life."

Struck by Brooke's resolve, Marika nodded. "I'd really like that."

They exchanged information, and after the formalities were taken care of, they faced each other. Marika opened her arms in invitation, and Brooke slid into her embrace. Finally Brooke broke away, mumbled goodbye, and left.

Marika followed her to the outer office, stood next to Rhiannon's desk, and watched her sister walk away.

"Everything okay?" Rhiannon asked.

Marika stared after Brooke. "Oh yes. Most definitely okay."

Hemmed in by Lee and Dana on one side and Marika on the other, Rhiannon leaned on the railing and stared down the oval track, awed by the thunder of hooves. Chuckwagons careened around the turn into the homestretch four abreast. Their outriders raced close behind them. The drivers stood and whipped their teams into a frenzy, striving for every last bit of speed.

Rhiannon gaped as they roared by her and crossed the finish line. She shook her head. *I certainly understand why they call it "half a mile of hell!" I thought nothing could top the bullriding, but this was unbelievable.*

Walking back to their seats, Rhiannon couldn't stop grinning. *This has been one of the best days of my life.* They'd started early, ridden most of the rides on the midway, checked out all the barn exhibits and animals, listened to the bands in the Nashville North tent, watched the rodeo, and eaten more food than she could remember ever putting away in a single day. Lee won Dana a large stuffed tiger that she carried around the entire day. Rhiannon tried her hand at the hoop toss. Her unspoken wish was to win something for Marika, but she came up empty, much to her disappointment.

"Well, that was the last race of the night," Lee said. "They're going to set up for the Grandstand Show now. D'you guys want to stay for that?"

Marika shrugged. "I've seen it many times, so I'm okay either way, but maybe Rhiannon would like to."

Rhiannon shook her head. "I don't think this day could be improved on, but whatever you all want is fine with me."

"What did you have in mind, hon?" Dana asked.

"I was thinking we could maybe drop into The Arc. They've got it set up like a barn dance, with a live band. I'd like to dance with my fiancée, and they've got the biggest floor in town."

Marika glanced at Rhiannon "Maybe that's not such a good idea."

"Why not?" Lee followed her gaze. "Oh, right, never thought of that."

"Thought of what? What are you two talking about?" Rhiannon asked.

"Unlike Oly's, which is a mixed bar, The Arc en Ciel is strictly a lesbian club, and they're worried that you might not be comfortable there," Dana said.

Rhiannon shrugged. "It doesn't bother me. Besides, it does sound like fun."

"Let's go, then," Lee said. "The night is young, and my boots were made for dancing."

They followed Lee down the aisle and out of the grandstands. As they ambled across the Stampede grounds, Rhiannon happily absorbed the atmosphere: carnival noises, country music, bright flashing lights, the smell of beer and fried food, and the rowdy ambience of throngs of people out for the city's annual party.

They set out for the car, which was parked blocks away. Lee and Dana walked ahead; Marika and Rhiannon followed.

"You're sure you're okay with this, Rhi?"

"Absolutely. Besides, would you deny Lee the chance to dance?"

They glanced ahead to where Lee had her arm around Dana's shoulders as they playfully tussled over the stuffed tiger.

"No, I wouldn't want to do that. But if you do feel at all uncomfortable, you'll let me know, right?"

"I will," Rhiannon said. "But really, what would make me uncomfortable?"

Marika looked Rhiannon up and down. "Well, for one thing, you might want to decide how you're going to handle all the invitations to dance."

Startled, Rhiannon glanced down at her clothes. She had splurged on a new pair of jeans and a stonewashed denim shirt that currently had the sleeves rolled halfway up her forearms, but she didn't think it was anything fancy, especially compared to what the others had on. She wasn't even wearing boots, just her old runners. Lee and Dana had flashy satin cowboy shirts—pearl buttons and all—with jeans, cowboy boots, and hats. She could tell they were having a great time playing dress-up. But Marika... Marika had almost taken Rhiannon's breath away when they'd met that morning. She wore an ivory-coloured silk blouse tucked into dark brown tailored pants, with short, low-heeled boots and dangling gold earrings. "I'll just stand behind you, and then I won't have to worry about anyone asking me to dance."

"What if I were to ask you to dance?" Marika asked. "Just to save you from the inevitable suitors, of course."

For a split second, Rhiannon imagined herself in Marika's arms and felt dizzy. "I don't know how to dance. I wouldn't want to embarrass you."

Marika murmured an indistinct response as they crossed another street.

Rhiannon kicked at a loose piece of pavement. *Dumbass. When will you ever get another chance like that?*

"It seems to me, this would be the perfect time to learn," Marika said, interrupting Rhiannon's brooding. "You're with friends. We won't laugh at you. I'll teach you how to two-step, if you like."

A frisson rippled through Rhiannon's body. "Yeah, I guess. If you're sure you want to risk your toes."

"They've been abused by bigger women than you, Rhiannon Davies." Marika raised her voice. "Isn't that right, Lee?"

Lee looked over her shoulder. "Isn't what right?"

"My feet have been danced on by bigger women than Rhi."

Dana started to laugh, and Lee groaned. "You're just never going to let me live that down, are you? It was my first Stampede. I didn't know a two-step from a foxtrot."

Marika tilted her head toward Rhiannon. "Lee is very... enthusiastic...on the dance floor. You'll notice that Dana is wearing her steel-toed boots."

Rhiannon chuckled. *This is going to be great. What a perfect day.*

They soon reached Dana's car and navigated through busy streets to the old converted warehouse down by the railroad yards. The Arc's entrance had been converted to look like a barn door, with hay bales, wooden barrels, and a section of plank fencing lining the way to the entrance.

Lee paid their cover charge and shook her head when Rhiannon tried to give her money. "Buy me a beer later. Now it's time to dance."

They were greeted by the sound of a country band. Dancers crowded a large wooden floor, many in garb that made Lee and Dana's look decorous. The stage was on one side of the dance floor, and a horseshoe-shaped bar bustling with patrons was on the other. The western theme continued throughout. Women were perched on the bales scattered around the interior. Servers with Calgary's iconic white cowboy hats circulated among the multitude of small tables that ringed the dance floor. Their black leather aprons were stuffed with bills that reflected the patrons' enthusiastic stampeding.

Lee led the way through the crowd. She greeted many of the club goers as she pushed through to a free table on the far side between the dance floor and the bar. Once they'd staked their claim, she and Dana tossed their hats on the table and headed for the floor.

Rhiannon sat beside Marika and watched the dancers and the band. Because she was accustomed to Lee and Dana's candid affection, Rhiannon wasn't taken aback at the sight of women dancing together and flirting openly. Her gaze drifted around the darker corners of the club, and she did a double take as she spotted AJ Darcy leaning against a pile of hay bales with a woman in her arms. Rhiannon looked away with a grin.

"What's so funny?" Marika's voice sounded right next to her ear, the only way she could be heard in the din of music and voices.

"A friend of yours," Rhiannon said. She leaned closer, catching the scent of Marika's hair, and pointed out the firefighter and her date.

Marika eyed the amorous couple and shrugged. "Not really a friend. I only talked to her once, though she did leave a phone message asking me out last weekend."

Rhiannon stiffened and glared at Darcy before she realized what she was doing and looked away. "Did you go out?"

Marika shook her head. "No. I had better things to do." She smiled at Rhiannon. "I had to teach a certain someone how not to run into dumpsters and how to appreciate Japanese cuisine."

She turned down a date with that...firefighter to spend the day with me? Rhiannon stared at Marika, but she had turned away to watch Lee and Dana.

A server stopped at their table. "What can I get you ladies?" Her eyes scanned her other customers as she waited for their order.

"A couple of drafts, whatever you have on tap is fine, and...Rhi? Do you want to try a wine cooler?"

Rhiannon nodded. She'd never had one but trusted Marika to choose.

"And two peach coolers," Marika said.

The server hurried off, and Rhiannon pulled out her wallet. When Marika tried to make her put it away, she shook her head. "No, this one is mine. I owe Lee a beer, remember?"

The out-of-breath dancers arrived back at their table at the same time as the drinks. Lee downed half her beer in one swallow, while Dana sipped hers.

Rhiannon signaled her approval of the cooler, and Marika smiled.

Lee and Dana alternated between the dance floor and their table, but it took the whole cooler before Rhiannon worked up the courage to dance. Marika led her to the least crowded corner of the floor.

When the ubiquitous two-step started up again, Marika positioned Rhiannon's hands and held her. "That's it, step, step, slide. You're doing great."

Rhiannon fell into the pattern easily and followed Marika's lead as they whirled around the edge of the crowded floor.

"It's easier if you don't watch your feet," Marika said.

Rhiannon looked at her partner and quickly forgot her nervousness. When the dance ended, Marika held Rhiannon's hand and waited for the next number. When it turned out to be a slow dance, she cocked her head at Rhiannon.

Rhiannon nodded, her heart thundering in her ears.

Marika drew Rhiannon into her arms and led them in a waltz.

Rhiannon stumbled. "Sorry." *Stupid feet.*

Marika chuckled and held Rhiannon closer.

Rhiannon forgot how to breathe. The warmth of Marika's body and the feel of her cheek against Rhiannon's hair overwhelmed her and she shivered.

Marika leaned back to look at her. "Are you okay?"

"Yes." *Oh, God. Am I?*

When the dance ended, Marika asked, "Want to sit the next one out?"

"Sure." *No, I want to stay right here.* Rhiannon followed Marika back to their table. She caught her breath and finished her cooler, but as soon as another dance started, she stood and extended her hand to Marika.

Marika accepted the invitation with a smile.

Four selections later, another slow dance began. Without asking, Marika opened her arms and Rhiannon stepped into them. It seemed the most natural thing in the world for her to rest her head on Marika's shoulder. Their arms tightened around each other. When the music ended they hadn't moved very far, but Rhiannon didn't mind. *Best dance so far.*

The pace picked up again, and for the next hour they stayed out on the floor. Rhiannon mastered the two-step, thrilled to each slow dance, and even tried a polka, hop and all. That attempt left them laughing and they went back to their table for a rest.

Rhiannon dropped into her chair, and Marika placed a hand on her shoulder. When Rhiannon looked up, Marika gestured toward the back of the club. "I'm just going to the washroom. I'll be back in a moment, okay?"

Rhiannon nodded, and Marika walked away. When Rhiannon realized where her gaze had settled, she flushed and stared at the tabletop. Grateful that Lee and Dana were on the dance floor, she breathed deeply and tried to collect herself. *I should probably stop drinking. It's making my head dizzy.* She rolled the bottle in her hands. It was her third, but she'd barely touched it.

"Hi, would you like to dance?" A sandy-haired woman with a friendly smile knelt beside her and waited for an answer.

"Um, I..." A familiar touch settled on Rhiannon's shoulders.

The stranger glanced up. "Oh, sorry. Didn't know you two were together." She gave an amiable nod and retreated into the crowd.

Rhiannon looked up at Marika. "Saving me from suitors?"

"Only if you want me to. Did you want to dance with her?"

Rhiannon laid her hands over Marika's. "Nope. I've just barely got you broken in."

Marika laughed and took her hand. "Then let's hit the floor."

By the time the band called last dance, Rhiannon's feet were sore. But held closely in Marika's arms for the final tune, she was thoroughly contented. When the song ended, they joined the crowd and exited the club. Outside, Rhiannon realized that Marika still held her hand. She glanced at her, then down at their interlocked hands.

Marika instantly relinquished her grip. "Oh, sorry."

"No problem."

They were silent as they walked to the car. Rhiannon curled her hand. It felt empty.

Once inside the car, Dana fastened her seat belt and asked, "Where to first?"

Marika turned to Rhiannon. "It's past two a.m. Why don't you stay at my place tonight, and I'll run you home in the morning?"

Rhiannon thought for a second. *I could sneak in without Hettie hearing me, but what a lousy way to end a perfect day.* "All right, but only if I take the daybed this time. I'm not putting you out of your own bed again."

Marika nodded. "Can you drop us both at my place?"

"Sure," Dana said and started the car.

The ride to Marika's condo was quiet. Once there, Rhiannon and Marika bade Lee and Dana goodnight, then left the car and entered the building.

Lee looked at her partner. "Am I right?"

Dana nodded. "Could be, love."

"You don't seem too happy about it."

"I like Rhiannon very much, you know that."

"But?" Lee caressed Dana's hair.

"But I'm worried. What if she's only experiencing her first crush, and it really doesn't have anything to do with

Marika? What if our friend loses her heart to that young woman, only to have it broken again when Rhiannon moves on?" Dana sighed. "I'm not sure how many more times that can happen before Marika doesn't have much left to break."

"From what I saw tonight, they at least deserve a chance," Lee said. "There was a helluva lot of chemistry crackling out on that dance floor."

"I'm not denying that, hon. I'm just not sure it'll be enough."

Lee groaned. "I'm too tired to think about this tonight. Let's go home."

"Okay. I have to soak my feet anyway."

"All that walking and dancing wore them out, eh?"

Dana raised one eyebrow. "Sure, love. Let's go with that."

CHAPTER 17

THE AIRCRAFT TAXIED FOR TAKE-OFF. Marika glanced at Rhiannon, who stared out the window. *I wonder if she'll be a white-knuckle flier.*

Their flight lifted off, and when they leveled at altitude, Rhiannon turned to her with a grin. "That was fun."

"I'm glad you liked it. Enjoy it while it lasts. It's not a long flight between Calgary and Vancouver." Marika enjoyed Rhiannon's obvious delight in their trip. What would normally have been routine business had turned into an adventure as Rhiannon reveled in every aspect of the journey. *She didn't even mind standing in line for forty-five minutes to check in. I wonder if I was this excited on my first flight.* Marika remembered her destination on that occasion and grimaced. *Geneva. No, I was definitely not excited about that flight.*

"Would either of you ladies care for a headset?"

Marika was drawn out of her memories by the flight attendant extending two headsets.

Rhiannon looked from the headset to Marika.

Marika smiled. "You'll need one if you want to listen to audio or watch video."

"Oh." Rhiannon shook her head and held up her book. "No, thank you. I brought along my own entertainment."

Marika declined a headset as well, and the flight attendant moved down the aisle.

Rhiannon left her book closed. "What is the hearing going to be like?"

"Well, we'll represent Dr. Tsang, his wife and children. The opposing counsel represents the Minister of Immigration, and the board hearing the case generally has one or two members. We'll present our case for refugee status, and opposing counsel will try to poke holes in our arguments. The board may rule immediately but more likely will reserve judgment for a few weeks."

Rhiannon nodded. "Okay. And what are my duties?"

"To tell you the truth, most of your work was done when we prepared the case. I'd originally planned to bring Marion along both as a reward for her hard work and as a training exercise. When you're doing the research I need, I think it's easier if you have a clear idea of what the end results are."

"So normally I wouldn't have come?" Rhiannon asked.

"That's right. Usually only the lawyer goes, but when the hearing was first scheduled, I secured permission for Marion to accompany me, so as her replacement, you received the same consideration."

"Are you sure it's okay with the firm?"

"Definitely," Marika said. "I talked to Daniel myself."

Rhiannon nodded at the invocation of the senior partner. She settled back in her seat and opened her book.

Marika took the Tsang file out of her briefcase but found herself unable to focus on it. Instead, her thoughts turned, as they so often did, to the evolving friendship between her and Rhiannon. When Rhiannon had stayed the night with her after they returned from dancing, it had taken stern resolve to simply make up the day bed for her guest and bid her goodnight before going to her own room.

Would she have come to my bed if I asked? Every now and then, Marika caught Rhiannon watching her with a confused look in her eyes, as if she was trying to comprehend something foreign to her. *She might've. Do I want to ask? Yes...no...I don't know. It's so unprofessional to even think about it.* Marika sighed. *Besides, with my track record, all I'd do is ruin another friendship.*

Rhiannon hadn't turned a page, and Marika glanced at her. Though she was looking at the book, she seemed a million miles away. *Join the crowd, my young friend.* Marika took a deep breath and forced her attention back on the file.

When they reached Vancouver, they checked into the Sandler Arms and immediately opened the connecting door between their rooms. Marika left her suitcase unpacked to lean against the doorjamb and watch Rhiannon examine all the features of her room. She chuckled when Rhiannon picked up the charge sheet for the courtesy bar.

"Geez, have you seen what they're asking for a can of Coke? Or a tiny bag of nuts?" Rhiannon glared at the charge sheet. "Who the heck would pay this when you can buy something five times the size for a quarter of the amount?"

"You'd be surprised. Sometimes when you get to your room after a long day of work, you just don't care about economizing."

Rhiannon frowned at Marika. "Well, I'm not going to be suckered."

Marika laughed. "Good for you. So still on the topic of food, do you want to go to dinner soon? When I talked to Len, he recommended a place on Burrard Street, not too far from here."

Rhiannon brightened. "Sounds good. Did Mr. Owen say if he'd see us in the office?"

"He's got a morning meeting, but he said he'd try to see us later in the day."

They left the hotel and found the recommended restaurant. They dined on sweet basil crepes and pan-baked fresh salmon filet with a blackberry-tarragon sauce. Marika managed to conceal the cost from Rhiannon by putting everything on her corporate card.

Despite a light drizzle, they walked the sea wall around Stanley Park to work off the fine dinner. The waves of the Pacific slapped a concrete barrier on one side. Stands of stately Douglas fir, hemlock, and cedar—broken periodically by lushly cultured gardens—grew in profusion on the other.

Marika enjoyed her own city, but had to admit that for sheer urban beauty, Vancouver won out.

Rhiannon had never seen the ocean, so she lay on the wall to dip her fingers in the water.

Marika didn't quite trust Rhiannon to not fall in, but she was amused by the face Rhi made when she licked her fingers.

"It really is salty." Rhiannon stood and wiped her fingers on her pants.

"Well, it is the Pacific." Marika nodded toward the bay, where a catamaran tacked to avoid a yacht under full sail. "Pretty, aren't they?"

"Yes. And there sure are a lot of them. I'm kind of surprised they go out in this weather."

"Living around here, you'd never get outdoors if you were afraid of a little rain."

Rhiannon laughed and pointed just ahead of them. A couple of seagulls squabbled over a piece of bread that had been dropped on the path. They watched until the dispute was resolved and the victor flew off with the crust in its beak. They resumed their walk.

"So, what's the schedule for tomorrow?" Rhiannon asked.

"I'd like to check in with the office by eight. The hearing is scheduled to start at nine thirty at the IRB," Marika said, referencing the Immigration and Refugee Board. "It's a fairly complex case. I expect it will take most of the day, but we should be done by dinnertime. I thought maybe we could go to Gastown for the evening, and then, assuming the hearing doesn't go into a second day, we'll fly home the next morning."

"Gastown?" Rhiannon cocked her head at Marika.

"Uh-huh. It's a historic part of the city, complete with cobblestones and fancy lampposts, and full of native craft shops, art galleries, and antique stores. It's a great place for people watching, and you can find anything from gourmet dining to bistros and sidewalk cafes, to pubs and comedy clubs. I thought you might enjoy checking it out with me."

"Sounds great." Rhiannon grinned and picked up a wet stone to skim across the waves.

The stone bounced twice and sank.

Marika smiled. *I know this is business, but I'll bet this is as close as she's come to a real vacation.*

Rhiannon picked up another stone and juggled it. "I should bring something home for Marion's baby. I definitely owe the little guy."

"Yes, the baby's timing was your gain...and mine."

Rhiannon glanced up, then looked away quickly.

Uh-oh. I have to watch that. I don't want her to worry for even a moment that I might take advantage of her. Marika shook her head. *And I won't. She'll never make the first move, so all I need to do is not make any advances, and all will be well.* "So do you think you have a good grasp of our case?"

Rhiannon nodded. "I think so. I spent quite a bit of time on the file last week."

"Okay, run through the high points for me."

"Tsang Ah-zhen was a doctor in southeastern China. Because he saw countless newly delivered infants murdered by regional family planning officers, he was well aware of the penalty for exceeding the official one-child policy. When his wife got pregnant a second time and someone turned her in, she was forced to have a late-term abortion."

"That was bad enough, but Dr. Tsang told me about some of the things he saw, and they were almost unimaginable." Marika shook her head.

"I know. I read the file. I haven't said this before, but working for you has really made me think."

Marika looked at Rhiannon. "About what?"

Rhiannon gazed out over the water. "When I ended up with Hettie, I thought I was in hell. It was the worst thing that had happened to me, aside from losing my parents. But then I read about a man who sees his wife raped by security forces or a doctor forced to stand aside while infants are killed, and I really didn't have it so bad."

Marika ached to put an arm around Rhiannon's shoulders. *You were a child. I may not know all the details, but I know a wounded soul when I see one.* She kept her hands in her pockets.

Rhiannon flashed a smile at Marika. "Sorry, I got off track there. Anyway, Mrs. Tsang got pregnant for a third time and though she hid in their home, someone ratted her out again. This time, though, they were tipped off and fled to Canada. They went to Calgary, where his brother-in-law helped them get established and file a petition for refugee status. The hearing was transferred to Vancouver when they moved here last year."

Marika forced herself to focus on the case. "What are the strongest points of our case?"

"First is their very real fear of prosecution should they be returned to China, with the possibility that their younger daughter, who was born in Canada, would be subjected to persecution as an 'illegal birth.' Also, according to our government guidelines, Dr. Tsang, as a physician, is a 'desirable' immigrant. Third, the couple has a strong support system already in place and hasn't drawn on Canadian social assistance programs." Rhiannon looked at Marika. "Will it be enough, do you think?"

"I think with the documents that Dr. Tsang brought with him, it should be. I expect a favourable result, but you don't always know how the board will rule. We just have to present the strongest case we can."

Rhiannon walked along for a few moments, then stopped and put her hand on Marika's arm. "Thank you for bringing me along. I'm really looking forward to watching the hearing tomorrow. Not to mention that I've been having a blast playing tourist. You're a wonderful guide."

"It's been my pleasure. You're a good traveling companion," Marika said. "I think you'll get a lot out of the hearing, and once the work is done, we can enjoy the evening."

"Sounds great."

They strolled on. Marika found that, despite the light rain, there was an inner glow keeping her warm. No matter how she might resist, the feeling was closely linked to the woman keeping pace beside her.

Marika began to place papers in her briefcase. It had been a long day, but she was pleased with their presentation.

Rhiannon took the briefcase from her to finish packing up the documents.

Marika turned to the Chinese man and his wife sitting at the long table beside her and offered her hand. "I think it went well, Dr. Tsang. As soon as I receive notification of the Board's decision, I'll contact you."

Dr. Tsang inclined his head and shook her hand. "Thank you, Ms. Havers. My wife and I are very grateful for your help. We look forward to hearing from you."

The couple made their departure, and Marika turned to Rhiannon. "We just have to make a brief stop at the office, and then we're free for the evening, all right?"

"Okay. Maybe Mr. Owen will be back by now. I'd like to see him before we leave."

Marika, too, hoped Len was around. *He's not even going to recognize Rhi. She's changed so much since she first started working for me.* The changes were most apparent when Rhiannon was with her, Lee, and Dana, but even around others, much of the stark suspicion that had clung to Rhiannon like armour had vanished. *I doubt the other assistants call her Miss Ice anymore.*

A brisk ten-minute walk brought them to the doors of the firm's Vancouver branch. After Marika left the documents with the office manager, they took the elevator to the ninth floor.

Len was in his office. "Marika! Rhiannon! I hoped you'd make it back before you left town." He hugged Marika and offered his hand to Rhiannon.

She beamed and shook his hand. "Hi, Mr. Owen. It's really great to see you again."

Len's eyebrows shot up. "It's great to see you, too, Rhiannon. Are you enjoying Vancouver?"

"Oh yes, and that restaurant you recommended was fabulous. We had a wonderful meal there last night, didn't we, Marika?" Rhiannon turned to Marika.

Len's jaw dropped.

Marika suppressed a smirk. "We did, and we hope to find a place just as good tonight."

"I just have to make a quick stop before we head back to the hotel." Rhiannon excused herself and left the office.

Len turned to Marika. "What the hell did you do to my assistant?"

Marika smiled. "Do? Whatever do you mean?"

"In two years I couldn't get her to call me anything but Mr. Owen, and she sure as hell never went out for a meal with me. Did you do a personality transplant or something?"

"No, that's all her. I didn't do anything special, really." Marika grinned at the disbelief in her colleague's eyes. Before he could grill her further, Harrison Kurst stepped through the door.

"Ah, Marika. I'm glad I caught up with you before you left." He held out his hand.

"Harrison. It's nice to see you, as always," Marika said, greeting the senior partner. They exchanged courteous chitchat on the disposition of her case and the latest news from the Calgary branch.

Harrison turned to Owen. "You'll be at the reception, Len?"

"Of course. In fact, I was going to suggest that I walk over with Marika. She and her assistant are staying at the Sandler Arms."

Harrison nodded. "Wonderful, then why don't you join us, Marika? It's being held in one of their conference rooms at the top of the tower. Wonderful view of the city and the harbour from there."

Oh no. No, no, no. I have plans! "I'm afraid I have no idea what you're talking about."

The senior partner smiled. "Sorry, we did rather spring that on you, didn't we? But it would be an excellent idea to have a representative from the Calgary branch there as well, and I can't think of anyone better. Right, it's settled, then. I'll see you two over there." Harrison left no opening for protests as he strode out of the office, past Rhiannon, who had slipped back in.

Marika turned on Len. "What the hell was that all about? I have plans for tonight, and I don't want to break them."

Len grimaced. "I'm sorry. I shouldn't have mentioned where you're staying. I never thought..."

Marika frowned and crossed her arms. "So, what is this stupid reception all about, and why is Harrison so keen on me being there?"

"It's just your basic suck-up assignment. Palmer DeAndre of DeAndre Shipping and Transport fame is one of the firm's biggest clients. He and his wife Sandra put on this annual reception to thank contributors to their charitable foundation. Attendance is pretty much mandatory for us since Harrison is on their board of directors, and a lot of McGregor, Cohen, and Kurst business is tied up with DeAndre Shipping." Len regarded Marika apologetically. "If it helps any, they do put on a terrific spread, and it's an open bar."

"I don't care. I don't want to go."

Len fidgeted. "I don't think it was a suggestion. Besides, all you have to do is make an appearance and schmooze for an hour, and then you can slip out. Hell, there are usually over five hundred people there, so no one's going to notice. Just make sure that Kurst sees you there."

Rhiannon crossed the room. "Mr. Owen, would you excuse us for a moment?"

He nodded and made a quick exit.

"Marika, it's okay."

Marika scowled. "No, it's not. I want to take you to Gastown."

Rhiannon laid a hand on her arm. "We can do both. You go to the reception for an hour or so, then come back and pick me up at the room. We'll still have lots of time. It's only six thirty now, so even if we don't leave until eight or nine, the night will still be young."

Marika shook her head. "This is not the way I pictured tonight."

"I know, but sometimes you have to be flexible. He is a senior partner, and he obviously expects you to be there. Go, and when you come back, we'll have some fun, okay?"

Marika looked at Rhiannon. "When did you get to be so darned persuasive?"

Rhiannon grinned. "Comes from hanging around lawyers."

Len poked his head back into the office. "Everything all right?"

"Yes, I'll play the stupid schmooze game...but not for long," Marika said. "And if Harrison has a problem with that, he can take it up with Daniel or Ian."

Len ignored her truculent tone and grabbed his suit jacket. "Let's go, then. The sooner we get over there, the sooner you can leave." He led the way to the elevators.

Marika lagged behind and whispered to Rhiannon, "When exactly did I lose control of our plans?"

Rhiannon said nothing, but her eyes twinkled and she linked arms to hurry Marika's pace.

Marika sighed. *Guess I'm going to the damned reception, but I'll be out of there inside of an hour come hell or high water.*

Marika set her briefcase and purse on a chair. She slipped her keycard into a pocket and went to the open door between their rooms.

Rhiannon had already changed into jeans and a casual shirt.

Marika shook her head. "Lucky girl."

Rhiannon grinned and flopped on her bed.

"I'll be back before long, okay?"

"Okay. Have fun, and I'll see you in a bit." Rhiannon waved and opened her book.

Marika lingered for a moment, then joined Len in the hall. They took an elevator to the twenty-first floor. "Tell me about our hosts. What exactly is the reception about?"

"Palmer DeAndre has made billions from his shipping and transport empire, so he and his wife set up a charitable foundation to spread some of the wealth around. She's the one who mostly administers the foundation, while he just keeps on making more billions."

"So they're the local power couple?" Marika asked.

Len nodded. "One of several. But they're actually quite low-key about it. They tend not to seek out publicity. From what I understand, they've set up a number of foundation offices across North America and even into Europe and Asia.

She travels a lot of on behalf of the DeAndre Foundation. You'll see the lower mainland's elite here tonight, which is why Harrison insists that we be seen as well."

The cream of Vancouver society can jump in the bay as far as I'm concerned. I'd much rather be in Gastown with Rhi. The elevator deposited them in a foyer crowded with elegantly dressed men and women. Marika sighed. *Oh well, I might as well get it over with.* She followed Len's lead as he greeted people and made small talk. Eventually, they made their way through the throng and into the huge reception hall.

A long buffet table—done up with white linens, fresh flowers, and heavy silver serving dishes—lined one wall. It was presided over by several men in tall chef's hats. A phalanx of black-clad waiters circulated among the guests, offering hors d'oeuvres and drinks.

Marika and Len snagged glasses of wine from a passing waiter and continued to network. They passed the floor-to-ceiling windows, and Marika stopped to admire the view. Outside, the sun still sparkled off the waters of English Bay, and a profusion of white sails dotted the waves. She quelled a desire to be out there or anywhere but here, as long as it was with Rhiannon. "Let's find Harrison, so he knows we've made an appearance."

Len scanned the large and growing crowd. "Over there." He tipped his glass in the direction of a small stage near the windows. "In fact, he's talking to DeAndre himself, so maybe you'll be able to kill two birds with one stone. I have to corner Harrison on another matter myself, since I didn't get the chance at the office."

"Then lead on." They walked toward the senior partner, who was conversing with a tall, white-haired man.

"Ah, good to see you two." Harrison turned to the other man. "Palmer, I'd like you to meet two of our brightest associates. This is Marika Havers from our Calgary branch and Len Owen from our Vancouver office. Marika, Len... this is Palmer DeAndre."

"It's nice to meet you." DeAndre extended his hand. Marika took it. "Mr. DeAndre."

He smiled. "Palmer, please." He nodded at Len and shook his hand as well. "I'm so glad you could join us this evening."

"Our pleasure." Len spoke for both of them.

The conversation resumed. Since the discussion revolved around the upcoming provincial election, Marika sipped her wine and listened. She was impressed that DeAndre didn't attempt to dominate the small group. He paid attention and didn't run roughshod over contrary opinions. *He seems like a nice enough fellow. Pretty down to earth for a multi-billionaire. I suppose this won't be as bad as I feared. It's like Rhi said. We'll still have lots of time to be together.*

They chatted for a while, and then Len said, "Palmer, would you excuse me if I borrow Harrison for a few moments? It's an office matter that unfortunately can't wait."

DeAndre nodded, and the men drew away. "So, what brings you to our fair city, Marika...business or pleasure?"

"Business, mostly. But I've also enjoyed a bit of playing tourist. It certainly is beautiful here."

"You know, I've traveled all over the world, and I've yet to see any place that can compare," DeAndre said. "My wife, Sandra, travels extensively on behalf of our foundation, and I know she misses home terribly when she's away. She's always so glad when she returns. I don't know how she keeps up the pace. I wish I had half her energy."

"She must be a remarkable woman to devote so much of her time and energy to philanthropic endeavours." Marika was impressed by the man's obvious admiration for his wife.

"Yes, she's incredible." Palmer smiled fondly. He nodded toward a group by the window. "She's just over there, no doubt twisting a few arms for her latest project. She's so good at it that they never even know what they've agreed to until she turns up at their door to collect. Oh, here she comes now. I'll introduce you." Palmer's eyes lit up as he looked over Marika's shoulder.

She turned to meet Sandra DeAndre, and froze.

An elegant woman of average height and build approached. Her brown hair was swept back in a chignon, and she wore a designer dress in black and silver, with diamond drop earrings and a matching pendant. Sandra nodded to Marika and extended her hand to her husband. "Hello, Palmer. Did you miss me?"

Palmer bent over her hand and kissed it. "Always, my love. I trust you were successful in prying open some wallets?"

Sandra laughed. "Oh, somewhat, but, darling, do introduce me to your lovely companion."

"I'm sorry, where are my manners? Sandra, this is one of Harrison's lawyers, Marika Havers. Marika, this is my wife, Sandra DeAndre."

Sandra extended a hand, and Marika forced herself to meet it, mumbling an inanity as she stared into familiar eyes. Numb, her mind tried to wrap itself around the reality that Cass stood in front of her.

Palmer frowned at Marika. "Are you all right, my dear? You look terribly pale."

"I...I..."

"She does look unwell, darling," Sandra said. "It's probably that flu that's going around. Why don't I take her to the ladies' room, just in case?" She wrapped a firm hand around Marika's upper arm and guided her away. Sandra nodded and smiled her way through the crowd to the corridor, never loosening her iron grip on Marika.

Inside the powder room, a middle-aged society matron touched up her make-up at the mirror. "Oh, Sandra, I was going to come see you. I'll have to postpone our luncheon at the club on Sunday—"

"Helen, would you mind terribly if I find you a little later?" Sandra asked. "I'm afraid my friend isn't feeling well and may have the flu, so if you would excuse us..."

"Of course, dear," Helen said. "I'll give you a call tomorrow if we miss each other tonight."

The matron left the room, and Sandra locked the door behind her. Then she whirled, grabbed Marika's jacket front, and slammed her against the wall.

Marika stared, her eyes wide. The benevolent philanthropist was gone, and in her place stood the woman who had held her in thrall for almost a year.

Flat, malevolent eyes pinned Marika, and a vice grip held her in place. "What the hell are you doing here?"

Marika shook her head. "I didn't know. My senior partner insisted I come."

"Jesus Christ. Of all the goddamned fuck-ups." Cass released Marika and paced back and forth.

Marika shivered. She hated to be in the vicinity when Cass lost her temper. Her gaze tracked the other woman, and her mind reeled at the realization of Cass' double life.

When Cass stopped and faced Marika, she tried to shrink away but had nowhere to go. Cass advanced on her, eyes glittering. Her left hand shot out and wrapped around Marika's neck.

Marika gasped but made no move to escape.

"You're not going to say a word about this, are you?" The tone was almost casual, but there was no mistaking the pressure that tightened around Marika's neck.

Marika tried to shake her head as she stared at Cass.

"Good," Cass crooned. "That's my good girl. Because if you did, I'd have to punish you." Cass' eyes gleamed, and she licked her lips.

Marika shuddered.

"And my baby doesn't like being punished, does she?" Cass' right hand deliberately unbuttoned Marika's suit jacket and pushed it aside. She viciously twisted Marika's nipple, then clamped her hand over the tortured breast.

Marika bit back a groan and held still. It would be far worse if she resisted.

The doorknob rattled, and Cass scowled. "I'm leaving now. I don't care what you tell your boss, but you're going to get your ass out of here, and I don't want to see you back again, got that?"

Marika swallowed against the constrictive hand. "Mmmph."

Cass released her throat and carefully re-buttoned her jacket. "Good, and just so we understand each other—" She lashed out and landed a brutal strike across Marika's face.

Marika choked.

Cass grabbed her hair and pulled her head back. "We do understand each other, don't we?"

Unable to stop the tears welling in her eyes, Marika mouthed the word "yes."

Cass pressed her body hard against Marika's and drew her tongue slowly down Marika's exposed throat to just above her collarbone. She lingered there for a second, then bit Marika.

Marika flinched but didn't make a sound as a trickle of blood ran into the collar of her blouse.

Cass pushed Marika aside. She wiped her mouth, straightened her dress, and unlocked the door. "Oh, Marge, do give it a moment, won't you? I'm afraid someone's been ill in there, and I think we should give her a few minutes to clean up."

The door closed, and Marika sank into a nearby chair, one hand on her collar and an arm wrapped tightly around her body as she tried to stop shaking. Several minutes later, someone turned the knob, so she stood and went to the door.

Marika averted her face from the women who entered and kept to the edge of the corridor. One of the elevators had just arrived and deposited more partygoers, so she boarded it and punched the button for the fourth floor. Marika stared blindly at the doors, and her mind began to retreat into itself. When the lift stopped, Marika stumbled down the hallway to her room. Her fingers trembled as she tried to insert the keycard. Once inside, she collapsed on the bed and curled into a ball. From a distance, she heard a voice calling her name, but she closed her eyes and shut the sound out.

Rhiannon was reading when Marika came in. Surprised, she glanced at the bedside table. *Wow, that didn't even take an hour. Excellent. We'll still have tons of time tonight.* She tossed the book aside. Her delight vanished when she got to the door and an ashen-faced Marika stumbled by, unfocused eyes staring right past her.

Rhiannon's mouth dropped open, and she stared as Marika collapsed on the bed, her knees coming up to her chest and her arms wrapped around them. "Marika?" Rhiannon advanced into the room. "Marika? Are you okay?"

There was no answer.

Rhiannon approached the bed. "Marika? Hey, what's going on?" Eyes which had looked at her so warmly were now blank and unseeing. Rhiannon was almost relieved when Marika closed her eyes. But then she saw the angry red mark on the colourless cheek. She had seen that mark on her mirror image often enough to know that someone had hit Marika—hard. *Jesus Christ! What the hell happened? I thought you just went upstairs.*

Rhiannon dropped to her knees and stroked Marika's hair. "Hey, c'mon, talk to me. Tell me what happened. Did someone hurt you? Please, Marika. You're scaring me here." To her horror, from that angle she also saw livid bruises on Marika's neck and a bloodstain on the collar of her blouse.

The silent, unmoving woman didn't respond. After five minutes of coaxing, wheedling, and caressing the pallid face, Rhiannon looked to the bedside phone and bit her lip. *This is way out of my league. I need to call someone. Cops? Ambulance? Hotel security? Jesus, what do I do?*

Aside from the angry marks on her face and throat, Marika didn't seem to be physically harmed. *No way would she want a stranger to see her like this.* Rhiannon brought her mouth close to Marika's ear. "Hang in there. I'm going to get some help, but I'll be right back." She returned to her room and left the door open in case Marika called. She crossed to the phone, noted the instructions for long-distance, and, blessing her eidetic memory, placed a call.

"Hello."

Rhiannon sighed in relief. "Lee? It's Rhiannon."

"Rhi? Where the heck are you? Are you guys back from Vancouver already?"

"No, we're still here. But there's a problem, and I don't know what to do."

"What's wrong?" Lee's tone sharpened. "Is it something with Marika? Is she okay?"

"I don't think so." Rhiannon's voice trembled. "I think there's something really wrong with her."

"It's okay, hon. It's going to be all right. Now start from the beginning and tell me everything."

Rhiannon quickly ran through the events of the evening. "And all I can see is the mark on her face, the bruises on her throat, and some sort of small cut that's already stopped bleeding. But she isn't moving, and she won't talk to me. It's like she's not even there, like she's spaced out. Should I call the police? Or tell hotel security? Maybe I should get hold of Mr. Owen and see if he knows anything."

There was a long moment of silence, but Rhiannon took comfort in it. *Lee will know what to do.*

"Did you try touching her?" Lee asked. "Did she respond to that?"

"I patted her hair and her cheek, but nothing."

A deep sigh came over the line. "Okay. I don't think we should call in the authorities quite yet. It could make the situation much worse than it is now. If she's not back to normal by morning, we will, but Dana and I have seen Marika like this before. I'm not sure if the cause is the same—frankly I don't see how it could be—but if you do what we did, then it should work again."

"What? What should I do?"

"Basically you're going to wait, but at the same time, talk to her, touch her, even hold her. Once Marika starts to come around, just let her know that you're there for her. Don't press her to talk about whatever it was, unless she's ready."

"I can do that." Rhiannon wiped her damp eyes. "Can you tell me what's going on? Why she's like this?"

"God, where do I start? Whatever happened tonight traumatized her, and this is the way she protects herself. She basically shuts down mentally and emotionally until she can handle it. The last time this happened, at least that we saw, it involved a woman who abused her. I don't see how she could've run into her out there, but if she did... Rhiannon, this woman is evil."

Rhiannon's breath caught. *Jesus. I've never heard Lee sound so serious.* "Should I call security or something? Do you think if it is that woman, she'll come after Marika?"

"No, that's not the way the bitch operates. She gets Marika to come to her, though I'm damned if I know how."

"What?" *Marika goes willingly to someone who left her in this state? That's fucked-up.*

"Look, I don't know if it's even the same thing, but when she starts to talk again, listen up for a mention of 'Cass,' okay? Don't let her know you know what's going on, but tell me, all right?"

"Definitely. I'm going back in there now. If I get a chance, I'll call you later. If not, I'll talk to you when we're back in Calgary. And Lee...thanks."

"You did right to call me. Marika is very lucky you're there. Now go look after our friend."

Rhiannon bade Lee goodbye and walked to the other room. Marika hadn't moved an inch in her absence. She contemplated her options, then crawled onto the bed and curled up behind the rigid form. She wrapped one arm around Marika's body and settled her other hand on Marika's hair. Snuggling close, she began to talk. She kept her voice soft and calm as she chatted about nothing and everything.

A long time passed before Marika finally relaxed. She didn't say anything but did straighten out her limbs and settle back into Rhiannon's embrace.

Relief flooded Rhiannon. "Welcome back." Her throat ached from the unprecedented talking marathon. Exhausted, Rhiannon dropped off, still pressed against Marika.

When she woke, hours later, Marika had rolled to face her. Through open curtains, city lights provided enough illumination for Rhiannon to see the eyes that gazed at her. Still mostly asleep, she smiled.

Marika caressed Rhiannon's cheek, then began to withdraw her hand.

Rhiannon reached for it and drew Marika's hand to her chest. As she drifted back to sleep, she felt long fingers tighten around her own.

"It went well this evening, don't you think, darling?" Palmer laid his hands on Sandra's shoulders as she sat at her dressing table, removing her diamonds.

Sandra patted his hand and smiled up at him. "Very well, my love." She stretched and yawned. "It was a long night, though, and you do have to be in the office tomorrow. Why don't you pour us a nightcap?"

Palmer dropped a kiss on her hair and left their bedroom.

She watched him go, then stared into the mirror as her mind worked furiously. She considered and discarded options until she settled on a course of action. She had successfully kept her lives separate for years, and the unexpected appearance of Marika at the reception had shaken her more than she had thought possible.

Cass had known from the beginning that consorting with Marika was not wise. But the refined woman was so far removed from the usual consorts Cass associated with that she had been unable to resist the challenge. Her eyes narrowed, and a half smile lifted the corner of her mouth. Marika had proved so...unexpectedly amenable to Cass' darker proclivities. The predator had known how to exploit every hurt, every pain in the woman's past to turn Marika to her pleasure.

Now that Marika was aware of her other life, Cass knew that she should cut any further ties. *But Marika so enlivens my stops in Calgary. Besides, she's not going to tell anyone. She's even more terrified of exposing our...relationship than she is of me. Still, a little insurance wouldn't hurt.* Cass opened a drawer and pulled out a cell phone. After glancing at the door, she placed a call. "I have a job for you. The instructions will be waiting for you tomorrow. And Gao—this gets the highest priority." Cass flipped the small phone shut and tossed it back in the drawer.

Then Sandra rose and greeted her husband with a smile as he returned to the room with two brandy snifters in hand.

CHAPTER 18

RHIANNON OPENED HER EYES, AND the wisps of her dream slipped away. She had been walking beside a waterfall with someone whose face she couldn't remember, but whose presence filled her with contentment. Rhiannon had resisted waking until she couldn't hang on to the dream any longer. Now, she was alone. The bedspread was folded around her, and she still wore the clothes she'd donned the previous evening in anticipation of going to Gastown. Marika's clothes were tossed across a chair, and the shower was running in the bathroom.

Rhiannon yawned, pushed back the covers, and swung her legs over the edge of the bed. She listened to the shower. *Wonder if I should check on her?* She glanced down at her rumpled clothes. *No, I think I'll get cleaned up first. She must be doing better if she's up and showering. I'm not quite ready to deal with it all.* She ran a hand through tousled hair and went back to her room. After a shower and change of clothes, she packed for the flight home. She returned to the dividing doorway but didn't see Marika, so she closed the door and picked up the phone.

Lee answered. "Hello?"

"Hi, it's Rhiannon."

"I'm so glad you called. Is everything all right?"

"I think so. I mean, I haven't seen her this morning, 'cause she's in the shower, but she did eventually relax last night."

Lee exhaled deeply. "Good. You did great. Look, did she talk at all? Did she mention Cass?"

"No, she never said a word, just let me hold her most of the night." The remembered warmth of Marika's body still filled Rhiannon's senses.

"Okay. We need to find out whether the authorities should be called in, but don't press her if she doesn't want to open up," Lee said. "I'll talk to her once she's home. What time is your flight?"

"We leave here at eleven Vancouver time, so I think that puts us in about one or one-thirty Calgary time. How should I handle things this morning?"

"Just be yourself. Let her set the pace, but don't be surprised if she doesn't say much about last night. Look, I have to get going. I'm late for work, but I'd hoped to hear from you before I left. If you get a chance, give me a call tonight, okay?"

"Okay. Thanks, Lee." Rhiannon hung up and struggled to make sense of her tumultuous emotions. *I was so scared, but it felt...good...right to hold her.* She almost missed the soft knock on their dividing door. "Come in."

Marika opened the door but stood in the doorway, her hands in her pockets and staring at her feet.

"Good morning." *Just be yourself. Let her set the pace.*

"Morning, Rhi." Marika took a deep breath and met Rhiannon's gaze. "Look, I owe you an apology."

Rhiannon shook her head. "That's not necessary. All I need to know is that you're okay."

"I am, and I do owe you an apology." Marika's voice was firm. "I ruined your evening. We didn't get to Gastown. Hell, you probably didn't even have anything to eat."

Rhiannon crossed to where Marika stood. "So I'll see Gastown some other time. As for eating, let's go find breakfast before we're off to the airport."

Marika studied Rhiannon's face. "Just like that? You're letting me off the hook?"

"You were never on a hook." Rhiannon's voice was gentle. "What happened, happened, but I have to ask—were you attacked? Should we be calling the police or at least hotel security?"

Marika shook her head and dropped her gaze. "No, nothing like that. I just… Something happened that triggered a very bad memory for me, that's all. I don't want to talk about it."

"Okay. I'm sorry. I wish I could've done more."

Marika raised her head. "Last night—Thank you for being there. You made me feel safe. You made me feel… well, I just really appreciate what you did."

Rhiannon reached toward Marika's pale cheek that no longer bore the angry red imprint of a hand. She stopped just short of touching. "Whatever happened, you didn't deserve that. No one does."

Rhiannon held Marika's gaze for a long moment, then she broke the tension with a grin. "I just have to throw a few things in my suitcase, and I'm ready to go." Rhiannon backed up a couple of steps. "And pick a good place for breakfast, because I'm hungry. I'm thinking eggs, bacon, hash browns, sausages, waffles, toast…"

Her lighthearted litany was received with a chuckle, and Marika walked back into her room, shaking her head.

Rhiannon's smile vanished. Memories of her early years in her aunt's "care" flashed through her mind. Her parents had never spanked her, and she'd endured extreme confusion and anguish when subjected to Hettie's harsh discipline. Rhiannon was fifteen the last time Hettie struck her. It was the first time she fought back. Rhiannon had sworn that day that no one would ever hit her again. She now expanded that promise. *If there's any way I can stop it, Marika, no one will ever hit you again, either.*

Gao sat motionless, his gaze fixed on the arrival gate for the Air Canada flight from Vancouver. His instructions from the Chameleon had arrived very early that morning, and he'd had to scramble to implement her orders. Gao had no idea why this lawyer was so important, but the Chameleon's commands were perfectly clear. She wanted to know every move Marika Havers made, every person she saw, and every place she went. He was to report comprehensively on a daily basis, until further notice.

Their electronics expert, Perry, had been annoyed at the hour of his summoning. But upon learning that the orders came directly from the Chameleon, he dropped his complaints. Gao had no doubt that the lawyer's home was already bugged, her computer searched, and her phone tapped. Gao's instructions were to forward Perry's transcripts unread. The Chameleon had been crystal clear on that point.

He glanced at the printout in his hand and reviewed again the information and photograph his boss had sent him, though he had already committed the lawyer's face to memory.

It wasn't long before Gao picked up his quarry, walking and talking with a shorter woman. He fell in behind them on the escalator to the lower baggage level. He leaned against a pillar and listened to their conversation.

"You've got the afternoon off, Rhi. We're not expected back in the office until the morning. I'm just going to go home and write up my notes from the hearing."

"I think I'm going to see if David's up for a driving lesson. We were going tonight anyway, but maybe he's free this afternoon."

The smaller woman moved forward to grab two bags off the carousel. She handed one to the lawyer and brushed past Gao with a murmured apology.

Gao stepped out of the way. He allowed them to get partway to the exit before he walked toward the same door. He hung back until the cabbie stowed their bags in the trunk and they climbed in the back of the taxi.

Gao crossed the road to where he had left his nondescript Honda in metered parking. He pulled out three cars behind the departing taxi and settled in to follow at a discreet distance.

The cab drove to the inner city and pulled up in front of a Victoria Park address.

Gao immediately pulled over, and his gaze swivelled from the taxi to a house on the other side of the street. *I'll be damned.* The woman getting out of the cab lived directly across from the King brothers.

The smaller woman exchanged a few words with her companion and then disappeared into a ramshackle yellow house.

Gao pulled out to follow the taxi from a few blocks back. He'd been to the lawyer's home several times that morning, so he drove by rote and concentrated on how to further implement the Chameleon's directives.

———————

Marika stared at her computer screen, her mind far away from the notes she'd been entering. She'd been home for several hours but found it almost impossible to concentrate as she grew progressively more upset with herself for her behaviour the previous night. *Why the hell didn't I just pull away from her? There's no way she'd have created a scene in front of Palmer and her guests.*

She fingered the small bandage on her neck, then slid her hand down to cover her breast. Far stronger than the memory of the pain Cass inflicted was the image of her eyes—those cold, mocking eyes. She had seen their expression too often in Cass' bedroom. *What the hell did I get myself into?* Marika shook her head. *How could I be such a fool? And why in God's name did I ever go back after that first night?*

Soon though, thoughts of Rhiannon drove out memories of Cass. *Rhi wouldn't have folded like a house of cards. She probably would've slugged Cass the moment she tried to lay a hand on her.* Marika pictured Rhiannon blackening Cass' eyes. "Rhi would never have ended up in Cass' bed in the first place. Why did I?"

Marika swiveled in her chair. *I can't believe how easily she let it go. She didn't say another word about that fiasco. It was like it never happened.*

Loud knocking drew Marika from her musings and to the door. She peered through the spy hole.

Lee stood in the hall.

She smiled and unlocked her door. "Hi, Lee. What brings you around at this time of day? Shouldn't you still be punching the time clock?"

"Yeah, yeah." Lee brushed by Marika. "What's the good of being your own boss if you can't set your own hours? Besides, I had to make up for being late this morning."

Marika followed her into the living room. "By leaving early?"

Lee raised an eyebrow. "I can tell you've never been in the military. You obviously missed learning that time-honoured principle in all those high-brow schools you went to."

Marika chuckled. "Can I get you anything?"

Lee dropped onto the couch. "Well, if you twisted my arm, I could drink a beer. It's been a long day."

Marika went to get one of the dark ales she kept especially for Lee. She was about to grab a juice for herself, then decided on a beer, too.

She returned to the living room and twisted the cap off one bottle. She handed it across Spooky, who had taken up residence on Lee's lap.

Lee nodded her thanks.

Marika sat on the other end of the couch and opened the second beer.

"How'd the trip to Lotus Land go?" Lee asked.

"Pretty good. I think the hearing went well, though we won't get the IRB's judgment for a few weeks. We had a wonderful time on Sunday night. We went out to dinner and then walked around Stanley Park for a bit."

"Sounds nice. So whad'dya do after the hearing?"

Lee's tone was casual, but Marika's gaze flashed to her face. "You talked to Rhiannon."

"She called me last night. You scared her pretty badly."

Marika's head and heart dropped. *So it was all a front. Oh God, I thought maybe I wasn't as bad as I'd feared. But if Rhiannon called Lee...* She was unable to meet Lee's eyes. "What did Rhi say? Did she think I was crazy?"

Lee reached over and squeezed Marika's hand. "No. All she wanted to know was how to help you. That kid cares about you a whole bunch."

Marika shook her head. "She shouldn't." She looked at Lee sadly. "She really shouldn't."

Lee studied her. "Why?"

"You know why."

"No, I don't. Well, apart from you being her boss, but that's not insurmountable. Marion is coming back eventually, and Rhiannon would've had to switch to another office anyway. She can always do that earlier than planned, if necessary."

Marika poked Lee's broad shoulder. "Don't be obtuse. That's not it, and you know it."

Lee shrugged. "If that's not it, what is?"

"I can't... She hasn't..."

"And you get paid the big bucks for this brilliant discourse, do you? Wow, Osgoode Hall really does turn out scintillating elocutionists." Lee grinned and took a sip.

"Scintillating elocutionists? Did you swallow a dictionary for breakfast?"

"Hey, I'll have you know there's just as much substance as style in this old gal."

Marika smiled. "All right, all right. I get your point."

"Do you want to talk about what happened?"

Marika started to shake her head, then paused. *Screw her threats. It's not like she'll ever know if I confide in Lee.* "Cass happened."

Lee scowled. "In Vancouver? Did you know she was going to be there?"

"No! For God's sake, I didn't go looking for her." Marika poured out the whole story.

Lee stared at her. "So you're saying that Cass and this socialite philanthropist, what's-her-name, are one and the same?"

"Sandra DeAndre, yes. They are unquestionably the same woman."

Lee shook her head. "Well, I'll be damned. What are you going to do now?"

"I want out. I don't ever want to see Cass or Sandra or whatever she wants to call herself again."

Lee's eyes widened. "Really? You mean that this time?"

"I mean it. I hate the way she makes me feel, and the other...it just isn't worth it. Rhi told me this morning that I didn't deserve that...what Cass did to me. She's right. I don't."

Lee whooped and pushed Spooky off her lap. She leaned over and wrapped Marika in a bear hug. "Finally! Hot damn, you have no idea how glad I am to hear that."

Marika laughed and winced at the enthusiastic hug. "Lee..."

"Oops, sorry." Lee mussed Marika's hair.

Marika smoothed her hair back into place.

"So, basically, you don't call her and don't go over to her place, right?" Lee asked.

"Right. She only came over here that one time." Marika shuddered at the memory of the night Cass had taken her to her psychological limits and beyond. "I always went to her place, so I simply won't call her ever again. I'm sure she won't bother me, especially now that I know her secret. She'll probably want to get a million miles away from me, not that I have any intention of telling anyone."

"You know you could press charges if you wanted," Lee said. "She did attack you, and from what you told me, there was at least one witness who saw you enter the ladies' room together. Not to mention what Rhi could testify to after you came back to your room."

Marika shook her head. "God, no. I'm not pulling Rhi into my mess any further than she already has been. I don't want anything more to do with Cass, and I sure as hell don't want the world to know I was ever involved with her."

Lee nodded. "I get it. No point in stirring up the hornet's nest, though there's a part of me that would love to see what would happen if her social circle found out what she was up to on her charitable rounds."

"Not to mention her husband." Marika had problems squaring the man's obvious devotion to his wife with Cass' double dealing. *Though given how thoroughly I've been manipulated, it's not really surprising that Palmer is under her spell, too.*

Lee beamed and leaned back into the couch cushions. "So then, there's nothing stopping you from exploring this thing with Rhiannon."

"There is no 'thing' with Rhi. It's all in your imagination."

"Nuh-uh, Dana thinks so, too. There's definitely something electric building between you two."

"Just friendship. And anyway, I'm not going to allow it to develop into anything more, got that?"

"Got it." But Lee's grin told Marika that her friend wasn't buying it for a moment.

David held his breath as Rhiannon steered the old Volvo into the rectory's narrow driveway, put the car in park, and turned off the ignition. "Excellent, Rhi. You're really coming along nicely. I'd say a few more weeks of practice, and you'll be ready to go for your test." He smiled. "So, can I interest you in staying for supper? I was just going to grill some burgers, if you're hungry."

"Sounds good, if you're sure you have enough."

"I've got enough." David exited the car.

Rhiannon got out and tossed the keys to him over the top of the roof.

David caught them. "C'mon. I'll put you to work."

"Oh, sure. You never said word one about making me work for my supper." Rhiannon followed him up the path.

David grinned. *It's like night and day. You'd never know she was the same angry young woman I met just last month.* Their driving lessons had become a highlight of his week. Rhiannon still challenged him at every turn, but without the former abrasive undertones. She appeared to relish their debates as much as he did. While David enjoyed a considerable educational edge, he often scrambled to counter her arguments. He was well aware that she liked to adopt contrary positions just to test the depth of his beliefs and suppositions.

Once inside, David listed what they needed. He left Rhiannon to dig things out while he started the charcoals on his cranky, old barbeque in the tiny backyard.

When she joined him, she handed him the Coke that had become an established part of their ritual. They sat in the shade of the old mountain ash and waited for the grill to heat up.

Unbidden, Rhiannon told him about her trip to Vancouver. When she glossed over their cancelled plans to go to Gastown, David's interest was piqued. "It's too bad you didn't get there. It was always one of my favourite spots when I lived in Vancouver. Not that I had much money to spend, but Hannah and I used to like to wander around and enjoy people-watching on a Saturday afternoon."

"Yeah, I'd have liked to see it, but there's always another time."

"True. Any particular reason you didn't get there this time?"

Rhiannon didn't immediately answer.

David tensed. She was much improved these days, but occasionally he inadvertently trespassed on her boundaries.

"Marika wasn't feeling well, so I stayed in to look after her."

David let out a long breath. "I'm sorry to hear that. I hope she was feeling better today."

"Yeah, she was." Rhiannon was quiet again. "I really like her."

"That's good. I'm glad you're getting along with her. I'm sure it makes work much more pleasant."

Rhiannon sighed. "No, David. I mean I really *like* her."

His eyes widened. "Oh! Um...oh."

She looked at him wryly. "That was insightful."

David tried to shake off the surprise. He had been pleased Rhiannon had made friends, but he never once considered this possibility. He held his tongue while he considered how to respond.

Rhiannon sipped her Coke.

"Are you sure?" David finally asked.

Rhiannon stared off across the yard. "I wasn't absolutely sure until last night."

David blinked and sat upright. "Did she do anything? I mean..."

"I know what you mean, and no. We did sleep together, but we *just* slept together. She wasn't in any shape to do anything more, even if we'd wanted to."

David pressed the cold can to his cheek. It wasn't the first time he'd counseled young people on exactly this issue, but this was Rhiannon. He had to step carefully. "How does she feel about it...about you?"

"There are times I see a look in her eyes that tells me she feels the same. When we were dancing last weekend—"

"You were dancing?" David wondered whether his voice had squeaked in actuality or just in his head. But judging by the emerging grin on Rhiannon's face, she had heard his mouse imitation.

"Yes." Rhiannon's eyes gleamed with mischief. "We went dancing at The Arc with Lee and Dana."

She went to a lesbian bar? When did all this happen?

Rhiannon leaned on the arm of his lawn chair. "She is the sexiest dancer. I even turned down other women, just to stay in her arms all night."

David summoned every bit of his pastoral experience and managed to keep a calm demeanour, although he downed the Coke in three quick gulps.

Rhiannon took her arm off his chair. She stretched out her legs and crossed them at the ankles.

David took a deep breath. "This isn't something to be taken lightly. I would hate to see you rush into anything—"

"I wasn't asking for advice. I was talking to you as a friend." Rhiannon frowned at him.

That stung. "And I'm listening as your friend, but that doesn't mean I'm not concerned about the impact this would have on your life or how suddenly it appears to be happening. I never considered that you might be...inclined that way."

Rhiannon shrugged. "Neither did I. Never had feelings for anyone either way before. But she's...special, David. And she makes me feel special. I like being around her. I can't stop thinking about her. I want to...protect her."

He raised an eyebrow. "Have you considered that maybe it's just because you're around her a lot and that you haven't really given young men your age much of a chance?"

Rhiannon looked at him with a half-smile. "Well, when the IT support guy was sniffing around me, I sure didn't feel anything like this for him."

"Perhaps he just wasn't the right one."

"What do you have against Marika being the right one?" Rhiannon's voice sharpened.

"If she really is, then nothing. I'm only concerned that you haven't thought this all out." David was floundering. He simply couldn't summon the cool impartiality he used when counseling young people in his church. *Not with Rhiannon.*

"I really don't think this is something that you can think out," Rhiannon said. "You either feel it, or you don't. You can't force something that isn't there, and you can't deny something that is."

"And this is?"

"And this is." Rhiannon nodded.

David absorbed the certainty in her voice. "So, what are you going to do about it?"

Rhiannon shrugged. "For now, nothing." She pointed at the smoking grill. "You might want to take a look at that."

David moved to the barbeque. As he poked at the charcoals with tongs, he considered his instinctive reaction to what Rhiannon had revealed. An image of Conor's thin face flashed through his mind, and he flinched at the comparison. *I can't fail her like I failed him.* He distributed the coals evenly, closed the cover, and turned to Rhiannon. "I'm in your corner, Rhi. No matter what."

She smiled and tilted her Coke can at him. "I never doubted that."

Cass was about to open a thick manila envelope when Palmer stuck his head into her office. She set the envelope down and slid it under a stack of papers. "Did you want something, dear?"

"Darling, I just got a call from Sharon," he said. "She said something about accompanying me to the mayor's reception next week? Are you not able to make that?"

Sandra sighed. "I did pencil that into your engagement calendar, Palmer. I have prior out-of-town commitments that couldn't be changed, so your daughter graciously agreed to escort you."

"Oh, all right. You know I'd rather go with you, my love, but if you can't make it..."

"I'm afraid not," Sandra said. "Foundation business, darling, and you know how seriously I take that."

"Yes, I do. You're a remarkable woman, and I'm a lucky man."

She gave him an indulgent smile. "You're slightly biased. Now, why don't you go up to bed, and I'll join you as soon as I catch up on some paperwork."

The thick carpeting muffled the sound of Palmer's retreating footsteps.

Cass crossed the room and shut the door. She returned to her desk and unsealed the thick manila envelope Liang had just delivered. She scanned Gao's first report, then stopped short at the transcript of Marika's conversation with someone named Lee. She seethed as she read the printout. *So Marika ignored my warning. She wants out of our...little arrangement, does she? And who is this annoying chit, Rhiannon, who planted that idea in my pet's brain?*

Cass scowled. The caution that had served her all these years warred with her irrational desire to keep Marika. Immediately after becoming involved with her, Cass had a thorough background check done. Initially, she had considered turning Marika to her professional interests, but all reports indicated that the lawyer was ethical and incorruptible, so Cass had contented herself with a strictly sexual relationship. *Surely this will simply be one more in her long string of failed, short-lived affairs. Nothing to be concerned with. Nothing at all. And yet...*

Cass re-read Gao's report on Marika's arrival at the airport. Her subordinate had provided a very comprehensive report, including the conversation he overheard and Marika's demeanour in addressing her companion. *Could this be more than a casual affair? The little bitch certainly seems to have some influence with her.* Cass stood and paced. *Unacceptable. I end relationships, not my pets. Marika will be allowed to leave my bed when I say so—not before.* Cass strolled over to the window and gazed out. She ignored the beautiful twilight view from the mansion's third floor. Instead, a vision of pleading eyes filled her mind. She closed her eyes and recalled the sensation of Marika's hair twisted around her fist and her velvet throat under her tongue. *Mine. She's mine. Perhaps it's time to remind her of that.*

CHAPTER 19

RHIANNON SUCCESSFULLY EXECUTED A PARALLEL park for the third time in a row and looked at Marika. *I think I'm getting the hang of this. That was pretty darned smooth.*

"Well done." Marika smiled. "You know what? I think it's time for some highway driving."

Rhiannon blinked. "Are you sure?"

"I am, but you need to feel confident, too. So what do you say? Are you ready to give it a try? In a lot of ways it's much easier than city driving."

Rhiannon gulped but nodded. "If you're game, so am I."

They headed for the busy Trans-Canada Highway. Traffic was heavy as it flowed west out of Calgary toward the mountains, but with Marika's encouragement, Rhiannon swiftly gained confidence.

"You're doing great. Just keep your speed steady at 110 and stay in the right-hand lane." Marika chuckled. "And you might want to loosen your grip a little, or your hands are going to be sore by the time we get to Banff."

Startled, Rhiannon shifted her gaze from the highway to Marika. "We're going all the way to Banff?"

"Eyes on the road," Marika said. "Sure, why not? It'll be great practice for you, and it's a beautiful drive. Did you have anything else planned for the day?"

"No, nothing at all." Rhiannon's smile grew. *I get to spend all day with her again.* She drove along the Trans-Canada, admiring scenery she rarely saw. Golden fields rolled on beneath cloudless azure skies, and the distant mountains extended their silent invitation to come and play. Her assurance grew with every passing kilometre. By the time they stopped to pay their admission at the park gate, Rhiannon was confident she had a good grasp of highway driving.

They spent the afternoon exploring Banff and rode the gondola to the top of Sulphur Mountain. On the return drive, they took the old, more picturesque highway north of the Bow River. They passed Ghost Lake, where boats and sailboards abounded, and entered the small town of Cochrane around supper time.

"I'd like to buy you dinner here," Rhiannon said. "You paid for the gondola tickets, and you wouldn't let me put any gas in the car, so I insist."

"Okay, but I get to choose the place."

"As long as it's not another hot dog stand." Rhiannon mock-glared at Marika.

Marika stuck out her tongue, and Rhiannon gave up. She was too happy to sustain even a semblance of pique.

"Turn right here." Marika pointed ahead. "Stop in front of that diner. That's where I want to have dinner."

Rhiannon shook her head but followed Marika's directions. *There goes the steak dinner and fancy restaurant I was going to treat her to.*

When they entered the 1950's-style diner, Rhiannon had to admit it looked like a fun place. It was authentic right down to the melamine counter, which was manned by a soda jerk dressed in a white shirt, black bow tie, and red-and-white-striped hat.

"Step right up, beautiful ladies." The young man laid two menus on the counter. "What can I start you off with tonight? I highly recommend the hand-dipped milkshakes. Best in the province, if I do say so myself."

"How can we say no?" They sat on the swivel stools. "I'll have strawberry, please. Marika?"

"Chocolate. A day like today just calls for chocolate, don't you think?" Marika smiled at Rhiannon.

"It was a fabulous day, wasn't it?" *I thought Stampede was a blast, but today...today was perfection.*

They passed the Calgary city limits sign about eight. "My condo's close," Marika said. "Rather than going all the way downtown, why don't you stay with me tonight? The daybed's already made up and ready."

Rhiannon nodded. "Sure. Sounds like a good idea." *Yes, yes, yes!*

Twenty minutes later, Marika had five CDs loaded, and they'd settled on opposite ends of the couch to read.

Half an hour later, the novel Rhiannon had started lay ignored on her lap. Instead, her mind was on the dream she had nurtured since the first week of being in Hettie's care. The dream had sustained her for over twelve years. It had been as vital a part of her existence as breathing, but now a new fixation dominated her days and nights. She fell asleep with the echo of Marika's voice in her ears and wakened to the memory of Marika's slender arms holding her close.

Rhiannon had never made allowances for anything or anyone disrupting her singular focus on achieving her goal. Her timeline was set; every penny she would need was accounted for, and she had already acquired her passport. But for the first time, depositing her most recent paycheque had not raised her savings bottom line by the customary amount. *And I don't even care. I've had so much fun. I love doing things with her—with Lee and Dana, too.*

The foot Rhiannon was resting her hand on nudged her thigh. She blinked and looked up.

Marika smiled. "You're a thousand miles away. You've barely turned a page since we sat down."

Rhiannon squeezed Marika's toes gently. "I was just thinking about what a good day it was, and I started daydreaming."

"It was a good day, wasn't it? Maybe we should drive to Lake Louise next weekend."

"I'd like that." The phone on the end table behind Rhiannon rang. "Want me to get it?" Marika nodded, and Rhiannon picked up the receiver. "Havers residence. How may I help you?"

Marika rolled her eyes.

There was an instant of silence. "Um, is Marika there?"

"One moment, please." Rhiannon tossed the cordless to Marika.

She caught it and accidentally hit the speaker button. "Hello?"

"You have a maid now?"

"Oh, hi, Terry. No, that was Rhiannon goofing around. What are you up to?"

Terry chuckled. "I might ask you the same thing."

"Teeeerrrrry." Marika's voice dropped two octaves, and Rhiannon grinned.

"Okay, okay. Look, I was just calling to see if you—and Rhiannon, if she's interested—want to come with Jan and me to the zoo tomorrow. We're babysitting my nieces and thought that might be a good way to kill a couple of hours. I know it's not normally your thing, but I haven't seen you in ages, and it will be a beautiful day for it. I promise you won't have to do anything with the rugrats. Just think of it as a walk in the park, with an unusual amount of exotic wildlife around."

"Just a sec." Marika raised an eyebrow at Rhiannon. "Are you interested?"

"Sure. If you want to go, I wouldn't mind tagging along. I haven't been to a zoo since I was a little kid."

"Excellent." Marika flexed her toes.

Rhiannon grinned. *Never let it be said I can't take a hint.* She picked up Marika's foot, rested it on her lap, and began a foot massage. *I could do this all day. Wonder what else she might like to have rubbed?* Her eyes widened. *Oh, God. I didn't say that out loud, did I?*

Marika blew her a soundless kiss. "Sounds wonderful, Ter. What time and where do you want us to meet you?"

"You'll come?" Terry's surprise was audible.

"Well, why'd you ask if you didn't think I would? I can always turn you down, if you'd rather."

"No, no, I'm glad you guys are coming," Terry said. "Why don't we meet at the entrance about ten thirty? That'll give us a couple of hours to wander around before the girls start getting cranky and need their nap."

"Take after their aunt, do they?" Marika winked at Rhiannon.

"Ha, ha." Terry blew a raspberry over the phone. "Besides, I have much better uses for naptime than sleeping these days."

Marika laughed. "I guess you do at that. We'll see you at ten thirty tomorrow."

"Great...and Marika, I'm really glad you're both coming." Terry hung up without waiting for a response.

Marika set the phone aside. "Mmm, don't stop. That feels fabulous."

Rhiannon took both of Marika's feet onto her lap. "So, we're off to the zoo, are we?" She glanced at a milkshake stain on her shorts. "I should really stop by my place to change first."

Marika grinned. "Sorry 'bout that. That soda jerk made me laugh so hard—"

"That you just had to spit your shake all over me. Yeah, I know. I didn't mind, but I don't want to go to the zoo in these."

"You could borrow some of my shorts."

Rhiannon eyed the long, slender legs that rested on top of hers. "No, thanks. I don't feel like wearing capris." She calculated rapidly. "It should work out fine. If we're due to meet them at ten thirty, we could go by my place about ten. My aunt will have gone to church, and the neighbourhood is really quiet on Sunday mornings."

Marika nodded and extracted her feet from Rhiannon's grip. "Don't get the idea that you're done. I'm just taking a brief raincheck so I can make some tea. Interested?"

"In the raincheck or the tea?"

"Brat." Marika stood and tossed a throw pillow at Rhiannon. "Both. You are not getting out of finishing that fabulous foot rub."

Rhiannon grinned. "I guess I do owe you for all those wonderful backrubs, so yes to both." She watched Marika walk toward the kitchen. *She's so beautiful.* A now familiar warmth swept through Rhiannon, and she smiled as she recalled how flustered she'd been at the Stampede dance the first time she caught herself ogling Marika. *How quickly things change.*

⬥

On the street outside the lawyer's condo, Gao had been parked for over an hour when his cell phone rang. His gaze flicked constantly between the entrance to the condo tower and the garage exit while he took the call. "Yes?"

"They just made plans to go to the zoo tomorrow," Perry said without preamble. "They're meeting friends at the main gate. Ten thirty."

Gao groaned. "Great, that's just how I wanted to spend my Sunday—going to the damned zoo. All right. Does it sound as if they are settled in for the night?"

"Yeah. Sounds like it."

Gao jotted a notation on his pad. "Fine. Let me know if it looks as if she's going to change her plans. I'm going to call it a night."

"Do you know how long we're gonna haveta keep this up?"

Gao frowned. "Until she says to stop, you know that."

"Fuckin' son-of-a-bitch. I'm bored outta my goddamned skull."

Gao's lip curled. "Tell you what. You include that in your next report. Tell the Chameleon how bored you are. I'm sure she'll be very interested in your opinion."

The line went dead.

Fool. As if I were any less bored. Unlike Perry, Gao had seen evidence of the Chameleon's displeasure up close and personal. *There is no way I will ever cross that woman. If she wants me to spend the next year tailing the damned lawyer, I'll do it.*

⬥

When Rhiannon pulled up in front of her aunt's house, Marika cocked her head. "Not going around back today?"

"No, we'll only be a couple of minutes, and Hettie's always at church by now." Rhiannon got out, walked around the car, and handed the keys to Marika. When she unlocked the front door, she cast an uncertain look at Marika, then pushed her way inside.

Marika wasn't surprised by the dark, shabby interior. *Lee was right. It is a dump. Hard to believe Rhi's lived here most of her life.* She remained impassive as she followed Rhiannon upstairs, down a narrow hall and into a locked bedroom.

This is a little better. Not exactly Ethan Allen furniture, but I can see Rhi all over this place. It's about as neat, clean, and organized as a military camp. Marika smiled at the stack of books on the table, and then her attention was drawn to the walls and the drawings that covered them. She moved closer and traced a finger over a laughing, dark-haired man and a woman who looked a lot like Rhiannon.

"My parents." Rhiannon zipped up her clean shorts. She nodded at the picture Marika was touching. "Those are my parents."

"I kind of thought so." Marika dropped her hand. "You look a lot like your mother."

"Yeah." Rhiannon peeled off her shirt and took a fresh one out of the legless bureau. "I've got Dad's eyes, though."

Marika crossed to Rhiannon. "Let me take a look at your shoulder before you put that on."

Rhiannon held still while Marika examined the healing shoulder. She pushed the bra strap to the side and ran a finger alongside the dull pink scar. A shiver rippled through Rhiannon's body, and Marika pulled her hand away. "I'm sorry. Did I hurt you?"

"No." Rhiannon pulled the T-shirt over her head. "Not at all. In fact, I went to the clinic on Friday, and the doctor cleared me to start swimming again. I thought I'd go Monday after work." Rhiannon tucked her shirt in and grabbed her backpack. "Let's go." She held the door open for Marika.

Marika exited into the hall and gasped.

A hulking woman stood right outside the door and stared at them.

A repressed growl came from behind Marika.

Rhiannon stepped out of the room. "I thought you'd be in church this morning."

"I'm sure you did." There was nasty glee in Hettie's voice.

Marika studied Rhiannon's aunt. Hettie loomed large in the dark hallway, almost as tall as Marika but twice her weight, with small piercing eyes and doughy features. Her sallow complexion and platinum-dyed hair did her no favours, but her malevolent air outweighed her physical lack. Marika shook off a shudder and offered her hand. "Hi. I'm Marika Havers, Rhiannon's boss."

The woman touched Marika's hand. "Hettie Walker, Anne's aunt." Hettie emphasized "Anne."

Before Marika could say anything further, Rhiannon took her arm and hustled her by Hettie. She just had time to call out, "Nice to meet you," before Rhiannon rushed her down the stairs and outside.

Marika had to work to keep up with Rhiannon's rapid strides as she covered the distance to the Lexus in seconds. Marika keyed the remote to unlock the car and walked around to the driver's side. It was a quiet drive to the zoo. When they arrived, Marika pulled into the parking lot and found a spot.

Rhiannon stared out the window. "I'm sorry. I thought she'd be gone. She never misses church."

"It's all right." Marika turned the engine off and laid a hand on Rhiannon's shoulder. "Don't let her ruin our day, okay?" It was several moments before she felt Rhiannon relax.

Rhiannon faced Marika and tilted her chin. "You're right. There's no way I'm going to let her mess up our day."

Marika gave Rhiannon's shoulder a squeeze and undid her seat belt. They were almost to the main entrance when they spotted Terry, Jan, and two toddlers waiting for them. Marika smiled as she watched the little girls scramble in and out of a large red wagon. "I don't think I envy Terry."

Rhiannon grinned. "But they sure are cute. Gotta love those glasses."

Both children sported bright pink sunglasses under white and yellow sunhats.

"Hi, guys," Terry said.

Jan waved, then took off after one of the twins who was heading solo for the entrance.

Terry sighed and shook her head. She picked up the remaining twin, who'd started to howl, and thrust the handle of the wagon at Marika. "Here, take this for a minute, will you?" She hurried after Jan and reunited the twins.

Marika looked at Rhiannon wryly. "It's not too late. You could save yourself, you know? Take the car and meet me later."

"Nope, can't even start the car without a licenced driver present, remember?" Rhiannon took one side of the handle and helped pull. They caught up with Terry and Jan and paid their admission fee.

Once through the gate, Terry settled the girls back into the wagon and took the handle. She grinned at her nieces. "They have a lot of energy."

Marika smiled at the understatement and fell into step with Rhiannon behind the wagon.

"How do they tell them apart?" Rhiannon asked as the excited toddlers bounced in the wagon.

"Kelly—pink shirt, Kerry—purple shirt," Terry said over her shoulder.

Rhiannon looked up at Marika. "What happens if they mix up the laundry?"

Marika chuckled. "I'm pretty sure their parents can tell them apart."

Even with the occasional dash to catch a fleeing child, Marika enjoyed the next couple of hours. Rhiannon had the same look of wonder as the twins when a hippopotamus rose out of the water, the giraffes reached for leaves on the highest branches of the trees, and the tigers paced their forested compound. Best of all was the primate house, where they spent half an hour watching the antics of the spider monkeys.

Rhiannon convulsed with laughter at one male who brazenly played with himself.

Amused as much by Rhiannon's reaction as by the monkey's antics, Marika winked. "Boys will be boys."

Terry nodded to where a small female sat in a larger female's embrace. She smiled at Jan. "And girls will be girls."

Marika's gaze turned to Rhiannon, who stood beside her, entranced with a monkey swinging across the large cage on ropes and vines. Lost in a study of Rhiannon's profile, she started when a hand patted her shoulder.

"Yes?" Marika turned. "Did you say something?"

"We were wondering if you two are ready for lunch." Jan shifted a squirming Kelly in her arms. "I think the kids are getting hungry."

"Sure. That okay with you, Rhi?"

Rhiannon nodded.

They left the primate house and made their way to the picnic area. Terry and Marika stayed with the twins at a table while Jan and Rhiannon went to the snack bar for hot dogs and drinks. Once the children were pacified with juice boxes and cookies, Terry turned to stare at Marika.

Marika raised an eyebrow. "What?"

"You remind me of me." Terry smirked.

Marika frowned. "What are you talking about?"

"You're smitten, my friend. You've got the same goofy look on your face that I can feel on mine every time I'm around Jan."

"I do not." Marika blew out her breath. "For heaven's sake, are you and Lee conspiring together or something?"

"Nope. I haven't talked to Lee recently, but if she figures you're smitten, too, then she's obviously a woman of equal insight and keen powers of observation. Though, to be fair, a blind man could see what's going on between you two."

Marika shook her head. "There's nothing going on. We're just friends. Why won't anyone believe me?"

Terry smiled at Marika. "Because we can see what's in your eyes and the way you look at her. I think it's wonderful. Why are you trying to reject something that makes you so happy? Why not relax and see what happens?"

Marika was about to rebut Terry's assumptions when she saw Rhiannon and Jan walking their way with trays of food. "Please don't embarrass her, Ter." Without waiting for a response, she jumped to her feet and went to help.

Gao lounged under a tree on the far side of the lunch area. He set the digital camera at his side with muted satisfaction. His boss would be pleased with the photographic record of the lawyer's weekend.

Gao took an energy bar out of his waist pack and surveyed the lawyer's party as he ate. *For God's sake, go home. I'm so tired of traipsing all over hell's half-acre. And who knows how many ways those idiots have managed to mishandle yesterday's shipment without me looking over their shoulders.* He brooded about the unfairness. *She will hold me responsible for them but prevents me from exercising supervision because of this ridiculous assignment. It's insane.*

Gao leaned back against the tree and closed his eyes. *Ours is not to reason why. I'll assign Perry the evening surveillance shift and go find the Kings—get their report in person. It will be a good opportunity to ask them about their neighbour as well.*

Sandra accepted Liang's hand out of the limo. Palmer followed. He took Sandra's hand and tucked it over his arm. They approached the door, and a servant opened it for them.

"It was a lovely service, don't you think, my dear?" Palmer asked as he escorted Sandra into their home.

"Yes, darling. I thought Reverend Grant quite outdid himself today. By the way, he asked me if we would be interested in supporting their inner-city teen-retrieval project this fall. I told him to send the information to the Foundation office, and I'd take a look at it."

"That's nice," Palmer said absently.

Sandra smiled and patted Palmer's arm. "Are you going to the club right away?"

"Do you mind?" Palmer asked. "I'm meeting Harvey, Brandon, and Peter for lunch before our tee time."

"Not at all, darling. I still have arrangements to make for the trip next week, so you run along and play. Perhaps I'll join you later for drinks, and we can have dinner there."

Palmer kissed her cheek. "You are the best. I'll see you at the club." He climbed the long, winding staircase.

Sandra turned to the hovering servant. "Tell Liang I want to see him in my office." She had scarcely arrived at her office before her chauffeur presented himself at the door with an envelope in hand. "Did you print them?"

"Yes, madam. Both days are accounted for."

She took the envelope. "Wait outside."

Cass fanned rapidly through the stack of colour photos, her anger rising by the moment. She ignored the zooscape and beautiful mountains and focused solely on the women who were together in almost every shot. Their expressions and body language infuriated her.

She selected three of the photos and pushed the others aside. The first was of Marika and her companion arm-in-arm as they emerged from an old-fashioned diner. The second was of the smaller woman laughing at some monkeys while Marika regarded her with an expression of affection and delight.

It was the third, though, that set Cass' blood to boiling. They stood at the railing of a mountain observation point. Cass checked Gao's report and discovered it was at the top of the gondola ride up Sulphur Mountain. They faced each other, and the interloper was tucking a lock of wind-whipped hair behind Marika's ear. The look they exchanged was so tender that Cass ripped the picture into tiny pieces.

Cass drew in deep breaths until she quieted herself enough to read Perry's electronic surveillance report. She whistled. Although Rhiannon stayed with Marika the previous night, they had not shared a bed. *So, you haven't fucked her yet? You're off your game, Marika. It usually doesn't take you half this long.* "Guess you never mentioned to your little whore that I had you in my bed two hours after we met." It was small consolation. Based on the photos and transcripts, it was a matter of "when" not "if" they became lovers.

She leaned back in her chair. The familiar rage swelled and exhilarated her. *Too bad I can't take care of this problem personally. I'd love to acquaint that little bitch with my favourite blade*. But while Cass ignored the rational inner voice that warned her to walk away from Marika, she couldn't entirely abandon the caution that had served her so well.

Cass took a cell phone out of the drawer and quickly punched in a number. When her call was answered, she said, "Eliminate the lawyer's companion. Make it look like an accident." She waited just long enough to secure acknowledgement of her order, terminated the connection, and picked up the photo of the women emerging from the restaurant.

A cold smile crossed her face as she studied the laughing couple. Very deliberately, she tore the picture down the middle, crumpled one half, and stared at the other.

Cass traced her finger over Marika's image. "You and I are overdue for a long conversation."

CHAPTER 20

LEE WALKED DOWN THE SEVENTH-FLOOR hallway to Marika's office, many of those she greeted familiar to her now. Marika and Rhiannon were conferring at Rhiannon's desk, and Lee grinned at their body language. Marika rested one hand on Rhiannon's shoulder, and Rhiannon leaned toward Marika, her gaze fastened on Marika's face.

Lee cleared her throat.

They jumped apart, a slight flush rising on Marika's face.

"Hey, wage slaves, the day's over. It's time to play."

"God, Lee. You scared me out of a year's growth," Marika said.

"You don't want to be any taller, anyway." Lee looked at Rhiannon. "How's it going, Rhi?"

"Great. You're in a good mood today, considering it's Monday."

"Why not? It's been a beautiful summer day in the best city in the country. And coincidentally, Eli's with his dad on their annual fishing trip, so Dana and I have the house to ourselves this week. I even talked her into going out for a nice long ride on the Suzuki yesterday. Really, can life get any better?" Lee beat out a drumroll on the corner of Rhiannon's desk.

Marika raised an eyebrow. "So you just came by to share the joy?"

"Nope. Came by to see if you two would like to join me at the Tudor Rose for a bite and a brew."

"What happened to you and Dana having the house all to yourselves?" Marika asked. "I wouldn't think you'd want to waste any of that alone time."

Lee frowned. "She's stuck on evening shift tonight." The frown vanished. "But then she goes on days, and we have four nights to play. So what about it? Can I tempt you into joining me?"

"Sure, I'd love to," Marika said. "Rhi?"

Rhiannon shook her head. "Thank you, but no. I brought my swim gear with me, and I'm going to the Y."

"Aw, are you sure? I was going to tell you guys all about the wedding plans," Lee said. "Dana's got everything planned to the nth degree. Which reminds me, you do know you're invited, right, Rhi?" There was an exchange of glances between her friends.

Rhiannon cleared her throat. "Well, actually, a couple of weeks ago Marika asked me to go with her, and I said yes."

Lee grinned and caught Marika's eye. "A couple of weeks ago, eh? My, my, wasn't that remarkable foresight on her part."

Marika glared at Lee. "I'll shut down my computer, grab my purse, and be right with you."

Lee looked at Rhiannon, who'd finished closing her files. "Are you sure you won't come? You could always go to the Y afterwards."

Rhiannon shook her head. "I'd like to, but I'm meeting David for a driving lesson at seven-thirty, and I really want to get in a swim first. I'm feeling sluggish after all these weeks off. Can I take a raincheck?"

"Sure. No problem. We can even walk partway together."

Marika rejoined them. They took the elevator to the street level and maneuvered through the five o'clock crowds that clogged the sidewalks. They had almost reached the corner when someone called Lee's name.

She turned.

Al, dressed in his city police uniform, approached.

Still on foot patrol, eh? Good thing he likes it. "Hey, Al. How's it going?"

"Good. It's great to see you, Sarge," Al said. "Me and the major were just talking about you the other day, wonderin' how the hell you were doing."

"Same old, same old," Lee said. "Not much different from our military days. Hurry up and wait, and God help the hindmost."

Al laughed. "Ain't that life in a nutshell?"

"So how is Marc these days? Still running his department with an iron fist?"

"Ah, you know the major. He may run a tight ship, but he's a good guy. He sure has a lot of respect for you, and he still dreams of recruiting you for the city police, you know?"

Lee chuckled. "Not going to happen, my friend. I like being the boss." She still held their former commanding officer in great affection. He'd come to her one day with a warning. In those less enlightened days, she had been about to be investigated and likely discharged for being a lesbian. It gave Lee a chance to put in her release voluntarily. She knew Major Manion pulled strings to protect her, and she'd never forgotten his kindness or his genuine regret that he was losing one of his best people. "So what've you been up to lately?"

Rhiannon tapped Lee on the arm and jerked her head down the street.

Lee nodded and Rhiannon walked away. Lee broke into Al's monologue long enough to introduce Marika.

There was a deafening squeal of tires and frantic yells. Lee spun toward the commotion.

Marika screamed and bolted to the corner.

Rhiannon was sprawled on the sidewalk. A nondescript tan car sped off down the street while people rushed to her aid. Marika reached Rhiannon as she struggled to sit up.

Lee turned to Al, who was already on his radio, calling in a description of the car and the direction the careless—or drunk—driver had fled. She dashed to where her friends sat on the sidewalk.

Marika clutched Rhiannon. "Are you sure you're okay?"

Rhiannon nodded. "He just missed me."

"Damned fool came out of nowhere." A businessman shook his head and helped Rhiannon to her feet.

The young woman who had retrieved Rhiannon's gym bag glared in the direction the car had gone. "He never even slowed down. The bastard just kept going."

Al jogged up, his radio chattering. He surveyed Rhiannon, who stood in the circle of Marika's arm. "They've sent a unit after him, ma'am. Do you need me to call EMS?"

Rhiannon looked at the raw palm of her right hand. "No, thanks. It's nothing a bit of first aid won't take care of."

Al began to gather statements from excited onlookers.

Lee moved closer. "Can you tell me what happened?"

Rhiannon shuddered, and Marika's arm tightened around her shoulders. "I'm not sure I know. I started across the street—I know I had the light. I was thinking about you two going to the Tudor Rose, and I decided that I wanted to go too. So I turned and sprinted for the sidewalk. The next thing I knew, I heard the sound of a car right behind me, and I jumped. Geez, I felt the wind as it roared by." Pale, Rhiannon looked at Lee with wide eyes. "If I hadn't changed my mind, he would've hit me."

"But he didn't. You're all right, and that's all that matters." Lee brushed a hand over Rhiannon's cheek. She got a shaky half-smile in response.

Lee looked over Rhi's shoulder into Marika's angry, fearful eyes. She laid a hand on Marika's shoulder before making her way to where Al was talking to witnesses and taking notes. She waited patiently until he was done, then looked at him with a raised eyebrow.

"Dunno, Sarge. This is a weird one. One witness is sure she saw the car parked just down the block before the accident. Said it looked to her like it was deliberate. Another fellow claims the driver was weaving all over the road, and he's sure he was drunk. Hopefully, the boys will nab him. I got a partial plate, but the description of the driver was pretty vague. About all everyone agrees on is that it was a male wearing a ballcap, hunched over the wheel."

"Will you do me a favour and let me know what happens with this? The almost-victim is a very good friend of mine." Lee handed Al her business card.

He tucked it in his shirt pocket. "No problem. Now, I gotta talk to your friend for a few minutes, so if you'll excuse me." Al wound his way back through the gathering of witnesses and lookie-loos to where Rhiannon and Marika stood together.

Lee turned and gazed down the street. *It had to be an accident, right? Just some dumbass drunk.* But the witness' statement about the apparently deliberate nature of the incident bothered her. *Who would try to hurt Rhiannon? And why?* Lee pushed the thought to the back of her mind and rejoined her friends, but the fine summer day had lost its lustre.

Gao pulled into the metered parking spot, turned off the engine, and exited the stolen Pontiac. He walked away at an unhurried pace, tossing latex gloves and a baseball cap in the nearest garbage can. Sirens sounded in the distance

He kept his expression blank though his thoughts roiled. The hit and run had been a spur of the moment plan instigated by the Chameleon's orders. *I should've taken time to plan more carefully. Next time.* He walked down the sidewalk, and the glimmers of a new course of action began to take shape. *Even better. No direct involvement.*

Rhiannon winced as Dana cleaned and dressed her scraped palm. After her near miss, Marika and Lee had insisted on walking Rhiannon to the downtown clinic where Dana worked.

"You know," Dana said. "You're making a habit out of this. I'm going to have to start charging for my services if you keep this up."

Rhiannon grinned. "I'll try to stay in one piece from now on."

Dana finished and set her materials to the side. She peeled off her gloves and gave Rhiannon a hug. "Good. I've seen enough of your blood to last me one lifetime." She walked Rhiannon out to the waiting room, where Marika and Lee waited.

"All better?" Lee asked.

Rhiannon nodded. "I'm fine. It was no big deal."

"Like hell it wasn't!" Marika flushed when the others turned to look at her.

Rhiannon smiled at Marika. "It's okay, really. I'm okay."

"Look, why don't we go to the Tudor Rose like we planned? I'm sure everyone will feel better once we have something to eat." Lee kissed Dana goodbye and herded Marika and Rhiannon outside.

When they got to the pub, Rhiannon borrowed Marika's cellphone and stepped away from their booth to make a call. "Hi, David?"

"Hey, Rhi. I was just going to phone you. My schedule has cleared, and we can go driving earlier if you want."

"That's what I'm calling about. I'm going to have to postpone our lesson tonight. I was sort of in an accident."

"What kind of an accident? Are you all right?"

"I'm okay, honest." Rhiannon glanced back at the booth. Marika and Lee were watching her. "Some idiot nearly hit me with his car, but all I got was a bit of road rash. Dana's already patched me up, and I'm going to have dinner with Marika and Lee."

"Good Lord! Are you sure you're all right?"

"I'm sure. I'll call you tomorrow to reschedule, okay?"

"Okay. And, Rhi, please take care of yourself. Look both ways before crossing."

Rhiannon flashed back on her father issuing those same instructions. She grinned. "Yes, Dad."

David harrumphed. "Talk to you later."

"Will do. Goodnight, David."

After they ate, Marika drove her home. She pulled into the alley, parked behind Hettie's house, and unbuckled her seatbelt.

"Um, Marika?"

"Don't even think of arguing. I'm walking you to the door." Marika opened her side and got out.

Rhiannon smiled and followed suit. *Not arguing. Nope, not in the least.*

When they reached the backdoor, Marika didn't say a word. She just reached for Rhiannon and pulled her into a long hug.

I am so not arguing. Rhiannon closed her eyes and absorbed the sweetness of Marika's embrace.

Finally, Marika eased away. She raised her hands to Rhiannon's face.

Rhiannon froze, every cell in her body on high alert. *Is she going to—?*

But Marika only stared into Rhiannon's eyes for a timeless moment, then her hands dropped away. "I'm so glad you're all right. Have a good night." With another quick hug, she spun on her heel and walked back down the path to her car.

Rhiannon waved as Marika drove away, then entered the house with a huge grin on her face. The house was empty, and she bounded up the stairs, humming.

Two hours later, stretched out on her bed in her pajamas, Rhiannon set aside her novel. She'd read until her eyes were heavy and she was ready for sleep. She opened her bankbook, a routine so ingrained that it was automatic, and reviewed the numbers she knew by heart. Then she set the passbook down and picked up her passport. Rhiannon flipped through the pristine pages. In the recent past, she'd have imagined the stamps of countless countries there. But tonight it was just a small, blue booklet—not the magic key to freedom and distant lands it had once been.

Rhiannon set the passport on top of the bankbook, too tired to think. She turned off her lamp, tucked her left hand behind her head, and rested her bandaged right hand on the passport and bankbook. The day's heat lingered even though dusk had fallen, and it was still hot in her room. She'd left her door ajar to increase the draft coming in the open windows, but it did little to stir the sluggish air.

Rhiannon shunned the blankets and drifted off to sleep. Her last waking thought was of Marika's embrace.

A violent fit of coughing woke Rhiannon from a deep sleep. Confused, she opened her eyes, but they stung from the thick smoke gathering in her room. Understanding sank in, and she bolted to her feet. She ran to her door and yanked it open to discover the hallway was filled with smoke and flames licked up the walls. "Hettie! Hettie, we have to get out!"

Unable to go down the hall, Rhiannon screamed her aunt's name over and over, but got no response. Within minutes, the heat and smoke drove her back into her room, and she slammed the door. Coughing hoarsely, she retreated until she bumped into the bed and fell onto the mattress. The discarded bankbook and passport were under her hand so she jammed them into her pajama pocket.

Rhiannon's thoughts careened. *There's was no way out. I can't get to the stairs, and I'm two floors up. Jesus!* A jump would mean multiple broken bones and potential death. Her heart raced. *Not now. Not when I'm finally having fun, when I have friends, when I have—* She flashed on Marika cupping her face and staring into her eyes. *No, not again. It's not going to end this way—not now. Think, damnit. Think. There has to be a way out!*

Rhiannon clenched the bedspread. Instantly, she dropped to her knees and stripped off the sheets and coverlet. *Please, let it hold me. God, don't let it break.* Rhiannon knotted the bedding together, tears streaming down her face. The smoke had thickened in the brief time she'd been awake. She choked and struggled for air as she crawled across the floor, desperately hoping she was on course for the open windows. Terrified, Rhiannon looked back. An eerie orange glow illuminated the door, and an ominous crackling resounded in her ears. Time was running out.

Rhiannon could barely make out shapes now, but the table leg she bumped into meant the windows were right above her. She scrambled to her feet and slid across the tabletop to reach an open window. She fought for air while thick reams of smoke poured out of the room. The narrow bit of wall between the two windows served as an anchor for her improvised escape rope.

"Mom, help me!" The unconscious plea escaped Rhiannon's lips as she tugged on the bedding. When it held, she swung her legs out the window. She descended amidst calls from below and the sound of approaching sirens. Hands reached to assist her just as the bedding parted and she dropped the last few feet. Louis, her across-the-alley neighbour, helped her away from the house.

"Oh my God—my aunt." Rhiannon looked back at the house, where flames shot out from under the eaves and swirled in a macabre dance across the roof. "Did she get out? Does anyone know if she got out?"

Louis steered her to the edge of the alley and gave her into the care of his wife, who stood with other neighbours watching the old house disappear in the roaring conflagration. "Shit. It's like settin' a haystack on fire." Louis spat. "All the damn houses around here ain't nothin' but fuckin' tinderboxes."

"My aunt?" Rhiannon's eyes widened. If Hettie was still in there, she didn't stand a chance.

"I'll go 'round the front and see if I kin find her," Louis said. His wife laid a comforting hand on Rhiannon's arm.

Rhiannon shivered and wiped a grimy sleeve across her burning eyes. Fire trucks screamed up in front of the house and lights flashed through the smoke and flames. Her stomach threatened to empty, and she gagged. She was hypnotized by the strobes at the edge of her vision and transported back to an earlier fire—the nightmare that had destroyed her childhood.

"You! You're the one who brought this catastrophe down on my house!"

Rhiannon blinked.

Hettie bore down on her like a battle cruiser under full sail and lashed out in a fury. She caught Rhiannon across the jaw, and Rhiannon's head snapped back.

Louis instantly stepped between them and pushed Hettie back.

Hettie shoved at his chest and tried to sidestep him. "You killed your mother, and now you're trying to kill me! You're evil, girl, evil! You stay out all night, doing God knows what. You brought His wrath down on my house! You're damned, Anne Davies! Have been since the moment your ungrateful carcass was dumped on my doorstep. I shoulda known you'd bring your curse with you—"

"Hettie Walker! That's enough." David's deep, angry voice rang out. He hurried up and scanned Rhiannon, then turned to confront Hettie. "I know you're upset right now, so I'll save the lecture on your unchristian attitude, but I suspect you'll find this tragedy had little to do with God and more to do with man's carelessness." David turned his gaze on Eugenia Carter, who stood with her hands clasped to her mouth. "Can you take Hettie home with you for now?"

Eugenia nodded and led the distraught woman from the scene. Hettie's wails and lamentations filled the smoky air.

"Jesus, I'm sorry, kid," Louis said. "I found your aunt standin' out front with Miz Carter, and I tol' her you was out back. I din't know she would hit ya."

"It's all right, Louis," David said. "There's no way you could've known." He took off his jacket and wrapped it around Rhiannon's shoulders. "I'm going to take her back to the rectory with me. Would you let the fire captain know that both inhabitants got out safely and where he can find Hettie if he needs to talk to her?"

Louis nodded. "Sure thing." He trotted off, dodging firemen and jumping over hoses.

David guided Rhiannon away from the scene. She leaned against him as he led her down the alley, avoiding the stones for the sparse grass as much as he could. "I'd loan you my shoes, but you could fit both of your feet into one of them, so I don't think you'd get too far."

Rhiannon managed a small grunt.

David didn't try to force further conversation. He supported her as the noise of the fire, firefighters, and onlookers faded behind them. Ten minutes later, they reached the church, and David steered her to the rectory door. He unlocked it and directed her inside.

Rhiannon walked into the kitchen and stopped.

David moved in front of her and took her hands.

Rhiannon focused on him. He wore a pajama shirt with jeans and runners on sockless feet. A smile glimmered as she took in his disheveled appearance. His thin, blonde hair stuck out at all angles, his glasses had slipped down his nose, and a light stubble covered his normally closely shaven cheeks. "How did you know?" Rhiannon asked. It had seemed so natural for him to show up when she was in need.

"Tupper called me as soon as he heard the ruckus, and I ran the whole way there." David squeezed her hands, then touched her jaw. "This is going to make for a nasty bruise."

Rhiannon realized why her head ached. *So much for never letting anyone hit me again.*

"There's some Tylenol in the bathroom cupboard if you need it. Why don't you go take a shower? You can use my robe—it's hanging on the back of the door. I'll make some tea, and we'll sit and talk a bit, okay?"

Rhiannon glanced at her soot-stained arms and nodded. Once in the bathroom, she stripped off her pajamas and something dropped from the pocket. She stooped to pick up the bankbook and passport. Rhiannon stared at the only things she had salvaged. *I wish I'd thought to grab my wallet.* She shook her head. *It's just stuff. You got out safely. That's all that counts.*

Rhiannon found the Tylenol, then pushed the shower curtain aside and climbed into the tub. She set the water on hard and hot. The sluice blasted the first layer of grime off her body. She picked up the soap and scoured away the last physical reminders of the fire. When Rhiannon finally turned off the water and got out, she could no longer smell the stink of smoke on herself, though her pajamas still reeked. She towelled dry and shook her head when she wrapped herself in David's robe. It dragged on the floor, the sleeves came down to her knees, and she was lost in voluminous fleecy folds. *I feel like the smallest dwarf.*

She picked up the remnants of her possessions and padded out of the steamy bathroom.

David sat at the kitchen table, toying with the teapot in front of him. He glanced up at her approach and grinned.

"Yeah, yeah, yuck it up, Ichabod." Rhiannon set her dirty pajamas by the kitchen door and slid into the chair opposite him.

David pressed a hand to his mouth, but finally lost the struggle in a burst of laughter.

Rhiannon joined him, and some of her stress washed away in the shared hilarity.

When his chuckles subsided, David poured a cup of tea and pushed it across the table to her. A third cup sat in front of him.

Rhiannon touched it and looked at him.

"I called Marika while you were in the shower," David said. "She's on her way over, and she's bringing some clothes for you."

Rhiannon's eyes filled, and she rubbed her sleeve over them. "Thank you. That was really thoughtful." Her heart beat faster. *Marika's coming.* She took a deep breath and laid the passport and bankbook on the table. "This was all I saved."

David looked at the documents, and picked up the passport. He glanced at Rhiannon, and she nodded. He flipped through the blank pages before setting it carefully back on the bankbook. "Want to tell me about it?"

She inhaled the fragrance of her tea. "It?"

"Must be pretty important to you if that's all you grabbed in your escape," David said.

"Actually, it was more an accident that I had them on my bed. I was looking at them before I fell asleep, so when the fire hit, I just grabbed them on my way out."

"Uh-huh. Any particular reason you were looking at them before you went to sleep?" David sipped his tea.

"I look at them most nights and dream of the day when I'll have enough money to use that passport." Rhiannon curled her hands around her cup and studied her tea. "I'm going away from here pretty soon. I've had it planned for years. First, I'm going to Wales. I was born there, in Aberystwyth, when my parents were visiting my dad's family. I can remember Dad talking about his family all the time when I was little. I vaguely remember meeting an uncle or a cousin who came over for a visit, but I've never met the rest of them. Dad and Mom always planned to take me there again when they could afford it."

"So you want to visit your family there?" David asked.

"I want to know why they abandoned me to Hettie," Rhiannon shot back, the old bitterness rising. "She was the only living relative Mom had, but Dad had a whole gang of them. Why didn't one of them come for me? It's not like Hettie would've fought them for custody."

David reached a hand across the table, and Rhiannon's anger subsided under his touch. She took a deep breath. "Anyway, from there, I'm going to start traveling. I'm used to living cheap, and I've got a decent nest egg to fall back on. I'm not afraid to work, and I thought I could pick up some extra money by drawing for tourists in the summer months. I'll stay in hostels or camp out where I can. I've got it all worked down to exactly what I'm taking with me."

"How far are you going, and how long do you think you'll be gone?"

"Well, my maps are burnt up now, or I'd show you some of the places I plan to go, but as to how far—pretty much wherever the winds and inclination take me. And I'll be gone until I'm ready to come back...if ever. I can tell you I'll never live with Hettie again."

The last was said so emphatically that David grinned, then his smile faded. "I'll miss you."

Rhiannon met his gaze steadily. "I'll miss you, too. You've been a good—if very unexpected—friend."

He tilted his head. "What about Marika?"

Rhiannon ran her finger around the edge of the cup. That was the question that echoed in her mind every night. Troubled, she looked up. "I don't know. I...just don't know." Her dream of escape was so old and deep-rooted; her feelings for Marika were so new. She'd been trying not to think about it too much, preferring to live in the moment and let the future take care of itself.

"Well, I'm glad you saved something," David said. "The church has an emergency community fund that I have discretionary use of, and I'll help you get some things together." When she began to protest, he held his hand up and shook his head. "No, not this time, Rhiannon Davies. You've nothing left, and I'm not about to let your pride stand in the way of helping you out. Got that?"

Rhiannon subsided with a chuckle. "All right. But I'll pay you back."

David smiled. "If you wish to make a contribution to the church fund someday, I certainly wouldn't deny you that right. I really am sorry that you lost everything, but I'm so deeply grateful that you got out safely."

"Thanks." Rhiannon patted his hand. "My stuff wasn't all that great, but I am sad to lose my pictures." Wistfully, she considered all the drawings that had covered her walls. "Strange, I lost my parents to a fire, and now I've lost all my pictures of them to another fire. Ironic, eh?"

"Can you draw your parents again?"

"Yes. That's how I first got started drawing. We lost all the family photos in the fire, and I didn't want to forget Mom, so I started drawing her over and over. I discovered I actually had a talent for it. When Dad died...well, it took me a while to stop being mad at him, but eventually I started drawing him, too."

"Do you want to talk about them?"

David wasn't pressing or prying. He simply offered her an option. *Do I want to tell him?* Rhiannon had never spoken to anyone about what happened all those years ago. School counselors had all abandoned the effort to open her up. *He's my friend. I trusted him with the dream. Can I tell him about that night*—all *about that night?* Rhiannon studied David. *How did I ever think he was the homeliest man I'd ever seen?* There was compassion in his eyes and lines of laughter in his face. *He cares—about everyone, but especially me.* Ultimately, it was simple. She could trust this man...this priest...this friend. "Yes. I do want to talk about them."

He nodded but didn't say anything.

"I was ten years old—" Lights swept across the kitchen as a car pulled into the driveway. "Hold that thought." She opened the door.

Marika ran up the pathway and swept Rhiannon into her arms. She held Rhiannon so tightly it almost hurt.

Rhiannon locked her arms around Marika's back and buried her face in Marika's chest. They stood silently in the doorway. When Marika pulled back, Rhiannon brushed the dampness from her cheeks.

Marika's eyes widened, and she held Rhiannon at arm's length. "What in heaven's name are you wearing?"

"The Friendly Giant's housecoat. It wasn't like I had a lot of choice."

"Well, not that you don't look adorable, but I can do something about that." Marika walked back to the car and returned with a plastic bag. "Here, I think you'll find something that'll fit you better in there."

Rhiannon left Marika with David in the kitchen and went to change. She found underwear, shorts, a T-shirt, and sandals that were much too long, but still wearable. She dressed and surveyed herself in the mirror, pleased with her more conventional appearance. She hung the robe back on the door and returned to the kitchen to find her friends deep in conversation.

They both looked up at her approach, their faces lined with worry and weariness.

Rhiannon glanced at the kitchen clock. It was almost two in the morning. "Look, I'm keeping you both up—" Before she could go any further, they shook their heads.

David pushed out a chair and gestured her into the seat. "Don't be silly. It's hardly your fault that your home burned down in the middle of the night." Rhiannon sat down. "Now, I believe you were about to tell me about your parents."

Marika didn't look surprised.

David must've told her. It didn't bother Rhiannon. She'd made the decision to open up. These two, above all others, would listen without judgement. David topped up their cups, and she began again.

"Well, like I was saying, I was ten years old. We lived in Toronto, quite close to the railway tracks. Dad worked the night shift as a baker, and Mom worked days in a dry-cleaning place. We didn't have much money, but I never felt deprived. Mom and Dad were great about finding things to do in the city that didn't cost much. When I think of my early childhood, I remember a lot of laughter and a sense of being loved and safe."

Rhiannon paused to take a drink. Her audience was fixed intently on her. "I can remember Dad dancing me around the kitchen while I stood on his shoes, but he really loved to dance with Mom. They'd turn up the radio, and I'd sit on the counter clapping as they danced and danced." She smiled. "Dad worshipped the ground Mom walked on, and Mom's eyes used to just shine when she heard him at the front door."

Rhiannon glanced at Marika. They looked at each other for a long moment before Rhi took a deep breath and went on. "Mom used to babysit for some of the people in the neighbourhood, and one night she was looking after this little kid who just wouldn't settle down. Dad was at work, Mom was occupied with the cranky baby, and when it came time for bed, she didn't have time to read me my usual stories. I was mad at her, and I stomped upstairs to my bedroom..."

"Stupid baby!" Rhiannon slammed the door behind her. She loved story time with her mother, and it was ruined.

She marched across the room and dropped to her knees in front of the cage. She opened the wire door and scooped out Elrod. Leaning back against her bed, she stroked the white mouse with one finger.

Elrod sniffed her palm, then tickled her as he ran up her arm and across the back of her neck. She giggled and plucked him off her shoulder. She gave him a goodnight kiss and put him back in his cage.

With a heartfelt sigh, she got into bed and picked up one of her books but tossed it aside and pulled the covers up around her neck. When her mother came in to say goodnight, Rhiannon pretended she was asleep and didn't react to the kiss on her cheek.

She was quite sure she wouldn't sleep, but she was wrenched awake hours later. Her mother grabbed her and pulled her out of bed while she cradled the wailing baby in the other arm. "We have to get out of the house...now! Hold on to my bathrobe and don't let go."

Scared into speechlessness, Rhiannon grabbed her mom's robe and trotted after her. They emerged into a smoky hall, and it was hard to see where she was going. She sensed her mother feeling her way with one hand. The baby's cries interspersed with coughs.

They were almost to the bottom of the stairs when Rhiannon remembered Elrod. She dropped the robe and ran back up the stairs. She burst into her room and grabbed the cage, but when she tried to leave, she was driven back by a blast of heat. She stared at the flames now visible in the hallway.

"Mommy, help me!" Rhiannon cast her gaze frantically about the room, seeking an escape. She ran to the window but couldn't get it open. Sobbing, she rolled under the bed and pulled Elrod's cage with her.

The window smashed, and strong hands pulled her out from under the bed. Still clutching the cage, she was carried to the window. Over the fireman's shoulder, she saw flames lick at her bed, and then she was outside, being carried down a ladder.

"When Mom realized we'd gotten separated, she gave the baby to a neighbour and ran back into the house. She didn't make it out a second time. Someone called Dad at work, and he rushed home. I'll never forget his scream when they told him that Mom was still inside." When Marika gently wiped at her cheeks with a tissue, Rhiannon realized she was crying. Marika used another tissue to dab at her own eyes.

David gazed at Rhiannon with compassion. "It's okay to stop—"

Rhiannon shook her head. "There's not much more to tell. Elrod died a few days after the fire. The same day we buried Mom, actually. Dad got an apartment, and he switched shifts so he could be home in the evenings and nights with me. But it was like everything good had gone out of his life. I never heard him laugh again. I tried so hard..."

Rhiannon's voice failed as she recalled the endless days she'd attempted to take her mother's place. She'd cleaned the sparsely furnished home and done her best to cook her father's meals. She'd talked to the silent man as they sat across the table from each other. One time, she tried to coax him into dancing, but he gently pushed her away and said, "Maybe later."

"One morning, he left for work at the usual time. I went to get my school lunch and I saw that Dad had forgotten his, so I ran after him. I was a block behind him and gaining when I saw—" Rhiannon paused, her voice cracking. "He stepped right into the path of a city bus. They tried to tell me later that it was an accident, that he wasn't paying attention, but I knew."

Her friends shifted uneasily.

"You knew what?" David asked.

Rhiannon's anguished gaze rose to meet his. "I knew he didn't love me enough to live for me. He walked into the path of that bus because he couldn't stand life without Mom one more moment. He didn't even last a year without her."

"I'm so, so sorry," Marika said, tears rolling down her cheeks. "To have that happen...and for you to see it..."

Rhiannon looked beyond them to a past she had never spoken of until now. "I always wondered if losing Dad was my punishment for killing Mom." There was an outcry of protests, and she shook her head. "No, it's okay. I do understand that I was a kid, and I reacted without thinking. That it killed my mother was a horrible accident." Rhiannon grimaced. "Mind you, when I got dumped with Hettie, I was pretty sure *that* was my punishment." Her weak attempt at humour failed to wring a smile from her friends. She looked at the clock. It was now almost three.

Marika followed her gaze and closed her hand over Rhiannon's. "I'm taking you home. You can stay with me as long as you want."

"I was going to keep you here," David said. "But I thought it might arouse less comment from the small-minded in the parish if you stayed with a female friend."

Rhiannon snorted at the irony. David's grin indicated he was well aware of it too. "I'll take you up on that offer for a few nights, but I'll get onto finding a new place in the morning."

Marika shook her head but stood when Rhiannon did.

David picked up her documents and handed them over before walking them to the door. "Call me tomorrow?" he asked.

Rhiannon nodded. "You mean today, but yes, I'll give you a call later on."

David opened his arms, and Rhiannon moved into them for a hug.

"Thanks, Ichabod," she whispered and squeezed him hard.

David hugged her back for a long moment, then released her. He stood in the doorway as Rhiannon got into Marika's car.

The last thing she saw before her eyes closed in exhaustion was David's hand raised in farewell as Marika backed out of the driveway.

A few tendrils of smoke still drifted up from the remains of the yellow house, but most of the emergency personnel had begun to pull back.

Pike sidled over to a fireman rolling up a hose. "Hey, pretty bad one, eh?"

"Yeah, but at least there was no loss of life." The firefighter slung the hose over his shoulder and walked away.

Pike's eyes widened, and he turned back to Eddie.

Eddie gaped at him. "Shit. What are we gonna do?"

"Shut the fuck up." Pike ran a hand through his hair. "I gotta think."

They crossed the street. When Eddie began to mount the stairs to their home, Pike shook his head. "Not a good idea. We gotta get outta here for a coupla days."

Eddie stared at Pike. "He ain't gonna be happy."

"Tell me somepin' I don't know, ya moron." Pike stalked over to the new pick-up parked behind their Harleys.

Pike didn't wait to see whether Eddie followed. He climbed in and started the engine. The truck was already in reverse by the time Eddie swung himself into the cab. Pike pulled out of the driveway, navigated around the pumper truck, and drove slowly down the street.

CHAPTER 21

MARIKA KEPT A CLOSE EYE on Rhiannon when they returned to the condo. "Are you sure there's nothing I can get you? Some warm milk, maybe?"

Rhiannon shook her head. "No, but thank you."

They made up the daybed in the den, a routine that had become second nature to them. Rhiannon shucked her clothes and climbed between the sheets.

Marika sat in the recliner, reluctant to leave Rhiannon alone.

Rhiannon's eyelids fluttered. "I feel like I've been up for a whole week."

"Go to sleep. And don't worry about going to work tomorrow. I'm going to call and book us off for the day."

"'Kay." Rhiannon's eyes closed. The hand that clutched the pillow relaxed. Her breathing deepened, and her features softened in sleep.

Marika studied Rhiannon's face. There was a shadow on her jaw where a bruise bloomed. Marika's anger flared. David had told her of Hettie's assault. *If I'd been there...* But thoughts of revenge melted away, replaced by sweeter memories of embracing Rhiannon. *Did she feel my desperation? I couldn't let her go. I needed to feel her warm, alive, pressed against me.* Marika closed her eyes and remembered how Rhiannon's arms had encircled her waist just as tightly. *She knew.* She sat in the chair for a long time, thinking about the story Rhiannon told her and David. *God, how did she survive? I can't even imagine a ten-year-old going through what she went through.* Marika shivered. *I should go back to bed. There's a lot to do tomorrow—or later today. I need some sleep.*

Marika rose to her feet. *Sleep, bedroom, down the hall, remember?* She shook her head, knelt by the daybed, and laid a hand on Rhiannon's hair. *They're right. I am so in love with her.* She tucked the covers around Rhiannon and softly kissed her cheek.

Marika's sleep was plagued by nightmares. Shortly after dawn, she gave up and formulated a plan. Then she got out of bed and went to the den.

Rhiannon had rolled in her sleep and faced away from Marika. The covers had slipped, leaving her exposed. Marika's gaze swept slowly across Rhiannon's back to the scar on her shoulder. *You got that protecting me. Now it's my turn.*

Lee folded the newspaper and drained her coffee. *Mmm, I should've taken today off.* She grinned, remembering why they'd been late to fall asleep. *Well worth a little exhaustion. I'll just hide in my office today.*

"Can I fill yours, too, love?" Dana extended the coffee pot toward Lee.

"You read my mind, thanks." Lee stacked their breakfast dishes while Dana poured the coffee.

The phone rang. Dana picked it up, and Lee returned her attention to the newspaper and her coffee.

"Hello." Dana balanced the phone between ear and shoulder while she transferred their bowls to the dishwasher. "Oh, hi, Marika. What's up?"

Dishes clattered on the counter, and Lee glanced at Dana.

"Oh, my God. Is she all right?"

Lee rose halfway to her feet.

Dana shook her head and motioned Lee back to her chair. "Well, thank heavens for that. Does she need a place to stay? We have lots of room here, and she would be most welcome."

Lee's breath caught, and she stared at Dana.

"All right, if you're sure. But you let us know if there's anything we can do. I mean that. In fact, do you know what her sizes are?" Dana jotted some notes on the phone pad. "Good, thanks. Look, we'll call you tonight, okay? You take care of her...and yourself. Bye, hon."

"What the hell happened?" Lee asked.

Dana sank down onto her chair. "Rhiannon's house burned down last night. She and her aunt both got out safely, but all she has are the clothes on her back."

An ominous chill went through Lee. *Two near misses in one day? Those are freakin' long odds.*

Dana rubbed her forehead. "I told Marika that Rhiannon could stay here if she wanted, but she wants Rhi to stay with her. She thinks she'll be more comfortable in familiar surroundings. She's going to take Rhiannon shopping for some clothes and things today. Apparently, David is going to help out with some church emergency funds. I'd like us to contribute too, all right? Lee? Lee?"

Lee blinked. "Yes, of course we'll help. Whatever you think best is fine with me."

"I wasn't sure if Rhiannon would accept cash, but Marika gave me her sizes. I don't have to be at work until noon, so I'll go and pick up some things. Maybe we can run them over after I get off tonight."

Lee nodded absently.

Dana sighed. "I know that look. You've got something going on in that head of yours."

Lee patted Dana's hand. "Just doing some thinking, sweetheart. Something about all this stinks like yesterday's fish. I think I'll do a little poking around."

Dana came around the table to kiss Lee. "Please make sure it's not a hornet's nest that you're poking. I'm going to shower. If you can be home about six-thirty tonight, we'll go over and see Marika and Rhiannon then."

Lee nodded, and Dana left the kitchen. Lee studied the tabletop, deep in thought, then she picked up the phone and punched in her business partner's home number. "Willem? I know it's early, but I need a favour."

"I have not even finished my breakfast, Lee. Couldn't this wait until we're in the office?" Willem asked.

"Not really. Is your cousin still with the city fire department?"

"Yes. Why do you ask?"

"A friend of mine lost her home in a house fire in Victoria Park last night."

"I'm so sorry. I heard of the fire on the news this morning. A three-alarm blaze, and apparently, they almost lost the houses on either side, as well. Your friend was lucky to get out alive."

"There's something more than a little suspicious about the fire, because my friend had another near miss with a hit and run earlier in the day." Lee's voice was strained. "I have a really bad feeling that she's in some kind of trouble. I'd like to figure out what's going on before there's another so-called accident. Can you get in touch with your cousin and find out what the unofficial word is on the fire?"

"Of course. I'll get the information as quickly as possible."

"Thanks, Wil. I'll be at the office in thirty minutes. See you there." Lee hung up. Willem would come through for her; he always did. Between the two of them, they had connections that covered most of the city, from boardrooms to back alleys—though Willem specialized in the former, while Lee was more at home in the latter.

Marika sipped her coffee at the kitchen table. Rhiannon was still asleep in the den, and she didn't want to wake her until absolutely necessary. She had called the office, explained the circumstances, and booked both of them off work for the day. She'd also let Dana and Lee know what was going on. Now she had nothing left to distract her from her thoughts.

When David called with the news the previous night, he'd taken pains to assure her that Rhiannon was fine and safe at the rectory. But that hadn't prevented Marika from being consumed with fear. Marika's frantic drive to the rectory took her near Rhiannon's house. Even from one street over, she'd become almost physically ill at glimpsing the smoking ruins. It was only when she pulled into David's driveway and saw Rhiannon framed in the light of the open door that she felt like she could breathe again.

Spooky announced Rhiannon's arrival with a crescendo of purrs. She came into the kitchen, knelt, and stroked his fur.

"Hey," Marika said. "How are you feeling this morning?"

Rhiannon straightened. "Not bad, I guess. Still a bit tired."

"You don't have to get up yet. We're off work for the day, if you want to go back to bed. You can use my bed if you'd be more comfortable."

Rhiannon took a cup from the cupboard and filled it from the carafe. "Thanks, but no. I'd rather be up. I've got to make some plans."

"I hope one of those plans is to stay here as long as you'd like. Dana said you're welcome to stay there, too, but I thought...well, you know. You're already familiar with the condo. Spooky likes you." Marika hesitated. "It's really no trouble. I mean, we get along well."

Rhiannon regarded her over the edge of the coffee cup

Under the table, Marika crossed her fingers.

Rhiannon set her cup down. "I really appreciate your offer. I can't even begin to tell you how much it means to me that you made it and that you came to my rescue last night, but..."

Marika's heart sank.

"I can't continue to impose on you. It wouldn't be fair to take over your office like that. I'd appreciate staying for a few days, but only until I find my own place."

Marika's head dropped.

"I...I really like being here with you," Rhiannon said. "But it just wouldn't be right to stay on."

"Why not?"

Rhiannon blinked. "Why not?"

Marika nodded. "Yes, why wouldn't it be right to stay here? You're not imposing, you're not being unfair, and it's no trouble having you...so why look for someplace else?"

"But..."

Marika took a deep breath. "You need some time to get back on your feet, and you can do that much quicker if you don't have to worry about finding a new home or spending a bunch of money to set everything up. You have everything here that you might need, except clothes, which we'll go and get today. We can ride to and from work together, so you don't need to be concerned about transportation. It's really very practical and absolutely logical for you to stay here."

Rhiannon chuckled.

Marika held her breath.

"So you *want* me to stay here?"

Marika raised one eyebrow. "Wasn't that what I said?"

"I suppose, in a roundabout fashion, you did."

"Then let me make it unequivocally clear. I want you here. I like having you around." Marika looked down at her hands, clasped tightly in her lap. "It feels more like home when you're here." There was a long moment of silence. *Too much, too soon?* Unable to look up, she waited.

Rhiannon laid a hand on her arm, then withdrew. "You'll tell me if I'm getting underfoot?"

Marika nodded.

"And you won't hesitate to tell me if I'm doing something that bugs you?"

A grin split Marika's face, and she nodded again.

"Then, thank you. I accept." Before Marika could say anything, Rhiannon raised a hand, "But, first, let's talk rent."

Marika frowned. "I'm not charging you rent, for heaven's sake."

"And I'm not letting you support me," Rhiannon said.

They glowered at one another for a moment, then Marika's lips twitched. "Is this our first fight as roomies?"

Rhiannon laughed. "Yeah, I guess so." Her smile faded, and she leaned forward. "I'm serious. I paid Hettie four hundred a month and bought my own groceries, so I figure I should at least do that here, too."

"You're only getting half a room, for heaven's sake." Marika shook her head. "Two hundred, and we'll put that toward groceries."

"It's a much nicer room than what I was living in, half or not," Rhiannon countered. "You have a pool and a workout room in the building, so I won't have to keep up my Y membership. Three fifty, plus I kick in for the groceries."

"Not a cent more than two seventy five," Marika said. "And we'll split groceries."

Rhiannon paused, then nodded and extended her hand. "Done."

Marika smiled, and they sealed the agreement. "Done. Now, why don't you have some breakfast, and we'll go shopping."

Rhiannon looked down at her clothes, the same ones Marika had brought her the night before. "I suppose they won't be too impressed if I show up at the office in this every day." She drained her coffee and rose. "I'm not really hungry, though. I think I'll just grab a shower before we go. I can still smell smoke on myself."

Marika hadn't detected any odour but understood. "Why don't you help yourself to some more of my clothes, so you can start out fresh today?"

"Thanks. I really appreciate that." Rhiannon left the kitchen. She had vanished down the hallway when the intercom signaled a caller from the lobby.

"Yes? Oh, hi, David. Come on up." Marika buzzed him in and went to unlock the front door. When he arrived, he carried a flat paper bag and a thick white envelope. Marika settled David in the living room and offered him a cup of coffee, which he declined.

"She's just in the shower." Marika sat on the couch. "She'll be out in a bit."

"I only have a few minutes before I have to leave for an appointment, but I wanted to drop by and see how she was doing. Did she sleep at all?"

Marika grimaced. "She seemed to sleep just fine. I wish I could say the same."

"I know what you mean," David said. "I kept dreaming about flames racing through the house and waking up in a cold sweat. I even got up about four thirty and went around to check all the appliances in the place."

"Uh-huh. About five a.m. I made myself a note to check the smoke detectors." Marika shook her head.

"Makes you think, doesn't it?"

"Makes me think how close she came to..." Marika choked on the words.

"But she didn't. And now we're going to help her put her life back together." David pushed the envelope across the cushions toward her. "There's one hundred and fifty dollars from the church emergency fund, and Tupper and I topped it up. She can use that in any manner she wishes."

"That's really sweet. I'm going to take her shopping for some clothes once she's ready, and this will come in very handy." Marika accepted the envelope and set it on the coffee table.

"Has she decided what she's going to do for a place to live? I have some connections in the community that might help."

"Thanks, but she's going to stay here for as long as she likes."

David raised one eyebrow but didn't comment. He looked at his wristwatch. "I'm afraid I'm going to have to get going, or I'll be late. Will you give her this, too, and tell her I'll call later?" He handed over the flat paper bag.

Marika nodded. "Sure, but are you certain you can't wait? She should only be a few more minutes."

"I wish I could, but I have a meeting with the bishop that I can't be late for." David stood, and Marika escorted him to the door. "Tell her...well, just tell her that I was thinking of her, okay?"

"I will. Thanks for coming by, and thank you for the money. That was very kind."

When David departed, Marika returned to the living room. With a quick glance down the hall, she took her wallet out of her purse, extracted a handful of twenties, and added them to the white envelope. She had just set it back on the coffee table when Rhiannon returned.

Rhi looked around. "Did I hear someone out here?"

"David dropped by, but he had to leave for an appointment. He left you these things." Marika handed over the envelope first. "He said to tell you that you could use that money however you see fit."

Rhiannon open the envelope and whistled. "Wow. This is all from the church?"

"Some of it, and others contributed. He mentioned someone named Tupper, and I think he put some in himself."

Rhiannon riffled through the money. "Geez, he didn't have to do that. I do have money in the bank, but that was awfully good of him. I'll have to call him later to say thank you."

Marika passed over the flat brown bag. "He left this, too. I don't know what it is."

Rhiannon set the envelope down and opened the bag. She held it open as she examined the contents. Then her eyes welled up.

"Rhi? What is it? What's wrong?"

Wordlessly, Rhiannon handed over the bag.

Marika pulled out a thick tablet of fine drawing paper, along with an extensive set of charcoal pencils and graphite sticks. Stuck to the tablet was a Post-It note, and Marika read the words aloud, "To recapture old memories and make new ones. Love, David."

Rhiannon hugged herself, and her tears flowed.

Marika dropped the art supplies. *It just hit her.* She gathered Rhiannon into her arms. "Shhh, it's okay. You're all right now. You're safe. I won't let anything happen to you."

Long after Rhiannon's tears stopped, they remained locked in an embrace.

Lee looked up from her desk when Willem entered her office.

He handed her a sheaf of handwritten notes. "I talked to Henrik. Unofficially, the preliminary indications are definitely arson. Cushions had been piled at the foot of the stairs and doused with some kind of accelerant. Those old houses all had lacquered staircases and lath and plaster construction, so the flames shot up the stairwell like a chimney. The arson dog found traces of accelerant in at least three other spots on the main level. Someone was unquestionably out to burn the place to the ground. I'm amazed your friend got out."

"No kidding." Lee scanned the notes. "Any ideas yet on possible suspects? Maybe the aunt going after the insurance?"

"Surely she would not have endangered her niece?" Willem shook his head. "She was out that night. Apparently she was playing canasta with some friends not too far away and didn't return home until she heard the fire trucks."

Lee leaned back in her chair. "I suppose her friends will alibi her whereabouts?"

Willem shrugged. "I assume so."

Lee stood and tucked the notes in her pocket. "I'm going to go take a look at the house. I may be out for the rest of the day. Can you cover my one o'clock for me? It's an initial intake, and you'll have to set a time for a follow-up assessment. Ann has the details."

"Of course. And if there's anything else I can do, don't hesitate to ask."

Lee patted her partner on the shoulder before she walked out. "I owe you one, Wil. You're the best."

"You owe me one hundred," Willem called after her. "But who's counting?"

Lee smiled.

A short while later, Lee parked down the street from Rhiannon's former home. She leaned against the hood of her truck and looked at the ruins. The roof had fallen in, and from what she could see, the interior was gutted. The firefighters had done well to prevent the spread of the flames to the neighbouring houses, but they never stood a chance of saving the old yellow house.

"Helluva mess, ain't it?"

Lee turned.

A thin, elderly woman in a plaid housedress watched her with inquisitive eyes. A cigarette dangled from her lips, a huge purse was over one arm, and she held the handle of a wire pull-cart.

"Yes, it sure is," Lee said. "Do you live around here?"

The woman jerked a thumb over her shoulder. "Two houses down. Damned glad that fire didn't spread. It ain't much, but it's been my home for over fifty years now. Raised my four kids there...buried my husband, too." She cackled. "Well, I didn't bury him there. Ya ain't gonna find him pushing up daisies in the backyard."

Lee smiled. "Do you know the people that lived there?" She gestured at the ruins.

"Yep." The woman squinted at her. "Why d'ya wanna know?"

"I'm a friend of Rhiannon Davies."

"Ya are if'n ya call her that." The woman tapped her cigarette. "She's a good girl, that one. Use ta come over in the winter and shovel my walks for me. Din't have any money to pay her, but I'd give her cookies hot out of the oven. Kid liked that. Don't think that bitch ever fed her enough."

"Bitch?"

The old woman pursed her lips. "Know it ain't charit'ble, but Hettie Walker's bin my neighbour for thirty years and there ain't no other way ta describe her. Use ta feel sorry for little Rhiannon, but tryin' to talk to Hettie only made it worse on the kid. So I just fed her along with my own gran'babies when I could, 'n let her stay at my place a few times when it was really bad."

"I'm sorry..." Lee was sorry for so many things: that her young friend had grown up in such harsh circumstances, that no one had stepped in to help her, that, as bad as it was, Rhiannon's home now lay in charred ruins.

The old woman shrugged. "Eh, that's life. None of us gets out alive, ya know? Still, I'm glad the girl is safe. Where's she now?"

"Staying with a friend of mine. She'll be fine there."

"Good. Ya tell her Grammy Olive says hi, all right?"

Lee nodded. "I'll tell her. Did you see what happened last night? I mean, were you around when the house went up?"

"We all were," Olive said. "Wasn't no sleepin' through all that fuss and commotion. Hell, even Pike and Eddie had their sorry asses over here watchin' all the excitement."

Lee straightened. "Pike and Eddie King?"

"Yeah, the rats came outta their hole." The old woman spat.

A thrill rippled through Lee. "Pike and Eddie live around here?"

"Right across the street from little Rhiannon. Born and raised right there, damn their worthless hides." Olive glared at a faded brown house on the opposite side of the road. "Had the nicest mother, but their daddy was a worthless lowlife. They're just chips off the old block. Wish ta hell they'd move away."

"So, when you saw them last night, did they seem...oh, I dunno...different or anything?"

Olive narrowed her eyes. "You some kind of cop?"

"No. I'm in private security, but I am worried about Rhiannon. She had two near misses yesterday, and that strikes me as more than coincidental."

"And yer thinkin' Pike and Eddie mighta had somepin' to do with it?" Olive took a final drag from her cigarette and ground it under her shoe.

"I don't know. I've had run-ins with them before." Lee watched Olive closely.

"Who hasn't?" Olive snorted. "The whole damn neighbourhood has crossed 'em one time or 'nother." She sighed. "Hell, if I knew somepin' to nail 'em, I would gladly tell, but they was just standin' here like the rest of us, watchin' the fire." She pushed her purse back on her arm. "Gotta get goin'. Bin nice talkin' with ya. Give my regards to little Rhiannon."

"I will." Olive walked away, and Lee stared at the King brothers' home. There was no sign of life about the place. Blinds were drawn, and the only living thing in the yard was a skinny mongrel nosing through piles of debris. Two motorcycles sat in the dirt driveway, and Lee crossed the street to take a closer look. She examined the Harleys and whistled. *These are top of the line. How the hell did those punks afford these?* A thin layer of soot coated the bright chrome. *They haven't been moved since before the fire.*

Lee climbed the two stairs to the porch and frowned at the flies buzzing around an overturned beer can and a half-eaten piece of pizza under a plastic chair. She knocked on the door. There was no answer, but she tried twice more before giving up. *They may have been here last night, but they sure as hell aren't here now.*

She returned to her truck and sat behind the wheel. *Why would arsonists choose this house to burn? Did Rhi anger the Kings somehow, enough that they took revenge? Did her aunt burn her own house for the insurance? Was Rhi's near miss with the car connected to the fire in some way?*

The first option didn't make much sense. "Pike and Eddie certainly aren't above arson. Hell, I don't think there's anything beyond those two if it's in their own interests. But unless there's some nasty history between them and Rhi that I don't know about, I can't see the risk being worth the reward."

Lee chewed on her lip. "Time to find out what Pike and Eddie have been up to lately." Lee started the engine. She knew the perfect place to begin her inquiries.

CHAPTER 22

LEE DROPPED HER CHANGE INTO the tip jar and nodded. "Thanks." She nursed her beer at the end of the bar. She'd spent most of the day calling in favours throughout the city's lower strata as she searched for Pike and Eddie, but the brothers had gone to ground, and she'd been unable to locate them. Now she was back where her search began in a seedy, smoke-filled bar that was the brothers' usual haunt.

For the countless time, Lee's gaze swept the interior of the bar. Each person who entered or left was evaluated and, thus far, dismissed. She was looking for a well-dressed Asian man who had been reported regularly in the brothers' company. None of her contacts were able to provide his name.

One informant told her that Pike and Eddie had been throwing money around on women, partying, and vehicles. They seemed to have a good deal that was putting a lot of cash in their pockets. Lee didn't doubt that. The Harleys in their driveway were almost brand new and definitely not cheap.

A newcomer entered the bar, and Lee's heart rate picked up. The slight Asian man was in khakis, a polo shirt, and a light jacket—a far cry from the standard leather, wife-beaters, and jeans most of the other patrons wore. His gaze darted around as if he was searching for somebody.

Maybe two somebodies? Lee leaned farther back into the shadowed corner.

The man completed his survey and, scowling, crossed to speak with the bartender.

Lee monitored their conversation for a few moments, then pushed her glass aside and walked out of the bar. She slid into her truck, put on her sunglasses, and waited, gaze fixed on the bar's entrance.

Her quarry exited and hastened to an older model Honda.

After he drove away, she waited a few beats before pulling out into traffic behind him. Lee was amused when he headed directly for a bar she'd already checked in her search for the elusive Kings. When he parked and entered the bar, she stopped behind his car long enough to note his licence number. She found a spot to park halfway down the block and made a call. "Vincent! My man!"

Vincent groaned.

"Aw, c'mon, Vinnie. Is that any way to talk to an old friend?"

"What friend? You only call me when you need something."

"Maybe so, but didn't I get you a month's worth of Flames tickets the last time we spoke?" Lee adjusted the rearview mirror for a better view of the bar's entrance.

"Yeah, yeah. So what you need, and what's in it for me?"

"I need you to look up a plate. I'll get you Stamps tickets for the next four home games and a twenty-sixer of your choice. Whaddaya say?"

"Make it a forty of Dark Horse, and you got a deal. What's the number?"

Lee rattled off the licence.

As Vincent pulled up the information for her, her target came out of the bar and headed for his car. He slammed his fist down on the hood.

Very interesting. He's definitely pissed about something. The brothers' disappearance, maybe?

Her mark stood motionless with his head lowered for a long moment, then he straightened and got into his car.

"Lee? You got a pen?"

"Yeah, go ahead."

"It's a mouthful so I'll spell it." Vincent gave her a name and address.

Lee nodded. "Thanks, man. I'll drop those tickets and the Dark Horse off later in the week." She ended the call as her target drove past. She pulled out several cars back of her mark, but this time when he stopped at a pool hall, she continued past.

"Have fun, Gao Qui-jian." Lee smirked. "I can tell you they haven't been there in four days. You're going to have about as much luck as I did." She left the inner city and drove to an apartment block in the southeast quadrant. She waited, assessing opportunities. Soon an elderly woman made her way from the bus stop to the door of the building, struggling with an armload of bags. Lee walked up behind the woman. "Looks like you've got quite the load there, ma'am. Can I give you a hand?"

The woman smiled as Lee took the heaviest bags. "Thank you, dear. I really shouldn't have spent so much, but I ran into the best sale and just couldn't resist." She unlocked the door, and Lee followed the woman in. The woman talked all the way to her ninth-floor apartment.

Lee set the bags inside her apartment and walked back to the bank of elevators. She took the lift down to the fifth floor, relieved to find the corridor empty. She was even more pleased to see that Gao's door had only a standard lock on it. Lee knocked twice, then pulled a lock pick out of her wallet and had the door open in thirty seconds. She stepped inside and held still while her gaze swept for any apparent security devices. *Confident bugger, aren't you?* When all remained quiet, she did a preliminary walk-through of the apartment. Satisfied that the residence was unsecured, Lee took stock of her surroundings.

The place was neat, clean, and sparsely decorated with generic furnishings. There was little to give away the taste or personality of the inhabitant.

Lee searched the apartment, careful to leave no indication of her intrusion. She found nothing of interest until she got to the bedroom. When she pulled open a bedside table, she discovered an H&K P7M13. German engineered with a double-stack magazine, it was an expensive and hard to acquire handgun. "Tchh, tchh. I bet you're breaking half a dozen laws owning that peashooter. Too bad I can't turn you in for it."

Lee closed the drawer without disturbing the weapon, then finished her search of the bedroom. She paused at the Powerbook G4 on the small workstation. *Wish I had Barb with me. She could make that baby give up every secret it holds.* Lee rifled through the three drawers but found nothing of interest until she came across a manila folder in the bottom drawer. It contained a sheaf of handwritten notes that listed times and places in a shorthand combination of Chinese characters and English. The topmost sheet contained the words, "lawyer, Banff, Cochrane, zoo." The dates were from the past weekend.

A chill rippled through Lee. Marika and Rhiannon had driven to Banff on Saturday and gone to the zoo with Terry and Jan on Sunday. She checked the earliest date on the notes, then replaced them in the folder and returned it to the drawer. *Wish I could take those with me, but I've pushed my luck far enough for one day.* She left the apartment without incident and returned to her car.

"Okay, you've got most of the pieces of the puzzle, you just have to put them together." Lee tapped her forehead. "Somehow, there's a connection between Pike, Eddie, Gao, and Rhiannon. What the hell could the kid have gotten mixed up in that she would be targeted by a bunch of thugs?" Lee shook her head. "Maybe she saw them doing something in the neighbourhood?" *I'll have to ask her. She might not realize what she saw.* "Or what about something at work?" Marika dealt exclusively in immigration cases, so Lee worried at it from that angle. *If the key is work, then Marika has to be involved, too, but she hasn't said anything about any problematic cases. She did have the hearing in Vancouver—*

Lee bolted upright. "Jesus! The date on the first notes." *That was the day Marika and Rhi came back from Vancouver.* "Oh, Christ." Lee stared across the parking spaces. *Cass!* Had Marika's discovery of Cass' other identity set off the chain of events endangering Rhiannon's life? *But why Rhiannon? Why not Marika?*

Unable to answer that question, Lee examined theories. *What if it's both of them, but Rhiannon just happened to be first in line?* "Would Cass do that? Kill two people because they found out about her alter ego?" Lee recalled the look of cold triumph in Cass' eyes as she'd left Marika naked and traumatized on the floor of her own bedroom. "Hell, yeah, she would." She took out her phone. "Willem? Is Barb in the office today?"

"She is. Do you require her services?" Willem asked.

"Yes. Tell her I'll pick her up in front of our building in twenty-five minutes. And, Wil? Tell her to bring all her equipment."

"Geez, do you think we've got enough here?" Rhiannon juggled half of the shopping bags. "I think there was at least one store with clothes still left in it."

Marika grinned at Rhiannon over the bags in her arms. "Well, cute as you look in my clothes, you really can't go back to work in shorts and T-shirts."

Rhiannon laughed and followed Marika out of the elevator. It had been a full day. They'd taken care of replacing Rhi's documents, then shopped all afternoon and capped off the day with dinner at an Italian restaurant.

Despite the trauma of the preceding twenty-four hours, Rhiannon hadn't stopped smiling. She was accustomed to shopping for her clothes in secondhand and low-end stores, so she initially balked at Marika's suggestion that she try some different shops. Rhiannon had always selected garments that allowed her to remain as invisible as possible. But for the first time, she wanted to look good. She'd accepted Marika's advice on colours and selections and thrilled to the admiration in Marika's eyes as she tried on various items. She spent all of the money in the envelope and several hundred from her own savings. *I'd have spent twice that for her to look at me the way she did. I could get used to that.*

"I'll clear out space in the walk-in and a drawer in the bureau for you to put your clothes in until we can pick up a freestanding wardrobe for the den this weekend, okay?" Marika inserted her key in the lock. "And don't let me forget to give you the spare key."

"Okay." Rhiannon trailed Marika into the apartment. She almost ran into Marika when she stopped short.

"Lee. Hi. I wasn't expecting you until later."

Rhiannon looked around Marika. Lee was seated at the dining room table with some items on a paper towel in front of her. "Hey, Lee." The serious expression on Lee's face took her aback.

"Come sit down," Lee said. "I want to talk to both of you."

Marika and Rhiannon shot a look at each other, set the bags down, and sat at the table. "What's going on?" Marika asked.

Lee rubbed her temples and winced. "I need you to listen carefully. First, let me tell you what I've found out and then we'll talk it over, okay?" She indicated the small metallic items on the towel. "I had Barb sweep your apartment this afternoon. She found bugs in every room, and your phone and computer were both tapped."

Marika gasped, and Rhiannon stared at Lee.

Lee outlined her investigation.

"But why? Why would anyone follow us?" Marika asked.

"I've thought about that a lot this afternoon." Lee scowled. "I suspect Cass is trying to cover the tracks of her double life by killing Rhi. If I'm right, she'll come after you next."

"Cass?" Marika knocked over her chair as she sprang to her feet. "Cass tried to have Rhi killed?"

Rhiannon shook her head. *Cass? Why would someone I don't even know try to have me killed?*

Lee reached for Marika's hand, but she backed away and crossed her arms over her chest. "Are you telling me that Cass sent someone to kill Rhiannon?"

"Sit down," Lee said.

For an instant, Rhiannon thought Marika would ignore Lee, but then Marika picked up her chair and sat down.

Lee sighed. "I don't have enough evidence to tell you for sure it was Cass. But unless something else odd happened in Vancouver, the only thing that stands out about the trip is that you discovered Cass and this society woman are one and the same. What if she would go to any lengths to ensure her secret doesn't get out?"

"But why me?" Rhiannon asked. "I've never even met the woman. I certainly couldn't identify her."

Lee looked at her. "You could be collateral damage control. Cass may think that Marika told you when she went back to her room that night, and she's covering all her bases."

"I told you." Marika's voice was flat. "If my home has been bugged since we got back, someone knows that I told you everything about that night."

"I know. I've thought about that, and I'll be watching my back," Lee said. "Look, whoever they are, they're going to realize that something is up, because their surveillance has gone dead."

Marika scowled. "Are you sure you got them all?"

"Yes. There's no one better at her job than Barb. She swept this place twice, just to be sure, and disabled all these. You're clean. And I've got a technician coming by tonight to install our best security system." Lee pinned them with a stern gaze. "You have to be hypervigilant from now on. Grow eyes in the back of your head and use 'em. Stick together, and watch each other's back. If you're going somewhere, ensure it's public. As much as possible, limit yourselves to going to work and coming home until I find out more. Marika, make sure you've always got your cell phone with you, and put my cell number on speed dial."

Rhiannon shivered. "What happens now?"

"Now I dig deeper. I want to find out more about the connection between Gao, the man who's following you, and Cass, and I want to know what rock Pike and Eddie have crawled under." Lee's eyes narrowed. "If I can find them, I can get them to squeal like a pair of stuck piggies. I'm also going to talk to my old CO to see if he can help me out." She stood and swept the useless bits of technology into her hand. "We'll get through this, don't you worry. I'm not going to let you down." Lee looked from one to the other. "Dana will be by after her shift. Will you tell her not to worry if I'm out late, that I'm working on something? She'll understand."

Marika nodded and walked Lee to the door.

Lee drew Marika into a hug before she made her exit.

Rhiannon rose and met Marika halfway.

Marika dropped her gaze. "I'm so sorry." The whispered words were barely audible.

Rhiannon took Marika's hand and led her to the couch. They sank into the thick cushions, and she took both of Marika's hands in hers. "What are you sorry for? None of this is your fault."

Marika shook her head. "If it is Cass, then it's *all* my fault. My weakness could have cost you your life." Her eyes filled with tears.

Rhiannon frowned. "If it is Cass, then she's the only one to blame. Not you."

"You don't understand." Marika stared at their linked hands.

"Then tell me." Rhiannon hadn't forgotten the loathing in Lee's voice when she described Cass as evil. She was baffled by how Marika could have fallen into the clutches of such a woman. *C'mon, Marika. Tell me. We'll lance this boil together.*

Finally, Marika looked at her. "How much do you know?"

"Very little, actually. I know that whoever this Cass is, she's bad *for* you and *to* you. I know that Lee and Dana hate her, which means a lot in my book, but I don't know anything beyond that."

Marika drew a deep breath.

Rhiannon tightened her grip on Marika's hands.

"It's not a pretty story, and I don't come off well in it."

Rhiannon shook her head. "I don't care."

Marika gave her a wry half-smile. "You might change your mind, but you deserve to know the mess your roommate has made, especially since it now involves you." Marika told Rhiannon of her life—of a bright, funny mother that spoiled her outrageously when she was drinking, and shut her out when she sobered up. She recounted the nights when she brought her mother home from the bars while her father worked late at his firm. She told of going to live with her father and his new wife after her parents divorced and of the scandal that saw her banished from the family.

Rhiannon listened to the recitation, and her heart ached.

Marika spoke briefly of the years away and the return to attend her father's alma mater in Toronto—graduating with honours, but with no one in the audience to cheer for her. She talked of coming to Calgary to start anew and of meeting Lee. She didn't spare herself when she detailed the litany of failed relationships, taking full responsibility for each of them.

"I met Cass last September. I'd gone with an acquaintance to a house party with people I didn't really know. I was feeling pretty lousy at the time, wondering if love was nothing more than a fairy tale told to gullible children. After a few too many, I started expounding on that theory to a stranger. She laughed, said she knew what I needed and that she could give it to me without all that love nonsense." Marika stared into the distance.

Rhiannon said nothing. It was up to Marika to find the courage to face why she went home with Cass.

After a long moment, Marika shook her head. "I sort of understand why I went to her place that night, but I'll never understand why I kept going back." She looked at Rhiannon with anguish in her eyes. "Lee and Dana were right, she was bad for me. Not just the things she did to me, but the way she made me feel."

"How did she make you feel?"

"Like the sum total of my worth was how I served her in the bedroom. Like no one would ever look at me as anything more than an available body and that love was out of the question for someone like me." Anger grew in Marika's eyes.

Rhiannon rejoiced at the sight.

"I don't think I'll ever forgive her for making me believe that."

"So, you know she lied, right?" Rhiannon needed to hear Marika's confirmation.

"I didn't for a long time, but recently...yes, I know she lied and manipulated me for her own ends. I doubt that I'll ever know why I fell for it for so long. I once worked up the nerve to ask her why she always let me come back if she had nothing but contempt for me. She laughed and said I was an amusing bauble, then she..." Marika shuddered.

"It's over," Rhiannon said. "Put it behind you. She doesn't deserve one more thought from you."

Marika squeezed Rhiannon's hands. "It's not over if she's the one behind the attacks on you. You don't know Cass. If she's set her mind on something, she won't stop." She bit her lip. "Maybe you should get out of here. You've got lots of holiday time coming. Let me send you to the other side of the country until it's safe for you to come back."

Rhiannon snorted. "Not likely. I don't run...especially from a bully like her. Sorry, you're stuck with me. Besides, I'm not worried. We've got Lee on our side."

Marika blew out a breath. "All right, but we follow her instructions to the letter. No playing Wonder Woman, all right?"

"I promise. I'll stick to you like glue."

Marika smiled. "Then how about we get your new clothes put away?"

Rhiannon released Marika's hands, and they picked up the abandoned bags. Rhiannon followed Marika down the hallway and made herself a promise. *Cass will never torment Marika again. Not if I can help it.*

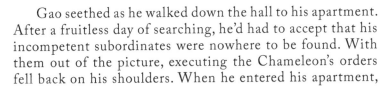

Gao seethed as he walked down the hall to his apartment. After a fruitless day of searching, he'd had to accept that his incompetent subordinates were nowhere to be found. With them out of the picture, executing the Chameleon's orders fell back on his shoulders. When he entered his apartment,

Gao checked the answering machine and found several messages from Perry. He returned the call.

Perry answered. "Yeah?"

"What do you want?" Gao did not waste pleasantries.

"The bugs ain't working."

Gao scowled. "What do you mean they're not working? None of them?"

"Yeah. All of them went dead, plus the taps are out, too."

Gao restrained an urge to tear into Perry. "When did this happen?"

"S'afternoon. I heard a couple of people moving around, but they wasn't talkin' or anything, and then...nothing. Couldn't hear a damned thing. You figure they found 'em all?"

"That would be the logical assumption," Gao said, chilled by the implications. "When do you normally send your report to the coast?"

"Midnight, but the Chameleon ain't in town right now. Liang's been handling things for the last coupla days."

Gao closed his eyes. He had a brief reprieve if his boss was away. As long as he executed her orders by the time she returned, she would be less likely to hold him responsible for the lapse in surveillance. "All right. Be candid in tonight's report. Tell Liang that the bugs have been deactivated, but that I'm on top of the situation and the Chameleon's order will be carried out as issued. Is that clear?"

"Yeah, okay. Did you want me to put more bugs in place?"

"No. If they have discovered them, they'll be hyperalert, and you won't get access easily. If the Chameleon wants surveillance continued once her orders are carried out, then you'll have to get back in somehow."

"Got it." Perry hung up.

Gao replaced the receiver and considered this turn of events. The Chameleon's original orders had been to make the hit look like an accident, but given two failed attempts, that was going to be virtually impossible. *It's time for direct action.* Gao retrieved his gun from the bedroom. He checked that the clip was fully loaded, tucked it in the back of his waistband, and zipped his jacket half closed.

Leaving the apartment, Gao decided that the troublesome and incompetent King brothers were officially expendable. *I'll see to that little matter after I conclude the Chameleon's business.*

CHAPTER 23

L EE STOOD IN THE OPEN office door. *His desk hasn't changed much in the past twenty years. Still as messy as ever.* She cleared her throat.

Marc looked up from his work and grinned. "Come in, come in. It's so good to see you again." He came out from behind his desk with his hand extended.

"Marc." Lee shook his hand. "Thank you for seeing me."

He motioned her to a chair and took one next to her. "I'm always delighted to see you, you know that. I'm just sorry I didn't get your message sooner. I've been away at a conference for the last few days."

Lee got to the heart of her visit. "I think I need your help. A couple of dear friends could be in serious trouble— life-threatening trouble."

Marc frowned. "More trouble than you can handle? That doesn't sound good. Tell me what's going on. If I can help, I will."

Lee laid out the events of the past week. When she brought up the possible involvement of Pike and Eddie King, Marc shook his head. "Well, there's a couple of names that are well-known to the police. Have you got anything concrete we can hang them on?"

"Mostly hearsay and circumstantial evidence, I'm afraid. I'm pretty sure I've got enough to shake their tongues loose if I could find them, but they've gone to ground. I haven't been able to find hide nor hair of them. That alone tells me that they're scared, because those two have never been noted for being inconspicuous or circumspect."

"They're not exactly the brightest bulbs in the box. Let me flag their names right now. If they turn up anywhere, I'll know about it." Marc returned to his desk and tapped commands into his computer. "Sorry, nothing new so far, but we can nab them on parole violations if nothing else. They won't be a top priority to anyone, but if they come up in the system anywhere, we'll be notified."

Lee nodded. It was a start. "Can you punch in Gao Quijian and see if anything comes up?"

Marc asked for the spelling and entered the name. When the information appeared, he gave a low whistle. "Jesus, what have you stumbled into? This is one of the bad guys. They've never been able to make anything stick to him, but he was a suspected Triad member in Vancouver. He disappeared off the radar for a year or two before surfacing in Calgary. The RCMP Major Crimes Unit was very interested in his arrival here, but he's maintained a low profile." Marc looked up at Lee. "And you say there's some connection between him and this woman in Vancouver?"

"Well, a lot of this is supposition. I'm still putting the pieces together. That's why I need to find Pike and Eddie. I'm sure they'll be the weak link." Lee shook her head. "I have to figure it out before my friends get hurt."

Marc tilted his head. "What steps have you taken so far?"

"I had a security system installed in their place—"

"They live together?" Marc asked.

"For now. Marika took Rhiannon in when her place burned down."

He nodded.

"I wanted to put a tail on Gao, but all our personnel are currently assigned. I've been digging like crazy trying to find the brothers. I've got my friends taking extra precautions, and I instructed our company electronics whiz to install a GPS locator on Marika's car."

"Sounds like you've done everything you can for now. I'll let you know immediately if the Kings show up." Marc glanced at his computer screen and frowned. "I think I'll talk to a friend of mine with the Major Crimes Unit. This could be the thread they've been looking for. I may be able to trade for some information on exactly what they think Gao is up to in Calgary and how it ties back to Vancouver. Those boys aren't always forthcoming with us locals, but it may be a case of one hand washing the other this time. The woman you were talking about with the dual identity—do you know her name?"

Lee searched her memory. "I just know her as Cass, but it's Sandra something—Sandra DeAndre, I think."

Marc's eyes widened. "DeAndre? Of the DeAndre shipping empire?"

"I don't know. All I know is that my friend said she was some big-shot socialite or something."

"Jesus, Lee, if she is one of the shipping DeAndres, we're talking a mess of hornets. Step very carefully."

Lee frowned. "I don't care if she's the prime minister's best buddy. If she's behind what's been happening, I'm going to take her down."

"Glad to see you haven't lost the old fire." Marc crossed his arms on his desk. "Look, protect your friends without doing anything illegal, but come to me when you get any hard evidence. Give me something I can use, and you know I'll help."

Lee stood with a sense of relief. "Thanks, Marc. This really means a lot to me. If I can ever return the favour, you know you only have to ask."

"Even if that means I want you back working for me?"

Lee grinned and shook her head. "You never give up, do you?"

Marc walked with her to the door of his office. "You have the best natural instincts for investigation that I ever saw. I'd love to have you working with us."

"No, thanks. I think I'll stick to the private sector. Business is booming for Willem and me. We've already planned a major expansion for next year, which will include a twenty-five percent increase in our work force."

"So when I retire on a cop's pension, you'll be retiring into the lap of luxury, is what you're saying." Marc heaved an exaggerated sigh.

Lee laughed. "Somehow I don't think you, Andrea, or the kids will ever starve."

"I expect I can keep us in beans and bacon, if nothing else. It's been great seeing you again. Don't leave it so long next time, okay?"

"I won't," Lee said. "We'll have a beer call sometime soon."

"Good. And if we learn anything about the whereabouts of those idiots, I'll let you know as soon as I hear."

They shook hands, and Lee took the elevator to the ground floor. She decided to touch base with Marika before going home for dinner. She hit the speed dial. "Hi, it's me."

"Hi, Lee. We're home safely." Marika's tone was amused.

"Glad to hear it." Lee wasn't going to apologize for hovering, even if the previous two days had been quiet. And she certainly wasn't going to relax her vigilance. "So you're in for the night?"

"Actually, David invited us for dinner, so we're just getting cleaned up to go over to his place. But don't fret. We'll drive directly there and then come right home again."

Lee frowned. She'd rather they stayed barricaded in the condo, but it wasn't reasonable to ask them to become hermits. "All right, but no stops on the way."

Marika chuckled. "Yes, Mother. I really do appreciate your concern, but you did say those brothers appear to have taken off. Maybe they've been frightened away and won't be back."

"Maybe. But that still leaves Gao, and we don't know what he's up to right now. I still want you to take precautions."

"We will. In fact, I'll call you as soon as we're home from David's, all right?"

"Good. I'll talk to you then." They exchanged farewells. *I hope you're right, my friend, but my gut says this is a long way from over.*

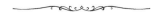

Gao slammed his hand against the steering wheel. He had tracked the lawyer and her companion for two straight days, looking for an opportunity to separate them and execute the companion. Mindful of the Chameleon's orders, he intended to keep the lawyer's involvement to a minimum. That eliminated a drive-by shooting as long as they were together.

Not like there's even been an opening for that. Gao hit the steering wheel again and ground his teeth. The only times he had seen them in the previous days had been when they drove out of the condo parking garage. He followed them to their office building, where they disappeared into the parking ramp, then he picked up the pursuit again when they drove home after work.

There was no doubt that his quarry was now aware of someone's interest. Gao hadn't seen them emerge from the office building with the rest of the lunch crew, nor had the lawyer made her usual trips to the coffee shop in the lobby.

Gao reached for his coffee and caught a glimpse of his reflection in the rearview mirror. He angled the mirror, studied his appearance, and scowled. Worry lines radiated from his dark, shadowed eyes, and his skin was sallow. Flesh had tightened across the bones of his face, and dim hollows were evident in his cheeks. *Damn them. I just need to get them out of my life and get back to normal.*

Rest was scarce, and dread grew by the hour as Gao was cognizant of time running out. Perry had informed him that Liang expected the boss back by the end of the weekend, which meant he was down to a day—two at best—before she learned of his failure.

Bile rose in his throat as he recalled his early days on the Chameleon's clean-up crew. The words of his partner then, a veteran of the Chameleon's organization, still haunted him. After a grisly clean-up of one of their own people, his partner said, "Remember what you seen here. You want to have grandchildren someday—don't ever cross her."

Gao batted at the rearview mirror. *Fuck it. If I have to break into their apartment tonight, I will. If the lawyer gets in my way, too bad. I'm not about to end up as some cleaning crew's assignment.* He took a deep swallow of his tepid coffee and almost spat it out as the garage security door opened and the black Lexus emerged. He set the coffee in the cupholder and started the engine.

A knot of excitement formed in Gao's belly. *Take it easy. Don't lose your head.* Gao hung back and tailed them to a church in the inner city. There they turned into the driveway of the church's rectory.

A tall, thin man came out of the side door to greet them.

Gao circled the block to drive by again. He pulled over at the end of the street and angled his mirror to have a clear view of the driveway and the Lexus. It wasn't an optimal situation, but it was a chance. Driven by the looming deadline of the Chameleon's return, he'd take it.

Gao glanced up at the street sign and punched Perry's number into his phone. "I'm in Victoria Park, at the corner of Twelfth and Fifth. Have my car picked up and returned to my apartment. I'll leave the door open and the keys under the floor mat. Don't waste any time." He closed his cell, turned off the engine, and deposited the keys under the mat.

Gao retrieved a long, hooked strip of metal from his glove box and slid it up his coat sleeve. He felt for the reassuring weight of the gun in his waistband and surveyed the street before exiting. He walked slowly toward the church, his gaze sweeping the area. The street was quiet and absent pedestrians, which suited his purpose. The Lexus could have an alarm, but if he had to run, he would come up with an alternative plan.

Laughter emanated from the yard behind the privacy hedge. He stopped on the driver's side of the Lexus, glanced around one more time, then tried the handle. When it unexpectedly opened, he almost giggled in disbelief. He scrambled into the car and sank into the space behind the driver's seat.

"Another piece, Marika?" David indicated the grilled chicken breasts.

Marika shook her head. "No, thank you. I think I've had enough."

Rhiannon held out her plate. "I'll have one more, please."

David forked a piece onto her plate. The week's events hadn't ruined her appetite or her disposition. Quite to the contrary, Rhiannon looked better than ever. She was relaxed, and her eyes sparkled with humour and happiness. In fact, both women exuded an unexpected sense of repose. When he'd met Marika previously, she had a brittle edge about her that was absent now. *I was wrong. They're good for each other.* "So, Lee figures the King brothers have hightailed it out of town?"

Marika nodded. "She thinks they got scared and ran. She's been trying to find them, but so far, without success."

David topped up everyone's iced tea. "I guess that must be a huge relief for you."

Marika and Rhiannon glanced at each other.

"Yes," Marika said. "But as our guardian angel points out, there was someone else involved, and she doesn't want us to get careless."

David frowned. "You are being careful, right?"

"We are," Rhiannon said. "Lee put a super duper security system in the condo, and we drive straight to work and straight home again. She won't even let us go grocery shopping." Rhiannon grinned. "She told Marika to give her the list, and she would get our stuff for us."

It was reassuring that Lee was watching over them. David had been impressed with Lee. She had a way of engendering confidence, and she was obviously devoted to her friends. He was grateful that she numbered Rhiannon among them.

"Sometimes it's hard to believe this is happening," Marika said.

Rhiannon laid a hand on Marika's forearm. "You're doing it again. This is not your fault, and I'm going to keep telling you that until you believe it."

Marika covered Rhiannon's hand with her own, and they gazed at each other for a long moment.

Hmm, think three's a crowd, Davie, old man? David cleared his throat. "You don't expect this Cass or Sandra or whatever she's calling herself to show up on your doorstep, do you?" They had filled him in on the whole story or at least most of it. He suspected that they had sanitized details of Marika and Cass' relationship.

Marika shook her head. "I really don't think so. I suspect everything that's happened is a warning, an attempt to scare me into keeping my mouth shut about who she really is." Her face hardened, and her eyes flashed. "She probably thought Rhi was expendable, that her death would serve as an object lesson to me."

David was fascinated by the fiercely protective way Marika looked at Rhiannon. He saw depths to the woman that he hadn't expected. *Rhiannon chose more wisely than I gave her credit for.*

"Shhh, it's okay. She's not going to hurt me." Rhiannon patted Marika's arm, then turned to David. "She's a bad one." She glanced at Marika.

Interesting. I don't think Marika knows exactly how much Rhi is aware of when it comes to her relationship with Cass. David smiled. *I think Marika and Cass might've met their match in my young friend, in very different ways.*

Rhiannon leaned across the table toward him. "Do you think there's such a thing as pure evil in the world?"

David recognized Rhiannon's philosophical mode, and he didn't have to contemplate his response for long. "Yes, I do." He settled back in his lawn chair. "I have a dear friend, a doctor who works with Doctors Without Borders. She was sent to Rwanda immediately after the genocide stopped. The second day she was there, the team leader dispatched her and another doctor to go with a man who'd come begging for help. The man took them to a village where there were about a dozen or so people with horrible wounds. They got them patched up as best they could, and she decided to do a quick walk around to make sure they hadn't missed anyone. She had pretty much covered the village, and she was just about to check out the small church when the man who'd originally come for them ran up to her and babbled that she didn't want to go in."

David paused, and he recalled the lost look on his doctor friend's face when she told him her story. "She told me that she would give anything if she had listened to him, but she was determined not to leave any stone unturned in case a survivor had been missed. So she shook the man off and opened the door of the church. She was overwhelmed with the stench—it hit her like a hammer, and she stumbled back, gasping for air. She covered her nose and mouth with her sleeve and went back to the doorway." He stopped.

After a long moment, Marika asked, "What did she see?"

"Bodies," David said. "Strewn through the pews, piled five and ten deep against the wall...men, women, children, babies...hacked to death and slaughtered in what they thought was a refuge. She couldn't force herself to go in. She turned away and vomited until she couldn't retch anymore. The man brought her water, then led her away. He explained that when the slaughter began, desperate people poured into the church, seeking sanctuary, but instead it was turned into a charnel house." David swallowed the lump in his throat. "She saw the results of evil that day, Rhi. How else to explain the collective madness that has periodically afflicted human beings from time immemorial and caused them to do these horrendous things to other human beings?"

"In a church?" Rhiannon shook her head. "They did that in a church?"

"A church is only a collection of bricks, mortar, and wood unless it's invested with the humanity of good people. Those that carried out that slaughter forsook their humanity for evil's sake."

They sat quietly, then Rhiannon excused herself and went to the rectory.

David winced. " I didn't mean to upset her."

"No, she asked," Marika said. "If there's one thing I've learned, she doesn't like things to be soft-pedaled. Besides, if I know her, she'll have a dozen more questions before the night is out. She does love to debate you, you know?"

"I've noticed." They chuckled together, and then he turned serious again. "Is Cass evil?"

"Yes." Marika's answer was instantaneous.

David frowned. "Are you sure you can keep Rhiannon safe?"

"I will...or die trying."

They regarded each other, wordlessly acknowledging their devotion to Rhiannon.

David nodded. "Good."

Marika eased back in her chair. "Besides, as Rhi likes to say, we have Lee on our side, and, to quote our young friend, 'Lee's not going to let some piss-ant psychopath get the best of her.'"

David laughed.

Marika joined in, and the tension dissipated.

"I think you're good for her," David said.

Marika glanced at David sharply. "She's good for me, too. She's a great person to be around."

He understood her caution but decided to have some fun. "I was going to introduce her to my son, Dylan, when he comes to visit me next month." David grinned at the look Marika shot him. "However, I've come to the conclusion she's never going to be my daughter-in-law."

Marika's gaze searched his face.

David took pity on her. "It's all right. Not that you've sought it, but if you did, I would freely give you my blessing."

"I...she...um, it's not what you think," Marika said.

Rhiannon returned and sat down.

"So, could I interest you two in some of my homemade pineapple upside down cake?" Without waiting for an answer, David headed for the kitchen. "Oh, you're a bad 'un, Davie. Put the cat among the pigeons now, haven't you?" He grinned and sliced three pieces of cake. "And darned well time that someone did." Not the slightest bit repentant, he made his way back outside with the plates.

Rhiannon and Marika were deep in conversation, their heads close together.

"Here we are." David set the plates down. "Sorry I didn't make up any whipped cream to go with it."

From Rhiannon's easy response and the way she dug into her cake, David suspected that Marika hadn't said anything about his comments to her, but that was fine with him. *They'll figure it out for themselves eventually. And if I put a bug in Marika's ear—well, even Cupid can use a helping hand now and then.*

The rest of the evening passed in laughter and conversation. They left the darker topics alone, and it was well into dusk by the time they rose to take their leave.

David walked them to the driveway. "I almost forget, Rhi. Your aunt needs you to come see the insurance people with her."

Rhiannon groaned. "Damn. I hoped I'd never have to see her again."

David smiled. "Probably better to get it over with, and then you're done. Besides, there may be some compensation in it for your belongings."

Rhiannon shook her head. "I'll bet you not a cent of the insurance money finds its way into my pocket."

"Then maybe you should take a lawyer with you to the meeting," Marika said.

"You'd do that? It wouldn't be pleasant, I can assure you."

"I'd do that."

David heard the unspoken "for you." From the way Rhiannon's eyes softened, she did too.

"Thank you." They gazed at each other for a long moment.

David smothered a smile. *Could they be any more obvious?* When Rhiannon turned back to him, he plastered an innocent look on his face. "So, shall I tell Hettie when I see her at Sunday services that you'll give her a call?"

"No. Tell her that she can call me at work," Rhiannon said. "Thanks for dinner, Ichabod. It was great."

"Always my pleasure."

Marika nodded. "It really was wonderful. Why don't you come for dinner on Sunday and let us repay the favour?"

They made plans to get together, and David waved as they walked to the Lexus.

Rhiannon opened the door, then stopped. "I forgot to ask—what happened to your flower gardens out front? They looked a mess when we drove up."

David grimaced. "Someone vandalized them this week, and poor old Tupper was heartbroken. He's going to replant them this weekend, and he swears he's going to stand guard over them for the rest of the summer if he has to. He does love his gardens."

Their murmurs of sympathy were cut short by the ringing of David's phone. "Oh, gotta go." He turned and hurried back to the door. "Call me tomorrow, okay?"

"You're as bad as Lee!" Rhiannon called after him. She and Marika laughed.

David smiled and dashed for the phone.

When the driver's door opened, Gao held perfectly still, focused on keeping his breathing calm and noiseless. For one panicked instant, he thought he had been seen when no one got in, but moments later, their laughter drifted over.

The seat moved against him as the smaller woman settled into it, then the distinctive click indicated that she had unlocked the passenger side door.

"Rhi," the lawyer said, "you didn't lock your door? Lee would have your head."

"I'm sorry. I didn't think...well, we're at the church, for heaven's sake." Rhiannon started the engine.

"Uh-huh, and you know what David said about that."

"Yeah, that was a pretty gruesome story all right."

Gao subtly worked muscles tight from being too long in one position as he prepared to move.

The car began to back up and then lurched to a halt as the driver half-turned, saw him, and screamed.

Instantly, Gao lunged forward and pressed the gun to the lawyer's head. "If you make one wrong move, I'll shoot her." Gao's voice was cold and calm. "Continue to back out and then drive away. I'll tell you where." He prodded the lawyer's temple with the barrel. "You, keep your eyes forward."

She did as he instructed.

"Drive to Macleod Trail and head south."

Gao intended to direct them south of the city to an isolated rural road where he would kill them both. When the Chameleon confronted him, he would explain that the lawyer had thrown herself into his path of fire and that her death had been an accident. If he sensed that she didn't buy his story or if she were enraged at his failure to follow her orders to the letter, he would vanish. Gao had planned for that eventuality ever since he had realized the hazardous nature of being in the Chameleon's service. Unlike Rhongji, he didn't spend his money lavishly and was well prepared to fund a life in exile...preferably on the other side of the world from his psychotic employer.

The car turned onto Macleod, and Gao brooded on the unfairness of it all. He'd had a tidy situation in Calgary until these two derailed it. Anger built and burned within. He contemplated their deaths with increasing pleasure.

Crouched between them, Gao pulled the gun down so the barrel was pressed against the lawyer's side, but not obvious to anyone passing by. To the casual observer, he would simply appear to be leaning forward. Gao kept an eye on the driver to make sure she didn't try anything.

She stole a look at him in the rearview mirror.

"Match the speed of traffic." Gao tapped the gun against Marika for emphasis, and the driver picked up the pace. He smiled coldly as she again glanced in the rearview mirror. *Study away, bitch. It won't matter in the least. You'll never get the chance to identify me.*

They had just crossed the major intersection at Glenmore when his cellphone rang. Irritated, he shifted his gun hand and reached into his pocket. He flipped the phone open. "Yes?"

"Gao. Have my instructions been carried out?"

The Chameleon's purr chilled Gao, and he had to force his words. "I'm in the process of doing so now, madam. They're in the car with me."

"They? What the hell are you doing? I very clearly told you to eliminate the lawyer's companion, not the lawyer."

Her snarl instantly made Gao rethink his plans. He would execute the small woman and merely knock the lawyer out. He'd transport her back to the city in the trunk of the car and leave her to be found. "Of course, madam, and I fully intend to carry out your orders to the letter." Cold sweat broke out on his forehead.

310

When his hostages exchanged a look, Gao hit the lawyer's temple with the butt of the gun, drawing a cry of pain and a rivulet of blood.

The driver hissed, but the blow served its purpose. His prisoners kept their eyes forward.

"Where are you now?"

"Heading south on Macleod, out of the city," Gao said.

"Have you passed Heritage yet?"

"No, madam."

"Three blocks past Heritage, turn right and go straight ahead to the Southfield Industrial Park. At the north end of the park, you'll find a shipping terminal—DeAndre Transport. Go around the back of the building and park beside the door. Someone will be there to let you and your prisoners in and show you where to go. Wait there for me and don't do anything to them for now. Is that clearly understood?"

Gao's eyes widened, and he swallowed hard. *She's here? In the city?* "Yes, madam." The line disconnected. He issued the new directions.

Within moments, they turned off the busy main road onto a side street leading to the industrial park. It was sparsely traveled at this late hour.

When they reached their destination, a man waited at the back door of the warehouse terminal.

"Get out of the car." Gao tapped the driver's shoulder. "You run, she dies. It's very simple."

The women looked at each other, opened the doors, and got out. Gao clambered over the seat to follow the lawyer, gun still jammed in her back.

The lawyer pressed her hand to the side of her head, and the smaller woman came around to take her arm.

Too taken up with his own concerns, Gao didn't bother to order them apart. He directed them to follow the man at the door.

They were led down a staircase to a sublevel jammed with shipping crates and freight dollies. The man opened a door and gestured them in.

Gao followed them into a small, almost bare storage room with metal shelving along one side and cases of office supplies amassed against the back wall. He motioned them to a patch of uncluttered wall. "Sit down."

They slid down the wall and huddled together. The small one used the bottom of her shirt to wipe away the blood on her companion's temple while keeping one arm wrapped around her waist.

Gao perched on a stack of boxes, his only concern to survive this night. He glanced at his watch and rested the gun on his thigh.

Ten minutes passed and then half an hour. The lawyer's head dropped onto her companion's shoulder.

Gao narrowed his eyes. *What if she's angry that I hurt the lawyer? Goddamnit. Why does she even care?* He worried at it as he contemplated the friendship between the lawyer and her companion. The weeks of surveillance had been illuminating. *I should've hit the small one instead. It would've been just as effective. Hurt one, the other bleeds.* Finally, he shrugged. *Fuck it. It's too late now, and I've got more important things to worry about.* His watch indicated a full hour had passed by the time he heard the door swing open. Gao's heart raced, and he jumped to his feet.

The Chameleon entered the room. She looked at the prisoners and sneered. "My, my...what a touching sight."

CHAPTER 24

"THANKS, GINO. IF YOU DO hear anything, let me know, okay?" Lee disconnected the call and rubbed her temples, trying to ease the dull throbbing that had developed after hours of fruitless phoning. Wherever Pike and Eddie had gone, they were smart enough not to contact any of their buddies. She'd pulled every string she could think of but hadn't been able to turn up even a hint of their whereabouts.

Arms closed around Lee, and she leaned back into Dana's embrace.

"Time to take a break, sweetie." Dana nuzzled Lee's hair. "It's getting late. You're not going to find them tonight."

Lee half-turned and pulled Dana around to stand between her legs. She caressed Dana's cheek. "I'm sorry, love. This didn't exactly turn out to be the romantic week to ourselves that I'd planned."

Dana captured Lee's hand and planted a kiss on the palm. "Don't worry about it. The important thing is ensuring that Marika and Rhiannon are safe. You're doing what you have to. You wouldn't be you if you didn't." She leaned down, and they indulged in a lingering kiss. Straightening, Dana smiled. "It's just one of the things I adore about you. But it's time to rest now. You've been going non-stop all week, and I know you're feeling it."

"True, I'm not as young as I once was," Lee said. "Okay, I'll just check on Marika, and then we'll go to bed."

Dana glanced at the kitchen clock. "Oh, hon, it's late. Why don't you leave it until the morning?"

"No. She promised she'd call when they were back from David's. She's probably fuming because she can't get through. You go get ready for bed. I'll be there in a minute."

Dana gave her another kiss and left the room.

Still smiling, Lee entered Marika's speed dial. Her smile faded as the answering machine picked up after four rings. "Marika, pick up. It's Lee. Hey, pick up. Look, if you're there, call me right back—home or cell, it doesn't matter."

When no one picked up, Lee frowned. She hung up and tried Marika's cell, with the same negative result. *They must've stayed late at David's.* She looked up his number and rang it.

A sleepy voice answered, and the fear in Lee's belly grew. "David? It's Lee Glenn. Are Marika and Rhiannon still there?"

"Lee? They left quite a while ago." David's voice sharpened.

"Damn it!" Lee's mind raced through the possibilities. "Exactly what time did they go?"

There was a clatter over the line. "Sorry. I dropped my glasses and can't see the clock without them. Goodness, it's been at least an hour and a half since they left." Anxiety laced David's words.

Lee didn't have time for blithe reassurances. Her gut told her that every minute counted. "Gotta go. I'll let you know what's happened when I find out."

"Is there anything I can do?"

"Pray." Lee hung up and looked for Barb's number. "C'mon, c'mon, be there." When a curt voice answered, she exhaled. "Barb? It's Lee."

"Boss? What's up?"

"Please tell me you installed a GPS in the Lexus like I asked you to." Lee held her breath.

"Of course I did. Put it in the same afternoon you told me about it."

"Thank, God! Remind me to give you a raise." Lee forced herself to loosen her grasp on the phone.

"Hell, yeah." Barb chuckled before sobering. "But why, boss? What's going on?"

"I think my friends are in trouble. They're not where they should be, and I haven't been able to locate them. It may be a false alarm—"

"Let me boot up and access the office interlink. Stay on the line. I'll have a location for you in a moment." Barb's phone clattered.

Lee began what felt like an interminable wait.

Still toweling her face dry, Dana walked back into the kitchen. "What's taking so long, love?"

Lee couldn't answer for the lump in her throat, so she shook her head.

Dana lowered the towel. "Oh no. What's going on?"

"I can't find them. They left David's over an hour ago, and they're not answering at home."

Dana sank into the chair opposite Lee's and twisted the towel in her hands.

Barb came back on the line. "Got 'em, boss. The car is in the Southfield Industrial Park on the north side of the lot."

"What's in that park?" Lee jotted down the location.

"Let's see... Okay, there are two main companies and a bunch of smaller ones. The big ones are Miller Petro-Industries and DeAndre Shipping, and the small ones..."

Lee straightened. "Did you say DeAndre Shipping?"

"Yeah. Their terminal is on the north side, according to the map I'm looking at."

"Jesus! Barb, stay on them, and if that car moves, call me immediately on my cell. I'm heading out now."

"Will do. Do you want me to contact the police?"

Lee agonized over that for an instant. Did she have enough to go to them? What if she sent the police in, and it endangered her friends? Knowing she could be at the facility in less than fifteen minutes decided her. "Hold off until I can get a look at what's going on, but be ready to notify them as soon as I give you the word."

"Okay, boss. I'll wait to hear from you."

Lee hung up and looked at Dana. "I've gotta go, hon."

Dana nodded. "I know, but you be damned careful, and you call me the instant you can."

"I will." Lee jammed the cellphone in her pocket, stole a precious couple of seconds to kiss Dana, and ran out, snagging the keys to the truck on the way. Within moments, she was barreling down quiet streets, headed for the south side of the city.

At the sound of the newcomer's voice, Rhiannon looked up to examine the woman who entered their storeroom cell. The unremarkable, middle-aged stranger was of average height and build, with drab brown hair and eyes. Then Rhiannon took a second look at those eyes, and a shiver ran up her spine. They were the eyes of a born predator, radiating cruelty and contempt from opaque depths. Rhiannon's fear increased a hundredfold. Gao was bad enough, but he didn't strike her as psychotic. She had held out some hope of reasoning with him, but a single glance told her there would be no reasoning with this woman.

Marika raised her head off Rhiannon's shoulder. "Cass. It figures. What the hell do you think you're doing?"

Rhiannon stared. *Oh, my God. This is Cass? Jesus Christ.*

Cass knelt in front of them. She reached out to touch Marika's face, but Marika jerked away.

For a brief instant, Rhiannon wanted to cheer, but rage flared in their captor's eyes, and Rhi chose the discretion of silence.

Cass turned her gaze on Rhiannon. "So you're the little thing that's caused me so many problems."

"So you're the piss-ant psycho bitch who can't take no for an answer." Rhiannon's imitation was dead-on.

Cass lashed out, but Marika blocked her hand milliseconds before it impacted Rhiannon's face.

Rhiannon didn't dare take her eyes off Cass, but she felt Marika's body quiver with tension as she fought to hold Cass' hand back.

A battle of will and muscles ensued until Cass smirked and pulled away. "Such an odd time to start showing a little backbone, my dear." She stood and strolled over to Gao, who had his gun pointed at Rhiannon and Marika. "Oh, do lower that." Her tone was one of faux amiability. "This is just a chat between old friends, an opportunity to arrive at... an understanding."

Gao did as he was told and sank back onto the stack of boxes.

Cass paced slowly in front of Marika and Rhiannon, never taking her eyes from them.

Was she thrown off by Marika's defence of me? Can we make that work for us? Rhiannon tried to come up with ways to exploit the changed dynamic.

Cass stopped pacing and again crouched in front of them. She gazed at Rhiannon but addressed Marika. "To answer your question, I've come to claim what is mine." Her gaze slid to Marika. "You."

Rhiannon's anger flared, but Marika's hand closed over hers with a warning squeeze.

Marika shook her head. "No."

Fury erupted in Cass' eyes. "I wasn't offering you a choice, dear. I'm not in the habit of allowing my chattel free will."

Marika leaned forward. "No, I'm not yours. I never was, and I never will be."

Cass' civilized façade slipped, and her eyes narrowed. "I don't think you quite grasp the situation." She gestured at Rhiannon and sneered. "You think this little thing can satisfy you? She would run screaming if she had even an inkling of the rot inside you."

"The only rot in her was the shadow you cast." Rhiannon glared at Cass. "She's free of you now. You'll never get to touch her again."

A malignant laugh rang out as Cass inclined her head at Rhiannon. "You are a fool, girl. She can't keep away. I never have to summon her. She keeps coming back. She knows she deserves what I do to her."

"Past tense," Rhiannon said. "Whatever you did to her, she's grown beyond you."

Cass' eyes blazed. "Would you like to know what I did to her, little girl? Shall I tell you the details of how I made her crawl and cry, of how sweet it was to make her beg for more and then beg me to stop?"

Rhiannon lashed out. Her foot caught Cass solidly on the thigh and sent her sprawling backwards.

Marika gasped.

Gao leapt up and aimed his gun directly at Rhiannon's head.

"No!" Cass pulled herself to her feet.

Terrified at what her instinctive reaction might have wrought, Rhiannon was nonetheless grimly pleased that Cass limped as she returned to her position in front of them.

Cass positioned herself to Marika's side and out of range of any flying feet.

Rhiannon read her death sentence in Cass' venomous gaze. Then, to her surprise, Cass ignored her and focused on Marika. "I believe we can come to an arrangement here. I understand this girl might be of some importance to you, so I'll offer you a deal." Cass' voice was calm and reasonable. "I've got an apartment waiting for you in Vancouver. You agree to fly there with me tonight, and we'll forget all about this nastiness. Your little pet can stay here, and you and I will pursue our...arrangement without her interference."

No! Don't do it! "Marika, don't believe—"

"Say another word, girl, and I'll cut your tongue out." Cass pulled a switchblade out of her pocket and flicked it open.

Rhiannon's mouth snapped shut. She didn't doubt that Cass would take profound pleasure in mutilating her.

"I don't even mind if you wish to continue your career," Cass said. "I can arrange for you to transfer to the top firm in the city. You'll have every advantage you could possibly desire."

"And all I have to do is be at your beck and call?" Marika asked.

No! Don't trust her! Don't go back to her. I couldn't bear it. God, Marika, don't— Rhiannon held her breath.

Cass laughed. "Oh, you needn't worry, dear. I won't make too many demands on your time. After all, I do have my own life to lead. You'll be free to live your life mostly as you choose. You can even bring your damned cat with you."

"You'd let Rhiannon go? She'd be safe?"

Cass nodded.

Rhiannon tensed, a new fear overwhelming everything else. *No, not even for my life. Don't go with that monster!* Knife be damned, she was about to plead with Marika, when Marika's gaze met hers. Instantly, Rhiannon calmed. The unspoken message in Marika's clear, peaceful eyes was one of love and indivisibility. Whatever happened, it would happen to them both.

Marika faced Cass. "No. I'll never be with you again, under any circumstances."

Cass' eyebrows shot up. "No? You understand that if you refuse, I'll kill the girl."

Marika lifted her chin. "You're going to kill her anyway, and I'd rather die with her than be with you."

Pride and defiance swelled in Rhiannon's chest.

The knife trembled in Cass' hand, and she pointed it at Rhiannon. "You'd actually choose dying with this...this nothing over living with me?"

"Yes." Marika smiled at Rhiannon. "She would never forgive me otherwise."

Rhiannon was awed at Marika's sang-froid, aware—even as she was convinced they were seconds from death—that something profound had changed.

Marika didn't flinch.

Cass stood and snapped her knife shut. "Kill them."

Terror flashed through Rhiannon. She tightened her hold on Marika. *No, not now. I never got to tell you—* She looked at Marika, trying to put everything left unsaid in her eyes.

Marika nodded slightly, and her lips moved. She clutched Rhiannon's hand.

Gao moved forward, his gun raised.

"Not here, you idiot." Cass glared at him. "Make sure there's no trace of them ever having been here. Everything else, I leave to your discretion." She fixed him with a cold stare. "Don't let me down, Gao."

"No, madam. It will be as you say." Gao inclined his head.

Cass strode to the door. She paused with her hand on the doorknob, turned, and looked at Marika. "It's rather unfortunate. You were an interesting divertissement." She shrugged and left the room.

Lee made it to the industrial park in record time and parked her truck behind one of the big transports lined up at the rear of the yard. She grabbed her steering wheel locking bar as a makeshift weapon and worked her way up the side of the building, cursing the security lighting that left so few shadows.

Marika's Lexus and another car were parked beside the back door to DeAndre Shipping.

When she was within twenty feet of the door, it opened. She flattened herself against the building.

"They'll be leaving in a few moments. When they do, double-check the room and then lock up for the night. Did you ensure the security tapes were replaced?" The woman's voice was clear in the night air.

Lee sagged in relief. *They're alive—for now. I'm not too late.* She tensed. She'd only have one chance, and timing was critical.

A man responded, but Lee couldn't make out what he said as he stood inside the building.

Lee waited until the woman's car pulled away, then covered the remaining distance. She paused under the floodlights nearest to the entrance and used the security bar to break two of them, covering her head against the shower of broken glass. Sheltered by the dark, Lee took up a position beside the door, weapon in hand as she waited.

Less than five minutes later, the door swung open. Rhiannon stepped out, followed by Marika and Gao, who pointed a gun at Marika's back.

Lee lashed out with the locking bar, smashing Gao's gun hand.

He howled, and the gun skittered away.

Lee swung the bar again and snapped Gao's head back. He collapsed in a heap.

A shout and the clatter of running footsteps sounded from inside the building.

"Go!" Lee shouted. "Now!"

Marika and Rhiannon sprang for the Lexus.

The second man burst through the door.

Lee met him with a solid blow to the stomach. He crumpled, and she dashed for the car.

Marika held the rear door open for her.

As soon as Lee dove into the back seat, Rhiannon hit the gas. The car roared off, tires screeching.

Lee looked out the back window.

The second man tried to get up. The first man stirred too.

Good. Not that I give a rat's ass if either of you assholes die, but I don't need the aggravation of an investigation.

"Where to?" Rhiannon sped away from the industrial park.

"My house." Lee's cell phone vibrated. "Yeah? Oh, thanks, Barb. I know it's moving. I'm in it, and I've got my friends with me. Thanks a million, kiddo. There'll definitely be a bonus in your next paycheque." Lee hung up.

She was surprised when Rhiannon abruptly pulled off the busy main road into a quiet side street, stopped at the curb, threw the car into neutral, and engaged the emergency brake. "What—?"

Lee's confusion cleared as Rhiannon and Marika reached for each other at the same instant. She leaned back against the seat and smiled as they clung together in wordless comfort. After a long moment, they drew apart, and Rhiannon gently touched the left side of Marika's face. "Are you okay? Does it hurt badly?"

Lee frowned. Marika's temple was streaked with blood. "Hey! Do you need to go to the hospital?"

Marika's gaze never left Rhiannon. "It's all right. I have a bad headache, but he didn't hit me that hard. I just want to go home."

Lee shook her head. "Not home, sweetie. You two are staying with us tonight, where I can keep an eye on you. We'll figure things out tomorrow."

Rhiannon reached back and gripped Lee's knee. "I don't know how you did it, but I'll never forget what I owe you."

Marika nodded. "We would've been dead without you. Cass told him—"

"So it was Cass." Lee slapped the back of Rhiannon's seat. "Then we can nail the bitch."

Marika sighed. "We can try, but she's very well-connected, and it'll only be our word against hers. How much do you want to bet that she's already set up a rock-solid alibi?"

Lee scowled. *No fucking way is that bitch getting away with this!*

Rhiannon disengaged the emergency brake, put the car in gear, and executed a U-turn to get back to the main street.

CHAPTER 25

O
N THE DRIVE BACK TO the house, Lee phoned first Dana and then Marc Manion.

"Lee? Don't tell me you've heard already," Marc said. "I was going to call you first thing in the morning."

Lee frowned. "Heard? About what?"

"About Pike and Eddie King."

A familiar tingle ran through Lee. She was closing in. "Did they find them?"

Marc chuckled. "You could say that. The idiots got picked up for shoplifting in Edmonton, and the arresting officer noticed the flag I put on them. They're in custody there now, and they'll be transferred back to Calgary in the morning."

"That's great news, but that's not why I called you." Lee laid out the evening's events in detail.

Marc whistled when she related Sandra DeAndre's involvement.

When Lee finished, there was a long moment of silence. "It's time to pull in the bigger guns, Sarge. After you left this afternoon, I talked to my friend in the Major Crimes Unit, and he was very interested in what you told me. It seems they've stumbled onto a link between Gao and a major Snakehead organization running out of Vancouver, one that they've been trying to get inside for a long time. He wanted me to set up a meeting with you next week to compare notes, but I think under the circumstances we should meet tomorrow before the King boys get here."

"Sounds good to me." Lee grinned. They were going to take Cass down. She could feel it in her bones. "Look, I know you'll need statements from my friends, but they're pretty shaken up right now. Can it wait until the morning?"

"You know the best time to get statements is while events are fresh." Marc was silent for a few moments. "We'll compromise. You interview them tonight, and I'll let the official statements slide until morning. I'll also arrange a warrant for Gao's arrest, though I'm sure he's long gone by now."

"Thanks, I sure appreciate it." Lee and Marc made arrangements to meet in his office in the morning and said goodnight.

By the time they reached the house, Dana and David were waiting. They all came together in mad crush of hugs and questions and reassurances until Lee shepherded them into the kitchen.

Lee signed the statements and set them aside. It had been harrowing to listen to Marika and Rhiannon recite their ordeal. Her hands curled into fists. *God, what I wouldn't give to be alone with Cass for five minutes.*

"What now?" Rhiannon's voice cracked.

Before Lee could answer, Dana broke in. "Now you two are going to march yourselves downstairs and go to bed. The guest room is made up, and I don't want to see hide nor hair of you until breakfast."

Marika nodded. "Thanks, Dana. And thanks for patching me up." She held a hand out to Rhiannon, who took it and followed her to the stairs.

David waited until they disappeared through the basement door. "What does happen now?"

Lee scowled. "Now we protect them until Cass' whole rotten house of cards tumbles down around her. What bothers me is the way Gao acted toward Cass. Going by what they said, he was scared shitless of her. I've always said Cass was a psycho, but this was way over the top, even for her."

"Can we protect them here?" Dana's brow furrowed. "I can have Eli stay with his father for another week or so, if necessary."

Lee nodded. "That might not be a bad idea until this is all settled. I was over there while Marika's place was bugged, and it wouldn't be difficult to figure out who I am or where we live. I want you taking extra precautions, too, hon. In fact, I'd rather you went and stayed with your mother until this is over."

Dana snorted. "Not happening, love. If you're here, I'm here."

Lee knew better than to argue.

David frowned. "If they can connect them to this house, then we'd better find Rhiannon and Marika a different refuge."

"Agreed," Lee said. "I'm just not sure where. Maybe put them in a hotel or something."

David raised a hand. "If I could make a suggestion? An old friend of mine owns a cabin at Shuswap Lakes in B.C. As long as no one else is in it at the moment, I know he wouldn't mind loaning it to them. I can call him first thing in the morning."

Lee nodded. "Good idea. That would get them well out of the city and safely away."

They brainstormed for another few minutes, then David drained his coffee and stood. "I'd better get going and let you two get some sleep. I'll call you in the morning as soon as I talk to my friend."

Lee and Dana walked David to the door and bade him goodnight. When the door closed behind him, they looked at each other.

"I have to say, life is never dull around you." Dana patted Lee's belly. "So, my hero, are you ready for bed?"

"Aw geez, I'm no hero," Lee said as she set their alarm system and wrapped an arm around Dana.

They walked down the hall to their bedroom. "You'll always be my hero, and I'm sure that Rhiannon and Marika would agree wholeheartedly."

"Mmm. Maybe." Lee grinned. "So, do you think they're doing it?"

"Lee!" Dana laughed. "You are so bad."

"I didn't see them protest sharing a bed," Lee said. "Besides, did you see the way they looked at each other?"

"Yes, I did, but then they'd just survived a terrifying situation. It could have been survivor relief."

"Nuh-uh." Lee stepped aside to let Dana precede her into their bedroom. "Those two are crazy about each other."

―――――――

In the basement guest room, Marika laughed out loud. "You look like one of the seven dwarfs." She couldn't remember when she'd last seen anything as adorable as the sight of Rhiannon draped in one of Lee's old T-shirts.

Rhiannon grinned. "Hey, Ms. Pot. Take a look in the mirror. You don't exactly fill out Lee's shirt either."

They turned out the light, slid under the bedding, and faced each other only inches apart.

Rhiannon's face was illuminated by the light from the small window.

"Are you all right?" Marika gently pushed Rhi's hair back off her forehead. Her heart overflowed with emotion—relief and exultation, but more than anything, love.

"Considering that it wasn't that long ago that I thought I'd be going to sleep permanently tonight, I'm doing pretty well." Rhiannon caught and held Marika's hand.

Awareness of their narrow escape thrummed just below Marika's skin and kept sleep at bay.

Finally, Rhiannon whispered, "I was scared."

"So was I. If Lee hadn't found us—"

Rhiannon shook her head. "No. I was scared that you were going to agree to her terms, hoping it would save me."

"I knew she was lying. I knew she wouldn't let you live."

"But *you* could've lived, if you'd agreed to her deal." Rhi's words were quiet. "I would've understood, you know?"

"Did you really think I'd buy my life at the cost of yours?" Marika's breath caught.

"No, I knew you wouldn't." Rhiannon caressed Marika's face. "And I don't know what I was more afraid of...that you'd die, or that you'd end up in her clutches."

The tension ebbed from Marika's body. "There was never any question. I wouldn't go back to her for any price."

Rhiannon smiled. "I'm glad."

Marika returned the smile and opened her arms.

Rhiannon snuggled into them, wrapping her body around Marika's.

Her warmth finally drove away the chill that had seized Marika the moment Cass walked through the door. *God, I almost lost you tonight. I can't lose you. I can't live without you.*

Rhiannon ignored the tapping on the door. She was warm and comfortable cocooned in Marika's arms and saw no reason to move. But when someone tickled her nose, she had to open her eyes.

Lee knelt at the side of their bed, sporting a broad grin. "Hey, sleepyheads. It's time to get up."

Marika yawned and nuzzled Rhiannon's hair. "Hey, yourself. I trust you have a good reason for waking us at the crack of dawn."

Lee chuckled. "It's past ten. Dawn was hours ago, and I can't let you sleep any longer."

"Why not?" Rhiannon wriggled closer to Marika. "It's Saturday, isn't it?"

Lee smiled. "Yes, it is. But we've got a lot to take care of, and then you two are leaving town for a bit."

"We are?" Marika propped her chin on Rhiannon's shoulder. "Where are we going?"

"I'll explain it all when you come upstairs. Dana went over to your place this morning and packed you both some clothes. She brought Spooky back, too. He's going to stay with us while you're gone." Lee retrieved two suitcases from beside the door and set them by the bed. "Don't waste any time, ladies. We're expected at the police station by noon." She left and closed the door behind her.

Rhiannon reluctantly swung her feet over the edge of the bed and sat up. She scowled at the suitcases. *Screw getting up. I just want to crawl back into her arms.*

Marika rubbed Rhiannon's back, erasing her frown.

Rhiannon looked back at Marika, who stretched lazily. "You don't appear to be getting up."

Marika grinned. "I lack incentive."

"Do you?" Rhiannon smiled and flipped the covers off, exposing Marika. "So you figure you're just going to lie there while I have to get up?"

Marika's eyes gleamed. "You don't have to." She extended her hand.

Rhiannon intertwined her fingers with Marika's. The air between them was so charged that she could barely breathe.

A gentle tug pulled Rhiannon forward and into Marika's arms. Rhiannon's heart pounded as soft lips tentatively brushed hers.

They started when a loud knock sounded and Lee hollered, "Get a move on, you two. David's waiting upstairs."

Rhiannon's head dropped onto Marika's shoulder.

Marika gave a strangled laugh. "We're coming." She stroked Rhiannon's hair. "Are you... Will you be all right?"

Rhiannon tried to slow her erratic breathing. "Only if you promise we can pick this discussion up later."

"I promise. First opportunity." Marika grinned. "Think you can remember where we left off?"

"Oh, I think I can." Rhiannon delicately kissed her way down Marika's throat, lingered in the hollow of her throat, and returned to her lips. She caressed Marika's mouth with her tongue, then drew away and sat up. "I think, right about there."

"Um, yeah...that would be it." Marika's eyes were wide.

Rhiannon laughed and knelt beside the bags. "I'll take a shower first. I'll be out in five minutes." She left the room, pretending that she didn't hear Marika's muttered suggestion that they could share.

Moments later, Rhiannon stood under the hot water, eyes closed as she imagined Marika stepping into the shower, her sleek naked body only inches away. She shivered and pressed her forehead against the wall.

It was such an unfamiliar emotion, the desire that surged through her, weakened her knees, and hardened her nipples. Rhiannon ran a wet finger over her mouth and recalled the sensation of Marika's lips on hers. When her other hand strayed down her belly, she caught herself. *Not now!* She redirected her disobedient hand to the shower control and forced herself to turn the water temperature down. Rhiannon squeaked as the blast of cool water hit her and drove all other thoughts out of her mind. *Jesus, I always thought that was a myth.*

It was a short-lived remedy. She finished and dressed, her mind on how it felt to hold Marika, to taste her lips and feel her body so close. *God, I've barely had my first kiss, and all I can think of is how much more I want with her. But what if—?* Apprehension over her inexperience battled desire, then she recalled the look in Marika's eyes. *She loves me as much as I love her.* Rhiannon hung up the towel and returned to the bedroom.

Marika still lay on the bed with her arms crossed behind her head, staring at the ceiling.

Rhiannon took a moment to admire the way the T-shirt fell just short of Marika's slender thighs. Then she shook herself. "Bathroom's all yours. I'll meet you upstairs, okay?"

"Okay." Marika didn't move. Her gaze caressed Rhiannon.

Rhiannon almost groaned aloud at the acute desire in Marika's eyes. She pulled away and headed upstairs. *Get a grip. You're going to embarrass yourself.* But she entered the kitchen with a broad smile on her face. She slid onto a chair opposite Lee and David. "Marika will be up in a few moments. She's taking a shower."

"Huh. I thought you'd share one," Lee said.

Rhiannon blushed.

Dana swatted Lee. "Behave yourself. Rhi, just ignore her."

Rhiannon took a deep breath. "So, what's happening today?"

"Why don't we wait for Marika, and then I only have to run through this once." Lee refilled her and David's coffee mugs.

"Okay." Rhiannon accepted a plate of eggs, sausages, and toast from Dana. She was cleaning up the final bites when hands settled on her shoulders. She looked up at Marika, who smiled back before taking the chair next to her.

Spooky padded in from the living room and promptly jumped up on Marika's lap.

"Over easy?" Dana placed a mug in front of Marika.

Marika shook her head. "No, thanks. Just coffee's good."

Rhiannon cleared her throat. "So, now that Marika's here, can you fill us in on what's happening?"

"You're going to finish breakfast," Lee said. "Then we're going to the police station to file formal reports on what happened last night. Once that's done, you're leaving town until everything is resolved. David will tell you what we've arranged."

David pulled a key and homemade map out of his pocket. "I called Conor this morning. His family has a cabin out at Shuswap Lakes. It's nothing fancy, but it'll give you a place to go where no one would ever think to look for you. You only have to buy food supplies. Make sure you pick them up in town before you head out to the cabin because it's on the far side of the lake and not easily accessible."

"Are you sure it's okay with Conor that two strangers stay at his family's place?" Marika asked.

David smiled. "You're not strangers to me, and that's good enough for him."

Rhiannon frowned. "What about work? How long are we going to be gone? We can't just not show up on Monday."

"I've already called Daniel Cohen and explained the situation," Lee said. "Both of you are on three weeks' holiday, starting now. He'll have a temp man your office and rearrange appointments. I've also rented a car under Barb's name, so there'll be no connection to you. You'll be driving it to the Shuswaps."

Rhiannon tilted her head. "Cass wouldn't be stupid enough to try again, would she?"

Lee's eyes narrowed. "I'm not sure what that woman would be crazy enough to do, but I'm not taking any chances." She leaned forward. "There's a lot more going on here than we know. Luckily, we caught a break yesterday. Pike and Eddie will be transported back to Calgary this afternoon, and Marc has agreed to let me sit in on their interrogation. I'm pretty sure we can crack this wide open once we put some pressure on those weasels, but I'm also concerned about Gao."

"Surely he's left town," Marika said. "He wouldn't stay around when he knows we can identify him."

Lee shook her head. "Dunno where he went. According to Marc, Gao never went back to his apartment, but that doesn't mean he isn't still around. He's a loose end that we have to take into consideration."

"Look at it this way," David said. "You're getting an unexpected vacation in one of the prettiest places around. All you have to do is relax and enjoy the lake."

Marika and Rhiannon glanced at each other. Marika flushed.

Rhiannon looked away, her heart racing. *Maybe going to the lakes isn't a bad idea.*

David tapped the key on the table. "Besides, after all I had to do to find this blessed thing, you have to accept the offer."

Rhiannon was grateful for the distraction. "Why? Couldn't you find it?"

"I still haven't unpacked all my boxes from my move here, and I knew the key was in one of them. After I talked to Conor, it took me almost an hour of searching before I found it. I even dragged poor Tupper in to help me. You should have seen the both of us in the basement, rummaging through a ton of boxes." David shook his head. "I think Tupper was about to shoot me by the time I finally found it." He went over his homemade map with Rhiannon and Marika.

Rhiannon leaned forward to examine the map, conscious of Marika's arm resting against hers. Marika's scent filled her senses, and she had to force herself to pay attention to David's instructions.

When David was satisfied that they could follow his map, he pushed it and the key across the table. "There's a canoe stored in the wood hut. Feel free to use it or anything else around the place." He smiled. "Seriously. Put everything else out of your mind, and just have fun."

"But make sure you take your cell phone, so I can reach you to keep you updated," Lee said.

Marika nodded. "I'll check in with you every evening before we go to bed."

Before we go to bed. The simple phrase took Rhiannon's breath away.

CHAPTER 26

R HIANNON TOYED WITH DAVID'S MAP, afraid to look up for fear that her thoughts were written on her face. *Before we go to bed.*

"Let's get moving," Lee said. "The sooner we get your statements filed, the sooner you two can get out of Calgary." She pushed back her chair. "I'm going to take a quick look around outside."

"I'll grab our bags." Marika stood. "Be back up in a moment."

Rhiannon took a deep breath and rose to clear the table.

Dana waved her off. "I've got that. Why don't you walk David to his car?"

Grateful for the distraction, Rhiannon followed David through the rear door.

"I parked in the back alley. I thought it might be less conspicuous there." David looked at Rhiannon. "Are you okay? You've been through an awful lot in a very short span of time."

They walked through the yard, and Rhiannon considered his question. "I feel like I've been on a roller coaster. Parts of the ride have been incredible, and I wouldn't trade those for anything. But I also feel like my whole world has been turned upside down and I'm stumbling around, just trying to get my bearings." She grimaced. "Does that make sense?"

David nodded. "Very much so."

They stopped at the fence, and Rhiannon leaned on the gate. "For so long, all I've been focused on is saving up enough money to leave. Nothing ever distracted me from that. I worked all the overtime I could get, took odd jobs, paid off my education loan within a year, never spent a single cent that I could avoid, and finally, I'm there. I could go today if I wanted. Just take a cab to the airport and be gone." Rhiannon shook her head. "But..."

"But?" David leaned on the gate next to her.

"But I didn't figure Marika into my calculations." Rhiannon shrugged. "How could I? Nothing in my life prepared me for what I'm feeling now."

David cocked his head. "Oh, I don't know about that. Wouldn't you agree that for the first ten years of your life, your parents gave you a daily exemplar of love? I know that it's been bleak since you came to live with Hettie, but maybe it's time to let the old dream go because you don't need it anymore."

Rhiannon rested her chin on her folded hands. "I'm not sure I can do that. It's kept me going through some really tough times."

"It was a crutch and a good one, but when we heal, we throw away our crutches."

Rhiannon sighed, and they were silent.

Finally, David asked, "Do you love her?"

"Yes."

"Does she love you?"

Rhiannon looked at David. "I think she does. I really think she does."

"Then you have to decide if she's worth throwing away that crutch for, because you can't have both."

David unlatched the gate, and Rhiannon pulled it open. He stopped on the other side and grinned at her. "Nervous?"

Rhiannon blushed. "God, yes!"

He chuckled. "I suppose it wouldn't do any good to give you my premarital counseling course in a nutshell, eh?"

Rhiannon rolled her eyes.

"Didn't think so." David placed one hand over hers and squeezed gently. "Just follow your heart, Rhi. It won't steer you wrong." He walked to his car.

A wave of affection swept over Rhiannon. *If he hadn't been so bloody stubborn about being my friend, I don't know if*

*I'd ever have opened up to anyone. If not for him, she might not
be in my life. I owe him so much.* "Thank you...for everything."

David smiled, got into the car, and drove off.

Rhiannon turned back to the house.

Marika stood at the back door, waiting for her.
"Everything all right?"

"Mmm-hmm." Rhiannon nodded. "We were just talking
about...life."

Marika raised one eyebrow. "Oh, was that all?"

Rhiannon chuckled, and they walked to the front door.

───────────

Rhiannon glanced at Marika as they followed Lee and
Dana into Lee's former CO's office in police headquarters.
"It's okay. We'll get through this—together." She put a hand
on Marika's back.

The furrow on Marika's forehead eased, and she nodded.
"Together."

The lean, white-haired senior officer stood as they
entered. "Ah, Lee, right on time as usual. I'd like to introduce
you to Keith Judson of Major Crimes. Keith, this is Lee
Glenn and her partner, Dana Cochrane. And I haven't yet
met these ladies."

Lee gestured Rhiannon and Marika forward. "Marika,
Rhi, this is an old friend of mine, Marc Manion. Marc,
Keith, this is Marika Havers and Rhiannon Davies."

They took their seats, and Lee handed over an envelope.
"These are the statements that I took last night. I'd like to
get Marika and Rhiannon's part out of the way, so they can
get out of here. They're going out of town for a few days."

Keith Judson took the lead. He questioned them on the
previous evening's events, as well as everything that led up
to the confrontation with Cass.

Rhiannon rethought her initial impression of the
balding, plain-clothed officer. His bland exterior concealed
an incisive mind, and his honed questions swiftly delved to
the meat of their story. *At least he's not judging us, or if he is,
he's good at hiding it.*

Marika faltered when she explained how she came to be involved with Cass, and Rhiannon laid a hand on her arm. Marika shot her a grateful glance.

Judson was most interested in the Vancouver encounter. "Are you sure it was Sandra DeAndre, Ms. Havers? There's no doubt in your mind that the woman calling herself Cass—the woman who ordered your death last night—was unquestionably Sandra DeAndre?"

"No doubt at all," Marika said. "The host was introduced to me as Palmer DeAndre, and he himself introduced me to his wife, Sandra. Trust me, when she dragged me off to the ladies' room, the facade came off and she was all Cass." She shuddered.

Rhiannon took her hand, and Marika clung to it. *Hang in there, love. It's almost over.*

Judson nodded grimly. "I'm sorry that you had to go through all this, but you may have given us the break we've needed for a long time." He shook his head. "I'm sorry. I can't go into it any further at the moment, but I will tell you that your testimony may be vital in a major bust of snakeheads and drug smugglers."

Rhiannon finally accepted that there was much more involved than simply a sociopath scorned. She glanced at Marika. *She has to be freaked out, though she seemed okay when we woke up this morning.* Rhiannon almost lost herself in that sweet memory before she tuned back into the conversation.

"Can you at least tell us if you looked into DeAndre's whereabouts last night?" Lee asked.

The men exchanged glances, and Judson said, "We did make some preliminary inquiries. Mrs. DeAndre has been in Montreal in connection with the DeAndre charitable foundation for the past week. Her secretary said she was expected back this weekend. But we also checked with the airport, and a private jet registered with the DeAndre foundation flew into Calgary in the evening and departed for Vancouver after midnight."

Lee nodded. "That matches Cass' movements as far as we know them."

Judson held up a cautionary hand. "We're going to have to proceed very carefully. The DeAndres have some powerful friends."

Lee snorted. "Which is no doubt why the bitch feels she can do whatever the hell she wants with people's lives."

Dana laid a hand on Lee's knee. "Are we done here, gentlemen?"

Marc looked at Judson, who nodded. "I think so. Nothing more we can do until the King brothers arrive. Lee, you're going to be in on that, right?"

Lee nodded, and Judson frowned.

Marc smiled. "Trust me, Keith. Lee is a skilled interrogator, and she has a psychological edge when it comes to Pike and Eddie. If anyone can, she'll have those two spilling their guts in no time flat."

Judson shrugged. "It's your ballpark. If you feel she can help..."

"I do," Marc said. He turned back to Lee. "Be back here by three, and we'll go over our strategy."

"I'll be here." Lee stood, and the others followed her lead.

As they started to leave the office, Judson asked, "Ms. Havers, will I be able to get in touch with you if I need to?"

Lee looked at Judson. "You can reach her and Rhiannon through me. Their whereabouts are on a need-to-know basis."

"And I suppose I don't need to know."

"No," Lee said. "You don't." She motioned the others to wait while she returned for a quick conference with Marc. He handed Lee a card, and she returned to lead her small band down the hallway to the elevator.

On the way back to the garage, Lee placed a call on her cell phone.

By the time, they got to their parking spot, an inconspicuous, late-model Buick was parked beside Dana's Taurus. A wiry, short-haired woman leaned against the trunk, smoking.

"Hey, Barb," Lee called as they approached.

Barb walked over to meet them and handed a set of keys to Lee. "All taken care of, boss. The bug was right where you thought it'd be. Oh, and I threw a couple of maps in the rental too."

"Thanks, kiddo." Lee smiled. "You really are worth your weight in gold. Go...have some fun."

Barb grinned and went to a nearby Taurus, identical to Dana's. She started it up and drove away.

Dana unlocked the trunk of her car and retrieved the bags. She set them behind the Buick. "Now you two be very careful, you hear?"

Lee nodded. "If you see anything at all suspicious, don't waste time. Get to the nearest police station and explain what's going on. There's an RCMP detachment in Sicamous, so after you pick up groceries, make note of its location before you go to the cabin." She pulled a card out of her pocket, wrote something on it, and handed it over.

Rhiannon peered over Marika's arm. It was one of Marc's cards, and Lee had jotted his cellphone number on it.

"That should be enough to convince any of the local constabulary that you're serious," Lee said. "If they need to call to confirm your story, Marc will back you up."

They looked at one another. Dana was the first to step forward. She pulled Marika into a fierce hug, then she turned to Rhiannon as Lee and Marika embraced. Enfolding Rhi, Dana whispered, "Please take of her."

"I will. I promise." Rhiannon drew back and was swept up in Lee's arms.

"Love you, Lady Mouse. You take care of yourself now. Come back safely." Lee wiped her eyes. "Wait for at least five minutes after we've left before you take off. And if I don't hear from you by ten every night, I'm sending the cops to check on you."

Marika smiled. "Ten at night, and I'll even call you in the mornings."

"Good." Lee grinned. "But you don't have to make it too early. I'm sure you won't be up with the roosters."

Dana grabbed Lee's arm and propelled her away.

"What? I only meant that they'd be on holiday and would want to sleep in."

Rhiannon couldn't hear Dana's rejoinder, but Lee's laugh boomed through the garage.

Marika smiled and shook her head. "I guess we should get going."

They got into the Buick and waited until Dana and Lee pulled out. Within twenty minutes, they were on the Trans-Canada, heading west toward the mountains.

Exhilaration swept over Rhiannon. *We're alive, we're together, and it looks like blue skies ahead. Could life get any better?*

Gao lay on Perry's couch and glared at the cast on his right hand. The bitch had hit him so hard that she'd broken three of his knuckles, his thumb, and forefinger. He'd had to risk going to a walk-in clinic after the fiasco at the warehouse. An overworked nurse set his hand, stitched the gash in his forehead, and warned of a probable concussion. Gao had subsisted since on over-the-counter remedies to ease the constant headache.

He kept trying to make plans, but thoughts slipped in and out of his mind like wisps of fog. The single concept Gao could fixate on was the need to find the women who had escaped from him. He and Perry used the information they'd accumulated on their targets to narrow their focus. With the description he got from the Chameleon's man who'd hauled him away from the industrial park after the women fled, it was easy to determine which of the lawyer's friends had thrown a wrench into his plans.

Barely able to move from Perry's couch, Gao had dispatched his reluctant host early that morning to find the lawyer and her annoying companion.

Gao's uninjured hand rested on the gun that lay on his stomach while he tried to plot his next move. His desire to execute the women had grown into an obsession with each hour he was stuck on the uncomfortable couch. *Goddamned bitches destroyed everything I've worked for. I can't go home.*

I can't report success to the Chameleon. And if that means I need to run, I won't even be able to. I can't fucking do anything but lie in this pigsty and hope Perry doesn't screw this up. He sought solace in imagining what he'd do once he had them in his control. *I'll kill the lawyer first and make her little friend watch. No, I'll kill the friend first and make the lawyer watch. No, even better—I'll make them watch each other suffer. I wonder how many bullets the human body can take before it dies. Bet the little one lasts longer.*

For the first time since Gao had entered the Chameleon's organization, her orders and wishes were not paramount. Had she instructed him to abandon his pursuit of the lawyer and her companion, he could not have done so. A part of his brain—a small, still rational part—fought to interject logic into his thinking, but the emotional tsunami that consumed him wouldn't allow it. *I will find them; I will kill them. Simple as that.*

Someone was at the door, and Gao readied his gun.

Perry entered, yelped, and threw up his hands.

Gao scowled and lowered the gun. "What did you find?"

Perry perched on the edge of a chair. "You were right about them being at Glenn's house. I saw them come out this morning."

"Did they see you?"

"Nope. I kept watch from a neighbour's garage. Dude wasn't home."

"Are they still there?"

Perry shifted and wiped a hand across his face. "Not exactly."

"What do you mean, not exactly?"

"I put tracking bugs on the Lexus and the Taurus and followed 'em downtown."

"Where did they go?" Gao asked.

"Police headquarters. I sure as hell wasn't going in there, so I walked around until they came out again. When they returned, I went back to my car so I could track them again." Perry fidgeted.

"And?" *He's fucked up. I knew it. I should just kill him now.*

"Jesus, how was I to know?" Perry stared at the floor. "I followed the tracker, and I caught up to it on the highway going north before I realized I was behind the wrong car. Christ, it was an identical Taurus, but it only had one person in it, and she wasn't one of the women I'd seen back at the house. I don't know what went wrong."

Gao closed his eyes and fought a surge of nausea. "They found your little toy, you fool. They put it on some other car to throw you off." He opened his eyes. "What did you do once you made the brilliant observation that it wasn't the right car?"

"I went right back to the Glenn house. I waited around for a few hours, but the only person that came out was Glenn. I followed her, thinkin' maybe she would lead me to wherever the others were, but she just went back to the police station. I didn't know what else you'd want me to do, so I came right back here. I'm sorry, man, but I don't usually do this kinda work, you know?" Perry ran his fingers through his hair.

Gao glared at him, anger and frustration warring for dominance. Finally, he acknowledged that he needed the other man for the time being and tamped down his emotions. "All right. It's clear that they've stashed them. Bring me all the printouts you have from surveillance on the lawyer's apartment. There has to be a clue in there somewhere."

Perry scrambled to carry out his orders, and Gao tried to concentrate on a course of action. Within moments, though, he was drawn back into a vision of the women kneeling before him, clutching each other, their eyes filled with terror as he aimed his gun at them. He savoured the image until Perry returned with a thick sheaf of printouts.

Gao pushed his mental meanderings aside for the more immediate business of analyzing data. *There has to be a way to find them.* He shuffled the sheets of paper with his left hand. *It's just a matter of time. It might take a while, but I will find them. And when I do...*

CHAPTER 27

LEE ENTERED MARC'S OFFICE FOR the second time that day and found him and Keith deep in conversation. Both men looked up and nodded at her.

"Hi, Lee," Marc said. "Keith's just received some very interesting faxes from Vancouver that might help loosen Pike's and Eddie's tongues."

Lee picked up a fax and whistled. "Damn. Someone must've hated this guy." The corpse's naked, mutilated body was bad enough, but his untouched face frozen in a rictus of horror turned her stomach. *Jesus, they kept him conscious while they tortured him.* "Who is he?"

"His name is Chai Rhongji. He's Gao's cousin," Keith said. "He was executed sometime this morning and dumped where he would be easily found. This was meant as a message."

"Gao's boss is not happy about the way he botched his orders last night." Lee pushed the faxes back across the desk. *That's the stuff of nightmares.*

The two men exchanged glances.

Marc said, "It's time to tell Lee everything you've told me. She'll be able to use it when she interrogates the King boys."

Keith leaned back in his chair, arms crossed, and shook his head. "I'm still not convinced, Marc. Bottom line, she's a civilian." He glanced at Lee. "No offence."

Lee shrugged. "None taken."

"A civilian now, but with an extensive background in policing, interrogation, and security issues," Marc said. "Look, I know it's not exactly conventional, but—"

"It's not that I don't trust you," Keith said. "And I'm sure that Ms. Glenn was an excellent officer at one time, but it's been what—a decade or more since she worked for you?"

"I need you to trust me on this, Keith. Lee's gifted. She can talk a lobster into a pot of boiling water." Marc frowned. "Pike and Eddie won't be afraid of us. They've been dealing with the law since they were kids. They're career criminals—not very good ones, mind you, but it does mean they're not intimidated by the police. We won't get to first base with them. Lee, on the other hand, scares the hell out of them."

Keith looked at Lee and raised an eyebrow.

Lee smiled. "Marc was my CO many years ago when Pike and Eddie were young hoodlums who thought it would be a great idea to sneak onto the base. I was on patrol that night and caught them assaulting a female private. I was alone, and they didn't see me as a threat. They were wrong."

Marc laughed. "Were they ever. They went from the base to the hospital to their first adult stint in prison, all compliments of then Corporal Glenn."

Keith studied Lee for several moments, then sighed. "All right, I'm going to trust both of you and hope to hell I don't end up losing the best lead we've had to date."

"A lead we wouldn't even have without Lee's intervention," Marc said with asperity.

"Admitted, but remember, this is for your ears only." Keith pointed at the faxes. "Every time we think we're getting close, something like this happens. Sources dry up, witnesses suddenly get amnesia, and it's like the whole underworld holds its breath until someone gives the word that they can breathe again." He looked at Lee. "We've been working on this thing for over a decade. Now and then we manage to pick off a few fringe players, but they never know enough to get us to the inner circle where the power is."

Lee frowned. "The inner circle of what?"

"The Chameleon."

The name meant nothing to Lee.

"The Chameleon is the intensely secretive head of a well-entrenched, international ring that specializes in smuggling drugs and people. Until your friends' information connected Gao and DeAndre, we couldn't even confirm that the Chameleon was a woman. Only a very small inner circle knows her identity, but everyone who works for her organization knows that crossing her in any way means a prolonged, gruesome death." Keith thumped his fist against the arm of his chair. "It's set up like resistance cells in a war zone. Each cell only knows the identity of the person they report to. If we manage to bust one part of the organization, the larger whole barely feels the loss."

Lee stared at Keith. "Are you telling me Cass or Sandra or whatever the hell her name is, is a mob boss? Is she Triad?"

Keith shook his head. "DeAndre's group is definitely trans-national, and they work closely with the local Triad. The Chameleon is as powerful as any Triad leader, maybe more so because she's concentrated power in her own hands. But ultimately, that could prove to be a mistake. I don't think she's dispersed the power through enough layers to conceal herself for much longer."

Lee scowled. "Seems to me that she's done pretty damned well hiding in plain sight. Who the hell is going to suspect some fancy do-gooder socialite of being a criminal mastermind?"

"We've not been very effective so far, but she rules entirely by fear, not through ethnic solidarity." Keith pointed at the crime scene photos. "There's exhibit one. All we've needed is one solid break—a trail that leads straight back to her—and even her inner circle will jump ship. Your friends gave us that break."

"Okay, I understand what you're saying," Lee said. "But you want to use this against Pike and Eddie how?"

Marc snorted. "Those two are the tiniest of fish, but we believe they worked for Gao, who apparently works for the Chameleon—assuming that DeAndre does turn out to be the Chameleon. They may be stupid, but they've got to understand that they're totally expendable. I've no doubt that's why they took off."

Lee nodded. "So, we convince them that the only way they can avoid Chai Rhongji's fate is to cooperate with us, that they'll be safer in our custody than out where the Chameleon can reach them." She thrust her hands in her pockets. "You know we're going to have to trade them protection for whatever information they have."

"We're prepared to do that if they cooperate," Keith said. "What we need is confirmation that they do work for Gao as part of the Chameleon's organization, and we can use that to implicate DeAndre."

"Then the best way to get their admission is to let them think we already know what's going on." Lee grinned. "I can do that."

Marc smiled. "I know. I've seen you work." The phone on his desk rang, and he picked it up. "Manion. Yes, all right. We'll be down in a few minutes. Oh, hold on a moment." He covered the receiver. "Do you want them together or in separate rooms, Lee?"

"Together for now, then we'll play it by ear."

Marc relayed the instructions and hung up. "They're downstairs whenever we're ready."

"No time like the present. Let's go have a chat." Lee stood and gathered the crime scene photos.

As they rode the elevator down to the basement interrogation rooms, goose bumps rose on Lee's arms. *I'm breathing down Cass' neck. I can feel it. We're going to shatter her whole fuckin' empire, and Pike and Eddie are going to help us.*

When they stepped through the door labeled "Interrogation One," Pike and Eddie sat in a small inner room behind a one-way window.

Lee studied the brothers.

Pike fidgeted incessantly, his gaze flicking around the room. Black, greasy hair hung in tangles around his thin face marked with deep shadows under his eyes and at least three days of beard growth. Eddie didn't fidget, but he kept his gaze fixed on Pike's face as if waiting for direction. His once-white T-shirt was grey with dirt, and his buzz cut had grown out enough to add to his unkempt appearance.

"We have to go in with you," Marc said as he activated the recording camera.

Lee shrugged. "No problem. Just let me talk first, okay?"

When they entered the inner room, Marc stood next to Keith against the back wall, out of the brothers' field of vision.

Pike's eyes widened. "What the fuck are you doing here?"

Lee pulled a chair out and settled into it. She crossed one leg over the other and made herself comfortable as she watched them.

The silence lengthened.

Pike squirmed, and Eddie shifted, his gaze jumping between his brother and Lee.

Finally, Pike said, "We ain't done nuthin'. It was just a lousy shoplifting rap, an' it was a mistake, anyways."

Lee smiled. "Well, actually, Francis, it *was* a mistake and rather a large one...on your part."

Pike glanced at Eddie. "Dunno what yer talkin' 'bout, cuz the most they got us on is boostin' a coupla bottles of booze. That's nuthin'.'"

"Sorry, Francis," Lee said. "Quite apart from you two breaking the terms of your parole, we've also found out some rather interesting things about you boys since your abrupt departure from our fair city." She set the photos down and pushed them across the table.

Pike didn't look.

Eddie reared back. "Jesus Christ!"

Pike's gaze darted to the photos. He slapped his hand on them. "We didn't do this! We ain't murderers."

"If Miss Davies and her aunt hadn't escaped the fire you set, you would be murderers. But as it stands, besides the shoplifting, you are at least guilty of arson and attempted murder." It was a well-aimed shot in the dark, and Lee was gratified by Eddie's blurted "How—?"

Pike glared Eddie into silence.

"But that's the least of your troubles." Lee nodded at the pictures under Pike's hand. "That is the late, unlamented Chai Rhongji, found rather publicly displayed on the Vancouver waterfront this morning."

There was no response to the name.

"It seems that the late Mr. Chai was the cousin of your immediate superior, Gao Qui-jian."

Pike wavered in his chair and grabbed the edge of the table. Even Eddie's dim eyes reflected panic.

Lee didn't give them a chance to recover. "It appears that Gao failed to carry out a pair of executions ordered by the Chameleon, and this was her warning."

Pike's olive-toned skin turned a waxy yellow.

He looks about one short step away from being a cadaver already. Lee had figured it was a safe bet that the brothers would assume they were Gao's new targets.

Eddie couldn't tear his gaze from the pictures while Pike refused to look at them again.

Pike tried to speak, stopped, and cleared his throat, then tried again. "Got nuthin' to do with us." Sweat broke out on his face.

"Francis, Francis, Francis," Lee crooned.

Pike flinched.

Lee slammed her hand on the table and abandoned her casual pose. She leaned across the table and grinned. "Let's get down to it, boys. I'm not in the mood to waste any more of my time. Here's how it is. You fucked up with the fire. The Chameleon does not tolerate those who can't follow orders, so she instructed Gao to get rid of loose ends...that would be you two. Now Gao, he looked all over town for you. But you boys actually showed a bit of good sense and took off in time. That made the Chameleon very unhappy, so she sent this...message of encouragement to Gao. I don't know a lot about Gao, but I do know that the Chinese place a lot of value on family. So I doubt that he's happy his cousin was killed because of you two." Lee glanced at Marc, who smirked. "So here you are. You not only have a very pissed off Gao hunting for you, you've also come very unfavourably to the Chameleon's attention. We all know what happens to loose ends in her organization."

"What...uh, what...?" Pike stumbled, then fell silent.

Eddie continued to stare—hypnotized—at the photos of Rhongji's mutilated corpse.

"That is the million-dollar question, isn't it, Francis?" Lee leaned back in her chair. "What do you do now? I guess the question you have to ask yourselves is—how far does the Chameleon's reach extend? How far can you run so she won't be able to find you?"

Pike trembled, and Eddie kept licking his lips.

There is no such place, is there, boys? "Okay then, assuming your goal is to save your sorry asses, what are you going to do?"

Eddie stared at Lee, and Pike swallowed convulsively.

Dumbass is trying to think his way out of this mess. Lee snorted. *Good luck with that, flea brain.* "As I see it, you have very few options. We can bust you on the shoplifting charges, which, along with the parole violations, will send you back to Drumheller." Lee invoked the name of the penitentiary from which the brothers had been released the previous year. "Of course, I'm not sure that you'd be safe from her even inside prison." *Barbed wire and armed guards won't even slow her down, will it, boys? And you know that sure as you know your own names.*

Pike's skinny chest heaved.

"I'm thinking the better solution would be for you to tell us absolutely everything you know about the Chameleon's organization, let us put you in protective custody until the trial, and then enter the witness protection program."

"We ain't snitches." Pike's voice squeaked.

Lee shrugged. "No skin off my nose." She looked past the brothers. "Marc, do you think you can get these two fine upstanding citizens released ROR this afternoon? After all, it's only a cheap shoplifting bust, and now that they're back in the city, they won't be too hard for us—or anyone else—to find when we need them."

Pike held up his hands. "Wait. Look, let's talk about it, 'kay? Ain't no need to get hasty here."

Lee glanced at her watch and yawned. "Got places to go and things to do, Francis. If you want to say something, you'd better say it now."

Pike hesitated.

"Tell her, Pike." Eddie gathered up the photos and shook them at his brother. "It's over. Either of 'em catch us, this is the way we end up. I don't want to die, man. 'Specially not like this."

Pike gaped at his brother, then his shoulders squared. "Ain't gonna happen, Eddie. I won't let it."

Lee's eyebrows rose. *Huh, who'd have thought it? Pike looking out for his little brother.*

"You guarantee protective custody and witness protection for both of us?" There was an undertone of desperation in Pike's question.

Lee motioned Marc and Keith forward. "Gentlemen, can the city police and the RCMP guarantee their safety?"

Keith maintained a poker face. "That will depend on the quality of their information and whether we can verify it as the truth."

Eddie clutched Pike's arm. "The tapes!"

"Shut up!" Pike drew a deep breath. "Could be that we have proof of Gao's involvement."

Lee shook her head. "You taped him? What did you think...that you could blackmail him?"

"Wasn't blackmail. It was insurance," Pike said. "And yeah, we got some tapes, but you don't get them until Eddie and me get some guarantees."

Keith nodded and took a seat. "All right. Let's talk."

Lee stood and motioned Marc out of the room. The adrenaline of the hunt ebbed, and fatigue was setting in.

Marc asked, "Tired?"

"Yes." Lee stretched. "It's been a helluva long week. I could do with some peace and quiet."

Marc patted her shoulder. "You did a great job in there, Sarge. You played those two like a well-tuned fiddle."

"Glad to help. I had a lot of incentive."

"We're going to get her," Marc said. "Don't you doubt it. Your friends will be fine."

"As you yourself pointed out, Pike and Eddie are small fish. We still have to connect the dots to Gao and then to Cass. We're a long way from proving that the eminent and highly regarded Mrs. DeAndre is the Chameleon."

"But we're on the right path. We use these guys to bring down Gao, and then we use Gao to bring her down. It's only a matter of time."

Lee grimaced. "Right. We don't even know where the hell Gao is. He could be on a flight to Outer Mongolia right now. And you can bet Cass isn't sitting still, waiting to see where the chips fall. She's way too smart not to have a back-up plan."

Marc smiled. "One thing at a time, my friend. We've got Gao's photo flagged at every point of departure across Canada and the US, so that should slow him down. As for the Chameleon, if it is Mrs. DeAndre, she's actually going to be handicapped by her visibility. Given her position, it's not like she can just drop out of sight. Her husband would raise holy hell to find her, and he has the clout to do so. No, I imagine she's going to proceed very carefully as she figures out her next move. Our advantage is that the dominoes have already started to fall, and they won't stop until the last one lands at her doorstep."

Lee forced a smile. "You're right. It's only a matter of time."

"Exactly. And meanwhile, your friends are safe and sound and out of her reach."

"Yes...out of reach." *Then why the hell does my gut feel like it's on a roller coaster?*

CHAPTER 28

MARIKA TORE HER GAZE AWAY from a sleeping Rhiannon to focus her full attention on the highway. They'd made excellent time, even through the twisting, narrow mountain passes, as she bent the speed limit in her eagerness to get away. *Three weeks with Rhi, isolated at a lakeside cabin. Life is good.* Again her gaze strayed from the highway to Rhiannon. *She look so innocent, but she's overcome so much: an abusive aunt, a knife-wielding attacker, a psycho killer—no wonder I fell so hard. She's the proverbial knight in shining armour.* Her smile faded. *But you really aren't invincible, are you, love? If they haven't caught Cass by the time we get back, I'm taking a leave of absence and getting you the hell out of here.*

Marika smiled. It might be difficult to convince Rhiannon that running away was an appropriate course of action. *Though she didn't mind leaving Calgary today.* She drew in a deep breath. It was getting more and more difficult to restrain herself. *Take it slow. You don't want to scare her. Let her set the pace. Though the way she kissed me this morning...*

Rhiannon yawned, stretched, and opened her eyes. She blinked and looked out the window. "Where are we?"

"Almost there. The last sign I saw said thirty kilometres to Sicamous. We'll stop for groceries there."

Rhiannon reached for the map and studied it. "It looks like the cabin is in the least populated area."

"David said the road in there isn't great, but we'll manage. It's probably better that it's not around the more popular beaches."

Rhiannon glanced at Marika. "You don't think we've been followed, do you?"

Marika slowed as they approached the town limits. "No, I don't. Lee was very careful to cover our tracks, and there's no way anyone could know where we went. Besides, these lakes are so big, it would be like looking for a needle in a haystack. We're just going to enjoy an unexpected vacation, and by the time we get back, the whole mess will be cleaned up."

Rhiannon smiled. "I can't think of anyone I'd rather be on vacation with."

"Me neither." Marika turned into the first large grocery store they came to. Once inside, she abandoned her intent to buy a balanced assortment of food groups. It was fun to give in to Rhiannon's irrepressible good humour as she tossed hot dogs, hamburgers, buns, chips, and pop into their cart.

By aisle five, Marika's conscience kicked in. "Do you think maybe we should put something green in there?"

"Nah. We'll eat healthily when we're home again. You're supposed to eat junk when you're on holiday." Rhiannon started down the aisle toward the marshmallows.

Marika shook her head and grinned. When she caught up, Rhiannon was contemplating two bags of marshmallows, her brow furrowed.

Rhiannon held out both bags. "Traditional white or fruit-flavoured—what do you think?"

"I think I love you." Marika's eyes widened. This was not the romantic setting she'd pictured for her first declaration of love.

Rhiannon dropped both bags into the cart and closed the space between them.

The heat of her body radiated through Marika. It was all she could do not to take Rhi in her arms.

"I love you, too." Rhiannon's eyes shone. "We need to get out of here soon. I want to...I need to—"

The spell was broken as a matron entered their aisle with three squabbling children in tow.

Marika shivered and stepped back. "Let's finish up here and get going."

Rhiannon nodded and turned back to the shelves. A bag of pretzels joined the marshmallows.

You don't even like pretzels. Marika smiled. *Mind somewhere else, my love?*

They checked out and had left town before it occurred to Marika that she hadn't located the RCMP detachment. *Oh well. It's not like we'll need them anyway.*

Inside of an hour, they'd turned onto a narrow gravel road. They searched for the turnoff to the cabin, catching glimpses of shimmering water through the thick forest.

"There it is." Rhiannon pointed to a small, hand-lettered sign that read "O'Reilly."

Just past the tree the sign was nailed to, a road wound its way down to a half-hidden A-frame log cabin.

Marika steered down a trail barely wide enough for the Buick. She winced at the sound of branches and foliage scraping the sides of the car, but within moments they emerged into a clearing behind the cabin.

They got out and picked their way down the steep path around the side of the cabin. Hand in hand, they came around the corner of the building. The lake stretched out in front of them, shining in the late afternoon sun.

The cabin was built into the side of a hill, and the incline to the lake's edge slanted steeply. The private beach featured a wharf jutting eight feet out into the water. Marika assumed that the shed on the edge of the property was the wood hut David had mentioned. She eyed a brick-lined fire pit on the verge of the small beach and pictured them roasting marshmallows.

Marika turned to examine the cabin. The place wasn't elegant like the grand cedar and glass chalets they'd passed coming around the lake, but she liked it immediately. The top floor of the A-frame had a walk-out balcony, and the entire face featured floor-to-ceiling windows with a stone chimney on one side of the cabin.

Rhiannon tilted her head. "Shall we take a look inside?"

"Why don't we grab as much as we can carry and get the groceries stowed away? That ice cream you insisted on getting isn't going to last long in the trunk."

Rhiannon grinned. "Oh, like I had to twist your arm."

They retrieved their grocery bags, and Marika unlocked the back door. It opened onto a hall that led to a spacious great room at the front of the cabin. A quick inspection revealed a modern washroom, laundry room, and storage space on the left side of the hall and two large bedrooms with four sets of bunks each on the right side.

They walked into the great room and stopped short. Through the windows, tall stands of Douglas fir and cedar framed the waters, the hills on the far side of the lake, and a brilliant blue sky. It was picture postcard perfect.

Rhiannon stared. "That's going to be an awesome sight at sunset."

"Mmm-hm," Marika said. "It'll be beautiful at dawn, too."

"But Lee said we didn't have to get up that early."

The mood broke, and Marika laughed. "I'll start putting away the groceries. Why don't you grab our suitcases?"

Marika stowed the groceries and held her breath when Rhiannon returned with their bags. David had told them that the master bedroom was the only room upstairs under the peaked roof, but she'd left their sleeping arrangements for Rhiannon to decide. When Rhiannon climbed the stairs with both suitcases, a smile broke out on Marika's face. *Guess that answers that question.*

Rhiannon returned from upstairs. "I thought we could unpack later."

"Sure." Marika's hands trembled. She emptied the last bag and turned to Rhiannon.

Rhiannon jammed her hands into her pockets and stared at her feet.

It's okay. You set the pace, love. There's no hurry. "Are you hungry?" Marika asked. "We could make a bonfire in the pit and roast wieners and marshmallows."

Rhiannon shook her head. "I'd like that...but later. I'm not that hungry right now. Would you like to walk along the beach a bit, maybe stretch our legs after the long ride?"

Marika nodded. "That sounds like an excellent idea."

They walked down to the lakeshore and turned east. The shoreline varied from boulder-strewn to fine grain sand to near marshy conditions. It took twenty minutes before they passed the nearest neighbouring cabin, a squat, mostly stone structure that loomed over its patch of hillside.

"Ours is prettier," Rhiannon said.

"I agree." Marika's cares slipped away, and her focus narrowed to Rhiannon and the lakeshore. A plethora of boats cut through the waves—graceful sailboats, raucous speedboats, and ungainly houseboats.

Rhiannon stopped every few metres as she discovered another item to examine. She found a perfect skipping stone, an exotic-looking chunk of driftwood, and a tiny thumbnail-sized frog that she gently carried back to Marika to display.

Marika admired every new find, though she shied away from handling the frog.

Rhi returned the tiny creature to the water, then bounded on ahead to see what lay around the next corner.

Rhiannon's delight in the shoreline's treasures enchanted Marika. *I wonder if she's ever been to a lake.* When Rhiannon returned with a particularly fine shell to show her, she asked.

Rhiannon shook her head. "Not like this. Mom and Dad used to take me to the lakeside park in Toronto, but Lake Ontario is pretty dirty. They'd let me swim in the pool at the park, but Mom didn't like me going in the lake." She looked at the crystal waters lapping at the shore, every stone of the lakebed clearly visible through gentle waves. "I've certainly never been anywhere like this."

They explored for almost an hour. Marika was about to suggest that they turn back when they came around a bend and saw a houseboat nosing in to shore. Several women pulled on heavy ropes which stretched from each corner of the boat.

Rhiannon ran to help the woman on the rope closest to them.

Marika hastened to follow, but by the time she reached them, they'd already looped the rope around a thick tree.

The tall stranger tied it off with an impressive set of knots. She finished securing the line and waved at the woman who'd steered the boat from the upper deck. "Good job, Karen. You can shut it down now."

The woman with a captain's hat pushed rakishly back on her strawberry blonde hair throttled down the engine.

Marika stared at the all-female crew. She estimated there were over a dozen of them, but it was hard to keep count as they swarmed all over the boat.

The stranger turned to them. "Thanks for the assist."

"No problem," Rhiannon said. "Glad to help."

"Are you some kind of club?" Marika asked.

The woman smiled. "No, just a gang of old friends that gets together every two years for a reunion." She watched her crewmates as they dragged out a metal gangplank. "We all grew up in the same small town and went to school together. Now we're scattered, but we always come back together again." She turned back to Marika and Rhiannon. "For one weekend, we leave husbands, kids, jobs, and everything else behind and act like a bunch of teenagers again."

"Minus the making out." A teasing voice came from behind her as another woman climbed the shore to where they stood. "Hi, sorry to interrupt, Janene, but they need you to turn on the gas."

"Oops, gotta go. That's my assigned duty. Thanks again for the assist." Janene walked away with her friend.

"At least your assigned duty doesn't include getting the damned boat going every morning," the other woman said. "I'd trade you any day." They laughed and returned to the boat.

A light melancholy settled over Marika. She loved her friends but had never experienced such uncomplicated, cheerful camaraderie within a large group of women. "That is amazing."

"Yes." Rhiannon gazed at the boat and her crew. "They're middle-aged, so they must've been friends for a lot of years."

Marika turned back in the direction from which they had come, and Rhiannon matched her pace. They didn't stop to explore on their return.

"Do you suppose that we'd have a big group of friends like that if we'd grown up differently?" Rhiannon asked.

"It's impossible to know what would've happened if you hadn't lost your parents and I hadn't been tossed out of my family." Marika shrugged. "But I think there's a point in everyone's life when they have to set the past aside and move on. Otherwise, you only hurt yourself and the people who care for you in the here and now." Marika stopped in the sheltering lee of a prominent boulder and took Rhiannon's hands. "My love, I can't change what's gone before for either of us, but I do know that we're responsible for what happens from now on. We have remarkable friends who've stuck their necks out a mile for us. It's up to you and me to cherish them...and each other."

Rhiannon's eyes sparkled with unshed tears.

Marika drew her forward, and Rhiannon came into her arms as naturally as if she'd done it all her life. Rhiannon initiated a slow, smouldering kiss that weakened Marika's knees. Their bodies pressed so fiercely against each other that Marika could feel Rhiannon's heart pounding against hers.

Lost in the sensual thrill of mutual exploration, Marika fought to summon her self-control. She longed to ease Rhiannon down and make love to her on the beach, but the roar of a motorboat a short way off shore restored her sanity. "Not here, sweetheart. Let's get back to the cabin." Marika took Rhiannon's hand, and they made much quicker time on their return.

They'd barely closed the cabin door before Rhiannon turned and tugged Marika's T-shirt over her head.

Marika rested her hands on Rhiannon's waist. *Let her set the pace. Let her...*

Rhiannon's lips parted, and she trailed her fingers down to Marika's cleavage and along the top edge of her bra before easing the straps off her shoulders. "You are so beautiful."

"As are you, my love." Marika released Rhiannon and undid her bra.

With trembling fingers, Rhiannon tugged it away and dropped it on the floor. She hesitated and raised her gaze to meet Marika's.

Marika guided Rhiannon's hands to her breasts.

For a long moment, Rhiannon didn't move. She cupped Marika's breasts and drew a deep breath. Then she lowered her head and began to explore with her mouth, slowly, thoroughly, until Marika's knees buckled.

"Oh, my God! Rhi, please…"

Rhiannon's teeth scraped her nipple as she reached for Marika's shorts. She undid the button and pulled the zipper down.

Marika tightened her hold on Rhiannon. The door behind her was the only thing keeping her upright. When Rhiannon slipped inside Marika's panties and eased them down with her shorts, Marika almost crumpled. "Sweetheart?" Marika's breath came in deep gasps now.

"Mmm?" Rhiannon moved to Marika's other nipple. She stroked down Marika's belly, over her thighs until her hands came to rest on her ass.

Marika shivered. "How is it that I'm naked and you're fully clothed?"

Rhiannon lifted her head and grinned. "Careful planning? Forethought? Luck?"

Oh, you imp. To hell with letting you set the pace. Marika whirled Rhiannon around and pressed her against the door. She seized Rhiannon's T-shirt and lifted it. By the time she had Rhiannon's bra off, Rhi had divested herself of her shorts.

Skin to skin they stood, touching, kissing, stroking.

Rhiannon's hand slid between Marika's legs.

"Oh, sweet Jesus! We've got to move this upstairs before I can't move at all."

Rhiannon's laughter tickled Marika's neck.

Taking Rhiannon's hand, Marika led them up the stairs. When they reached the bedroom, she turned to face Rhiannon. "I love you." They were simple words, and Marika had never meant them more.

Rhiannon's eyes shone. "I love you, too."

Marika took both of Rhiannon's hands. "You're sure, Rhi? This is what you want?"

"God, yes!" Rhiannon steered Marika backwards until her legs touched the bed.

Marika fell back on the mattress, bringing Rhiannon with her. She rolled them over and delighted in the feel of Rhi's body beneath hers. *Go slow...slow and easy. Don't scare her.* Marika closed her eyes. "Slow."

"No, not slow." Rhiannon arched upwards. "Please?" She raked her fingers over Marika's back.

Marika opened her eyes and stared into Rhiannon's. Her nostrils flared, and she slid slowly downward.

Rhiannon's legs parted.

Easing between them, Marika captured a nipple and revelled in the sensation of Rhiannon surging beneath her.

Rhiannon cupped Marika's neck and urged her breast into Marika's mouth.

Dizzy with joy, desire, and amazement, Marika abandoned any hesitation. She swivelled to the side, keeping Rhi's breast captive, and began to stroke her inner thighs. She teased Rhiannon with soft touches that danced over her clit until Rhi seized Marika's hand and pressed it against her.

Instantly, Marika responded, her strokes firm and fast.

Soft cries burst from Rhiannon's throat, then she erupted in a throaty growl and strained against Marika's touch before she slumped to the bed, gasping for air.

Marika eased her hand away and embraced Rhiannon. "I love you, sweetheart. God, I love you so much."

"Love you, too. Love you..." Rhiannon's voice was barely audible.

"Every day I wake up grateful that you're in my life." Marika nuzzled Rhiannon's damp neck. "You're incredible... so beautiful...so responsive. God, how did I get so lucky?"

Rhiannon's breathing evened, and her limbs relaxed. "Oh...wow..."

Marika hugged her more tightly. "I take it that you liked that?"

"Oh...wow!"

Marika buried her face in Rhiannon's hair, unable to stifle her laughter at her lover's inarticulate eloquence.

A few minutes later, Rhiannon rolled Marika on her back.

Marika's heartbeat quickened.

Rhiannon's eyes sparkled above her. "I think I've only had half the experience." She trailed her fingers up Marika's belly and curled her hand around one breast. "Allow me?" She grazed Marika's nipple.

Marika quivered. "I wouldn't say no."

"No?" Rhiannon replaced her finger with her tongue for long, slow, sensuous moments before she raised her head. "Then what would you say?" Her hand slid between Marika's legs.

"I'd say...oh my!" Marika bucked as Rhiannon entered her.

"Hmmm, 'oh my'? That's interesting. What else would you say?" Rhiannon transferred her attention to the other breast.

"Uh...God!" Marika's hips rose.

Rhiannon's thumb caressed Marika's clit in time with her thrusts. "How admirably spiritual, my love."

"Oh, Jesus! Please, Rhi...harder...please!" Marika soared as Rhiannon possessed her, driving her higher until the cabin echoed with the sounds of her pleasure. Marika's tears flowed, impelled by emotional overload.

Rhiannon tenderly wiped Marika's eyes and curled around her.

This is her first time? My God, I may not survive. Rhiannon's warm body and soft touches soon lulled Marika into slumber. When she woke, the sun had begun to sink, illuminating the lake with a rosy light.

Rhiannon raised her head and smiled. "Hey."

"Hey, yourself." Marika ran her fingers through Rhiannon's hair. "Did you sleep?"

"Mmm-hmm. For a little bit." Rhiannon traced Marika's collar bone. "Mostly I listened to you sleep."

"Did I snore?"

Rhiannon chuckled. "No, though you did wuffle once or twice. It was cute." She lowered her head back to Marika's shoulder.

Marika wrapped her arms around Rhiannon. *She listened to me sleep. No one's ever done that before.*

They cuddled until the shadows had lengthened halfway across the room.

"I hate to say it, but I think I need to move," Marika finally said.

Rhiannon shifted and sat up, crossing her legs in a lotus position.

Marika stared.

Tilting her head, Rhiannon grinned. "I thought you were going to move."

"You take my breath away. You really do."

Rhiannon blushed and ducked her head.

"You have no idea, do you?" Marika rose on one elbow.

"Um..." Rhiannon pulled a pillow into her lap.

"Uh-uh." Marika laughed and tugged the pillow away. "You don't get to cover perfection." She piled it with the rest of the pillows behind her and sat up, comfortably cushioned. She spread her legs. "C'mere, you."

Rhiannon slid between her legs and leaned back against Marika's chest.

Marika wrapped her arms around Rhiannon. "Happy?" Marika nuzzled her ear.

"I can't remember ever being happier." Rhiannon wriggled.

Delightful sensations rippled through Marika's body. *What she does to me. Please, don't let this end.*

An osprey landed on the dock and flew off again. A boat, its white sails catching the sun's fading rays, tacked by and disappeared from view.

Finally, Marika asked, "Are you hungry? We could start a bonfire."

"We could." Rhiannon made no move to extricate herself from Marika's arms.

Marika stroked Rhiannon's hair. "It's been a long time since we ate. You must be getting hungry."

"Oh, I'm hungry all right." Rhiannon's voice was throaty. She began to stroke Marika's thighs.

Marika shivered, and her desire ignited. She drew her fingertips along Rhiannon's belly, up to explore the soft undersides of her breasts.

Rhiannon's nipples hardened under her touch, and she lifted her legs over Marika's.

Marika caressed Rhiannon from her breasts to her soft, inner thighs and back again but didn't stray between her legs.

Rhiannon's breath shortened. She captured Marika's hand and tried to direct it.

"Patience, my love." Marika traced along Rhiannon's folds but resisted her urging.

"Marika..." Rhiannon's voice was desperate.

"Mmm-hm?"

Rhiannon stiffened as Marika toyed with her clitoris. "Please."

"Please?"

"Oh, God...now...please, love, please..." Rhiannon clutched Marika's thighs as she brought both hands into play. "Yes...oh, God...I love you! I love you!" She went rigid against Marika's chest for long moments, then slumped.

Marika held her in complete contentment until Rhiannon shifted again. She started when Rhi rolled, slid down, and pinned her hands. "What...?"

"Patience, my lover said." Rhiannon grinned up at Marika. "Patience, she counselled while she drove me out of my mind."

Marika smiled. Wherever this was going, she was definitely along for the ride.

"If you move your hands, I'll stop." Rhiannon tucked Marika's hands under her thighs, then slid lower. She took her time, learning, loving, laving.

The sweetness of her touch brought Marika to the edge, but not over. She clamped a hand over Rhiannon's head.

Rhiannon reared back. "Uh-uh-uh. What did I say?" She put Marika's hand back under her thigh. "I believe patience was the operative word."

Marika's breath came hard and fast.

Rhiannon's tongue did not. She tantalized Marika, holding her apart as she leisurely explored.

"Oh, my God, Rhi—" Marika's hips bucked, and her hands clenched. "Please, sweetheart. You're going to give me a heart attack." *Patience, she says. Sweet Jesus, she's going to kill me.*

"Mmm, can't have that." Rhiannon stopped teasing and settled on Marika's clitoris.

It's never been like this—never. No one's loved me like you. Marika lost herself in a sensual fog, aware only of Rhiannon's touch holding her at the crest. Then she was over as wave after wave of delirious sensation wracked her body. When she finally opened her eyes, Rhiannon was watching her with a big grin.

Marika could barely summon the energy to lift an eyebrow.

"You were right. Patience is a good thing," Rhiannon said.

Marika chuckled. "It is, is it?"

Rhiannon's eyes gleamed. "Uh-huh. Like right now, I'm patiently waiting to do that all over again."

She is going to kill me! But what a way to go.

───────※───────

Lee frowned at the clock. It was twenty minutes past Marika's calling deadline. "Damn it. Why hasn't she called?" She picked up the phone and entered Marika's cell number. By the seventh ring, she started to get worried.

"Hello?" Marika was breathless.

"It's well past ten," Lee said, her worry slow to fade. "Everything okay?"

"Oh shit! I'm sorry. I forgot about calling. Yes, everything's okay. Cabin's great. Lake is great."

A distinct giggle sounded in the background.

Lee's eyebrow shot up, and she smiled as the picture came into focus.

"Can I call you tomorrow?" Marika asked. "I promise... first thing in the morning."

Lee chose to be merciful. "Okay. Just make sure you plug your cell in overnight."

"Rhiannon!" When Marika's voice came back on the line, it had gone up an octave. "Plug in... Oh, hell, I forgot to bring the charger."

"No, you didn't. Dana packed it in the side pocket of your suitcase."

"'Kay."

Lee said with feigned sternness, "Do not do anything else before you plug the phone in, Marika."

"Right...phone...plug in." There was a muted gasp. "Gotta go. Talk to you later."

The connection terminated abruptly, and Lee broke out laughing.

Dana poked her head around the door. "What's up, hon?"

Lee hung up the phone. "Let's just say that Marika and Rhiannon are enjoying their vacation." She grinned. "Told you that you didn't need to pack jammies for them."

CHAPTER 29

G AO SLAMMED HIS UNINJURED HAND down on the stack of papers. He'd combed through them at least a hundred times over the past couple of hours. *Not one goddamned clue—nothing!*

Perry wandered in from the kitchen, slurping soup from a stained mug. "Want some?"

Gao glared. "No."

Perry cringed and edged away.

Irritated by a blurry left eye, Gao returned his attention to the printouts.

"Did you get any ideas?"

Gao shook his head. "It's obvious that Glenn has them hidden, but there is nothing in these papers to indicate where they might be."

"Maybe they went with the tall, skinny guy who was there yesterday." Perry drained his soup with a loud slurp.

Gao's eyes narrowed. "What tall, skinny guy? And why the hell am I just finding out about him now?"

Perry quailed. "When I was watching the Glenn place, some tall, skinny guy came in through the backyard. He was there for over an hour, and when he left, one of the women walked him out. They talked for quite a while before he drove off."

"You're sure?" Gao felt a stirring of hope.

"Well, yeah. I had my binoculars."

Gao closed his eyes. *It was a tall, thin man who greeted them at the church.* He opened his eyes and smiled. "It's the priest. They went to stay with the priest, or he'll know where they are."

Perry flinched. "You going after a priest? Dude, that ain't right."

"You are a fool." Gao rose to his feet and awkwardly tucked his gun in the back of his trousers. "He's a chess piece, nothing more. But if he gives me the information I require without trouble, I will grant him a clean, swift execution. If he doesn't—" He shrugged.

"Jesus, man," Perry said. "He's a priest. He ain't gonna give 'em up."

Gao sneered. "Courage is a hollow philosophy when a man is confronted with an agonizing death. He'll give me what I want. Now get ready."

"Huh? Why?"

"You're driving." Gao eyed Perry and moved his hand to his gun.

Perry hastily set the soup mug aside, wiped his hands on his pants, and went to get his keys.

Gao grimaced. He'd have preferred to keep Perry out of this venture entirely. But his head still pounded, and his left eye was unreliable, so, for the moment, he needed him.

Under Gao's direction, Perry drove into the inner city.

Gao pointed ahead. "Turn there and slow down." The church's driveway was empty, and the windows of the rectory were dark. The only one around was an old man working in the flower gardens that fronted the building. Despite his scrambled cognition, Gao shifted gears on the fly. "Pull over up the street and wait for me."

Perry did as ordered.

Gao walked down the street that led to the church, scanning for anything out of the ordinary. All was humdrum, so he crossed the lawn to where the plaid-shirted man planted brightly coloured petunias.

Gao drooped his head. "Sir? Excuse me, sir?"

The man pushed himself up from the garden and turned. Resting on his haunches, he tipped a stained cowboy hat back over his grey hair and whistled. "Good Lord, lad. Did ya get the number of the truck that hit ya?"

Gao produced a rueful smile as he halted and squatted on the grass a short distance away from the old cowboy. He touched the bandage on his forehead. "It was five teenagers. They mugged me last night. I tried to give them my wallet, but they beat me anyway."

"Damnation." The cowboy shook his head. "Makes ya wonder what the world is comin' to, don' it?"

"Yes, sir, it does," Gao said.

"Eh, don't be callin' me sir. Name's Tupper." The cowboy held out his hand, then pulled it back when Gao raised the cast on his right hand. "Sorry, lad." He jerked a thumb at the flowerbeds. "T'were a buncha kids done this, too, just for the helluvit. It's taken me two days to clean up the mess, and now I'm tryin' to get the flowers in before services t'morra."

"My name is Charlie Liu, Mr. Tupper. I live not too far from here, and I wondered if I might speak to the minister. I've never gone to church, but the mugging made me think..."

Tupper nodded. "Yep, I know what ya mean, Charlie. Sometimes things come along makes a man ponder. Makes ya think there might be more ta life than puttin' yer next meal on the table. Why, I remember when I was riding range—"

Gao restrained his impatience. "I thought perhaps if I might speak to the minister, I would know whether this is a good church to attend."

Tupper bristled. "Ain't none better, lad. And we got the finest priest in the city here. They jus' don' make finer men than David Ross, let me tell ya." He laughed and rubbed his jaw. "Min' you, I mighta had a diff'rent opinion if ya'd asked me this mornin'. That man had me going through a hundred boxes looking for one blessed key. Then he finds it goin' back through the very firs' one he checked. Glory."

A thrill rippled through Gao, but he was careful to allow only polite interest in his voice. "Had he misplaced his house key?"

"Nah, though sometimes I swear that man couldn't find the glasses on his own nose. He was lookin' for the key to a buddy's cabin so he could loan it to some friends."

Suppressing a desire to punch the air, Gao remained motionless. "That was very nice of his friend to loan his cabin."

"Yep. Of course, he's a priest, too, so bein' nice is sorta in the job description. From what David says, though, this Conor darn near walks on water."

"Conor? I knew a priest named Conor Williams in Edmonton once. I wonder if it's the same man."

"Don' think so. David's friend's name is Conor O'Reilly." Tupper laughed. "Now there's a good Irish name for ya. My mother was a Reilly. Right straight from the ol' country, she was."

Gao shook his head. "No, that wouldn't be the gentleman I knew, then, though he did have a cabin as I recall. I'm afraid I don't remember what lake it was on."

"Mebbe it was on the Shuswaps, too. I know lotsa folks go there for holidays. David says the cabin is a real beaut, too, right down on the waterfront."

Gao could have kissed the garrulous, old cowboy. So his prey had fled to a waterfront cabin on the Shuswaps, owned by a priest named Conor Reilly—and he hadn't even had to pull his gun to get the information. *Time to wrap this up and get on the road.* He glanced up at the sky, still light in the summer evening. "I'm afraid I must get going. I take it your priest is out tonight?"

"'Fraid so. Miz Hancock took poorly s'afternoon, and the family asked David to come sit with 'em. Knowing him, he'll be there 'til the wee hours and then come d'rectly here for services."

"Then I shall attend services in the morning and speak to him afterwards." Gao stood up.

"Good idea," Tupper said. "I think ya'll like it here. Great priest, good buncha folks. They'll make ya feel right ta home."

"Thank you for taking the time to talk to me." Gao inclined his head in a little bow.

"My pleasure, Charlie. Be seein' ya around."

Gao scowled as he approached Perry's car and felt the vibration of the stereo through the pavement under his feet. *Oh, that's inconspicuous.*

Perry drummed wildly on the steering wheel.

Gao briefly considered throwing the man out of the car and driving himself to the Shuswaps. But he knew he needed to rest on the drive there so he would be in top form when he located the women. He wrenched open the passenger door.

Perry yelped and banged his head on the side window.

Gao snapped off the blaring stereo. "Drive."

Perry fumbled for the ignition. "Where?"

"Shuswap Lakes." Gao fastened his seatbelt.

Perry gaped at him. "Shuswap? In B.C.?"

"Yes, now drive."

"But—"

Gao pressed the barrel of his gun to Perry's head. "You were saying?"

"Nothing." Perry shook his head. "Didn't say nothing."

"You didn't say anything." Gao pulled the gun away, flipped the safety on, and set the weapon on his lap. "Get moving. We're going to drive straight there, no stops."

Perry scowled at the dashboard display. "I gotta get gas and take a leak."

"All right." Gao relaxed now that he had a destination. "But don't be foolish. You really don't want to become an added complication."

They stopped at a gas station to fill up and use the facilities. Gao stood at a urinal next to Perry. Even with the awkwardness of using his left hand, Gao was finished, washed up, and back in the car long before Perry. He took off his jacket and folded it on his lap to cover his hands— one in a cast and one holding the H&K P7M13.

When they got out on the highway, the setting sun bothered his eyes. Content that Perry was sufficiently cowed, Gao closed his eyes. Visions of cringing women soothed him as the sky deepened to night and the kilometres slipped by.

Rhiannon woke in a tangle of sheets and arms and legs. She allowed her eyes time to adjust to the morning light. Her mind wandered over every moment of the previous day—from waking for the first time in Marika's embrace to long after the stars came out when they'd finally settled down to sleep.

The hollow sensation in Rhiannon's stomach reminded her that they hadn't eaten since a roadside sandwich the previous afternoon. She smiled. *I'll just live on love.* She twisted in her warm cocoon.

Marika mumbled and tried to pull Rhiannon closer, but she resisted. She studied Marika: the way pale lashes fluttered and then subsided as if Marika defied waking from a wonderful dream, the strands of hair that had drifted over her face, the tiny blue veins at her temple.

Rhiannon's eyes narrowed at the bandage that Dana had placed over Marika's wound. *That son of a bitch. I'd like to meet him in a dark alley with a baseball bat. We'd see how he likes being hit in the head.* She forced the residual anger down. *Don't let that bastard ruin this.* She pushed back silken hair and traced her finger down Marika's jaw to her neck. She paused at the pulse point before continuing her downward path. Her caress came to rest on the side of Marika's breast.

"Are you having your way with me, sweetheart?" Amusement coloured Marika's sleep-raspy voice.

Rhiannon looked up into twinkling eyes. "Yes?"

Marika leaned forward to capture her lips in a lingering kiss. Then she took Rhiannon's hand and placed it over her breast. "Good."

Rhiannon's stomach rumbled loudly in the quiet room, and they started to laugh. She slid her arm around Marika's back. *I love feeling her against me. I am never going to get tired of this.* "Can we make a pact to never, ever wear pajamas?"

Marika chuckled. "We can. Did you intend that we stop wearing any clothing at all around each other?"

"Mmm, you come up with the best ideas." Rhiannon inserted her leg between Marika's.

Marika ran a hand down Rhiannon's back. "So you're proposing that I present my cases to the IRB in the nude, are you?"

"Well, I'd certainly rule in your favour if you did." Rhiannon nibbled on Marika's neck. "In fact, I'll bet you'd never lose another case."

"Brat. Well, if I'm going to be naked, then I think my assistant should be, as well."

Rhiannon giggled. "That's going to go over well when Marion comes back to work." She sobered. "I'm going to hate not being your assistant."

Marika eased back and covered Rhiannon's face with kisses. "Will being my lover make up for it?"

"Hmm, let me think..." Rhiannon slid her hand down to Marika's ass and lingered there. "I'm thinking, I'm thinking..." She came over Marika's hip and worked her hand between Marika's legs. "Still thinking..."

Laughing, Marika rolled Rhiannon onto her back and straddled her on hands and knees. "I don't think I've ever known you to be so slow coming to a decision."

Rhiannon licked her lips and eyed Marika's breasts. *Oh, this is even better.* But before she could take advantage of the new position, her stomach gurgled.

Marika laughed and stretched out over Rhiannon. "I suppose we really should eat, eh?"

Rhiannon waggled her eyebrows.

"Breakfast, my insatiable little darling, breakfast."

"Hmm. I guess that would be acceptable." Rhiannon's hips began a rhythmic motion. "For now." Her stomach rumbled again.

"Ooooh, that tickled." Marika grinned.

Rhiannon swirled patterns over Marika's body. "Tickling can be good."

"You want tickling, do you?" Marika's fingers flew over Rhiannon, driving her into squirming spasms of laughter.

They bounced out of bed and stood with their arms around each other as they surveyed the room. Pillows were tossed haphazardly, and half the bedding was on the floor.

"Sorta looks like a tornado hit it," Rhiannon said.

Marika smiled. "It does, doesn't it? I wonder how that happened."

"Probably the same way that pillow got all the way over there." Rhiannon pointed at a square cushion balanced precariously on the edge of a chair.

Marika blushed.

Rhiannon grinned, remembering the circumstances that had sent that pillow flying through the air. "I think a shower is in order. Join me?" She knelt by her suitcase to get fresh clothes. When the expected concurrence didn't come, Rhiannon glanced over her shoulder.

Marika hadn't moved.

Rhiannon cocked her head. "Marika? Everything okay?"

"Are you all right? I mean, with all this. I didn't rush you last night, did I?"

"Rush me?" Rhiannon blinked. "In case you didn't notice, love, there was a whole lot of mutual rushing going on."

Marika dropped her gaze.

Rhiannon rose and cradled her hands. "Hey, what's wrong? What are you thinking?"

Marika shook her head. "I'm sorry. I'm being an idiot."

"No, you're not," Rhiannon said. "If something's bothering you, I want to know what it is."

Marika drew a deep breath. "I wonder if everything has happened too fast, because of what we went through."

Rhiannon stared. "You think I made love with you as a reaction to surviving Gao and Cass?"

Marika nodded, her eyes averted.

Damn Cass to the ninth level of hell. I will never forgive that bitch for making Marika doubt herself. Rhiannon cupped Marika's chin and tilted her face until their gazes met. "I love you. And I fell in love with you long before last week. You said yourself that it's up to us what we make of our lives. Well, I want to make my life with you, not because of Cass or Gao or even Lee and Dana. I want to make a life with you because I love you and I can't imagine being without you." *David was right. I don't need the old crutch. I made my choice long before our first kiss.* "Do you believe me?"

Marika's gaze searched Rhiannon's face. Her smile dawned slowly. "Yes."

"Good, because I'm going to keep telling you until you believe me and not her."

Marika drew Rhiannon into her arms. "Thank you for being patient with me, love."

Rhiannon rested her head on Marika's shoulder and smiled. Patience had taken on a delightful new meaning in the past twelve hours.

They stood in the morning sun, arms locked around each other.

Finally, Marika broke the contented silence. "So... shower, then breakfast?"

Rhiannon nodded and stepped back. "Sounds good."

Marika stooped to sort through her suitcase. "I suppose you're going to have that chocolate marshmallow cereal you picked out."

"Of course." Rhiannon found the shorts she wanted at the bottom of the bag.

"You do realize that stuff is pure sugar."

"Yup. I figure I'm going to need all the energy I can get."

Marika groaned.

Rhiannon grinned.

CHAPTER 30

"**G**ODDAMNIT!" GAO GLARED AT THE map and local information pamphlet they'd picked up from a Shuswap gas station. "Did you know there are over a thousand kilometres of shoreline?"

Perry leaned his head on the steering wheel. "It's after two a.m., and I've been driving for hours. I don't know my own fucking name right now."

"Stop whining." Gao studied the H-shaped chain of four large lakes. *This is going to be much harder than I thought.*

"Dude, I gotta get some sleep."

Gao shook his head.

"Man, please. I'm fucking exhausted."

Gao looked up. *Huh, he does look like he's about to keel over.* "All right. Find a motel—a cheap one. And pay for our room in cash." He resumed his perusal of the map under the interior light.

Perry stopped at the first motel that had a vacancy sign. Ten minutes later, he was snoring on one of the beds.

Gao found a local phonebook in the room. After opening to the "R" section, he scanned the listings and found eight Reillys. *Yes!* He tore out the page, studied the addresses, and meticulously charted the location of each. *Goddamnit, all of the Reillys live in town.* He closed his eyes and breathed deeply. *That doesn't mean they don't have a cabin on the lakeside as well.* He set the map aside. *We'll leave early and check every cabin on the lake if we have to.*

The next morning, they began their search, but many hours later, they were no further ahead than when they'd started. Many of the cabins were nestled in the thick woods that covered the hillsides surrounding the lakes, and while he was able to eliminate those with family names displayed, the majority had no such identification.

Gao slammed his uninjured hand against the dashboard. *All right, relax. There's no deadline. They don't know I'm here. I just need a better plan.*

"Okay with you if I pick up some lunch?" Perry asked, gaze averted.

"Make it fast." *I can—if necessary—continue the cabin-by-cabin search, but I want a more effective way to search.* Gao's eyes widened. "The lakes."

Perry glanced at Gao. "Huh?"

Gao smiled. "The lakes. They're in a lakeshore cabin with a private beach. On a sunny afternoon like this, they're not going to be inside. All we have to do is rent a speedboat. We can cover the lakes much faster that way."

"Do you know how to drive a boat?" Perry asked. "'Cause I sure don't."

"How hard can it be?" Gao shrugged. "As soon as we've had lunch, we'll find a boat rental outlet. Are your binoculars still in the car?"

"Yeah. I left 'em in the trunk yesterday."

"Excellent. You'll drive; I'll scan the shoreline."

"Be careful, Rhi," Marika said. "I don't want to have to pull you out of the water again." *Not that you didn't make a very cute mermaid.* She grinned. *And I'm the lucky sailor that gets to take you home.*

"No worries." Rhiannon leaned out of the canoe and grabbed the end of the wharf to pull them alongside.

Marika propelled them forward with her paddle. "Uh-huh. That's what you said when you tried to catch the turtle. No worries."

Rhiannon chuckled. "It was shallow water. Besides, I almost had him." She crawled out on the wharf, tied the canoe, and extended a hand to Marika.

Marika stood and had one foot on the wharf when the wake of a speeding motorboat rocked the canoe and she almost fell.

Rhiannon grabbed Marika's arm and glared after the boat. "Stupid asshole." She helped her onto the wharf. "You okay?"

Safely on the dock, Marika smiled. "How could I not be after a day like today?" She drew Rhiannon into her arms and kissed her. "I've wanted to do that for hours."

"Me too, but I figured the canoe was too tippy for us to fool around out there."

"Agreed, oh great turtle hunter," Marika said. "And in case you hadn't noticed, you're very wet."

Rhiannon raised an eyebrow.

Marika laughed and turned Rhiannon in the direction of the cabin. "I meant that your clothes are still damp from your fishing expedition. Why don't you go change while I get the bonfire set up?"

Rhiannon collected the paddles and life jackets, walked to the end of the wharf, and looked back over her shoulder with a grin. "And you're right on both counts."

I've created a monster. A darling, adorable, horny monster. Marika smiled, watching Rhiannon climb the hill and stow their gear on the porch. *You'd never know we spent most of the afternoon in bed.* She went to the wood hut to gather kindling, old newspapers, and some small logs. Mentally crossing her fingers, she assembled the bonfire. *I hope I remember how to do this.* She struck a match. When a flame flickered and caught, she pumped a triumphant fist. *All right! You'd be proud, Dad. It worked just like you taught me.*

For a moment her smile faded, then Marika shook her head. "Rhi's my family now. That's all that matters. Forward, not back."

"Hey, love? You want me to bring down the food?" Rhiannon called from the cabin door.

"Sure. Do you need a hand?"

"No, I got it. You're the fire-maker, I'm the food-taker." Rhi disappeared back inside.

Marika sat on a log that had been left near the fire pit. The flames waned, then caught and grew, and she lost herself in their dance.

"What so funny, love?" Rhiannon approached with a tray.

"Sorry?"

"You had a big grin on your face." Rhiannon set the tray on the ground and took a seat beside Marika.

"Oh, I was thinking about us trying to get the canoe launched." Marika shook her head. "I'm amazed we didn't tip the thing over before we were four feet from the dock."

Rhiannon chuckled. "True, but for a couple of women who'd never canoed before, I thought we did okay." She popped a marshmallow into her mouth.

"That's because you're so quick to pick up new skills."

Rhiannon choked.

Marika pounded her on the back. "Are you okay?"

Several coughs later, Rhiannon nodded. "Sheesh, give me a double entendre warning next time."

"I have no idea what you mean." Marika raised her eyebrows. "I was just complimenting you on your technique, especially given that you'd had no experience."

Rhiannon burst out laughing. "Oh, you are so bad."

And you are so good for me. Marika smiled, locked her hands around one knee, and looked up at the sky. It wasn't dark enough for the stars to be out, but the light had faded to a soft blue with scattered orange-limned clouds.

"You're beautiful."

Marika turned her head.

Rhiannon regarded her seriously. "You really are. Anyone with eyes can tell that by looking at you, but I love knowing how beautiful you are on the inside, too."

Marika's breath caught. "That has to be the nicest thing anyone has ever said to me." She reached for Rhiannon, and their lips met.

Flames crackled and licked at the logs as soft sighs and murmurs filled the air.

Gao grinned as they sped away. *I have them!* After a fruitless afternoon of cruising up and down the waterways, all the hours of searching finally paid off. He'd had to restrain himself from screaming in triumph when he saw the lawyer's companion helping her out of a canoe.

"Where to?" Perry asked, his pasty skin burned bright red from unprotected hours on the water.

"Back to the marina. We'll return the boat and take the car." Gao marked the approximate position of the women on his map.

Back at the rental dock, they returned the boat and climbed the hill to the parking lot. To Gao's amazement, Perry balked at getting into the car.

"No. I'm not going along on this." Perry's gaze flitted from Gao to the few other people in the parking lot. "I do electronics. I've never killed anyone."

"I have." Gao's eyes narrowed. "Now get in the car."

"Nuh-uh." Perry's voice shook, but he maintained eye contact. "I'll wait for you back at the motel."

Now? You decide to grow a backbone now? Gao glared at him.

Perry flinched but didn't succumb.

"Fine." Gao scowled. "You would undoubtedly be more of a hindrance than a help. Give me the keys."

Perry slid them across the roof of the car and backed away.

Gao got in the car and adjusted the seat for his shorter frame. After he started the ignition, he powered down the window. "I won't be long, and I won't wait for you if you're not ready to go when I get back. Is that understood?"

Perry nodded.

Gao put the car in gear and pulled away. In the rearview mirror, Perry slouched off in the direction of the street. *I'm better off without him. He served his purpose, and now it's up to me.* He squinted. *Fucking eye. Perry's fortunate I'll need him for the trip back, or I'd abandon him in that fleabag motel.* He steered with his knees as he rubbed his temples and between his eyes. The hours of straining his good eye to compensate for the fuzzy vision in his bad eye had aggravated his ever-present headache.

Gao turned onto the main highway that circumnavigated the lakes. *It's almost over, then I can relax and report success to her. My life will be back to normal.* He smiled. *And their lives will be over.*

The boat rentals were on a different arm of the lake, and Gao estimated it would take him almost an hour to get to the arm where their cabin was, but that suited him. He glanced at the sky. *It won't be completely dark by the time I get there, but it won't be full light either. Doesn't matter either way. The element of surprise is the most important thing. This shouldn't take long at all.*

Marika grinned. *She is so impatient. Well, sometimes. Definitely with marshmallows.*

Rhiannon stripped her fifth blackened marshmallow from the toasting stick. Rather than keeping her stick over the embers to toast the white confection to a golden brown, she preferred to plunge the marshmallow into the flames for a quick charcoal effect. Sticky white tendrils coated her chin. She tried to clean them off but only managed to smear the marshmallow over her fingers, as well. "I think I'd better go get washed up." Rhiannon sucked one marshmallow-coated finger into her mouth.

"The lake's right there." Marika pointed down the beach.

"This is going to require soap." Rhiannon rose from their log. She leaned over with a grin and tried to kiss Marika.

Marika shrieked with laughter and held her at bay. *Thank God for longer arms.* "Go get cleaned up, brat, or no more kisses for you."

Rhiannon chortled and started up the trail to the cabin.

"Can you bring the cell back with you?" Marika asked. "I want to call Lee early so she doesn't interrupt us later."

Rhiannon grinned over her shoulder. "I like the way you think." She disappeared into the cabin.

Marika looked up at the emerging stars. A profound sense of contentment welled up within. *I don't remember the last time I was so—happy.* Her gaze settled back on the fire.

It wasn't long before Rhiannon returned, considerably cleaner and carrying the cell phone.

Marika accepted the phone and the kiss that went with it. She almost got lost in the soft sensations of Rhiannon's lips before she reluctantly pulled away. "If we keep doing that, I'm going to forget to call again."

Rhiannon sat down beside her. She stroked Marika's thigh and let her hand drift to the inside of her leg, wriggling the tips of her fingers under the edge of Marika's shorts. "Lee's timing definitely left something to be desired last night, so it's a good idea to check in with Mom first."

"Mom?" Marika laughed as she hit Lee's speed dial. "She would cuff you a good one if she heard that." The line was busy, so she set the phone on the ground while she concentrated on the delightful way Rhiannon had burrowed under her shorts. She put one hand behind Rhiannon's neck and gently rubbed the nape. She'd learned the previous night what a sensitive area that was for her lover.

They leaned toward each other. Just as their lips met, the phone rang, startling them apart.

"Damn! Told you she had lousy timing." Rhiannon shook her head.

Marika reached down to pick up the phone. "Hi, Lee." She winked at Rhiannon.

"Marika! You've got to get out of there!"

"What? Lee, what are you—?"

"Get out! Leave everything, and get the hell out of there. Gao knows where you are!"

Marika shot upright. "What do you mean he knows? How could he?"

Rhiannon bolted to her feet, eyes wide.

"David just called. Tupper told an Asian man with a cast on his hand and a bandage on his forehead where you two were. Gao doesn't know precisely, Marika, but you've got to get out of there as fast as you can. Go to the RCMP detachment in Sicamous. I'll have Marc call them right away to tell them what's going on. Don't stop to pack, just get moving. And call me when you're there!"

Marika instantly cut the connection, grabbed Rhiannon's hand, and ran for the cabin.

Rhiannon didn't ask what was going on; she matched her stride for stride.

After slamming through the door, Marika dropped Rhiannon's hand and raced up the stairs to get the car keys. She was back in seconds.

Rhiannon had turned off the lights. "Gao's coming?" She stood at the edge of a window and scanned the area around the cabin.

"Yes. We're going to the RCMP right now." Marika's voice cracked, and her heart pounded.

Rhiannon followed as they darted out the cabin's rear door.

Marika stopped short and frantically backpedaled. "There's a car coming down the road with its lights off."

They ran around the side of the cabin, and Rhiannon grabbed one of the paddles from the porch.

Marika pointed in the direction they had walked their first night there. "That way. Neighbour's closer."

They bolted down the hill to the beach.

Marika looked back.

Gao stood at the corner of the cabin, a gun pointed directly at them.

Two figures were running down the hill.

For a split second, Gao froze.

The lawyer led their flight. She glanced over her shoulder at him, and the campfire illuminated the fear on her face.

They're getting away! He shot wildly in their direction.

They disappeared behind a hut and then reappeared as they dashed for the forest.

He fired again and ran after them.

By the time Gao reached the forest, they'd disappeared. *Damn them! Damn their ancestors, and damn the children they will never have when I catch them!* He hurtled into the brush.

A city boy, born and bred, even he couldn't miss snapped branches and broken foliage. *Count your life in seconds. That's all you have left.*

<hr>

When Rhiannon finally pulled Marika to a halt, her lungs burned and her legs trembled. Bent double, Marika sucked in air. "We should head up the hill for the road."

"Listen to me," Rhiannon whispered hoarsely. "We have to stop him."

Marika stared at Rhiannon, just able to make out her features in the gathering gloom. "Are you crazy? We have to get out of here!"

"No, listen, love—we can get away, but by the time the police come, he'll be long gone. He'll come after us again and again. He'll never stop, unless we stop him."

"He's got a gun, we've got a paddle." Marika desperately wanted to take Rhiannon's hand and run. *I did this. I brought this danger down on her.*

Rhiannon dropped the paddle and grabbed Marika's arms with both hands. "We can do this. We can! No more running, Marika. Never again."

Rhiannon's grip was so tight it hurt. Marika shook her head. *This is insane!* She took a deep breath. "How?" Even as the question was out of her mouth, Marika couldn't believe she'd asked it.

Rhiannon quickly laid out her plan.

"No! I'm not letting you do that." Marika shook her head. "It's too dangerous. What if he shoots first and doesn't ask questions? You can't dodge a bullet!"

"He's not going to shoot until he tries to find out where you are. That gives us time."

"Then let me be the bait."

Rhiannon smiled. "I'm a smaller target." Her smile faded. "We don't have time to argue. You need to trust me, just like I'm trusting you to keep me safe."

"You're trusting me with your life." Marika trembled.

"I've already trusted you with my heart." Rhiannon raised a hand to caress Marika's face. "I believe in you. Believe in yourself, okay?"

Dear God, don't let me let her down! "Okay. I love you. Let's do this."

Rhiannon strained to pick up sounds of Gao's pursuit. When branches snapped ahead of her position, she took a deep breath. *Here goes. Stay safe, love.* She rose from her crouch and moved toward the sound.

A shot rang out, and she flinched. *I just had to wear white today.*

"Stop!"

Rhiannon halted, then stepped out to face Gao across the small clearing.

Gao glared at her. "Your friend...where is she?"

"Long gone." Rhiannon's whole body trembled, and her heart beat so hard it pounded in her ears. "She's out of your reach, you fucking dirt bag, and she'll have the police down on you so fast, you'll be rotting in Drumheller before you know it. You lose, asshole. She beat you." Despite the penumbra, she knew her taunts were getting to him. His hand shook and his face was a rictus of rage. *Good. The more off-balance the better.* "Your boss is going to turn you into fish food before you even make it to the pen."

"At least you'll be dead." He raised his gun.

A shadow moved to Gao's left, and Rhiannon dove to the ground.

The paddle smashed on his gun hand, and Marika screamed.

Gao howled and dropped to his knees, scrabbling after the fallen gun.

Rhiannon jumped to her feet and raced for the gun.

Marika slammed another blow against Gao's back.

He dropped like a stone and writhed on the ground.

Rhiannon picked up the gun and leveled it at Gao. She held a hand out to Marika.

Still holding the paddle, Marika jumped past their prone pursuer.

"Are you okay, love?" Rhiannon slipped an arm around Marika's waist.

"Am *I* okay? You're the one dodging bullets, Supergirl!" Marika threw an arm over Rhiannon's shoulders. "Lee was right. She should've called you Mighty Mouse."

Rhiannon grinned. *We did it. We won!*

Gao struggled to his knees and groaned. "You won't shoot." His breath came in deep gasps, but his tone was defiant.

"I can and will if I have to. There's nothing I wouldn't do to protect her." Rhiannon aimed the gun at Gao's head. *Better believe it, buddy. There's no question who's going down if you threaten her.*

"My hero," Marika whispered. Her arm tightened and her breathing began to even out.

Gao slumped to the forest floor and cradled his left hand with the cast on his right hand.

Marika caressed Rhiannon's hair.

Rhi stole a quick glance at her and smiled.

Gao's eyes widened. "You're lovers?"

Rhiannon glared at him. "No shit, Sherlock."

He shook his head. "That wasn't in the transcripts."

"Not that it's any of your bloody business, but you're interfering with our honeymoon," Marika said.

Wow, our honeymoon. That is so cool. Rhiannon squeezed Marika's waist.

Gao stared at Rhiannon. "The Chameleon—I thought you were simply foolish in defence of a friend."

"She is my friend. She's also the woman I love. You and your psycho boss never stood a chance," Rhiannon said. "We had luck and love and Lee on our side."

Marika laughed. "I couldn't have said it better, sweetheart."

Gao rolled onto his back and stared up at the sky, his arms limp at his side. The light of the full moon illuminated his face. He closed his eyes.

Rhiannon looked at Marika and raised her eyebrows.

Marika shrugged.

They both stared at Gao. His face and form had slackened, almost as if he'd gone to sleep.

Well, I'll be damned. Rhiannon shook her head. *Who naps at a time like this? Sonuvabitch looks downright...peaceful.*

CHAPTER 31

"**I** REALLY APPRECIATE YOU ALLOWING ME to watch," Lee said. She followed Marc into the outer interrogation room.

"It's a little unorthodox, but I know Keith won't mind. If it weren't for you, we wouldn't have Gao in custody. I thought you might enjoy seeing the fruits of your labours." Marc nodded at a uniformed officer sipping coffee and watching Gao and Keith Judson through the one-way mirror. "Lee, this is Constable Eade from the Sicamous RCMP detachment. He and his partner brought Gao back to Calgary."

"Bill, please." The young officer offered his hand with a smile. "So, it was your friends who caught this snake?"

"Yes, it was." Lee shook his hand. "I'm just thankful I found out he was on his way in time to warn them."

The constable chuckled. "I have a feeling those two would've handled themselves in any event. By the time me and my partner got to the cabin, they were sitting by the bonfire with Gao across from them, trussed up in duct tape tight as a Thanksgiving turkey. They'd even knotted his shoelaces together so he couldn't walk. Ms. Davies had his gun pointed right at him, and she looked ready to use it if she had to."

Lee expelled a breath. It had been the worst forty-seven minutes of her life until Marika called back. From the moment David phoned, alarmed about what Tupper had inadvertently done, until the moment Marika reported that they were both safe and Gao was incapacitated, Lee and

Dana had been terrified. Worst of all, there was nothing Lee could do after she notified Marc, who'd alerted the Sicamous RCMP.

"The funny part was, once we took control of the situation, I asked Ms. Davies for the gun. I teased her that it was a good thing she didn't need to use it since it was almost as big as she was. Well, damned if she didn't look at me and say it was a good thing mostly because she didn't have a clue how to use it and probably couldn't have hit the broad side of a barn door." The constable laughed out loud. "I thought Gao was going to have a stroke."

Lee chuckled and turned her attention to the interrogation room, where Keith was questioning a stony-faced Gao. "Geez, he looks like he came out on the losing end of ten rounds with Tyson."

Eade nodded. "We had him checked out before we left Sicamous. He's got a concussion, serious bruising on his back, and two fractured hands. Teach him to go up against a pair of helpless females. Uh-huh, 'bout as helpless as a coupla badgers."

Marc observed the interrogation intently. "Has he said anything yet, Constable?"

"No, sir. But then he's barely said a word since we picked him up. Wouldn't even tell us about the car he was driving. It's registered to some guy here in Calgary, but we haven't been able to locate him. Could be we'll be looking at another body eventually." Eade drained his coffee and tossed the empty Styrofoam cup into a garbage can. "On the drive here, all he did was stare out the window. Wouldn't say a word even when we asked him what kind of sandwich he wanted for lunch. Silent as the Sphinx."

Keith stood up and left the room. He joined the others in the outer office. "The man's a goddamned clam." He nodded to Lee. "I don't suppose you want to try your magic on him?"

"Sorry, Keith. I smashed his gun hand and gave him a concussion. I doubt that would encourage him to spill his guts." Lee narrowed her eyes at Gao. "Have you shown him the pictures of his cousin?"

Keith shook his head. "Hell, no. The last thing I want is for him to get the Chameleon's message. As if he's not already silent enough."

"Try it. Put the pictures on the table, ask him why he remains loyal to someone who would do that to his cousin, and then leave him alone." Lee shrugged. "What do you have to lose?"

When Marc gave him an encouraging nod, Keith took the pictures out of his briefcase. "I oughta have my head examined." He returned to the room, tossed the crime scene photos on the table, repeated Lee's words, and walked out.

It was several moments before Gao's gaze dropped to the pictures. He dragged them closer and slowly fanned the photos out across the table.

Lee smiled.

The flesh around Gao's eyes tightened, and his lips thinned and parted. His shoulders twitched as he studied the pictures. Finally, he lifted his head and stared at the two-way mirror. "She should not have done this. It was not necessary."

"Give him a try now," Lee said. "I think he might be ready to talk to you."

Keith shook his head. "Damn, Glenn. If you're ever interested in a career—"

"No way," Marc said. "I've got first dibs on her. Right, Sarge?"

Lee shook her head. "I'm very happy where I am, gentlemen, but thank you."

Keith put his hand on the doorknob, then turned to Lee. "I misjudged you. I'm sorry. If there's ever anything I can do, please let me know."

Lee allowed a wicked grin to spread across her face. "There is one thing you could do for me."

Keith cocked his head.

"Give me an hour's notice when you're going to bust DeAndre."

"You do know that's totally against procedure."

Lee crossed her arms and raised an eyebrow.

Keith smiled. "We'll see." He returned to the interrogation room.

This time, Gao responded to the methodical questioning with curt answers.

As Lee listened to his stark, graphic responses indict the woman known as the Chameleon, she could almost hear the steel bars clanging into place around Cass.

Rhiannon looked out across the lake, mirror perfect in the early hours of the morning. *It's so beautiful. We have to come back here someday.*

Marika approached from behind and wrapped her arms around Rhiannon.

Sighing, Rhiannon leaned back against Marika's body.

"Are you sorry to be leaving early, sweetheart?" Marika kissed the top of Rhiannon's head.

"No, not really. But it's been such a beautiful week—Gao aside—that I'm sad to see it end."

"We have two more weeks if we want to take them," Marika said.

Rhiannon turned and slid her arms around Marika's neck. "No, love. I like the idea of saving the rest of our holidays. We can use them to go somewhere special later on."

Marika studied Rhiannon. "Maybe Wales?"

"Maybe." Rhiannon shrugged. "Or even better, we could take a cruise someplace warm this winter. I always thought that would be a lot of fun."

Their lips met, and they stood together for long moments. Finally, they drew apart.

Rhiannon tilted her head. "Is everything locked up?"

Marika nodded. "Uh-huh. We're ready to leave whenever you are."

"Then let's go home."

Hand in hand, they walked up to the car.

The long drive back to Calgary was made shorter by animated chatter over everything from when Rhiannon would take her driving test to Lee and Dana's upcoming nuptials. The only topics they avoided was anything to do with Gao or Cass. By unspoken agreement, they refused to allow those baleful spectres to intrude on their bliss one instant before necessary.

They were approaching the city limits when Rhiannon yawned and stretched.

Marika smiled. "Hey, I've been doing all the driving. How come you're so tired?"

"It's hard work being a passenger," Rhiannon said. "Wish I could've helped with the driving, though."

"I know, sweetheart, but rental insurance doesn't cover you. Besides, I don't mind. It was a beautiful drive."

"It was." Rhiannon smiled. "Beautiful scenery inside the car and out."

Marika chuckled. "Are you sure you don't have an Irish heritage?"

"Just calling them like I see them, Ms. Havers." Rhiannon looked ahead. "Are we going to stop for a few minutes at Lee and Dana's before we go home?"

"Yes, we should pick up the Spookmeister, switch cars, and see how things are going."

"We owe them an awful lot, don't we?"

Marika nodded. "Yes, we do. I don't think we can ever repay them, especially Lee. Without her intervention, we'd be dead."

A shudder rippled through Rhiannon. She turned to gaze at Marika. *To have missed this—*

For an instant she found it hard to breathe, then Marika glanced at her. *Stop it. The worst didn't happen. We're together, and that's all that matters.*

"Are you okay?" Marika asked, braking for a stoplight.

Rhiannon reached across and trailed her fingers through Marika's hair. "I'm fine."

Marika closed her eyes. "Mmm. Let's not stay too long before we go home, okay?"

The light changed. They began to move, and Rhiannon dropped her hand to Marika's thigh. She traced delicate circles, slipping farther and farther under Marika's shorts with each loop.

Finally, with traffic getting heavier, Marika covered Rhiannon's hand and held it still. "Behave, love. You're not having your way with me in a moving vehicle."

Rhiannon grinned. "Does that mean I can have my way with you when the car stops?"

Marika shot Rhiannon an amused glance. "We'll see."

They held hands as they drove toward Lee and Dana's home.

When they pulled into the driveway and stopped, Lee came out of the front door, a huge grin on her face. "What's the matter? Paradise get boring?"

Rhiannon circled the car, threw her arms around Lee, and found herself hoisted in an enthusiastic bear hug. When she was returned to earth, Marika received the same treatment.

Laughing, Marika kissed Lee's forehead. "Let me down, you big goof."

Lee set her down. "It's great to have you guys back." She scowled. "Don't ever scare me like that again."

Marika and Rhiannon exchanged glances.

"Scare *you*?" Marika said. "Try being in our shoes."

Lee smiled. "I'm just so goddamned glad that you're still around to fill your shoes."

Rhiannon was about to second that sentiment when Dana burst out the front door.

"It's on! Come quick! You've got to see this." Dana darted back into the house, and they followed.

In the living room, Dana pointed at the TV. Newsworld's breaking news logo faded to an image of a perfectly coiffed, well-dressed anchorwoman and a society pages picture of Cass in the corner of the screen.

"This report just in from our Vancouver affiliate. A sensational arrest in that city this afternoon as Cassandra DeAndre, wife of shipping magnate Palmer DeAndre, has been charged with numerous counts of kidnapping, drug smuggling, human trafficking, and murder. Her chauffeur, Liang Zhaoxing, was also taken into custody."

The picture switched to a live external shot of the DeAndre mansion, where several police cars and a police van with its lights on were parked in the expansive circular driveway. A handful of officers in SWAT gear milled around the entrance.

"CBC reporter Vanessa Schroeder is on the scene. Vanessa, can you give us an update on the situation?"

An attractive, dark-haired woman stepped in front of the camera. "Yes, Diane. Approximately forty-five minutes ago, we received an anonymous tip that Cassandra DeAndre, well-known Vancouver socialite and head of the DeAndre Children's Charitable Foundation, was to be arrested on several serious charges, including drug smuggling and murder. When we arrived at the DeAndre residence, police were already on scene and had the suspect in custody."

The camera panned to a close-up of Cass being led from the house in handcuffs. She struggled furiously but futilely against the officers holding her. As she was forced toward the police car, her head snapped up and she glared at the cameras, a feral snarl twisting her lips. Behind her, two other armed officers escorted a sullen and shackled Liang.

Lee, Dana, Marika, and Rhiannon hooted and cheered as the CBC commentary continued.

Rhiannon remembered how terrifying it had been to fight back the night of their capture. *You ordered our deaths like we were nothing more than mosquitoes. Well, guess what, bitch? Your days of ruling the roost just came to an end.* She grinned.

An officer pushed Cass' head down to get her into the car. She fell forward against the car and lashed out with her feet. Her escorts fought to force her inside. Once she was stuffed into the back seat, the camera zoomed in on the door of the mansion.

Palmer DeAndre stared after his wife, tears running down his face.

They sobered at the sight.

"I feel sorry for him," Marika said. "He was a nice man, and I'm sure he was as taken in by Cass as I was."

Rhiannon put her arm around Marika's waist and hugged her. *My tender-hearted woman. I'd probably be more pissed that his money and prestige protected Cass for so long.*

Marika settled her arm around Rhiannon's shoulders.

Onscreen, the police cars began to move. Reporters milled around the slowly moving vehicles, and the camera picked up vivid footage of Cass inside the back seat. Though there was no sound, she was screaming, her face contorted in rage.

The camera followed the procession as it turned onto the street, then it panned back to show a large crowd of gawkers and a mass of media trucks lining the street outside the mansion.

"Aw, poor old Cass...the whole world is seeing her humiliation." Lee smirked.

Lee, did you...? Rhiannon cocked her head. "You wouldn't know anything about that anonymous tip to the TV people, would you?"

"Who, me?"

Rhiannon grinned. "Yes, you."

"I'm taking the Fifth."

Marika raised an eyebrow. "You know we don't have a Fifth Amendment in the Canadian Charter of Rights."

"Oh. Are you quite sure about that?" Lee winked.

Dana and Rhiannon laughed.

Marika smiled and shook her head.

Dana turned her back on the screen, where the tape of Cass' arrest was already being replayed. "Will you stay for dinner?"

Rhiannon and Marika looked at each other.

Marika shook her head. "Thank you, but I think we'll pass this time. Maybe next weekend? We'll just pick up Spooky and my car tonight."

Lee grinned. "I guess the honeymoon isn't quite over, eh?"

Marika gazed at Rhiannon. "Not for a long, long time to come."

Rhiannon nodded. "Let's go home, love."

They turned to see Lee and Dana smiling at them.

"Before you lovebirds take off, I swung by your office yesterday and picked up your messages." Lee crossed to the sideboard to pick up a small stack of notes. "Might as well take 'em with you."

Marika glanced at the top one and raised an eyebrow. "There's one here from your aunt, sweetheart. She wants you to meet her at her insurance agent's office on Tuesday." Marika held out the slip of paper to Rhiannon.

Rhiannon groaned. "Ughh. What a way to end a nearly perfect week."

"You were going to have to see her sometime, and I'll go with you," Marika said. "Don't worry. Once this matter is closed, you'll be done with her forever."

Can forever start now? Rhiannon sighed and followed Marika. They collected Spooky's things, picked up the smallest member of their household, and went home.

CHAPTER 32

RHIANNON BIT HER LIP AS she followed Marika off the elevator. *I so don't want to see Hettie.*

Marika stopped and put a hand on Rhiannon's arm. "You don't have to do this, sweetheart. I can handle it alone, if you'd rather."

"I know, and I love you for making the offer, but I need to put all this—to put her behind me, once and for all." Rhiannon tried to smile. "You've already done so much. I have to do my part, too." Marika had gathered all the documentation they would need, including affidavits from Lee and David as to what they'd seen in Rhiannon's room. "There's nothing she can do to me anymore, is there?"

Marika shook her head. "No. Not anymore. Just let her try, and see what I do to her."

Rhiannon took a deep breath. "Right. Then let's get this over with."

They opened the door on a plain, functional office.

A receptionist looked up. "May I help you?"

Marika nodded. "My client and I have an appointment with Mr. Reynolds about the Walker insurance matter."

"Of course. Miss Walker is already with Mr. Reynolds. Please go on in."

Rhiannon led the way. She pushed open the door.

Hettie turned to look at them.

A harried-looking man behind a paper-strewn desk glanced up at their entrance and stood.

Hettie glared at Marika. "Who is she?"

"I'm Marika Havers, Ms. Davies' attorney, Miss Walker. We've met before, but just in passing, so perhaps you don't recall. How do you do?" Marika extended her hand.

Hettie ignored it. "Attorney? What does Anne need an attorney for? This doesn't even concern her, 'ceptin' Mr. Reynolds needs her signature on some papers."

Mr. Reynolds offered his hand to Rhiannon and Marika. "Ladies, thank you for joining us. I've gone over the basics with Miss Walker. If I may recap?" He gestured them to chairs and began to cover the administrative details.

Rhiannon covertly studied her aunt. Hostility clung to her like cheap perfume. *I wonder if she's ever been genuinely happy.* She blinked at an unexpected rush of sympathy. *Huh. I never thought I'd feel compassion for the old bat.* Rhiannon just wanted to sign the papers and leave. *Hettie won't change. She thrives on negativity. She probably always will, but that's not my problem now.*

"Miss Walker," Marika said. "Ms. Davies has a valid claim against your insurance. She lost everything she owned and barely escaped with her life. She then had to find a new place to live and replace her destroyed wardrobe before she could return to work."

Hettie scowled. "I took Anne in outta the goodness of my heart and gave her a home all these years. Arsonists burn down my house, and she thinks she should get some of the insurance? No, sir, she gets not one penny that's rightfully mine!"

Marika smiled. "Actually, since Ms. Davies graduated from her legal assistant program three years ago, she's paid you four hundred dollars a month for the privilege of living in one small room. That means she contributed over fourteen thousand dollars to your income—money you would otherwise not have had and which you had a legal obligation to declare."

Rhiannon suppressed a smile at the consternation on Hettie's face. *And there's the shot across Hettie's bow. There was a reason she insisted I always pay in cash.*

"I've calculated her losses and replacement costs and arrived at a figure of eighteen hundred dollars, which I consider extremely fair." Marika shot Rhiannon a glance.

Rhi stifled a grin. *Good thing Hettie doesn't know Marika wanted to press for triple that. She'd have had a heart attack.*

"Eighteen hundred dollars!" Hettie squawked. "That ungrateful little—"

"Additionally, though the fire department report clearly identifies the cause as arson, they also note that the single smoke alarm in the dwelling had no batteries in it. It was your responsibility as the landlady to ensure a working alarm. Thus you are liable for the fact that Ms. Davies had no early warning and barely escaped with her life. She could, if she chose, sue you for negligence in civil court, but she has agreed that eighteen hundred will be adequate compensation."

Her aunt flushed a deep scarlet, and her chest heaved.

Rhiannon raised an eyebrow. *Damn, Hettie's going to stroke out if she doesn't calm down.*

"That is more than fair, Miss Walker," Mr. Reynolds said. "I would recommend that you accept the division. With the final papers signed today, I can issue both cheques before you leave." He pushed the papers across the desk and offered Hettie a pen.

Hettie snatched it out of his hand and scrawled her signature where he indicated. Then she lurched to her feet and lumbered out of the room.

"Miss Walker, your cheque—?" Mr. Reynolds stared at the door.

Rhiannon shook her head. "Don't worry. She'll be back. She's busy making a point."

Mr. Reynolds raised an eyebrow. "A point?"

"Yes. That I'm a greedy, ungrateful, unfeeling wretch, who spent the past dozen years sponging off her largess and doesn't deserve to breathe the same air as her."

"Oh." Mr. Reynolds shuffled the papers. "Um, if you'll excuse me, I'll have the cheques cut." He exited the office and closed the door behind him.

Marika knelt in front of Rhiannon and took her hands. "Are you okay?"

"I am. I didn't care about the cheque, but I'm glad I faced her one last time."

"You finally banished the boogeyman." Marika raised Rhiannon's hands to her lips.

"I did, and all thanks to you." Rhiannon leaned forward and kissed Marika.

The door opened. "I left my—" Hettie gasped.

"Figures. She always did have the worst timing." Rhiannon rose and turned to face Hettie with Marika standing at her back.

Hettie clutched her chest and stared. "Well, I never!"

Rhiannon laughed. "No, I expect you haven't." Marika's hands settled on her shoulders, and she covered them with her own.

"You...you're..."

"In love? Yes, very much so. In fact, I intend to spend the rest of my life with this amazing woman."

Hettie's eyes bulged, and her mouth fell open.

Marika chuckled quietly.

"I always knew there was something wrong with you." Hettie sneered. "Knew you weren't right. You're your father's daughter, through and through."

"Why, thank you. I take that as a great compliment." Rhiannon surprised herself with an absence of anger. *Hettie's opinion just doesn't matter.*

Mr. Reynolds returned. Two cheques in his hand, he edged by Hattie, who stood in the doorway. "Ms. Davies, if you would sign these papers, too?" He indicated the same papers that Hettie had signed before she stormed out of the office.

Rhiannon added her signature and accepted the cheque he extended. She smiled at Marika. "Shall we go, love?"

Marika nodded, picked up her briefcase, and followed Rhiannon to the door.

Hettie stepped back and pulled her dress aside. "You're going to hell, Anne Davies. You're going to hell!"

Rhiannon glanced at her with a grin and winked. "See you there, Hettie."

Hettie huffed loudly.

Rhiannon continued walking—out of the office and out of her aunt's life.

When they reached the elevators, Marika burst into laughter. "Oh, sweetheart, if you could've seen her face. I thought her head was going to explode."

Rhiannon chuckled. As they waited for the elevator to arrive, she studied the cheque. *This will put my account over ten thousand dollars. Two months ago, this cheque would've set me on my journey.*

Marika tilted her head. "Do you know what you're going to do with it?"

Rhiannon folded the cheque and tucked it in her pocket. "Dunno. Can't think of anything in particular." She checked her watch. "It's too late to go back to work. What would you say to just going home?"

"I'd say that sounds like a wonderful idea. Did you have any particular plans for our early return home?"

Rhiannon waggled her eyebrows.

Marika laughed. "Thought so. Insatiable wench."

They entered the elevator, and Rhiannon leaned against the back wall. "Did you hear that an Italian court recently ruled sex in an elevator is not cause for arrest?"

Marika put her briefcase down. "Really? So were you looking for my legal opinion on their judicial ruling? Or is this more what you had in mind?" She pressed her body against Rhiannon; her hands cupped Rhi's face, and she lowered her head.

The elevator doors closed as their lips met.

Spooky's head poked under the edge of the Saturday newspaper, and Marika chuckled. She shifted the paper and allowed him to curl up next to her on the bed. "You know Rhi's going to kick you out of that spot when she comes back." She returned to her perusal of the news and folded the paper so she could read one article of particular interest.

Rhiannon walked through their bedroom door, balancing two glasses of orange juice and a sheet of paper.

"I was beginning to wonder if you were squeezing the oranges yourself," Marika said as she accepted a glass.

"Nah. Just stopped to check our e-mail." Rhiannon set her glass on the bedside table and scooped Spooky away from Marika's thigh. She took up her favourite position, angled across the bed with her head in Marika's lap. "We got another letter from your sister."

Marika smiled. She and Brooke had built a relationship since July. When she told Brooke about Rhiannon, she'd instantly adopted Rhi as a sister-in-law and now addressed her e-mails to both of them. "What does she have to say?"

"Well, apparently the jerk that was bothering her in chemistry class is no longer quite as jerky. He invited her to the fall dance, and she's agonizing over whether or not she should go. She wants to know what you think." Rhiannon looked up at Marika. "So, what do you think, love?"

"I think he's probably nowhere near good enough for her and that she shouldn't even consider dating until she's at least twenty-one."

Laughing, Rhiannon captured and kissed Marika's hand. "You're going to be ruthless if we ever have kids, aren't you?"

"Mmm-hm. Our children are all attending parochial school, and there'll be no dating without chaperones. After all, they might take after you." *God, I'm actually joking about having children. Will miracles never cease?* She smiled. *Not around her, they won't.*

Rhiannon raised an eyebrow. "And that would be bad how?"

"Not bad, just challenging." *And I'm starting to think I might like that challenge someday.* "Hey, there's something in the paper you'll be interested in."

Rhiannon snorted. "Like I don't know a change of subject when I hear one." She grinned. "What is it?"

"It's an update on Cass' case. Her army of lawyers again moved that bail be granted, given that it'll be at least twelve more months before the case goes to trial. They argued that holding such a fine, upstanding citizen as Mrs. DeAndre on unproven charges for that length of time would be an affront to justice."

Rhiannon rolled her eyes. "Don't tell me they got her out."

"No, they didn't," Marika said. "Cass is still securely locked up."

They exchanged a high five. They'd avidly followed the sensational events of Cass' arrest and the subsequent dismantling of her criminal enterprise. DeAndre's former chauffeur and right-hand man secured a plea bargain in exchange for testimony against his employer. According to Lee's sources, between Liang and Gao, the Crown was wading through a mountain of incriminating evidence that had forced several delays in proceeding to trial.

"I hope they gave her Biker Bertha as a cellmate." Rhiannon snickered.

"That would be bad luck—for Biker Bertha."

They read quietly for a while until Marika noticed Rhiannon circling several ads. "See anything interesting?"

"Mmm-hm." Rhiannon tapped her pen against the paper. "I'm trying to decide between a '97 Civic and a '96 Cavalier." Since getting her licence, she'd fixated on buying a used car.

"You know, love, you could save your money and use mine whenever you want."

"I know, and I do appreciate it. But I have the money, and I'd really like my own car. It wasn't long ago that I couldn't even dream about owning one." She flashed a grin at Marika. "Besides, all the other kids have one."

Marika smiled. *Sometimes I forget how little she had in the way of a normal upbringing.*

"I think I'll call tomorrow about the Civic. Do you want to come with me to take a look at it?"

"Sure, but I don't know anything about cars," Marika said. "You might want to take Lee or David."

"David drives a Volvo." Rhiannon wrinkled her nose. "He would probably advise me to buy a safe, dull, four-door sedan. And Lee will be on her honeymoon for the next two weeks."

"Would the world end if you had to wait two more weeks to buy a car?"

Rhiannon sighed. "I suppose not. But what if this Civic is the best bargain I'd ever get, and I miss out on it because I don't move quickly enough?"

Laughing, Marika tugged the paper out of Rhiannon's hands and tossed it aside. "Honey, I'm pretty sure there will be lots of other once-in-a-lifetime-bargains available once Lee is back. Come on up here, and let's talk about other things."

Rhiannon sat up with a familiar gleam in her eyes and shifted to straddle Marika's legs.

Marika grinned and ran her hands up Rhiannon's thighs and under her long T-shirt. She took full advantage of the absence of undergarments, enjoying the now familiar curves and dips.

Rhiannon squirmed closer and rested her hands on Marika's shoulders. "So you want to talk about other things, do you? What did you have in mind?" She untied Marika's short robe and folded back the silk, exposing her breasts.

"Well, let's see—" Marika waited for Rhiannon's touch. It didn't come. She arched her back.

Smiling, Rhiannon drew a finger down the centre of Marika's torso. "Politics, perhaps. Maybe religion, recent movies, restaurant reviews?" She avoided Marika's breasts.

This is a new game. Marika's breathing quickened. She tried to grab Rhiannon's hands.

Rhiannon sat back, then very deliberately raised her T-shirt, pulled it off, and tossed it aside.

Marika threw off her robe and reached for Rhiannon.

Rhiannon caught Marika's hands and kissed each fingertip. She drew her tongue down Marika's hand and focused on her inner wrist, swirling her tongue in elaborate patterns. Then she switched hands and did the same thing in reverse.

Jesus, who knew wrists were an erogenous zone! "Rhi, please—"

"Uh-uh-uh. What's our mantra?" Rhiannon lifted her head and grinned.

"If you say patience, I may have to hurt you." Marika glared, but to no effect.

Rhiannon continued to take her own sweet time, lingering over the most unlikely spots—the inside of Marika's elbow, the indent of her clavicle, the base of her ribcage. She rolled Marika over and tenderly explored the base of her spine, the back of her knees, and the arch of her foot.

Mother of God! She's going to drive me insane! Marika writhed under the delicious torture. She tried to slip her hand down between her legs.

Rhiannon chuckled and trapped Marika's hand. "Oh no, love. I reserve that to my pleasure."

"Then for sanity's sake, take your pleasure!"

"Believe me, I am." Rhiannon's tongue traced the curve at the base of Marika's buttocks, then she rose and stretched out over her back. Her hips began to move, first with languor, then with lust.

Marika buried her head in a pillow and whimpered. *If she ever touches me, I'm going to last about half a second.*

"Would you like to roll over?" Rhiannon whispered next to Marika's ear. "Would you like to spread your legs for me? Would you like me to bury my fingers deep inside you and whip my tongue over your clit?"

"God, yes!" Marika panted and squirmed.

Rhiannon brushed Marika's hair to the side and nibbled on the nape of her neck for a long moment. "Then turn over, my love." She slid off Marika's back.

Coherent thought had ebbed, but Marika retained enough awareness to roll over.

Rhiannon eased between her legs.

Marika held her breath. *No more teasing.* "Please—Rhi, I need you."

"I know, love." Rhiannon's head and hand dipped between Marika's legs.

"Oh, sweet woman. Thank you, thank you, thank you." Marika's hips surged, and thought spiraled into sensation. Consumed with joy, she soared into an orgasm. When her body slumped, Marika gasped for air. "Oh, my God. Sweet Jesus, Rhi! What did you do to me?"

Rhiannon crawled up the bed and wrapped an arm and leg around Marika. "Loved you."

Marika barely had strength to put an arm around Rhiannon. "You're going to have to give me a few minutes."

"S'okay. I, um, kind of took care of both of us at the same time." Rhiannon burrowed her face into Marika's neck.

Marika laughed. "You are one talented woman." *God, are you ever!* She looked over at the bedside clock. "Four hours until the wedding. I hope that's enough time."

"Enough time for what?" Rhiannon yawned.

"To regain the energy to stand up with Lee!"

Rhiannon laughed. "Go to sleep, love. I'll make sure you're awake in time."

Marika closed her eyes. "'Kay."

CHAPTER 33

RHIANNON SAT ON THE EDGE of the neatly made bed while Marika finished dressing for the wedding. *God, she's gorgeous. I'm a lucky, lucky woman.*

Marika slipped on her pumps and moved to the dresser.

"You look fabulous," Rhiannon said. Marika's new peach and grey dress flattered her. *Hell, she could wear a paper bag and still look smashing.*

Marika smiled. "You look wonderful too, love."

Rhiannon glanced down at her burgundy wool trousers and pale grey blouse. *Definitely a step up from what I used to wear.* "Thanks again for helping me pick out this outfit."

"You're welcome." Marika affixed pearl clusters to her ears. "I hope my dress is okay. Given Lee's lack of information, I'll just be grateful if I don't clash with whatever they're wearing."

"What did she say?"

"I believe her exact words were, 'Wear something pretty, and be on time.'"

Rhiannon laughed. "That sounds like Lee. Do you know if there's going to be a lot of people there?"

"I expect so." Marika smoothed the fabric down over her hips. "I know Dana invited everyone on her team, and Lee invited her staff, not to mention all their friends and family."

"I bet Eli will look cute. I think it's great that he's standing up with his mom." Rhiannon frowned. *Oh, damn.* "Did you say *all* of Dana's team? Does that mean Darcy will be there?"

Marika leaned back against the dresser and tilted her head. "Sweetheart, I assume she'll be there, but why would it matter?"

"I dunno." Rhiannon scuffed at the carpet with the toe of her shoe. "I guess it's stupid." She and Marika had lived together for several months, but she'd never completely gotten past her overwhelming jealousy when Darcy had propositioned Marika.

Marika crossed to stand in front of her. "How can you make love to me the way you did this morning and still think that I'd have eyes for anyone but you?"

Rhiannon looked up, abashed.

Marika's eyes shone.

Darcy's no rival. What in heaven's name was I thinking? Rhiannon put her arms around Marika's waist. "Because I'm an idiot."

"Then you're my idiot, and I adore you." Marika smiled and smoothed strands of hair behind Rhiannon's ears. "We should probably get going. I want to get there a bit early in case Lee is having any pre-wedding jitters." She stepped out of Rhiannon's embrace, grabbed her purse, and took one last glance in the mirror.

Rhiannon took Marika's hand.

They stopped to pick up their wedding gift on the way out of the condo. Dana and Lee had told their guests not to bring gifts because they already had everything they needed. But Rhiannon spent weeks working on a large charcoal and ink portrait of them, which Marika then had professionally framed. They were both delighted with the way it had turned out and knew that their friends would be, too, gift restrictions or not.

When they arrived at Lee and Dana's, David's car was parked in front of the house along with several others.

"I'm really glad that David is going to perform the ceremony," Rhiannon said.

"Mmm-hm." Marika parked behind the Volvo and turned off the ignition. "Lee said they didn't want to put him on the spot so they weren't going to ask, but he volunteered."

Rhiannon nodded. "I hope he doesn't get in trouble for it. He's kind of side-stepping the church's 'don't ask, don't tell' policy."

Marika smiled. "I doubt that possibility made him hesitate for even a moment."

Rhiannon shook her head. "Nope. He'll always do what he thinks is right. It's who he is." She looked at Marika and smiled. *And maybe one day he'll be able to marry us. But today belongs to Lee and Dana.*

They left the car, and Eli met them, nattily attired in a brand new suit, with a big grin on his face. "Hi, guys. Lee said you're to go right downstairs, Marika. She's getting ready in the guest bedroom. Rhi, the others are gathered in the backyard."

"Thanks." Marika took their gift from Rhiannon. "I'll leave this in the house. See you after the ceremony, okay?" She kissed Rhiannon and walked to the front door.

Rhiannon walked around the house. A large group of people chatted in the backyard. Rows of chairs were arranged in front of an arbour with fall-coloured foliage twined through the trellis. A long table covered in white linen and manned by a formally clad waiter was set back against the house and offered a selection of beverages and finger foods.

Rhiannon made her first stop there. She requested two Cokes and stopped the waiter from pouring them into glasses. "No, thanks, I'll just take them in the can." She picked up the Cokes and carried them to where David stood with his back to her, on the edge of a circle. She tapped him on the shoulder. "Hey, Ichabod, can I interest you in a cold Coke?"

David turned and smiled. He accepted the can and tilted his head at the front row of chairs with a raised eyebrow.

Rhiannon nodded and followed him to the seats. They sat down beside each other, and she studied David. He wasn't wearing his formal vestments, but he did have on a dark blue shirt and trousers, with the white badge of his office affixed to his collar. "So, are you ready?" She took a sip of her drink.

David nodded. "I think so. I've never done a commitment ceremony, and a lot of the usual texts don't apply, but the basic principles do." He chuckled. "I was informed that it was to be short and sweet, so everyone could get to the real reason they came—to party."

"That's our Lee." Rhiannon grinned. *I love that some things never change.*

David held up the Coke. "We've come full circle, haven't we?"

"We have. You know, I thought you were the most irritating man I'd ever encountered when we met. I was so sure you had a hidden agenda. I tried and tried to figure out what you wanted."

David smiled. "I had an agenda, but it wasn't hidden. I simply wanted to be your friend."

Rhiannon shook her head. "I don't know why. I was the orneriest kid on the block." A deep, rich laugh greeted that statement, and Rhiannon couldn't help joining in. "Yeah, yeah. I know I was a pain in the ass."

David, chuckling, did not disagree. "I can't say you were the easiest person to get to know."

They sipped their Cokes, and Rhiannon recalled those hot summer days when they'd bickered, bantered, and learned about each other—only several months ago in reality, but eons ago in terms of their friendship. "Thank you."

David raised one eyebrow. "For what?"

Rhiannon stared at the lawn, now losing its lustre in the last days of autumn. "For sticking with me, for not giving up on me when most people would've in a heartbeat. I don't know if I'll ever understand why you decided I was worth your attention, but I'm profoundly grateful that you did."

"I just used the eyes that God and Conor opened. What I saw was a wounded human being with huge potential for being more than what she was."

"And what was I?"

David smiled. "A lonely, bitter, angry young woman who bordered on misanthropy."

Rhiannon snorted. "Geez. Sugar-coat it, why don't you? I'm amazed you came back."

"Ah, but I didn't tell you about what happened when the chrysalis fell away. I didn't tell you about the beautiful butterfly that emerged, the courageous, intelligent woman with a vast capacity for love and devotion who sits beside me today."

It was a moment before Rhiannon could get her throat to cooperate, but finally, in a shaky voice, she said, "You saved my life."

His warm hand closed over hers. "No, Rhiannon. You saved your own...and Marika's. And you know I'm not just talking about the Shuswaps."

Blinking back tears, Rhiannon drained her Coke.

David did the same. "So, will you be asking me to perform a ceremony for you two any time soon?" He rolled the empty can between his hands.

"Could be...someday." Rhiannon matched his casual tone, grateful for the change in conversation. "Maybe we'll wait until it's legal here. You know, if I were a traditional 'walking down the aisle' kinda girl, I'd want you to be the one walking with me. My dad's been gone many years, but I know he would approve of you standing in for him."

It was David's turn to be speechless. His prominent Adam's apple bobbed convulsively. "I...you honour me. I would be proud to do either—walk you down the aisle to meet Marika or perform your service." He smiled. "Or both. I can be very flexible, you know."

Rhiannon grinned. *Not as flexible as my partner.*

Eli popped up in front of them. "Excuse me, David. Mom wants to see you, please."

David nodded and handed his empty can to Rhiannon with a wink. "Duty calls. I'll talk to you later."

Rhiannon tucked both cans under her seat and turned sideways to survey the yard, which had steadily filled with people while she and David talked. Most of Dana's teammates were present. Willem chatted with Marc Manion on the far side of the yard. A couple of shady-looking characters huddled by the back fence. She grinned. *Want to bet they were on Lee's guest list?*

Darcy engaged in conversation with Lee's employee, Barb.

Rhiannon frowned reflexively, then caught herself. *Oh, for heaven's sake. Grow up.* She waved to Jan and Terry, who had just arrived.

They made their way over to her.

"Hi, guys."

They took the seats beside her.

"How's it going?"

Jan smiled. "Well, and with you?"

"Couldn't be better," Rhiannon said. "It looks like it's going to be a perfect day for a wedding."

They passed the next fifteen minutes in small talk until David emerged from the house and made his way to the arbour. The crowd fell silent as he raised his hands. "Could you please take your seats, and we'll get underway."

People filed into the rows of chairs as the strains of soft classical music filled the air. David gave everyone a moment to get settled, then, as Eli, Marika, Lee, and Dana appeared at the rear of the runner bounded by the banks of chairs, he said, "Would everyone please rise?"

The crowd stood, and Rhiannon smiled. Eli marched as stiffly as a wooden soldier with Marika on his arm. Lee and Dana stood, allowing their attendants to move ahead. *I wonder if Lee is as nervous as Eli.* Joy beamed from Lee's face. *Nope, no nerves there.* Dana, too, sported a radiant smile as she stood with her arm linked through Lee's. *No nerves there, either.*

"They look great, don't they?" Jan whispered.

Rhiannon nodded. Lee cut a sharp figure in a dark blue suit and white shirt while Dana wore a champagne-coloured dress and carried a bouquet of miniature white roses.

The music swelled, and Lee and Dana began their walk down the aisle. They took their places under the arbour, facing David. Marika stood beside Lee, and Eli flanked his mother.

David motioned for everyone to take their seats, then turned his attention to Lee and Dana. "Today you have entered this place together to stand before God, your family, and your friends, prepared to pledge each to the other your love and loyalty, your constancy and commitment, through whatever your lives may hold. It is not an easy road you embark on, but it is one of the most satisfying and fulfilling that life offers. As you journey this road together, sometimes you will go hand in hand, sometimes one will support the other, but never will you travel that path alone. God and your partner walk with you...always."

Lee reached for Dana's hand. They looked at each other, and Lee winked.

Rhiannon smiled. *Were ever two people so perfect for each other?*

"As your hearts have summoned you here, called by the need to fully and formally join your lives from this day forward, we are here to bear witness to the depth of your love, devotion, and commitment, one to the other. When heart calls to heart and two become as one, God rejoices, for God has fashioned eternal laws which transcend the laws of man. He commands you to cherish each other...to treasure the bonds you now willingly embrace...to honour each other always, and never forget that the love you share is a reflection of His vast, eternal, and immeasurable love."

Out of the corner of her eye, Rhiannon saw Terry take Jan's hand. *If Marika was sitting beside me, I'd be doing that, too.* Her eyes glistened as she listened to the soaring words that echoed the depth of her love for Marika. *Someday we will make this same commitment.* Rhiannon smiled when she noticed that Marika's gaze was focused on her. *Yeah, you're feeling it too, aren't you, love?*

"Lee and Dana have prepared their own vows." David nodded at the couple.

Dana handed Eli her flowers, then turned to Lee. They joined hands.

"My love, my Dana." Lee's voice rang out with clarity and confidence. "When I first met you, you were picking gravel out of my hide, mopping up my scrapes, and lecturing me about the dangers of riding motorcycles."

A chuckle ran through the crowd, all of them familiar with Lee's love affair with her bike.

She shot them a grin. "I don't think I heard a word of it 'cause all I could think of was how cute you were, even when you were chewing me out. You've enchanted me from the day we met. When I finally convinced you to go out with me, I think it was the third happiest day of my life. When you said you'd marry me, it was the second happiest day of my life. This day, when I stand before you, Eli, and our friends to declare my forever commitment, is the happiest day of my life." Lee's expression grew solemn. "Dana, I promise to love, cherish, and care for you and for Eli. You are my family, and nothing is more important than family. I freely pledge you all my tomorrows, for they're already yours. Without you, my days would be nothing. Thank you for giving me *your* tomorrows, my love. It is the greatest gift anyone has ever, or could ever, give me."

Lee raised Dana's hands to her lips, and Rhiannon's tears overflowed.

It was Dana's turn to speak, but she, too, was in tears. After one false start, she began again. "My love, my Lee...I recall our first encounter, too. I thought you were reckless, arrogant, cocky, and irritating. Thank God you persisted, though I brushed you off time and again." Dana's voice was quieter than Lee's but carried every bit as much conviction. "But even as I said 'no,' I was looking twice and liking what I saw. I'd never met anyone with such integrity and such joy. I'd never met anyone who so lived her life to the fullest, even when the consequences were painful."

Another ripple of laughter ran through the crowd.

"The day I said 'yes' to our first date, I know you thought you'd just worn me down. But in truth, if you hadn't come back, I'd have sought you out. I wasn't just saying yes for that date. I knew even then that you were a keeper...the woman I wanted to spend the rest of my life with." Dana's voice grew soft and serious. "You were right with me through some very hard times, as I knew you would be. I'm going to spend the rest of my life repaying the devotion you've shown me with an equal commitment to you and our family. Lee, I promise to love and cherish and care for you to the end of my days, for those days would be nothing without you."

David nodded at Marika and Eli, who produced the wedding rings and passed them over. He closed his fingers around them and looked at Lee and Dana. "These rings are a symbol and, as a symbol of what lies within your heart and the commitment you have made this day, must be honoured as you honour your wife and the vows you have made to her." He opened his hand and extended his palm to Lee.

She selected the smaller ring and slipped it on Dana's finger. "With this ring, I thee wed."

Dana took the matching ring and slid it onto Lee's finger. "With this ring, I thee wed."

David invited them to sign the document of commitment that he had drawn up. Marika and Eli added their signatures as witnesses. David completed the form with a flourish, then rolled it and tied it with a ribbon. He handed it to Dana and placed a hand on each woman's shoulder. Beaming out over the crowd, he pronounced, "I call on all of you to bear witness to the joining of these women today. Whom God has brought together let no one put asunder."

Without waiting for the customary permission, Lee pulled Dana into her arms and kissed her thoroughly. The crowd erupted in applause and cheers. When they parted, Lee pumped her fist into the air victoriously. "All right!"

That drew another round of laughter. Lee and Dana walked hand in hand into the crowd, and their guests surged forward to congratulate the couple. Rhiannon was one of the first to reach them, and she hugged each of them. Lee's eyes sparkled, and her grin stretched from ear to ear. Dana was almost as effervescent when she accepted Rhi's good wishes.

Rhiannon backed out of the way and looked for Marika. She found her with David under the arbour. Rhiannon crossed to them, wrapped an arm around Marika, and grinned at David. "You did well, Ichabod. That was beautiful."

"Lots more where that came from." David winked and moved away, leaving the two of them standing together under the arch.

Marika turned and locked her arms around Rhiannon's neck. "It was beautiful, wasn't it?" Her voice was soft as she gazed at Rhiannon.

"Almost as beautiful as you are to me," Rhiannon said. She stepped forward and buried her face against Marika's neck.

Marika's arms locked her in a tight embrace, and her breath caught.

Rhiannon pulled back to see tears rolling down Marika's cheeks. She brushed them away. "I hope those are good tears."

Marika nodded. "I was just thinking about this backyard and all the things that have happened here. Do you remember the first time you came for dinner?"

"Of course. I was scared to death. I sat in the park, wondering if I should just get back on the bus and go home. But then Lee and Eli showed up, and running away was no longer an option."

"I was annoyed because it felt like Lee and Dana were forcing us to socialize, but that was the night I started to see you with new eyes."

Rhiannon smiled. "And look at us now."

Marika's expression sobered. "I don't think I've ever told you that a week before that night, I was here for their big anniversary party. It didn't go well. I overheard some eye-opening opinions about my behaviour that really shook me up. I ended up leaving early and going to Cass' place."

Rhiannon growled.

Marika covered Rhi's lips. "No, wait, love. That also turned out to be the last time I slept with her. Not the last time I saw her, as you well know, but it was the beginning of the end of that warped and twisted relationship. When I got home the next morning, Lee and Terry were waiting for me. I had a huge fight with them, which I deeply regretted afterwards, but it did plant a seed."

Rhiannon gently removed Marika's fingers from her lips. "What kind of seed?"

"The kind of seed that made me focus on the way I was living, who I had sex with, and why I couldn't seem to find love like Lee and Dana or Terry and Jan. The kind of seed that you nurtured with your kindness, compassion, and utter lack of judgment when I zoned out in Vancouver. The kind of seed that blossomed into what I see in your eyes when you look at me and what I feel every morning when I wake up next to you."

"That sounds like a very good seed."

"The best, Rhi, and it all started here. I didn't think this kind of happiness was even possible for me. I believed it could be for everyone else, but never for me. You changed all that."

Rhiannon tilted her head. "You know you've done the same for me, don't you?"

Marika cupped Rhi's face. "I do know that, love. Without question. And I hope you know that I'm in this for life—our life. The good, the great, the maybe not-so-great—we're in it together. Always." She capped her promise with a deep, tender kiss.

The sweetness of Marika's declaration sank into Rhiannon's soul. It grew and expanded, and healed all the fissures left by the empty, arid years. Her heart filled with a profound sense of completeness. They had come through the fire together, and it hadn't destroyed them. Instead, it burned away the dross and left the diamond.

Marika's mouth moved from Rhiannon's lips to her ear. "I can hardly wait to see what comes next, sweetheart."

"Neither can I, my love. Neither can I."

ABOUT LOIS
CLOAREC HART

Born and raised in British Columbia, Canada, Lois Cloarec Hart grew up as an avid reader but didn't begin writing until much later in life. Several years after joining the Canadian Armed Forces, she received a degree in Honours History from Royal Military College and on graduation switched occupations from air traffic control to military intelligence. Having married a CAF fighter pilot while in college, Lois went on to spend another five years as an Intelligence Officer before leaving the military to care for her husband, who was ill with chronic progressive Multiple Sclerosis and passed away in 2001. She began writing while caring for her husband in his final years and had her first book, *Coming Home*, published in 2001. It was through that initial publishing process that Lois met the woman she would marry in April 2007. She now commutes annually between her northern home in Calgary and her wife's southern home in Atlanta.

Lois is the author of four novels, *Coming Home, Broken Faith, Kicker's Journey, Walking the Labyrinth*, and a collection of short stories, *Assorted Flavours*. Her novel *Kicker's Journey* won the 2010 Independent Publisher Book Award bronze medal, 2010 Golden Crown Literary Awards, 2010 Rainbow Romance Writer's Award for Excellence, and 2009 Lesbian Fiction Readers Choice Award for historical fiction. *Coming Home* (revised third edition) will be published in print and e-formats in spring 2014.

Visit her website: www.loiscloarechart.com
E-mail her at eljae1@shaw.ca

OTHER BOOKS FROM YLVA PUBLISHING

http://www.ylva-publishing.com

WALKING THE LABYRINTH

Lois Cloarec Hart

ISBN 978-3-95533-052-1
Length: 267 pages

Is there life after loss? Lee Glenn, co-owner of a private security company, didn't think so. Crushed by grief after the death of her wife, she uncharacteristically retreats from life.

But love doesn't give up easily. After her friends and family stage a dramatic intervention, Lee rejoins the world of the living, resolved to regain some sense of normalcy but only half-believing that it's possible. Her old friend and business partner convinces her to take on what appears on the surface to be a minor personal protection detail.

The assignment takes her far from home, from the darkness of her loss to the dawning of a life reborn. Along the way, Lee encounters people unlike any she's ever met before: Wrong-Way Wally, a small-town oracle shunned by the locals for his off-putting speech and mannerisms; and Wally's best friend, Gaëlle, a woman who not only translates the oracle's uncanny predictions, but who also appears to have a deep personal connection to life beyond life. Lee is shocked to find herself fascinated by Gaëlle, despite dismissing the woman's exotic beliefs as "hooey."

But opening yourself to love also means opening yourself to the possibility of pain. Will Lee have the courage to follow that path, a path that once led to the greatest agony she'd ever experienced? Or will she run back to the cold comfort of a safer solitary life?

KICKER'S JOURNEY
(revised edition)

Lois Cloarec Hart

ISBN 978-3-95533-060-6
Length: 472 pages

In 1899, two women from very different backgrounds are about to embark on a journey together—one that will take them from the Old World to the New, from the 19th century into the 20th, and from the comfort and familiarity of England to the rigours of Western Canada, where challenges await at every turn.

The journey begins simply for Kicker Stuart when she leaves her home village to take employment as hostler and farrier at Grindleshire Academy for Young Ladies. But when Kicker falls in love with a teacher, Madelyn Bristow, it radically alters the course of her tranquil life.

Together, the lovers flee the brutality of Madelyn's father and the prejudices of upper crust England in search of freedom to live, and love, as they choose. A journey as much of the heart and soul as of the body, it will find the lovers struggling against the expectations of gender, the oppression of class, and even, at times, each other.

What they find at the end of their journey is not a new Eden, but a land of hope and opportunity that offers them the chance to live out their most cherished dream—a life together.

SOMETHING IN THE WINE
Jae

ISBN: 978-3-95533-005-7
Length: 393 pages

All her life, Annie Prideaux has suffered through her brother's constant practical jokes only he thinks are funny. But Jake's last joke is one too many, she decides when he sets her up on a blind date with his friend Drew Corbin— neglecting to tell his straight sister one tiny detail: her date is not a man, but a lesbian.

Annie and Drew decide it's time to turn the tables on Jake by pretending to fall in love with each other.

At first glance, they have nothing in common. Disillusioned with love, Annie focuses on books, her cat, and her work as an accountant while Drew, more confident and outgoing, owns a dog and spends most of her time working in her beloved vineyard.

Only their common goal to take revenge on Jake unites them. But what starts as a table-turning game soon turns Annie's and Drew's lives upside down as the lines between pretending and reality begin to blur.

Something in the Wine is a story about love, friendship, and coming to terms with what it means to be yourself.

L.A. METRO
(second edition)

RJ Nolan

ISBN: 978-3-95533-041-5
Length: 349 pages

Dr. Kimberly Donovan's life is in shambles. After her medical ethics are questioned, first her family, then her closeted lover, the Chief of the ER, betray her. Determined to make a fresh start, she flees to California and L.A. Metropolitan Hospital.

Dr. Jess McKenna, L.A. Metro's Chief of the ER, gives new meaning to the phrase emotionally guarded, but she has her reasons.

When Kim and Jess meet, the attraction is immediate. Emotions Jess has tried to repress for years surface. But her interest in Kim also stirs dark memories. They settle for friendship, determined not to repeat past mistakes, but secretly they both wish things could be different.

Will the demons from Jess's past destroy their future before it can even get started? Or will L.A. Metro be a place to not only heal the sick, but to mend wounded hearts?

COMING FROM YLVA PUBLISHING

http://www.ylva-publishing.com

SEE RIGHT THROUGH ME
L.T. Smith

Trust, respect, and love. Three little words—that's all.
But these words are powerful, and if we ignore any one of
them, then three other little words take their place: jealousy,
insecurity, and heartbreak.

Schoolteacher Gemma Hughes is an ordinary woman
living an ordinary life. Disorganised and clumsy, she soon
finds herself in the capable hands of the beautiful Dr Maria
Moran. Everything goes wonderfully until Gemma starts
doubting Maria's intentions and begins listening to the
wrong people.

But has Maria something to hide, or is it a case of
swapping trust for insecurity, respect for jealousy and
finishing with a world of heartbreak and deceit? Can
Gemma stop her actions before it's too late? Or will she
ruin the best thing to happen in her life?

Given her track record, anything is possible …

COMING HOME
(revised edition)

Lois Cloarec Hart

A triangle with a twist, Coming Home is the story of three good people caught up in an impossible situation.

Rob, a charismatic ex-fighter pilot severely disabled with MS, has been steadfastly cared for by his wife, Jan, for many years. Quite by accident one day, Terry, a young writer/postal carrier, enters their lives and turns it upside down.

Injecting joy and turbulence into their quiet existence, Terry draws Rob and Jan into her lively circle of family and friends until the growing attachment between the two women begins to strain the bonds of love and loyalty, to Rob and each other.

IN A HEARTBEAT
RJ Nolan

Veteran police officer Sam McKenna has no trouble facing down criminals on a daily basis but breaks out in a sweat at the mere mention of commitment. A recent failed relationship strengthens her resolve to stick with her trademark no-strings-attached affairs.

Dr. Riley Connolly, a successful trauma surgeon, has spent her whole life trying to measure up to her family's expectations. And that includes hiding her sexuality from them.

When a routine call sends Sam to the hospital where Riley works, the two women are hurtled into a life-and-death situation. The incident binds them together. But can there be any future for a commitment-phobic cop and a closeted, workaholic doctor?

CONFLICT OF INTEREST
(revised edition)

Jae

Workaholic Detective Aiden Carlisle isn't looking for love—and certainly not at the law enforcement seminar she reluctantly agreed to attend. But the first lecturer is not at all what she expected.

Psychologist Dawn Kinsley has just found her place in life. After a failed relationship with a police officer, she has sworn never to get involved with another cop again, but she feels a connection to Aiden from the very first moment.

Can Aiden keep from crossing the line when a brutal crime threatens to keep them apart before they've even gotten together?

Broken Faith
© by Lois Cloarec Hart

ISBN: 978-3-95533-056-9 (paperback)

Also available as e-book

Published by Ylva Publishing, legal entity of Ylva Verlag, e.Kfr.

Ylva Verlag, e.Kfr.
Owner: Astrid Ohletz
Am Kirschgarten 2
65830 Kriftel
Germany

http://www.ylva-publishing.com

First Edition: 2002 by Renaissance Alliance Publishing
Revised Second Edition: November 2013

Credits:
Edited by Sandra Gerth and Judy Underwood
Cover Design by Streetlight Graphics